GARAGE SALE
Stalker

To Judy!
a fellow garage
sale enthusiast —AND R
of MYSTERIES!!

Suzi
Weinert

SUZI WEINERT

International Standard Book Number 13: 978-1-60452-090-3
International Standard Book Number 10: 1-60452-090-6
Library of Congress Control Number: 2014933889

BluewaterPress LLC
52 Tuscan Way Ste 202-309
Saint Augustine, Florida 32092

http://www.bluewaterpress.com
This book may be purchased online at

http://bluewaterpress.com/GSS

Editing by Carole Greene

To Don,

For his unfailing encouragement, clever suggestions,
computer rescues, patience and love.

TO MY READERS

Jennifer's passion for garage sales is shared by millions around the globe. For centuries, people have bartered or sold possessions by laying items on a blanket or table top in front of their home or at a local market. Today, garage sales—also known as yard sales, rummage sales, tag sales, attic sales, moving sales, barn sales and estate sales—thrive in the United States. Add flea markets, swap meets, consignment shops, thrift shops and recent internet venues such as Amazon, Craig's List and E-Bay and the result is *"big business."* Besides bargains, a bonus by-product of the second-hand market is that goods are recycled, not trashed. If you haven't tried these sales yet yourself, don't miss the adventure!

We like to sweep unsavory issues like child abuse, neglect and exploitation under the rug, but these serious problems exist and are on the increase. Almost daily, the media feature stories about such offenses. Several ideas for this book sprang from just such news coverage. While it's unpleasant reading, much of the public does so with shocked disbelief, doubting an individual concerned citizen can make a positive difference. Any situation producing traumatized, dysfunctional or dangerous people impacts society adversely. Consider contacting your local, county or state child protective service or a national group like Childhelp to learn how you might participate in constructive ways.

Thank you for reading my book. You may wish to e-mail me at: Suzi@GarageSaleStalker.com

—Suzi Weinert

PROLOGUE

His hands gloved against the cold, the dead woman's lawyer pulled his overcoat tighter against the winter chill, trying to dispel his growing uneasiness about the impending meeting. Gray-haired and well-dressed, he stared at the farm's weathered buildings as he stood in the upper driveway between the dilapidated barn and the old house. Flanking the back door, daffodil shoots emerged just above the cold February ground; perhaps a metaphor for the young man arriving today to bring new life to his deceased mother's home.

Beyond the tangle of overgrown brush and trees, tires crunched in the pebbles far below, where the property's gravel driveway touched the county road. He watched a black pickup truck appear at the top of the long incline and park beside his car. A tall, thirtyish man, built-like-a-tank with erect posture, beefy arms, a bull neck and blond crew-cut hair, stepped out of the truck.

"You must be Ruger Yates." The gray-haired man forced a convincing smile and extended his hand. "Welcome to Virginia. I'm Greg Bromley, your mother's attorney and old friend. After our letters and phone calls about her estate, you're here at last."

Ruger Yates shook his hand. Something about that contact made Bromley shiver. Was it this man's uncanny resemblance to his cruel father or just a reaction to the frosty wind?

A scuffing commotion in the truck bed drew Bromley's attention to a dog's muzzle poking over the edge.

"Hey," Bromley said, "looks like you brought a friend with you."

As he moved closer to see the animal, the large dog growled a warning, leaped out of the vehicle and squared off to confront him. Used to pleasant encounters with friends' pets, Bromley stepped back in surprise, observing this aggressive dog's battered condition. "Whoa, fella! I mean you no harm," he soothed, again trying to befriend the animal by slowly extending his hand to pat its head. But the dog growled louder, lips drawing back to expose menacing teeth and warning the stranger to come no closer.

"Is this dog a rescue?" he asked Ruger. "I mean... the scars and all?"

Ruger stiffened. "The pup found me. I just trained him."

What kind of training produced a dog looking like that? Bromley wondered, but instead he asked, "How long did it take you to get here from Texas?"

"About a week – I camped along the way. Lots of lonesome country between there and here."

"Right," Bromley nodded, wondering if this told as much about the traveler as the land he traversed. "Does the old homestead here seem at all familiar?"

Ruger looked around solemn-faced, almost trance-like, Bromley thought. Did this young man project negative vibes or was it his own over-active imagination? When at last the silence became awkward, Bromley spoke again.

"Your mother and I were classmates and friends for many years. We graduated in the same college class and then both worked in McLean. She taught school here. I always admired your mother. She was such a lovely person then, friendly and bright and very beautiful."

Seeing the blond man register no interest in his mother, Bromley changed the subject. "Hard to believe from what you see here now, Ruger, but this part of Fairfax County was all countryside forty or fifty years ago with lots of farms like your family's big spread." Bromley shivered again as the brisk winter breeze swirled around them. "Here, let's sit in my car while I tell you more about why you're here."

"Stay!" Ruger ordered the dog, with a simultaneous hand gesture. The animal obeyed instantly.

When the two men sat comfortably in Bromley's car, he started the engine and adjusted the heater knob for warmth. "Now where was I? Oh yes, so when she married your father, I was, well, surprised and maybe even a little jealous." His hope to create a friendly relationship with this young man faded further as the expressionless face stared back at him.

Bromley returned to facts. "I didn't see Wendey - that was your mother's name - for many years after she married until she needed legal help when your father was, ah, arrested and charged." He proceeded carefully; for despite his own revulsion, the man *was* Ruger's father. "Do you know the story?"

Raised an orphan, Ruger knew nothing of his family or early childhood except occasional wisps of frightening recall. Seared somewhere in the childhood recesses of his mind, their terror *demanded* repression.

"No," he answered.

"Well, it's like this. Your three-year-old sister died under... ah... unusual circumstances. Your father said it was accidental, but the prosecutor looked at the case differently and charged him with... um, a very serious crime. I convinced the jury that your father was mentally incompetent to stand trial, so rather than convicting him of mur... of the greater crime, the state sent him to a nearby mental institution where, as you may know, he died two years later."

Listening raptly, Ruger reacted with surprise. He did *not* know. "My father was insane?"

"That's the verdict I fought hard to get — instead of the alternative of life in prison or, ah, worse." Bromley changed the subject again. "Now that was a bad time for your mother. Her physical and mental health declined markedly during that period, what with mourning her daughter's...*untimely* death and her husband's, ah..." Bromley chose his words tactfully, "predicament. She tried to run the farm by herself and, as it turned out, was also raising two young boys alone. I offered many times afterward to get her professional psychological help, but she adamantly refused."

Ruger stared blankly at the older man. "Raising two young boys?"

"Yes, you and your older brother. Mathis was his name. Apparently she hid you boys somewhere here at the farm during the police investigations pursuant to your father's case, so at that time no outsiders knew you even existed. She had no phone, never left the farm and wrote me to come to the house to talk with her when she needed help or legal advice. Maybe you thought only doctors made house calls in those days." Bromley smiled at Ruger before deciding that humor, which sometimes lightened awkward situations like this, brought no response from this man. "Because I knew her from earlier days and saw how emotionally fragile she'd become, I dropped by often to make sure she was okay."

"Is that when you found my brother and me?"

"Ah, not exactly. On one visit, after my first distant glimpse of the two of you out by the barn, your mother said you were her sons and told me your names. On every visit after that I asked to meet you boys, but she always said you were busy elsewhere. Then one day when I inquired as usual, your mother said Mathis had 'gone.' I pressed her about where, but she looked frightened and wouldn't discuss it. He was six or seven, so this seemed odd but I dropped it, in order not to further upset her. She gave the same explanation about him on my future visits. To this day I don't know what happened to him.

"Mathis..."Ruger said, reaching for an elusive memory.

"What?"

"That name... I've heard that name," Ruger said aloud, but to himself.

Even if Ruger was only five or six then, Bromley thought it odd not to immediately recognize his brother's name. But he put that aside and continued. "She could live on food from her garden, meat and eggs from the chickens and water from the well, but she still needed money for electric bills, roof repair and so on. So we discussed selling a few acres of her farm. To help her, I networked in town to find a buyer, who paid her an excellent price." He chose not to mention that he didn't profit from these transactions, despite spending considerable time brokering deals to bring Wendey top dollar for her land.

Bromley returned to his story, "When I finally saw you up close for the first time, you didn't look so good." His voice faltered as he remembered the emaciated, unkempt, wild-eyed boy with a welt on his face, a bruise on his arm and a festering burn scar on the back of one hand. "In fact," Bromley feigned cheer, "I thought it might be a good idea for a bright boy like you to attend a military school I knew about, so I made a quick phone call. It took all my persuasive powers to get the school to accept a six-year-old."

After a pause, Ruger asked, "How did I get to the school?"

"Well, I took you with me that very day, bought you new clothes and shoes and then we had haircuts together at the barber shop.

We ate lunch and I drove you to the school." Bromley frowned as he recalled the clothing store clerk's offer to discard the tattered outfit Ruger wore into his shop… and how oddly the barber eyed Bromley upon seeing the condition of the boy's arms and legs, never mind his matted hair. Nor did he describe the restaurant experience, where Ruger wolfed down his food, his thin arms curled protectively around his plate lest it be snatched away and his eyes wary of danger as he ate. "Do you remember any of that? The shopping, getting your hair cut, eating lunch together?"

"No," Ruger answered, although each of Bromley's descriptions lasered a pinpoint of light on forgotten pockets deep in Ruger's subconscious.

"Your mother paid for that schooling by periodically selling off more farm acreage, and the school sent your progress reports to me."

"To you?"

Bromley nodded. How could he explain to this young man that his mother, her neglect of her son already apparent, told him she hated the boy and wanted nothing more to do with him? In the ensuing years, her distaste for the child didn't waiver, despite Bromley's urgings to the contrary.

"Yes, the school sent me your papers, saved for you in this file." He handed Ruger a folder. "She wasn't well," Bromley said and, reshaping the ugly truth into something kinder, he added, "so she asked me to make sure you were provided for financially and pay your school bills." Should he tell the young man that he paid those bills from his own pocket when his mother's payments lagged? Would it help this man to know at least one person in the world had cared what happened to him? Probably not…

"How did she die?" Ruger asked.

"She wrote me that she was very sick and couldn't remember if she'd executed a Will. She had, but since I couldn't phone to tell her so, I went by. I knocked and knocked but she didn't answer the door. Over the years she'd become a hermit and didn't believe in medicine or doctors. Before driving away, I opened her mailbox and found some bills collected there so I went to the McLean post office. Her letter carrier told me she picked up her mail every day during the twenty-odd years he'd delivered it. Then I drove to the police station and brought a patrolman back here with me to force our way inside. We found she'd passed away in her bed. The autopsy determined she died of pneumonia the day before."

"And you found me through the Army?"

"That's right, Ruger. The military school said you enlisted after graduation. 'Yates' is not a common name, which helped. Years earlier, we'd drafted her Will on one of your mother's good days. Since your parents had no other relatives and your brother had disappeared, you were the obvious beneficiary for the estate. The Will also provided guidelines for her burial, which I oversaw in your absence. The ashes from her cremation are in this box." He reached into the back seat and handed a package to Ruger.

With tightly compressed lips, Ruger took the box, holding it as if scorpions might cascade from beneath the lid and swarm across his body.

Ruger's reaction to his mother's remains increased Bromley's unease, but he cleared his throat and pressed on. "The Yates family has owned this house at least a hundred years, although someone added electricity and plumbing along the way. You don't know the McLean or Great Falls areas yet, so I'll just tell you that your farm's fifteen acres lie between two very desirable residential locations. This property is worth a small fortune. The buildings show little attention for at least the last thirty years. The land is far more valuable than the structures, so if you sell in the future, a builder will demolish everything here for new construction. Knowing this may help you decide how long to keep it and whether major repairs make sense."

Making ready to leave, Bromley added, "Here's a northern Virginia book map which might help initially as you find your way around town. I've marked my office location on this page. We need to sign some papers there tomorrow if that's convenient. Two o'clock good?"

"Yes."

"Oh…I hired a cleaning woman to tidy up, empty the refrigerator and wastebaskets and dispose of the linens in your mother's bedroom. Otherwise, it's as she left it. Here are the keys. Good luck to you."

Bromley waited as Ruger climbed out of his car, anticipating a civil good-bye or thank-you, but none came. Was Ruger Yates always a boorish cold fish or did this return to his childhood home distract him from otherwise conventional good manners?

To avoid the need for facing this man again, Bromley would instruct his secretary to handle the estate document signing at his office tomorrow. Driving away from the farm, he shivered again, this time with relief.

***

Ruger watched the attorney's car disappear down the driveway before depositing the noxious box of ashes in the farthest recess of the barn, nowhere close to the house. Putting the file of school reports in the cab of his pickup, he again instructed his dog to "stay" and, with a trembling hand, unlocked the back door of his mother's house.

The door creaked eerily as Ruger pushed it open. Cautious, he stood at the threshold several minutes before stepping inside. Silence filled the space around him as dust motes spun in the weak sunlight filtering through filthy windows. The rear entryway, a mud-and-laundry room, led into the kitchen. Ruger waited expectantly for some familiarity to kick in, but none did.

Wary, he advanced into the kitchen and glanced around the room. As he focused on the shabby table and four rickety chairs, an unwanted snapshot of memory flashed into his mind. He and Mathis did school lessons there, the success of which determined whether or not they ate. But failure at lessons meant more than hunger; it meant beatings with any tool accidentally convenient to their irate mother's grasp—a coat hanger, an extension cord, a wooden spoon, a hot pan.

Ruger felt apprehension grow, as if an unstoppable living object had broken free inside him and begun to move—something getting bigger and rising higher within, something that would not remain suppressed any longer. His throat tightened and he drew his arms protectively close to his body as a second memory hurtled up and exploded into his conscious mind. He stared numbly as the vivid old tape replayed in his brain. At this very table his raving mother chopped off one of Mathis' fingers to punish him for spelling mistakes. The gushing blood, the wrenching screams, the total terror...

Ruger stood motionless several minutes, paralyzed by these violent recollections and feeling again the fear and pain inflicted then. Suddenly he strode across the kitchen and dry-heaved into the sink. Recovering at last, he slumped onto one of the ancient chairs, leaned forward on his elbows and covered his eyes with his hands.

He'd successfully blotted out the old terror these many years. For all his military toughness, he still wasn't ready for this inner child's sickening journey through horrifying past events. Stop this, he ordered himself. That was then, this is now. She's gone; you can do this. Focus on the situation at hand—the same single-minded focus that marshalled you through the near-impossible military assignments where you excelled. Form a plan, eliminate distractions, go!

He stood, did a disciplined 360-degree take of the kitchen and walked across the hall to the parlor. The boys were never allowed into this room. Even now, he stepped back from the forbidden threshold. Finally prodding himself forward, for the first time in his life he entered this area of his childhood home. Like a museum still-life with everything in place, the room was frozen in time. He swept a finger through dust on the nearest end table. Clearly his mother also avoided this room, keeping it perpetually unused and pristine for company who never came.

Returning to the hallway, he followed the threadbare carpet runner's trail from the kitchen to the first bedroom. As a child, he'd peered into but never entered his mother's room. Hesitantly, he opened the door to reveal a bed with bare mattress, an austere dresser, a listing lamp and a tattered floor rug. Adding to the unwelcoming dimness from tightly drawn shades covering otherwise bare windows, an unpleasant sick-room odor assaulted his nostrils. He'd later find that smell concentrated in the mattress when he threw it away. He choked, gripped by unbearable claustrophobia. Backing out rapidly, he lurched heavily against the wall and closed his eyes to gather courage and resolve.

The next bedroom triggered yet another memory. He and Mathis had shared this room with twin beds when one wasn't punished by imprisonment elsewhere in the house or outdoor sheds. "Elsewhere in the house" shook a kaleidoscope of crisscrossed, nauseating images through his mind. He glanced anxiously at the closet and cringed at a vision of the cellar.

Suddenly he couldn't breathe. Clutching his chest, he hurried down the hall, through the kitchen, wrenched open the back door and gulped in the cold winter air. Still sitting in the previously ordered position, his dog studied him, alert for the next command.

"What the hell are you looking at, you mangy hyena?" Ruger shouted, booting the animal fiercely in the ribs. Propelled into the air by the vicious kick, the dog yelped sharply, landed hard and scrambled to recover footing. With an anxious look at its master, the dog eased itself back into the "stay" position again.

His anger relieved by action, Ruger took more deep breaths before finally reentering the house. The second time was easier. He walked back down the hall to the third bedroom, pushed open its door and gaped at a room outfitted for a little girl—a room he'd never seen. Faded hand-sewn gingham curtains hung limply at the window and a matching drab coverlet lay on the simple twin bed beside a scuffed chest of drawers. On a child's chair sat the shabby remnant of a worn teddy bear, the penetrating stare of its remaining eye aimed straight at Ruger.

He drew back and shut the door hard. Despite no memory of her room, he vaguely recalled a little girl. From Bromley's story, she must have been his young sister.

Returning to his truck, Ruger sat down to think. Should he stay here tonight or go to a motel? Should he move in here at all or rent a flat in town? Admittedly, this isolation provided privacy and security for his clandestine computer work, never mind rent-free. Until he sold this property, money might get scarce once his military pay ran out and before his "consultant fees" rolled in.

Hadn't he survived Navy Seal training to which his Army Special Forces unit was attached? Hadn't he accepted military assignments so risky that only he volunteered? Hell, if he could do that he could take on an empty old house and in the process rid himself of whatever demons it held. The sensible solution was to stay and come to terms with the violent memories.

A simple, constructive plan dawned. He could erase the past by erasing everything in the main part of the house that pertained to it. He'd ditch his mother's furnishings and substitute his own stuff. He'd transform what was hers into his. He'd take control!

No need for *new* furniture with the length of his living situation here uncertain, but he would need *different* furniture and used would work just fine. Salvation Army and Goodwill sold what he needed. He'd donate this existing furniture while there. Newspaper ads listed household items for sale and didn't he remember something about garage sales? He considered selling his mother's old furniture at such a sale of his own but dismissed this idea. A loner, he didn't like people, didn't want them near this house and certainly didn't want to draw any attention to his living at this location. Still, he might attend other people's sales to find what he needed at reasonable prices.

He'd first transform the girl's room into an office because his on-going work eclipsed all else. He'd sleep in a twin bed in the room once shared with Mathis until refurnishing it as his own sleeping quarters. Next, he'd replace everything in the kitchen and redo the parlor into a comfortable place to watch TV. But the third bedroom, where his mother slept for forty years and where she died, awaited a yet uncertain use. Maybe if he scrubbed every inch of it and let the room stand empty for weeks until he was certain his mother's purged spirit joined her belongings clustered in the cellar, then he could turn her bedroom into a gym. Add a thorough house cleaning and window washing—how long would the whole refitting take? Ten days? Two weeks? Three? As for the cellar, he shuddered, much later, if ever at all...

His face set with resolve. He wouldn't let exposure to gruesome memories change his plan. He wouldn't let their accumulating horror take on a power of its own. He wouldn't let that power push him in directions he didn't want to go. He *wouldn't*...

CHAPTER 1

Jennifer Shannon threw a cardboard box into the passenger side of the vehicle, raced around to the driver's side and jumped into the front seat of the white Cadillac Crossover SUV. Revving the motor, she needed to move fast with only an hour to complete her plan.

Barreling down the street, she glanced at the notebook on the seat beside her to verify her destination. No need to consult the book map since she'd driven that neighborhood before. She fingered the zippered fanny pack belted around her waist, in which she'd stuffed small bills and coins. Earlier she'd locked larger denomination "backup bills" in the glove compartment.

Several turns, a glance to verify the correct street name at the corner, and she slowed to identify house numbers, odd/even, ascending/descending, to establish the correct direction and which side of the street. A cluster of parked cars a block ahead confirmed the location even before the street address appeared on the mailbox. Seconds later, she swung into an open parking spot in front of the house.

From the number of parked cars and array of items strewn before the house, this might be a winner. Jennifer glanced at her reflection in the rear-view mirror. In her rush to get away this morning, rather than dealing with "bad hair" she covered her honey-colored bob with a scarf moments before leaving the house. Now she tightened its knot at the back of her neck and applied the lipstick forgotten in her hasty no-makeup departure. Rubbing her lips together to spread the color evenly, she turned her perceptive bright blue eyes toward the first garage sale of the day!

She was early — at 7:45 a.m., fifteen minutes ahead of the 8 a.m. start listed in the newspaper ad which, along with numerous others, she'd cut out and taped in her notebook. With luck, she'd hit most, maybe all these close ones, even in this morning's abbreviated time. Out of her car and moving rapidly along the sidewalk, she blended with other shoppers advancing toward the house.

Lots of potential "treasures" here — pieces of quality furniture spread across the front lawn, household knick-knacks heaped on tables along both sides of the driveway, a makeshift clothes rack on a pole suspended between two ladders — items stretching from the curb, up the driveway, back into the garage and even laterally across the front porch. Her pulse quickened!

Sliding purposefully around other shoppers, she began her initial "overview scan" to quickly identify any standout — a piece of furniture, painting, lamp, or other unusual item inviting a hasty claim. She'd disciplined herself to pause briefly like this at the outer edge to scope the scene first, stifling a nearly overwhelming urge to dash instead toward whatever beckoned first. Later, she'd look over the remaining items in more detail. A thorough inspection of a sale this size should require less than ten minutes for her practiced eye.

She noticed the random scatter of "merchandise," *not* arranged into like groups of furniture, luggage, books, jewelry, sports equipment, clothing, appliances, shoes, baby items, tools or household goods. Few were pre-priced, and those tagged bore post-it-notes. A poor sticker choice for uneven surfaces, humid summer temperatures and tag-switching customers, she thought.

The seller, a pinch-faced middle-aged woman, appeared to be running the sale by herself — also not a good idea, Jennifer knew. Aside from answering questions, demonstrating how things work, and keeping an eye out for shop-lifting, cashiering for a busy garage sale crowd required full-focus vigilance. Jennifer hoped the woman had helpers coming soon because even before the 8 a.m. start, Seller was already outnumbered. An amateur operation, Jennifer concluded — hard on the Seller but perhaps advantageous for the Buyer!

Spotting a luxuriant six-foot tall artificial bamboo tree rooted in a handsome brass planter, Jennifer instantly envisioned it gracing a waiting corner in her living room. Trying to control her eagerness as another shopper appraised the tree by touching its leaves, Jennifer pretended to study a china plate. As soon as the other shopper moved on, Jennifer grabbed the tree, inspected it top to bottom and wrestled it over to Seller, who stood near her garage entrance with one hand clutching a cash box and the other pushing wisps of hair back from her nervous face.

"Good morning," Jennifer began conversationally. "Great weather today for your sale, isn't it? It's a lot of work getting it all ready." She gestured toward the yard. "Are you moving?"

"Well, yes, I...I've sold the house to move to a smaller place," Seller's downcast eyes brimmed with tears. "I recently divorced my husband, and," suddenly her chin came up with resolve, "and the house sold so fast that now I have to be out in just three weeks!"

Maybe priced the house too low? Jennifer wondered to herself. Instead she said, "A garage sale is a great way to clean out the house and make some money in the process. Good idea!"

Seller managed a self-conscious smile. "Thanks, I hope so. I... I've never held one before; actually I've never even been to one, but a friend suggested I try it so... " her voice trailed away.

"After today, you'll be very experienced. How much are you asking for this tree?"

"Oh, I'm sorry it's not priced," Seller apologized. "I ran out of time after midnight getting everything ready."

"Hey, no problem! What amount do you have in mind?"

"I guess $40. It cost $80 new and half price seems about right," the Seller reasoned.

Jennifer knew some garage sale buyers thought bargaining tacky and paid the asking price while others considered bargaining practical and even entertaining. The worst the Seller could say was "no."

Classic bargaining strategy dictated offering about 50% of the asking price for a good-condition item. Seller might agree, but if not they usually negotiated toward a compromise figure less than Seller's original price but more than Buyer's original offer. Exceptions included items already very fairly priced or ones priced so ridiculously low that the buyer snapped up the purchase without hesitation.

"Yes," Jennifer pointed to the tree offered for $40, "but after all, this is a garage sale where people look for real bargains." Per formula, she offered half the asking price. "Would you accept $20? You don't want to cart it back inside after the sale if it doesn't sell, do you?"

Seller offered a thin smile. "That's true," she hesitated as other buyers jostled toward her, items in hand. "How about $30?"

"Sold," Jennifer agreed, thinking the brass planter alone was worth that much. She gave Seller the money and began lugging the cumbersome artificial tree toward her car.

And that's when it happened!

CHAPTER 2

Something thudded hard against Jennifer, knocking her completely off balance! The bamboo tree fell from her grasp and she stumbled awkwardly, wind-milling her arms in a frantic effort to stay afoot. "Why don't you watch out where the hell you're going?" a cross male voice snarled as a burly man with a blond crew cut muscled past her. He carried a huge, heavy TV set without apparent effort. Reaching a black pickup, he deposited the TV lightly onto the truck bed as only a powerful weight-lifter could... and without a glance of concern in her direction.

Jennifer quickly looked back toward the sale to see if someone witnessed what happened, but all were engrossed in shopping. She turned again toward the man who'd slammed into her. Despite his gym-trim muscles and hulking football player physique — which might be admired under other circumstances — he accepted no responsibility for the incident he'd just created, moved to the driver's door of his pickup and climbed inside.

Politeness characterized most garage sale shoppers, and, frankly, everyone Jennifer knew, so she half-expected him to call out an apology or even return to help pick up her fallen tree. Instead, his truck motor roared to life and she heard its gears shift. That he ignored his role in nearly decking her upset Jennifer; but this coarse disregard paired with his startling strength reminded her that raw power in irresponsible hands spelled danger! A look at any day's newspaper underscored that chilling observation!

This guy acted very differently from the well-mannered men Jennifer only now realized she took for granted. The men she knew not only behaved politely but large physically-intimidating men *doubled* their efforts at respectful, non-threatening behavior around women. Never would her husband, sons, male neighbors or business associates treat a woman so crassly.

Considering this, she felt a new relief that he sped away instead of returning, perhaps to confront rather than assist her. She shivered, the hair on her arms prickling alarm as she watched his truck disappear down the street, grateful that he didn't know or care who she was.

What was going on here? Jennifer liked people, made friends easily and avoided the rash judgments of flimsy first impressions. Was he just a jerk or maybe a nice guy having a bad day? Was the TV heavier than he let on, forcing him to concentrate more on hefting his burden than finding a clear path to his truck? Why did she even attempt plausible explanations for his callous behavior when her intuition told her this man spelled trouble? She'd steer clear of him if he appeared at other sales — or anywhere else for that matter!

Enough time wasted on this. She struggled to her van, stuffed the tree inside and took a tape measure from the box on the front seat. Checking the furniture measurements written this morning in her notebook, she locked the van's doors and returned to the sale. Now for a close look at what remained.

Her eyes darted across the jumbled sale items. There — the bench she'd noticed earlier! She whipped out her tape measure. Darn, too long for the mud room that needed seating space. She walked a last once-around the driveway, porch and garage.

Of the dozen shoppers here, she recognized several "Regulars" as she called them because of their frequent attendance at these sales. There was "Englishman," a quiet fellow concentrating on reusable construction materials and "Stevedore," a large man with an angular face and thick, white hair, who typically bought furniture. She'd observed him consigning some at the local Treasure Trove thrift shop and guessed he refurbished and sold pieces found at these sales.

She noticed "Duchess," a tall, elegant-looking middle aged woman with dark brown hair piled into a tall beehive atop her head, who moved regally among the wares, fingering better quality jewelry, linens, china, silver and leather and buying upscale items.

Sometimes Jennifer saw friends or neighbors at these sales. For instance, that man with the curly black hair and scimitar-shaped scar on his lower left cheek. He looked familiar, but why — a distant neighbor, a clerk in a store she patronized, a waiter in one of the many local restaurants she and Jason frequented? She'd certainly seen him more than once!

Wait! A month ago at an estate sale, they passed on the stairs when she started down as he came up — and more recently, last week at a moving sale. Now it all came back: she'd seen him prior to that in Great Falls and again in Vienna. But wasn't something about him different then? She thought she remembered the scar but his hair... was her memory failing?

If a Regular, he needed a name. His cheek blemish reminded her of the dueling scars from centuries earlier when fencing was commonplace. Though not likely what disfigured this young man, Jennifer nevertheless chose "Swordsman."

Refocusing on the sale, she spotted a new-looking four-slice toaster, but did it work? She moved toward Seller who, without a calculator, attempted to total the prices of numerous items a Buyer handed her. As she waited in the check-out line, Jennifer's eyes surveyed the other shoppers to assure that the ill-mannered blond body-builder wasn't there. Mercifully, her turn came next.

"You have such great stuff that I'm back again!" Jennifer said to Seller, trying to sound cheerier than she felt. She held up the toaster. "What are you asking for this?"

"How about $4.00?"

Great price, but Jennifer knew that purchasing used items cautioned "buyer beware." In their zeal to complete a sale, some Sellers couldn't resist stretching the truth a little and, unlike protocol for store purchases, you couldn't return faulty merchandise the next day. All electrical appliances invited testing, as did anything battery-operated. The cardboard box in her van held aids to cope with this need, such as light bulbs to test lamps, various batteries, a flashlight and screw drivers, together with rope to tie down the SUV 's tailgate if something large had to stick out, a bungee cord, packaging tape, newspapers for wrapping glass or ceramics and a blanket/pillow combo to cushion fragile cargo.

"Do you mind plugging it in, please, to make sure it works?" Jennifer asked.

"I guess it is only fair to test it," Seller acknowledged, "although I didn't really set up for that..."

"Have you an extension cord or maybe there's an electrical outlet in the garage?"

"Let me think," said the bewildered Seller. "I'm pretty sure there's no plug in the garage. I... I guess you could try an outlet in the kitchen. I understand you want to be sure. Just go on in...."

"Thanks!" Jennifer hurried to the back of the garage, through the kitchen door into the house. "Hello," she called, not wanting to startle anyone inside. "Hello," she called again. Silence.

Plugging the toaster into the first outlet she saw, she depressed its plunger and watched closely as the coils inside glowed. Though grateful to test it out, she knew it risky for Seller to allow a stranger into her house unsupervised! Jennifer posed no problem, but others might. How could Seller know the difference? Should she share this thought or keep it to herself?

When the toaster popped its imaginary bread to the surface, she wrapped the cord around one hand and, gripping the appliance by the handles, hurried back outside.

"Thanks so much for letting me try it. It works perfectly. I'll take it." Jennifer fished $4.00 from the purse fastened around her waist, paid Seller and then hesitated as several customers pressed forward to pay for their items.

Shielding her words from the others with a cupped hand, Jennifer whispered to Seller, "I just want to mention that it's probably not a good idea to let anyone into your house unless you or someone you trust is there. Good luck and I hope you do really well today."

Seller's startled gaze followed Jennifer down the driveway to her car, before other Buyers jostled forward, demanding check-out attention. Now she probably wonders if I took something — the messenger never wins, Jennifer thought! Still, the woman needed warning...

Jumping into her van, gunning the motor and simultaneously glancing at the notebook on the seat beside her, Jennifer placed a finger on the ad listing her next stop. Two garage sales on the same street and only a few minutes from her current location. As the

SUV's motor roared to life, she executed a remarkably close U-turn and sped down the street.

Jennifer's mind wandered as she drove, thinking that behind every garage sale lay a story. At the last house, the story was doubly unfortunate—an obviously painful divorce and a sorely needed, if poorly executed, sale of belongings. Jennifer sincerely hoped happiness lay somewhere in Seller's future.

But what was happiness anyway? If you couldn't achieve it in privileged and affluent McLean, Virginia, where the heck could you? The third world's desperate poor who scrabbled in gritty poverty for daily survival surely imagined if they lived in safe and beautiful homes with plenty to eat they'd be happy forever. Yet she knew from newspaper accounts and neighborhood stories that the full gamut of crime—domestic abuse, child neglect, fraud, theft, arson and even murder—surfaced right here against McLean's backdrop of comfort and wealth!

She sighed as her thoughts turned again to the last Seller. If fifty percent of today's marriages ended in divorce, what future did that suggest for her five grown children, three of whom already had spouses? And what of the ups and downs in her own forty-year marriage to Jason?

Thinking of his familiar craggy face, balding head and warm grin, she smiled and then chuckled aloud as she drove. Somehow, they'd survived those frenetic early years together, enduring each other's foibles, building Jason's business and raising a big family. Now they found themselves sharing a particularly comfortable time with each other and with the life they'd shaped together.

As the congestion of parked cars just ahead signaled her upcoming destination, she pushed aside her thoughts to concentrate on finding a place to wedge her crossover. Since every sale reflected a story, what tale would unfold at this next stop?

CHAPTER 3

Jennifer maneuvered her car smoothly into an opening among the vehicles clustered in front of the next sale. The later on a Saturday morning, the more Buyers are awake and on the prowl! Knowing that choice stuff sells fast, she jumped out and hustled up the driveway.

An entirely different scenario here—these Sellers were NOT novices. The two of them seemed relaxed as they looked out confidently over their well organized, pre-priced merchandise.

Jennifer dodged through the large crowd of buyers to approach the comfortably seated sellers. "What a lot of effort you've put into getting ready for this!"

"You're so right! We're recently married and so we're combining two households," the man said pleasantly, beaming at his new bride. "For instance, I thought I had a lot of exceptional bachelor stuff, but I'm told now," he winked at his wife, "it's *inappropriate!*"

"Well," added his wife, "besides the usual duplication we have some one-of-a-kind things that just couldn't work in the new house," she glanced at her husband mischievously.

"Such as?" Jennifer queried with friendly interest.

New Wife cradled a coffee cup in one hand and gestured with the other. "Such as everything on that side of the driveway from my husband's old apartment! Such as that oil painting of a nude woman, coincidentally also an old girlfriend," she shot her spouse a meaningful glance. "Such as all this ultra-modern black and chrome living room furniture, the zebra rug and pillows, and all those chrome accessories. And," she wrinkled her nose, "and not least, such as these stacks of *Penthouse* and *Playboy* magazines."

"A fifteen-year classic collection of both," New Husband remarked wistfully, reminiscing as he riffled through one of the magazines. Dropping it back on the stack, he sighed. "Perfect for just the right guy."

The sign on the husband's orphaned items read:

COUCH - $100

2 MATCHING CHAIRS - $40 each

3 GLASS/CHROME COFFEE AND END TABLES - $30 each

CHROME 4-PANEL ROOM DIVIDER - $75

PAIR CHROME TABLE LAMPS - $30 each

CHROME FLOOR LAMP - $40

CHROME SHELVING - $85

FRAMED ORIGINAL OIL PAINTING - $100

MEN'S MAGAZINES $1 each or all 360 for $200

The painting caught Jennifer's eye right away. She'd immediately divined the bamboo tree's place in her living room, but where could she hang this intriguing art? She walked around the sale thinking this over before again returning to study the painting: a nude woman seated with her back to the artist, delicate flesh tones accentuating her hour-glass figure, her long, tawny hair cascading from the crown of her head down over her shoulders. Because of the subject's unseen face, the picture embodied every woman who had ever sat in that classic pose. She definitely wanted it, but where to display it? Her mind flipped through possible places in the house and then it came to her — their spacious master bathroom was the perfect location. But $100?

Jennifer approached New Wife, "What's your best price for the old girlfriend you don't want."

"I especially want THAT to disappear today," New Wife confided. "Hey, make me an offer!"

"Okay, how about... um... $50?"

"I think it's worth way more than that."

Jennifer smiled craftily, "Ah, but what is it worth to you to have this abomination gone forever?"

"Sold!" laughed New Wife. Jennifer paid her, awkwardly hefted the large painting as best she could and sidled slowly down the driveway with her oversized trophy.

Suddenly an obstacle blocked her way and a rough male voice commanded, "Put that down. It's mine!" Hardly a polite suggestion, this was an *order!*

"Pardon me?" Jennifer said politely, "I've just bought this and am taking it to my car." As she tried stepping ahead, her path was again blocked. Now she lowered the large frame slightly, her blue eyes barely peering over the top.

Those same blue eyes widened in shock as she stared directly into the face of the brawny, blond muscleman who'd crashed into her at the last sale—the man she'd vowed to avoid! A thick neck topped the tall man's square torso and the beady eyes in his obstinate face glared coldly straight down at Jennifer across the top of the picture frame. Only inches away from him now, she shuddered as her initial apprehension from that first sighting escalated into fear. Big and nasty, he reminded her of a wrestler, which confirmed this as the right name for him.

Wrestler barked at her, "I just bought everything listed on that sign from him," he pointed toward New Husband. "That means *all* of it—the furniture, magazines, lamps AND this picture."

Her logical mind commanded her to defuse this risky situation fast, but incongruously she did not. Summoning courage born of the conviction that she was in the right and reinforced by the illusion of safety with at least twenty people at the sale who could come to her rescue, to her surprise she said, "But I've already paid for this. I think that makes it mine!"

Wrestler's expression turned malevolent as his large, powerful hand encircled and squeezed her small wrist. He spoke in a measured, demanding voice. "I bought it and I'm taking it *now!*"

He was hurting her arm! Frozen, she still clung to the painting, unable to move away from this menace. Heads turned in the direction of their raised voices and New Husband hurried toward them.

Jennifer had already mentally hung the painting in the chosen room at home and knew that at these sales whoever paid first became the new owner! To her amazement she stubbornly repeated to New Husband, "I believe I bought it first and if so, I think it's mine."

Wrestler's face reddened as he fought for control. His arm muscles twitched, his fingers clasped and unclasped, his already thick neck seemed to swell as his frustration increased.

"Hey there," New Husband said to them both in a congenial, relaxed tone. "I bet we can work out this little misunderstanding. As you both can see, my wife and I are each trying to sell everything out here today and sometimes people come to us separately with offers." Turning to Jennifer, he continued. "I'm sorry but my wife made a mistake offering the painting to you. She didn't realize I'd already sold it to this guy. We really apologize to you for the confusion. Of course, we'll return your money. No harm done?"

"But money changed hands. I think it's mine!" Jennifer protested to New Husband, careful to avoid Wrestler's glare.

"May I talk to you privately for a moment over here?" New Husband asked Jennifer.

Carrying the painting with her, she walked a few guarded steps to the side with New Husband.

"Look," he said, "I understand that you like it, you paid for it and you want it, but here are three things to think about. First, you can understand that we hope to get the best price offered today for our stuff. That's just common sense. Wouldn't you feel the same way if you were giving this sale today? And you know he paid us twice as much as you did. Second, we can't know which of you bought it first. Let's imagine that my wife sold it to you at the same moment I sold it to him. You can't both take it — unless it's cut in half, which makes no sense. And third," he glanced toward Wrestler, "frankly, this guy makes me very uneasy. You know what I mean? What happens if we try to take it away from him?"

Peering sidelong at Wrestler, reluctantly, she *did* understand. His intransigent scowl, his body radiating bottled energy and his next move ominous and unpredictable, never mind that piercing stare...A barrage of thoughts tumbled through Jennifer's mind. Was this the kind of nut who would follow her home, stalk her or the children, bash her car windows or poison her cat?

New Husband continued calmly, "Look, agreed, this isn't the outcome you'd like, but here is your money back with an extra five dollars," he pressed it into her hand, "and we'll make you the deal of a lifetime on anything else you buy here today. How does that sound?"

Vacillating, her focus flicked from New Husband to the glowering Wrestler and back again.

"This isn't fair," she said in a quiet voice to New Husband.

"No, it isn't. But it is a good decision," New Husband assured her, pressing the money into her pocket and gently easing the picture from her loosening fingers. "Now go look around and find some good stuff. Then see me for a REAL deal!"

Turning back to the sale, she tried to refocus yet couldn't help glancing sideways as Wrestler loaded his purchases into the black pickup truck, mercifully ignoring her. Relieved at his rapt absorption with his task, she realized now the idiotically stupid risk she'd taken. She had pledged to avoid him and instead confronted him! Madness! What was wrong with her today?

Still, she memorized his license plate number to record in the notebook in her car, an act giving her the illusion of a strategic edge: she knew his vehicle plate number but, thank goodness, he didn't know hers! Also this information doubled as insurance against any possible future trouble from him, in which case she could tell police exactly how to trace him.

Shaking these uncomfortable thoughts as best she could, Jennifer forced her attention back to the sale. Soon she noticed a bench which her tape measure confirmed fit her space perfectly. With a little paint and simple upholstering she could turn this into a decorator piece to transform her mudroom in a practical yet custom way. The tag read $20.

Looking around, she observed that Wrestler's truck was gone. Relieved, she lugged the bench and some other small items into the line of buyers to pay New Husband for their purchases.

When Jennifer's turn came, New Husband patted her arm and without even cataloging her items said, "You just take these with our compliments. No charge at all! And again, I'm sorry for what happened earlier. But that guy was, well, strange! You know what I mean?"

"Here's your $5 bribe back," she said with a twinkle, "and thanks for your kind offer, but of course I'll pay for my purchases," and when she insisted, New Husband finally agreed. Jennifer continued, "That dreadful guy had no sense of humor at all, but clearly you do!"

New Husband chuckled appreciatively, "God knows I try, and I admit that bachelor stuff held warm memories for me. But my future's going to be way better than the past." He glanced happily toward New Wife, busy selling items on the other side of the yard.

Jennifer started to leave, but on impulse turned back. "I've been thinking about the way you handled that situation with the painting and I must ask—what do you do in real life?"

New Husband threw back his head and broke into a hearty laugh. "Funny you should ask! I'm a professional mediator."

CHAPTER 4

Checking her watch, Jennifer realized with regret that only 20 minutes remained to shop if she were to return home by 9 a.m. as planned. She pulled into the knot of cars at the next sale and parked quickly.

Three gloomy middle-aged couples conducted this sale. They'd neatly categorized and priced the items around them, but these dejected Sellers were not happy campers.

"This represents a *whole* lot of work," Jennifer commiserated, surveying the scene.

"Yeah, but not because we wanted to," said the woman in orange. "After Mama died, Daddy just couldn't keep on by himself. He forgot to pay bills, so the utilities got turned off a couple of times and he blazed up a few pots of food on the stove. We were afraid he'd set the house afire and burn himself to a bacon-crisp if we hadn't finally put a stop to it by finding him a nursing home."

"Assisted living," corrected the tired-looking man in green, who wore a straw hat.

The woman in yellow said, "It's been a nightmare going through all their things, and were they ever savers: old bills, receipts and magazines dating back fifty years! Besides all we put out for this sale, there's a ton more to go through inside before we can sell the house. Because some of us grew up here, that's yet another nightmare." Yellow sighed heavily.

The man in the red shirt glanced at the other two. "Lucky for us, Reba knows all about giving garage sales, which saved us a pile of money because those estate sale folks charge a bundle to do it for you."

Orange said, "We had a devil of a time pricing stuff because we're not from around here and not real sure what's right for these parts. So if the price doesn't look right, make us an offer."

About fifteen other shoppers milled around now. Spotting Swordsman again, Jennifer watched him peripherally. What set him apart from the other shoppers? Not focused on the sale's merchandise like everybody else, instead he looked around the house and yard as if in the first upscale residence he'd ever seen. Nor did he fit the bored husband stereotype— one dutifully accompanying his shopper wife but with no shred of interest himself. No, Swordsman seemed alert to the surroundings, but if not a shopper or the spouse of one, then why repeatedly visit these sales? An architect looking for new ideas? That seemed farfetched.

Was she just edgy from her earlier encounter with Wrestler? Once suspicion clouds your mind your perceptions change. Different from the in-her-face prickly danger radiated by Wrestler, Swordsman's unlikely behavior triggered her curiosity — something *odd* about him!

Enough. Didn't curiosity kill the cat? Her smile faded. She *was* that curious cat!

As if reading her interest, Swordsman turned to look directly at her and their gazes locked. To break this uncomfortable contact, she consulted her watch—her time was running out!

Ignoring Swordsman now, she stepped forward for a better overview of the sale. Her glance moved across the merchandise, stopped, then riveted. Could it be true? At the end of the far table sat a collection of Blue Danube china! She could hardly contain her excitement!

Years ago, she inherited her mother's Blue Danube place settings for eight and using it brought back warm childhood memories. Adding extra settings to accommodate her large family was easy back when it sold open-stock in department stores. But the now-discontinued pattern was no longer available retail, even though breakage and chips required frequent new additions. A company called Replacements, Inc. charged dearly since the current demand exceeded the existing supply, forcing the price up. Now occasional lucky finds still occurred at antique and thrift shops or estate and garage sales.

She moved swiftly past the other displays to the table. There they were! Turning the gravy boat upside down, she verified the maker's mark on the bottom. Calm, be calm! Check each piece for chips, cracks, maker's mark and price. The gravy boat sticker read $10 , salt and pepper $7, candle sticks $5 each, filigree serving dish $15, cream and sugar $15, cake plate $15, jelly jar $5, pitcher $10, coffee pot $15 — and all in mint condition. She felt pricks of adrenalin rush down her arms to her fingertips as she gently eased past another shopper who reached for one of the pieces.

"Excuse me," she smiled politely at the shopper, "but I'm already buying these," and then a bit louder to Yellow and Red, "Would you please help me collect them and wrap them up for me?"

Yellow hurried to assist. "Well, they sure are pretty little blue and white dishes, aren't they? You want them all?"

"Yes, please. Was this part of a whole set of china?" Jennifer probed.

"Well now, a lot of it sold about 30 minutes ago but I think another piece is still inside the house unless Reba's keeping it — a sort of casserole dish with a cover on it. Let me ask her about it."

Jennifer wondered at the connection between the upscale items at this handsome house and the folksy heirs unloading them. Certainly a story here, but probably not one learned diplomatically. With an important purchase in progress she must not risk alienating them, despite her curiosity.

A moment later Blue walked over to Jennifer. "You the one interested in more of these dishes?"

"Well yes, I might be. I..." Jennifer hoped her voice didn't reveal her true passion as she made a Herculean effort at casualness. "I sort of like blue and white and think I *might* be able to find a place for some of them," she somehow managed.

"Seems like you sure love dishes! While they're wrapping up your other things, come on in the house with me to take a look at it, but I don't know for sure yet if it's for sale."

Nearly trembling, Jennifer followed Blue into the house, through the box-strewn kitchen to the cluttered dining room with paintings stacked against a wall. And there it was. Jennifer couldn't suppress a sharp intake of breath. To cover this betrayal, she faked a small cough.

Like a museum piece atop the credenza sat the graceful Blue Danube soup tureen, a replica of the emperor's own Meissen original. She'd often ogled its photo in the brochure. Steadying herself against the door jam, she felt her pulse race. What pleasure to gaze upon this beautiful piece, never mind the intoxicating possibility of *owning* it! How could she persuade Blue to let it go?

"Oh, my," Jennifer whispered. "Looks like your mother owned a lot of nice things."

Rather than accepting the intended compliment, Blue's face became even sterner. "Actually, she's my husband's mother, not mine. He's sitting outside there with the rest of us, the one in green, wearing the straw hat. Yes, she did have a lot of right pretty dishes and statues and such, but just between us she always acted real snooty."

Doubting its wisdom, Jennifer risked a curious, "Oh?"

"Yep, she was always uppity with me, like I wasn't good enough for her son. Tried to like her but just never could. My dander went up every time she put me down: how I set a table, the way I cooked, the music I liked, how I dressed. Truth is, I'm not real sorry she's finally gone."

Thinking of no discreet response, Jennifer instead reached for the tureen. "May I?"

"Here, let me do it for you," Blue responded protectively. "This here is the lid, and this is the bowl part. I'll turn it over for you because I saw you doing that with the other pieces outside. And that's the big saucer that sits under it." Blue replaced the tureen and its parts on the credenza. "And this here is the dipper," she held up the soup ladle.

"Did I understand you to say this is for sale?" Jennifer inquired politely.

"Maybe, but first I want to see how much you like it, cause that would mean you'd pay... I mean, you'd take real good care of it. And next, I'd be asking a lot for it because I'm just as happy to keep it myself. So I might sell it to you but not for less than..." she'd pick an outrageous price, doubting anyone foolish enough to buy it for that, "not for less than $100," she said smugly.

"A hundred dollars? I... is that your best price?"

"Not a penny less. Yep, that's it, take it or leave it," said Blue with finality.

Jennifer frowned, "Then I guess...I guess I'll take it!"

Surprise spread across Blue's face. What kind of place was this McLean, Virginia? Who ever heard of paying that much for a darned old dish, even one with three parts and a dipper? Should she have asked more? A crafty expression flickered across her face. "I meant to say $125."

"But you just offered it to me for $100 and I agreed."

"Yes, I know that but I made a mistake. And we don't take checks! " Blue warned.

"I understand about preferring cash, but... well, I mean... you changed the deal."

"Yes, I did, but I'm just as happy to keep that casserole myself. And they need me outside! Do you want it or not?"

Jennifer stared at the tureen. Explaining this impulse purchase to Jason would require creativity. But just look at it—she might never ever stumble upon another such chance! Straightening with decision she said, "I'll take it."

"You got the money with you?"

"Yes, in the car."

"Better get it and pay me then before I even carry it outside the house," Blue added with caution.

Hurrying outside, Jennifer whispered to herself over and over: Don't let her change her mind! *Please*, don't let her change her mind!

Five minutes later, with the packaged Blue Danube china braced safely in cardboard boxes on the van's floor, she gloated. Even if you were lucky enough to *find* them, these pieces cost more than double what she just paid and the four-part tureen more yet!

Euphoric, Jennifer turned toward home!

CHAPTER 5

Her time-sensitive jaunt finished and aglow with her success at the sales, Jennifer relaxed on the drive home. Gliding past the well-kept McLean houses surrounded by manicured lawns, she reflected that this community "showed" well today just as it had twenty-five years ago when Jason's new job first prompted their springtime visit to the Washington, D.C. area.

After a week of fruitless house-hunting but still seeking a roomy, affordable home for their five young children, they extended their search to a Virginia suburb of D.C. called McLean. That morning their agent showed them a house new on the market—colonial-style on a quiet cul-de-sac where springtime flowers splashed glorious colors across the yard. With a large yard bordered behind by wooded park land for their kids to explore, two blocks from pool and tennis and three blocks from an outstanding Fairfax County elementary school, this property seemed *perfect*. But the cost! Would they sacrifice the kids' college funds to buy it? They moved in a week later.

Jennifer smiled. Despite a tight budget in those early days, time proved this decision wise. Their family thrived in this congenial neighborhood and the property's price quadrupled in the intervening twenty-five years. Eventually, they financed their children through college after all.

Nearing home, Jennifer snapped out of her reverie, pressed the remote control to open the iron driveway gates, maneuvered the van through the tall brick columns on either side, pressed a second remote to open the garage door and drove inside. Jumping out of her SUV, she picked up the toaster, piled an armful of her other purchases atop it and hustled them into the house.

She found Jason drinking coffee and reading the newspaper on the long glass-enclosed sun porch covering the entire back of their house. "Hello, Hon," she called. "Are the children up yet?"

"Just me, but I heard the shower, so at least one's awake." Jason looked up from the paper and added, "The girls usually sleep late like all college kids—lucky if we see them before noon. Aren't you home sooner than usual?"

"Becca's summer job interview is this morning. Her car's in the shop so she asked to borrow mine because you need yours for golf at ten."

Though eager to tell him about her buys, she knew function equaled desirability to her engineer husband: something to *use* ranked higher than something to *see*. So she needed to apply some finesse. Ignoring his skeptical frown, she held up two sturdy garden trowels and said, "Here's something for you! Didn't your last one break yesterday? They're new and only a dollar each!"

"Great," he said without enthusiasm, but she knew he'd garden with them before the day ended.

"And a lot of 'smalls' plus these nice earrings!" She pointed to her earlobes. "The clip-on's I wear are nearly impossible to find retail any more. And a bamboo tree that will look stunning in the living room and a bench for the seating we need in the mudroom."

He grunted and lowered his eyes back to the paper. "Need help bringing anything in?"

"Thanks, Jay. Just the tree and bench." She poured herself some coffee, wanting to share what weighed uppermost on her mind: the scary encounters with Wrestler! But she hesitated. This would worry him and maybe further dampen his marginal enthusiasm for her garage sale hobby. She valued his love and protectiveness, but why alarm him with information that might elicit strong objections or even challenge her cherished independence?

And in the unlikely event she ever saw Wrestler again, she'd *really* avoid him this time! Since most garage sale buyers had specific goals, such as replacing a lamp or a chair, they shopped no more after achieving their objective. Regulars like her were the exception, not the rule.

Jennifer's own garage sale experience began as a practical shopping choice when her children were young and the new-house budget tight. Later, this habit blossomed into genuine treasure-hunting because people sell what people have. Wealthy McLean and surrounds offered excellent "gently used" merchandise and finding quality bargains is ever popular, as perpetual sales at retail stores and car lots prove. She'd found many unusual and useful items to benefit her home, her life-style and her family; and the sale "stories" intrigued her.

She knew long established markets existed for "used" houses with several previous owners, for "pre-owned cars" and for antique shops where merchandise is necessarily second-hand. Garage and estate sales were the same idea. Since Wrestler had likely completed his shopping, little probability existed for their paths to cross again. Regulars like Jennifer looked for fun, adventure, practical finds and unique treasures...not trouble.

So unlike what was actually on her mind, she asked her husband, "Find any interesting news in the morning paper? I only grabbed the classified section earlier to locate the sales."

"Ways to solve Old Dominion Drive traffic congestion," he droned, "a new store at Tysons Corner; critique of a new local restaurant, a burglary in Great Falls and another in Woodlea Hills..."

"Woodlea Hills! That's just down the road. We'd better lock our doors religiously. I must be sure to alert the girls about that. Anything else?"

"Another McLean woman is missing."

Jennifer looked up sharply. "Don't I remember headlines about a teenager disappearing a month ago? What ever happened with that case?"

"Don't think she turned up—maybe a runaway? Who knows better than we do what parents face raising kids these days."

"Hey, I didn't know you had five in mind when we married!" she needled.

He stifled a smile. "If I'd known about the five I might not have proposed." Seeing her raised eyebrow, he conceded, "Well, *maybe...* " He winked and she strolled over to kiss his cheek.

"Okay, break it up, you two!" Daughter Becca strolled into the kitchen dressed for her upcoming appointment. "Coffee seriously needed!"

Jennifer gestured toward the coffee pot. "Ready and waiting for you. Good morning, Sweetie! Not quite awake yet?"

"Barely! Thanks for coming back early, Mom. Any garage sale goodies for show-and-tell?"

"Well, funny you should ask! *Hold onto your hat!*" Jennifer smiled and bustled away to her car in the garage.

Jason groaned. "Oh no! When she says *'hold-on-to-your-hat,'* years of experience tell me I'm in for a fast ride. I fear that phrase! What wild and crazy thing did she find this time?"

Becca laughed. "Dad, how can she still shock you after more than forty years together?"

"Shock hardly covers it! Life with your mom isn't boring, but that phrase *always* means steeling myself for a major jolt!"

"While she's still out in the garage, Dad, does she suspect anything about tomorrow?"

"No, I think we're really going to surprise her!"

Moments later, Jennifer reappeared and placed the bulky newspaper-wrapped bundle housing the tureen on the kitchen counter. She'd sneak the other Blue Danube pieces into the china cabinet later, confident Jason wouldn't notice those additions once ensconced.

As she pulled away the wrapping, Jason sat bolt upright, his eyes on the tureen and his voice rising an octave. "Oh geez, I'm afraid to ask the cost of that *glorified soup bowl.*"

Anticipating his bluster, Jennifer purred, "Look, today is the last day ever that I'm fifty-nine years old. Tomorrow is the big six-oh! Isn't this the ideal birthday present for me, Jason?"

Now he pushed back from the table, cast long-suffering eyes toward the ceiling and whistled a loud note. "The price must be a whopper because you just pulled out the big cannons."

She chuckled and lightly kissed his forehead. "Thank you, honey; it's *exactly* what I wanted most." She smiled so happily and Jason moaned in such painful mock distress that they all had to laugh.

As Jennifer handed her the car keys, Becca giggled and pointed to the new tureen. "Bet I can guess what we're having for lunch."

"You're exactly right!" her mother confirmed, "...and sandwiches, too!"

CHAPTER 6

Jason grinned at how willingly their grown children embraced his surprise party idea for Jennifer's 60th birthday. The Blue Danube tureen aside, he thought a party at home with her loved ones gathered was the perfect gift for his dear wife, who doted on her family.

All their married children lived within a two hours' drive, remarkable in today's mobile society. Hannah, Becca and their close friend Tina MacKenzie had whisked Jennifer away to morning garage sales on the pretext of furnishing the college apartment the girls would share in the fall. They pledged to return her at noon, their arrival signaling the birthday feast to begin. Meantime, the "fam," with their spouses and the Grands, began arriving at the house late-morning, bringing covered dishes for the event.

Brown-haired Tina MacKenzie visited the Shannon girls so often—for meals, overnights, video-watching, studying and celebrations—that her presence seemed as normal as if she were just another child of their family. Quiet and friendly but more serious and reserved than the Shannon girls, Tina recently always wore the same unusual gold filigree dangling earrings.

As with many of Jennifer's astute observations, Jason hadn't noticed this until his wife pointed it out. "Her dad brought the earrings to her from his last trip to China. When he had the heart attack and died only a week after returning, Tina began wearing them constantly in his memory. Her dad's death hit her very hard and widowhood's tough for her mother to shoulder, too." Then, with eyes full of tears, Jen said to him, "I can't even imagine life without *you*, Jay!"

Gently pushing that memory aside, Jason basted more sauce onto chicken marinating in two big pans, about to take them outside when he heard, "Here, Dad, let me help with that." His twenty-eight-year-old son Mike offered as they each carried a large pan out to the patio grill.

"And where's Bethany?"

"My wife is picking up the cake and should return any minute now." Kaela swept past them, jostling scissors and an armful of fresh-cut flowers from the garden. "Dad, do you know where Mom's vases are?"

"In the laundry room cupboards. Here, I'll show you," Jason said. "Be back in a minute, Mike."

After producing the vase, Jason closed the laundry room door on the noisy crowd for a quiet moment, grateful that his children seemed grounded and happy, except perhaps for Hannah.

Five months ago Hannah discovered the boy she dated exclusively through six years of high school and early college had multiple other love affairs going during that same time. At a party she attended with college girlfriends, a stunned Hannah stumbled upon Kevin kissing his newest "squeeze."

As Hannah's beau, Kevin had been welcomed into their home for years. His deception startled them all, but the betrayal broke Hannah's heart. She closed herself in her room for days. When the crying finally stopped, she emerged haggard, depressed and disillusioned.

"I'll never trust my own judgment... or any man... again," she sobbed against her father's shoulder when he tried consoling her.

"Hannah, Hannah. Honey, time *does* heal; broken hearts can mend to love again and judgment grows from experiences like this one. Someday you'll find just the right trustworthy guy, I promise. They do exist, you know!" He looked into her tear-filled eyes.

"Oh, Daddy," she wailed, "why couldn't Kevin be like you?"

"We're all who we are! And some good may come out of this if Kevin realizes his behavior cost him a wonderful girl and he decides to change that behavior. You've moved past someone who didn't share your expectations and freed yourself to find someone who does, someone you can respect and who feels the same about you."

Wiping a tear from her cheek, Hannah asked, "Is that how it is for you and Mom?"

This unexpected question from his twenty-year-old daughter caught him by surprise. Blowing her nose into the handkerchief he'd handed her, Hannah didn't notice his smile grow as he reflected upon how he and Jennifer had stretched, changed, grown and merged in their forty-one years together. Some coincidental mix of intelligence and humor miraculously buoyed them through those harried years of marital adjustment and child-raising. Overcoming rough patches and sharing precious moments forged them together, so that now they felt closer than ever. "Yes it is that way for us," he answered honestly. Hannah seemed comforted, whether by her parents' affection or by his honesty, he wasn't sure which.

Intuitively, he thought Hannah would survive this temporary shock and hurt, land on her feet, emerge wiser for weathering the difficult lesson and some day reach for love again. He reminded himself that people heal differently, but five months of this sadness did seem a *long* time….

Jason returned to the dining room in time to hear a six-year-old Grand shout, "Auntie Bethany brought the birthday cake," as the youngster rocketed past the table on his way out to the back yard goldfish pond. A fancy chocolate cake with "Happy Birthday, Jennifer" frosted across the top dominated one end of the buffet table; and, if not 60, a large number of candles promised a warm glow.

The front door opened as Dylan and family arrived, with plans to stay several days to visit local museums. After hugs all around, they hustled their suitcases to appointed bedrooms and returned to the main floor just as a scout at the front window ran through the house calling, "She's here, quick, she's here!"

Stopping tasks and conversations, parents herded their children together into the dining room where numerous young Grands danced around in barely-contained anticipation. They listened as the automatic garage door droned open to admit Jennifer's car. Kaela whispered loudly to the group, "Okay, everyone, this is it! Get ready. It's *party* time!" Seconds later, the door from the garage to the house opened and Jennifer stepped in, followed closely by the three girls. Startled at the unexpected crowd in her house, she stopped in her tracks, amazement showing in her wide-eyed, open-mouthed expression.

The room echoed as shouts of "Surprise!" erupted in various octaves. Jennifer stood transfixed in the open doorway, a widening smile animating her face as a lively high-low chorus of voices launched into an off-key but enthusiastic rendition of "Happy-Birthday-To-You."

Delighted, she touched Jason's arm. "I'll bet you masterminded this, you rascal," she whispered to him and joked to the group, "Can't sudden shocks like this level a tottering 60-year old?"

"Speech, speech," someone called.

Emotional now, she managed to say, "I must be the luckiest person on Earth to have all of you in my life. Sharing this day with me is the very best possible present. Thank you! Thank you!" Approving hoots, foot stomping and whistles followed from the crowd.

Emerging from an impromptu conference with his siblings, Dylan stepped forward. "Mom, this gift is from all your children, but since I'm the oldest they want me to present it." He read the tag attached to a colorfully wrapped package, "For the woman who already has almost everything, here's one thing she doesn't." He handed her the box.

Fumbling the wrapping open, she drew out a metal rectangle and held it up for all to see. "YRDSALE" said the vanity license plate for her car. She burst into appreciative laughter and the rest joined in.

"Virginia doesn't allow enough spaces to spell out both words, so we had to abbreviate!" chirped another Grand, twelve-year-old Rachel.

"This is perfect! There'll be no hiding my madness from the world now."

"Time to eat!" Mike called, hustling to the barbeque to wield tongs transferring chicken from grill to serving platter. Lunch proceeded with noisy exuberance, followed by candle-lighting of the cake, wish-making and a circle of excited grandchildren helping Jennifer blow out the tiny flames. Afterward, the adults relaxed to talk together while the children played outside.

During a lull in activity, Tina approached Jennifer. "Mrs. Shannon, I have a little present for you also, to celebrate your birthday and to thank you for welcoming me so often into your home."

Touched, Jennifer hugged Tina, thanked her and opened the small gift box. Inside sat a tiny red cloisonné frog. Reading Jennifer's puzzled expression, Tina explained, "Shopping for someone like you is hard because you already have so many unusual things, but frogs are good luck omens in the Orient. Red is also a good fortune color there, so it's a double dose! My dad brought this one from China. It's small enough to carry with you as a little talisman. I hope you like it."

"Oh, Tina, thank you so very much. What an original present! You can be sure I'll cherish it because it comes from you and because nobody can have too much good luck! Look, I'm putting it into my pocket right this minute. He's on duty as of now!"

A little later, Kaela took her mother aside. "Mom, I'd like to have a garage sale next weekend but my house is too far away. Your address is a better draw if we could have it in your driveway. The other girls want to join in and we thought you'd probably have some things to contribute from your stash in the garage. We'd do everything: put the ad in the newspaper, put up signs and clean up afterward. Even the Grands could sell toys they're bored with at their own little tables."

Jennifer looked doubtful, "Remember two years ago how much work that last one was? Are you sure you want to take this on by yourselves?" Bethany, Kaela and Becca all nodded.

"Then if Dad doesn't mind, it's fine with me. And you're right," she added with a twinkle, "I certainly do have a few items to contribute!"

CHAPTER 7

Delighted that Dylan's family stayed on after her party, Jennifer marveled at how quickly their three-day visit sped by. She still felt the damp farewell kisses from little Asa, Christopher, Ethan and Gabe. Such cute little Grands! But after their noise and energy, returning to quiet, normal routines also had definite rewards. Win-win, Jennifer thought.

When the phone rang, she rushed from folding sheets in the laundry room to get the call before the answering machine kicked in. "Hello," she said.

"Jennifer Shannon?" a male voice asked and when she acknowledged that she was, he continued, "This is Ronnie Williams over at Forensic Labs. Remember me?"

"Of course I do! How could anyone work at the lab for three years and not remember you, Ronnie? What's new?"

"Pretty much the same except Heather, who we hired when you left, must start maternity leave next week... sooner than expected, doctor's orders. So, we wonder if you might like to temp for her during the two months she's gone. Returning short term might fit your schedule and since you already know the business office routine, we wouldn't have to train someone new. What do you think?"

Jennifer mused, "Interesting, Ronnie. You know I left only because I didn't want full time work any more. How many days a week?"

"We could probably get by with four because, if I remember, you work like a house afire!"

She laughed, " Well, I like keeping busy! Four days a week for two months sounds possible."

They discussed salary and recent office chatter about other employees she knew. "This is a tentative 'yes' but I want to discuss it with Jason first. I'll call you back within the hour! And Ronnie, thanks for thinking of me for this job!"

"Jennifer, I'm always thinking about you!"

"You're incorrigible!"

"I try to be."

How pleasant! She warmed to the idea of working again in the lab's business office—a stimulating environment, pleasant staff, extra income for her garage sale mischief and… how nice to be wanted back. Ronnie, the office manager, hadn't changed a bit: still flirty but in the nice way, not the harassment way.

Jason encouraged her to do what she wanted, so she and Ronnie decided she'd start on Monday.

Smiling at this unexpected surprise, Jennifer poured a cup of coffee and sank into a chair in the quiet kitchen. Realizing she hadn't looked at the morning newspaper, she opened the *Washington Post.* A few pages inside the first section, an article immediately drew her attention: a burglary in nearby McLean Hunt. She attended a sale in that neighborhood just a week ago and something about the address looked familiar!

On impulse, she found her garage sale notebook, flipped pages until she located the McLean Hunt sale and compared the house number to the newspaper information. An exact match! She cut out and dated the newspaper article. Didn't Jason mention a robbery in Woodlea Hills last Saturday when she returned from sales with the soup tureen? Rushing to the newspapers stacked in her garage for recycling, she pulled out the previous weekend's *Washington Post* and *Times.*

Paging through, she found Jason's article and checked it against addresses from the last few weeks in her notebook. Comparing the Woodlea Hills address in the paper to her notebook, she couldn't believe it: another match!

The newspapers in her garage went back about a month. Dragging them inside, she began with recent dates, looking for a very specific type of news article. When she glanced at the clock, an hour had passed. Unsuccessfully comparing several more articles with notebook entries, she cursed herself for a waste of time and was about to stop when she found yet another match.

How many incidents form a pattern? Three surely defied random coincidence. Her mind raced as snippets of TV police dramas came to mind where crimes were examined for — what was it? — method-motive-and-opportunity. So if the motive was stealing, and the method involved something happening at a garage sale, that left only opportunity.

Carefully marking the three targeted pages in her notebook, she wondered what commonality might link these entries with the crimes. All upscale neighborhoods offered promising pickings for a greedy thief. Two of the ads described moving sales. The third, an estate sale, must have been run by an amateur because professional groups typically put their company name in the ad.

Trying to match specific sales with the newspaper addresses was daunting because she visited so many. Would a drive through those neighborhoods refresh her memory? Grabbing the newspaper articles and her notebook, she jumped into her car and sped off on her mission. An hour later, she walked into the McLean Police Station on Balls Hill Road.

CHAPTER 8

Jennifer entered the police station for the very first time. Talk about a sheltered life! Once inside, she spoke to the uniformed policeman behind the glass reception window. "Hello, there! I think I may have some information about the recent string of residential robberies in McLean and surrounding area. May I speak with the person working those cases?"

"That would be Detective Adam Iverson," he explained pleasantly. "May I have your name, please?"

She told him.

"Have a seat and I'll see if he's available."

Should she have discussed this with Jason rather than acting on her impetuous decision to rush over here? If her information seemed less logical to the police than to her, how foolish she'd look and feel!

She hardly sat down in the empty waiting room when a pleasant-looking young man dressed in street clothes strode in. "Mrs. Shannon? I'm Adam Iverson."

Grabbing her purse and notebook, she shook his offered hand. He looked maybe thirtyish, about the age of some of her children. Though only half her age, this policeman doubtless saw more violence and the seamy human behavior in his years on the force than she in her entire sixty years. Bless these guys for what they do, she thought with gratitude and respect.

His hazel eyes, neatly combed wavy brown hair and trim civilian clothes that fit his six-foot frame created a good first impression, but it was his congenial smile that dispelled her police-station nervousness and restored her sense of purpose. He'd put her completely at ease.

"Please come on back to my office," he invited and she followed him down the hall to his cubicle, where he indicated a chair. "Please have a seat," he said before sitting opposite her behind his desk. "What can I do for you, Mrs. Shannon?"

"Detective, I notice you're not in uniform like the policeman at the front desk. Why is that?"

"Detectives wear plain clothes so we don't stand out while investigating cases. You seem pretty observant," he added diplomatically but he would size her up as he listened. Her well-groomed appearance and sincerity appeared normal enough, but he knew that façade could hide a real fruitcake underneath. In this affluent area, some people—especially older retired ones—had too much time on their hands or felt lonely and hungered for attention. Others, who read too many mystery thrillers and spy novels, perceived sinister activity everywhere. Some already were, or bordered on, certifiable mental cases. Occasionally, an actual perp "volunteered" information to ensure his crime wasn't overlooked or to ostensibly transform his role from "bad guy" to "good guy."

The flip side was that police sometimes got from the public, and occasionally even requested, tips that broke stalled cases. Because of this, you had to hear each one out. Where would this older woman fall on the rating scale? Who knew?

"I hope I'm not wasting your time with this information today, but I'm naturally curious about situations and people and this concerns recent robberies described in the newspaper over the past couple of months." Jennifer put the three newspaper clippings on his desk, which he recognized as reporters' accounts of one group of cases keeping him guessing at the moment. "Do you know what garage sales, estate sales and moving sales are?" she asked.

Where the hell is *this* going? he wondered. Instead he said, "I've never actually been to one, but I think I know what they are."

"Well, I go to lots and keep a record of them here," she tapped the notebook in her lap. "This record goes back over a year, listing the local advertised sales I visit most weekends."

He nodded to encourage her.

"Look at this, Detective," she pointed to three pages marked in her notebook. "In the last month, these houses had sales followed by," she shifted to the newspaper articles, "robberies. Seems like someone attending these sales later returned to rob the house! What do you think?"

Iverson cleared his throat. "First, let's use the same vocabulary. To police, robbery means a crime against a person involving a weapon or threat. Burglary means a theft from a residence or business. Okay?"

"... and return later to burglarize the house," she corrected.

He smiled approval. "Thanks. Now, may I take a closer look?" He pointed to the book on her lap.

Placing her spiral binder on his desk, she rotated it 180 degrees for him to read while she pointed as she described. "See, I typically cut out the newspaper ads describing each sale and tape them down the left side of the page. Because the print is too small to read while driving, I print the prime info just to the right of the ad in larger letters: the address, the hours of the sale surrounded by a circle and the book map coordinates surrounded by a rectangle."

"What's this list on the opposite page?"

"What I bought that day at those sales and how much it cost."

"Is this some sort of code after each purchase?"

She laughed, "I can see why you'd think that. If the item is for a particular person, I write the name after it. If it's for a room at home I put LR for living room, K for kitchen and so on."

"What are EB, SS and UTPG?"

"Easter Baskets, Stocking Stuffers and Under-the-Pillow-Gifts," Jennifer explained.

"Under-the-pillow-gifts?"

"If any of my ten grandchildren spend the night at my house, they get an under-the-pillow-gift."

"Must be nice to be your grandchild." The detective turned back to the notebook. "Now which sales match the burglaries?"

She showed him and he verified their connection. Surprised at this new possibility for cases so far going nowhere, he felt genuine interest. "I think we should check this out."

"There's more! These sales attract a few Regulars—I call them that because they regularly visit this area's weekend sales—and any one of them potentially might be the thief."

"But you're a Regular so you could be the thief yourself."

She snorted with disdain at the very idea before realizing he had a valid point. "Of course, you're right! I'm not suggesting that every Regular *is* guilty... perhaps none or perhaps just one... but if so, which one? If not them, who would fit such coincidences?"

"I don't believe much in coincidence," the detective said.

"Then how should we proceed?" she asked.

He leaned forward at his desk. "These sales are on weekends, right?" She nodded. "Then why don't I come to your house in my own car? I follow you on your rounds that morning. You point out these Regulars. I see the cars they return to and run those license plates. That tells me who they are and if they have a rap sheet. Could I copy your notebook pages for the last few months? I'll compare the sale addresses against our crime reports for more possible matches."

"Please do! If you follow the newspaper trail, you should know their ads for these kinds of sales aren't necessarily under one heading in the classifieds."

"What does that mean exactly?" the detective asked.

"Some are listed under 'Estate Sales,' some under 'Moving Sales,' or 'Household Goods' or 'Garage Sales.' The rob... that is," she corrected, "burglary connection could surface under any of those headings. You might want to check the *Washington Times* as well as the *Post*." Then frowning, she remembered, "I almost forgot, this Saturday my daughters are holding a garage sale at my own house. But wait, they won't need me for that, so we can still follow your plan."

"Here, please write down your address and phone number and what time should I arrive on Saturday?"

She did. "I get an early start so please be there by 8 a.m. or I'll already be under way!"

"Not a problem, Ma'am. And thank you for coming in with your information."

"You're welcome. Nice to meet you, Detective Iverson," she smiled and shook his hand before leaving the office. "See you Saturday," she called over her shoulder.

The detective knew police don't routinely release to newspapers the addresses of victims of burglaries, but in this situation increased protection from the Neighborhood Watch's high alert justified the temporary decision to do so. If Mrs. Shannon's tip resulted from that choice, it was a good one.

After she left, he ran her name through his computer. With the only blemish a speeding ticket four years ago, he viewed her police record as a virtual zero. Next, he flipped through his Rolodex, picked up the phone and dialed his contact at *The Washington Post* to get a list of their relevant ads for the last six months. *The Washington Times* would be next.

CHAPTER 9

The daughters masterminding the Saturday garage sale in the Shannon driveway stayed overnight on Friday, ready for a very early start the next morning. Up at 6:30 a.m., they wolfed down breakfast and bustled to their pre-sale tasks. Earlier, Jennifer priced her own contributions for the sale, items the girls promised to peddle in her absence.

She told her family about her visit to the police station, so when Detective Iverson rang the doorbell at 7:45 a.m. and introduced himself, Jason promptly invited him inside.

"Some news," the detective volunteered when Jennifer joined them in the foyer. "We found two more hits from those notebook pages of yours that we copied. This looks like a connection we hadn't considered until you pointed it out. Good work!"

"The same to you for following through," she said. "You don't waste much time, do you?"

"I try not to, Ma'am. I see a sale set up in your driveway. Could that be my first garage sale experience?"

She glanced at her watch. This meant getting a late start for the other sales, but catching a real criminal overrode catching a first look. "Of course," she agreed. "Good idea!"

Iverson cautioned, "Outdoors let's not say much about why I'm here. A garage sale is a public place. I assume your family already knows about me but we don't know who else might be listening. Maybe the very person we're trying to find... or one of his associates."

Jennifer nodded understanding. Walking the detective along the driveway's merchandise-covered tables, she introduced him to her daughters. They hurried about putting final touches on their displays, erecting signs at the head of the cul-de-sac, moving attention-getting furniture toward the front sidewalk and arranging a jewelry display on the "check out" table. But the novelty of a detective on the premises distracted them from their work long enough to make him feel welcome. Before they could object, he graciously moved several pieces of furniture for them and was rewarded with a donut in one hand and a mug of coffee in the other.

Though scheduled to begin at 9 a.m., these sales invariably drew early-birds, who began arriving today at 7 a.m.. Jennifer knew dealers often scoured better neighborhoods for under-priced antiques and "collectibles" to resell in their stores at healthy markups. Besides professional or amateur antique hunters, other early-birds typically searched for certain specifics: military paraphernalia, cameras, certain kinds of glassware or china, old books or records, photography equipment, tools, postcards, cigar boxes or whatever fueled their passion.

Jennifer handed the detective a copy of her proposed morning "itinerary," grouping prospective sales by neighborhood and numbered in the order she expected to reach them. When Hannah returned from positioning signs at nearby intersections and pulled her mother aside briefly to whisper in her ear, Jennifer answered, "I don't know. Let's find out."

Walking to where Iverson stood by his car, Jennifer said, "Um, two more things, Detective. First, if we stumble upon an Unadvertised Special not already on my list, I may stop rather suddenly, so please watch my turn signals."

"Ma'am, I'm a cop! I have a pretty fair idea how to follow a car. And what's second?"

"One of my daughters asks to ride along with me today," and as the 20-year-old girl approached them, Jennifer said, "Hannah, this is Detective Iverson."

"Hello, Hannah!" He stared with immediate interest at the brown-eyed girl with shoulder-length hair almost the same honey-color as her mother's. This daughter wasn't in the driveway earlier with the others. Thinking fast, Adam said, "How would you like to improve my cover today by riding to the first sale in my car?"

"Well, I...I guess that's okay," she agreed somewhat reluctantly, and he helped her into his car.

No, Jennifer thought as she climbed into her own van. No, he doesn't waste much time!

***

Ten minutes later, after both their cars parked at the first sale on the list, Jennifer strolled up the driveway, chatty as usual. "Hello," she began, "You're so well organized; did you own a store."

"Didn't own one," said the lady-seller, "but I spent *many* years working retail."

"Oh? Where?"

"Penney's, Sears and Montgomery Ward. My husband was in the service so I stuck with the big chains likely to have stores wherever we were stationed. That way I complemented his career with one of my own, and in the service the double income helped."

A large black Labrador scampered excitedly around the side of the house, galloping straight for Jennifer. She froze rigid, a hand at her throat and her eyes widened in panic as they riveted upon the black streak closing in upon her.

"My god, what's wrong?" cried Seller with obvious concern.

"I...I'm afraid of dogs," Jennifer stammered in a high voice choked with fright. "Sorry, but... if you have the fear, it's real."

"Baron," shouted Seller seconds before the dog reached Jennifer. "Into the house this *minute!*" The dog jerked to a stop, head hung in disappointment. With reluctance, he walked toward the opened kitchen door. He cast a last, long appraising look at Jennifer before disappearing inside.

Was it just superstition or could they smell fear?

"Forgive me," Jennifer apologized, breathing deeply to calm herself, "but dogs are territorial and can get upset about strangers on their turf. Even the cute little ones have a full set of teeth."

This amused Dog Owner. "My fault," she apologized. "He shouldn't have been out here today."

"Thanks for your understanding!" Jennifer calmed enough to change the subject. "With the beautiful weather this morning, bet you've had a lot of customers."

"You wouldn't believe it. Our ad said 8:30 a.m. but the early birds began at 6:30 a.m.. Waking up to the chiming doorbell surprised us, but luckily we organized everything yesterday. So we just threw on our clothes and started the sale two hours early."

"Good for you." Jennifer glanced about for Regulars while scoping the sale merchandise.

Over the years, she'd made some amazing purchases, not just for her own house but for her family and even for friends. Once she took an "order," success was usually only a matter of time! And they "shopped" risk-free because if they didn't like what she brought, she fielded it later at a consignment shop or a future garage sale of her own. The four-slice toaster requested by a neighbor was such an example.

Daughter Kaela asked her to look for a room divider and here stood a four-panel folding screen in mint condition. It exactly matched Kaela's description and price range: "natural wicker, tall and the Victorian curlicue style for $50 or less." So handsome was it that she momentarily tried to craft a spot for it in her own house. "What's the price for this?"

"How about $50? Actually, it's probably one-of-a-kind. We brought it back from our tour in Hawaii and even there, I bought it at a military thrift shop for that price ten years ago." Dog Owner ran a hand over the wicker. "It's in perfect shape and they're hard to find now."

Jennifer examined the hinges and made sure the screen unfolded smoothly and stood level. Satisfied, she thought it well worth the money but remembered to bargain, especially acting as Kaela's "broker." "Would you take any less?"

"Not now, because I think it's fairly priced. But you might stop back at 4 o'clock when the sale ends. If it's still here then, I could negotiate."

Other buyers arrived and Jennifer didn't want to lose this screen. "You drive a hard bargain," she smiled, "but I'll take it. Will you please hold it for me while I look at the rest of your sale?"

Dog Owner nodded and taped a "sold" sign on the screen as Jennifer moved among the furniture and tables of doo-dads while keeping a peripheral eye out for the Regulars.

Having accompanied her mother to many past sales, Hannah schooled the detective in shopping for used items.

He asked, "Is all this second-hand stuff really usable?"

"Buyer beware." She repeated her mother's counsel. "Especially if it's electric or battery operated. Don't accept what the seller says;

try it out yourself. With clothes or rugs or linens like bedspreads or table cloths, inspect every inch. For lamps and other electric appliances, cord condition is a potential safety issue unless you know how to replace it yourself."

"Hey," Iverson exclaimed, "I've always wanted one of these." He studied a tie rack which, when screwed into the wall, held at least twenty ties. "Couldn't belts hang on these hooks, too?"

"Why not? How much is it?"

"The tag says $2. Luckily, I've been saving up!" They laughed. He tucked the item under his arm and they shopped further.

"And here's a treasure for me," cried Hannah, picking up a book of poems.

"Do you like poetry?" he asked.

"Yes," she read the sign over the pile of books, "especially at fifty cents a book."

"This could become habit-forming," he said.

"Detective Iverson…" she began.

"Please call me Adam."

"Is that your real name or an undercover alias?"

"Nosy, aren't you?"

"Yes, and I'm not even the detective," she teased and they laughed again.

Jennifer hefted the folded screen toward her car. "No Regulars here.

Ready for the next sale?"

"As soon as we make our purchases," Hannah said.

"If you get lost, remember we have cell phones to reconnect," Jennifer said.

According to Jennifer's notebook, the next stop on their itinerary would be an estate sale put on by professionals. She drove to this location, watching in her rearview mirror for the detective's car to follow and realized she was somewhat annoyed not to see it behind her. After all, wasn't this police business? Maybe he just wasn't a very dedicated cop. Maybe he didn't share Jennifer's own urgency for cramming as many sales as possible into whatever time she allotted. Maybe Hannah's banter distracted him from his professional focus.

Or maybe something else?

CHAPTER 10

At last, Jennifer saw Iverson's car pulling onto the road to follow her as she drove down Balls Hill Road toward Georgetown Pike. When she parked at the next destination, they were right behind her. She hurried up the sidewalk toward the sale while the detective and Hannah strolled leisurely behind her. Before entering the front door, she glanced back to see them laughing and pointing to something in one of the enormous old trees shading the house.

Once through the door, Jennifer found herself in a serious house: easily 15,000+ square feet with gray stone facing, a jumbled custom roof-line including a turret with curved windows, beautifully crafted landscaping and a meticulously groomed lawn. She bet herself that this one sported a handsome pool-patio arrangement in the back yard.

Jennifer and the detective agreed to conceal their connection while at sales. She'd use a hand signal to identify a Regular. Almost immediately she saw the Englishman and there was the Yugoslavian, as usual, concentrating on clocks, watches and cameras, but still investigating every room. Seeing Iverson enter the huge, high-ceilinged, marble-tiled foyer, Jennifer signaled him, identifying both men. Exciting, playing spies!

Staying close in this mansion was impossible. Besides, Iverson left periodically to follow Regulars outside to their vehicles! Jennifer thought Adam appeared more attentive to his non-stop conversation with Hannah than to his police assignment. Or was this truly part of his cover? As they all moved further into the large house, she decided to roam about looking at the merchandise and find him only if she spotted another Regular.

Touring the home at an estate sale always intrigued Jennifer. With far deeper exposure than a docent-led tour of a famous person's house, these sales gave one the cupboards-open run of a complete stranger's home: the books they read, the movies they collected, the music they liked, the art they selected, the china and silver they used and even the clothes and shoes they wore. Open pantries housed the spices and foods that sustained them, kitchens held the pans they cooked with and bathrooms stood wide to reveal their cosmetics, soaps and vitamins. This inside peek at another's life story intrigued Jennifer. Equally fascinating was the chapter explaining their departure, which resulted in the sale itself.

During her own major household moves, each new empty house seemed a canvas inviting her artistry. These owners followed the same route, as their decorating solutions revealed, but unlike traditional house or museum tours, if you admired an original item here, you could *buy it!*

Wandering into the wood-paneled study where floor-to-ceiling book shelves lined the walls, she approached the large carved wooden desk to price ornate matching brass accessories for sale on top. Beside the brass-edged blotter-holder stood a brass pencil cup, letter opener and scissor set, double pen stand and the framed photo of a young couple posed in front of a yacht.

The woman in the picture stood in front of a man whose arms encircled her, touching her clasped hands as the camera captured forever this moment in their lives—a charming photo in a frame exactly matching the rest of the most unusual, classy-looking brass desk set. With only weeks until their anniversary, Jennifer wanted an unusual gift for Jason and this functional but handsome grouping would look fabulous on his home or office desk. Priced as a set, the tag read $150. She hesitated only seconds before loading the components into a nearby empty cardboard box.

Buys at these sales, with each item one-of-a-kind, pivoted on swift decision-making. If you left the merchandise for even a few minutes, someone else might scoop it up! No retail store's stockroom backup or reorder option offered a second chance. Here, if you snooze, you lose.

In their early McLean days with an expensive new house, large family and careful budget, Jennifer hated passing up extraordinary one-time purchases like this one in lieu of the more practical household and children's necessities relevant then. As with the recent tureen, now she struck when a seductive find surfaced. This freedom heightened her zeal to prowl more sales for more treasures. You had to be in the ballpark to hit a home run!

She looked around the den. What could she learn about the person who'd spent so many hours here? Like Iverson, she became a detective trying to translate clues into profiles of those they reflected.

The book shelves held both decorative old leather bindings and contemporary fiction. Other than several encyclopedia sets and a surprising number of dictionaries, she saw no law, medical or other professional books hinting at the owner's occupation.

Wandering back to the desk, she was drawn to two tall stacks of identical brand new books, each titled "Thinking and Writing Creatively" by Professor Gilbert Snowden. She picked up the top copy, turned it over and scanned the blurb on the back cover beneath the author's photo.

> *"Gilbert Snowden, professor of English at Georgetown University, is a leading writer and lecturer in North America on the use and role of language, past and present. Popular with his students, this author of six books lives with his wife in McLean, Virginia."*

She studied the photo, comparing it with the framed picture on top of her box: recognizably the same man at a different stage of life. She tucked the top copy of the book into the box with her brass items and climbed the majestic curving staircase.

On the second floor, she perused the bedrooms and baths, decorated with rich colors, elegant fixtures and expensive taste. She made mental notes about the display of art objects, placement of flower arrangements and unique window treatments, any of which she might copy.

After roaming through the many upstairs bedrooms, including a breath-taking master suite, she descended the massive carpeted staircase back to the main floor. A line of buyers clutching their purchases flanked a check-out table near the front door. Throughout the house, Jennifer had noticed "helpers" circulating among the rooms, refolding scattered linens, rearranging silver and china on tables where a recent purchase left a conspicuous void, hovering over jewelry and watching for shoplifters. These busy professionals knew their job!

Jennifer passed through the formal dining room and into the large kitchen, where a bent old man sat on a corner stool in the adjacent butler's pantry. She shoved her heavy box onto a counter near him in order to better inspect the kitchen merchandise. "Are you okay?" she asked.

The frail, stooped man nodded affirmatively and resettled himself but didn't answer.

"Looks like someone here really enjoyed tennis," she said aloud, fingering the sport-related collection of ashtrays, mugs, trophies and a clock centered in a ceramic tennis racket base.

"Yes, he certainly did," said the man in a voice surprisingly clear for his aged body.

She looked up. "You?"

"One and the same," he said, stirring to life.

"So... is this your house then?"

He sighed, "For forty years it was and will be for two weeks more, until July first."

"And then?"

"And then a new owner will grace these premises."

"But this is such a magnificent home." She tried to imagine tearing oneself away from this spectacular setting as she marveled aloud. "Glorious views from every window, the waterfall swimming pool in the back yard... "

"Lots of life lived here. Children raised here. Good times here. Rich memories here," he smiled thinly. Observing her questioning look and palms-up hand gesture he continued. "Then why leave? Why indeed," he sighed again. "There is a time and a season for every purpose," he began and then paused. "A new season is about to begin for me."

Curious, Jennifer perched on a stool nearby to give this man her full attention. "A new season?"

"Yes." He sat quietly long enough that she feared he'd forgotten their conversation. At last, he continued. "Surprising how few sentences describe the years of one's life."

"For instance...?" she encouraged.

He continued haltingly, "My wife died of cancer a few months ago. After bravely battling the beast for fifteen years, those last two *awful* years drained the very essence of her soul. Watching her helplessly, I... the experience nearly snuffed mine, as well." He stared around the room. "Now, the house is too big, too empty and too quiet. All the beauty we gathered to enrich our life here didn't halt its recent transformation into a mausoleum." He drew a labored breath, "The real essence isn't in what you find left here, it's in the energy that's moved on."

In a wash of insight, Jennifer pictured life's continuum from birth to death and for the first time recognized her own advanced progress on that path. In twenty years, maybe less, she or Jason would *be* this person!

"The circle of life," she mused, adding playfully, "as the Lion King would say!"

But instead of warming to her humor, the hunched man focused intently on his own world of thoughts. "I... I loved her very much," he croaked, fumbling a handkerchief from his pocket and wiping his eyes with the soft linen cloth.

Filled with empathy for this well-spoken, dignified old gentleman approaching the end of his years, Jennifer felt tears sting her eyes. He didn't seem a stranger she'd just met but rather someone with whom she shared some inexplicable connection.

"Forgive my nostalgia, but memories comprise the only genuine value left here," he rasped.

He looked so fragile and pathetic that Jennifer put her arms around him in a compassionate hug, willing strength to flow from her healthy body into his drooped bony shoulders. He folded his own arms around her and clung tightly, as if his life depended on it.

At last, she pulled back and stared into his rheumy brown eyes as he gave her a weak but sincere smile. She smiled warmth and compassion back at him.

"As they say in the vernacular," his old eyes twinkled, "thanks, I needed *that!*"

They both chuckled. Besides his intelligence and articulateness, his photo nestled in her box on the counter reminded her of the handsome fellow this wrinkled man once was.

His wave of nostalgia past, he spoke with a bit more enthusiasm now. "I'm moving to California to be near my daughter and live in a cottage on a vineyard she owns there. My several grandchildren promise to entertain me until I cry for peace, and the bountiful surrounding nature should energize what's left of my soul. Mark your calendar to think of me there in one month. I will mark mine to think of you! Let's shake on it." He extended his bony hand and they did, but afterward he didn't release her hand.

On impulse she asked, "What made you decide to stay in the house during this sale? You could have gone somewhere else instead of watching your precious belongings disappear one by one."

"Watching this unravel," he spoke softly so she had to lean forward to hear him, "... provides needed closure. *Seeing* it happen helps me believe it and thus accept it."

She sat back, her eyes moist again with tears. Would she feel this same way when she and Jason finally left their cherished McLean house? What unthinkable future circumstance would trigger that departure?

With the old man's gnarled hand clinging to hers, they shared a wordless communication. At last she broke the spell and stood.

"Just a minute," he said as she gathered up the box. "Are these your selections?"

"Yes," she answered.

"What interested you?" he asked, and she showed him.

He scribbled something quickly on a small notepad and, still brandishing the pen, he asked, "Would you like for me to autograph my book for you?"

Drawing upon what she'd learned while in his library, she smiled, "Well, if you're the famous Professor Snowden, yes definitely. Would you, please?"

"I *am* and I *would!* It's my great pleasure, Madam, and, you are...?"

She told him her name and handed him the book, which he opened with a flourish before pressing pen to paper. Finished at last, he placed the closed book back into her box. From the pad, he tore off the note written earlier. "Please, take the contents of this box with my grateful compliments. By-pass the check-out line and if stopped, show them this paper."

"Why, thank you kindly, Professor, but this isn't necessary." She touched his shoulder. "Meeting you is already the high point of my day! Great happiness to you in your new life!"

"And happiness to you also, my dear! My life has been grand and yours is... charmed."

Confusion played across her face. "Charmed?"

"Yes, you'll see. Perhaps you think I'm a rambling old coot, and actually you'd be right about that too," he chuckled at his own humor, "but sometimes one well advanced in years learns during that sojourn to observe and to detect... forces not everyone sees."

"You mean, like gravity or electricity?"

"Yes, but instead I refer to the electrical energy people radiate. Some call it 'auras', though it's more than that. Yours is... " He shook his head as if to get a clearer picture. Then his expression sobered, as if he just understood something very important. Putting a gnarled hand on her arm and looking straight into her eyes, he spoke with surprising intensity. "Remember our date one month from today! *Remember...*"

"You can count on it." She hugged him good-bye; his thin arms encircled her once again, capable of more strength than she expected. Or was it desperation?

"Farewell, dear Lady," he managed and then, as if an urgent last thought revealed itself to him, "Be careful. Be very *careful!*"

"You too, kind Sir," she replied. His eyes followed her every move as she slipped quietly out of the room, turning at the doorway to wave one last time.

Who would believe this encounter if she described it? Frankly, she didn't understand it herself. What did he mean about auras? Long before receiving Tina's frog, Jennifer felt luck in her life — great health, a good mind, a rewarding marriage, bright children, financial comfort and living the good life in a land of opportunity. But "charmed"? And why the warning to be "very careful"? Was the old professor more eccentric than prescient?

Back in her car, she pulled the pocket calendar from her purse, flipped it a month ahead and marked the date when she would warmly remember this day's improbable connection with a most unusual withered old man, by then 3,000 miles away in a California vineyard. You just never knew what might happen at one of these sales, Jennifer marveled yet again!

While waiting for the detective and Hannah to reappear, she opened the professor's book. On the blank opening page she read his handsome handwriting:

"To Jennifer Shannon,

Rudyard Kipling wrote, 'Words are, of course, the most powerful drug used by mankind.' But then, he had not experienced your hug.

With gratitude, Gilbert Snowden"

CHAPTER 11

Hannah's tap on the car window jerked Jennifer as she said, "Mom, how about just one more sale so Adam can run the license numbers at his office? Then shouldn't we get back to see what's happening in our own driveway?"

"Sounds reasonable," said Hannah.

Iverson asked, "Which of these addresses left on your list do you suggest for the last one today?"

"We want to find Regulars," she considered. "Where might they be? Let's try this one." She tapped Number 7 on her itinerary. "Hannah, would you like to ride with me this time?"

Iverson interrupted, "Um, actually she's teaching me important things I need to understand about these sales. Why doesn't she continue with me to this last one?"

Looking for and getting positive confirmation from her daughter, Jennifer nodded and sped off.

So, it's "Adam," is it?

Jennifer arrived first at their next stop. "Moving sale" could mean one household member moving out or *everyone* leaving or even a moving-in sale. "Everything must go" usually translated to, "Everything-we're-not-taking-with-us must go." With a closed garage and empty yard, she wouldn't know until inside. This upscale address in the Evermay development drew a big turnout today, judging from the number of cars parked around the house.

As Jennifer climbed out of her van, an idea popped into her head. She grabbed the cell phone from her car charger and stuffed it into her pocket.

The detective's vehicle nosed into a nearby parking spot just as she opened her van door. Assuming they'd be right on her heels, she paused to hold the front door of the house open for them until she realized they still sat in the car, talking.

Once inside, Jennifer learned the home's entire contents were indeed for sale. The first bedroom contained linens, many with original price tags attached. Recognizing a long-time Regular, Jennifer watched the Duchess examining the table cloths and impulsively implemented her plan. Raising her cell phone Jennifer said loudly, "Excuse me." When the Duchess looked up to see who spoke, Jennifer took her picture.

"Oh, sorry." She invented a quick alibi. "I was trying to get a shot of the... er, lamp behind you."

Duchess frowned annoyance but resumed her quest.

The similarly crammed second bedroom held elaborate Christmas décor and more furniture. Fur jackets, coats and clothes hung in the open closet.

Then Jennifer visited the master bedroom, roomy and beautifully decorated with a gorgeous comforter set on the bed, lamps, statuary and elaborate furniture. The walk-in closet housed pricey ladies clothes, hats and shoes, most in their original boxes.

Some lucky little lady occupied the next room, straight from *Better Homes & Gardens:* pink and white striped curtains and complementary bed linens, a white canopy bed and matching dresser, mirror and chest, a Victorian doll house, white book shelves displaying toys, games, books, dolls and a white plastic bin overflowing with stuffed animals. Finding a big plastic bag, Jennifer filled it with small horses and riders plus fences, corral, barn and other equestrian accessories to become an under-the-pillow-gift for a granddaughter.

Moving to the kitchen, she almost recognized someone but not his straight blond hair. Although nearly disguised with cover-up, the barely visible cheek scar looked like Swordsman's. But wearing a wig? Why would a guy with curly black hair change to a blond wig and lightened eyebrows except for a costume party? Or was the curly one the wig? She watched him stare at the back yard through the sliding doors, his hand upon the locked handle.

When Hannah and Iverson walked in, she gestured with sign language their need to talk. In the hall, she alerted them to the two Regulars at the sale and described her photo of Duchess. "Do you want one of Swordsman, too?"

Iverson nodded.

"Snapping Duchess was easy but Swordsman could be trickier, so I may need your help."

Looking again for Swordsman, they checked the dining and living rooms before descending to a thickly carpeted family room with stocked wet bar, fancy pool table in a separate alcove and a home theater arrangement with comfortable reclining chairs and a movie-room television. Everything was priced. On one of the couches sat an oversized, stuffed orange orangutan, and a middle-aged man lounged in an adjacent chair, but no sign of Swordsman. Had he slipped past them to his car?

"What a beautiful home!" Jennifer said to the man in the chair. "Is this entire level finished?"

"No, just the family room, theater area and the exercise and billiard rooms. The utilities and workshop are in the unfinished section through that door. If anything you want isn't priced, let me know."

"This place is huge," Iverson observed, entering the unfinished area where tangles of electrical wires and cables crisscrossed the ceiling. Swordsman stood beneath them, looking up.

They'd found him, but could they get his picture? As Iverson stepped back into the family room, cautiously followed by Swordsman, Jennifer tossed the stuffed orange monkey to the detective, calling, "Here, catch!" Hearing this, everyone in the lower level watched the airborne orangutan sail across the room, deftly caught by Iverson as Jennifer snapped his photo with Swordsman right behind him, looking directly into the camera.

The middle-aged man stood. "I won that handsome beast at the county fair five years ago. At first, he was a glorious memento of my triumph and after that, a very large dust-catcher cluttering the garage. Would you like to buy a prize orangutan?" he asked Jennifer.

"Actually, I would," she replied, "for one of my Grands who collects monkeys." Jennifer fingered the price tag as Hannah and Iverson nonchalantly followed Swordsman up the stairs.

Adam whispered, "Hannah, would you follow Duchess to her car and get her license number while I do the same with this guy? Can you do it without her noticing?" Hannah nodded.

Still downstairs, Jennifer read the price tag. "You're asking $10 for this orange animal? How about $5 if it goes to a really good home where a little girl will give it lots of love?"

"How about a compromise at $7.50?" the man countered.

"Sold," Jennifer agreed, pulling the cash from her fanny pack. "By the way, I'm just curious and if you don't mind my asking, clearly you're moving, but why would anyone leave such a wonderful house in a great neighborhood like this and sell virtually the entire contents?"

The man smiled. "Remember the fairy tales that end with 'they lived happily ever after'? My wife and I married ten years ago and had a little girl, but we didn't do the fairy tale bit. In fact, we separated, for four years. She stayed here while I started a new job and a new life up in New York. "Then about a year ago, my wife and I talked about mending fences and we did and now we're back together again. Our little girl is thrilled about our reconciliation and we're pretty amazed and excited ourselves. So we're moving to my upstate New York house and going to do just what the fairy tale promised!" He grinned as if owning the best secret in the world.

"What a wonderful story," Jennifer said. "I love happy endings. Now, Handsome Prince, make sure that fairy tale ending comes true."

"Why, you sound a lot like our fairy godmother," he joked back and waved warmly as she walked up the steps.

Outside, Hannah held the enormous orangutan as Jennifer unlocked her car. Finally seated inside the vehicle, Jennifer started the motor and pulled into the street, "Will Detective Iverson let us know what he learns when he runs those plates?"

"It's an active case but he'll tell us what he can. I'll e-mail them to him when we get home."

Jennifer nodded and they drove along in silence a few minutes, before Hannah spoke again, "Mom, don't you... don't you think he's kind of... interesting?"

Keeping her hands tight on the wheel, Jennifer gave her daughter a sidelong look, noticing Hannah's relaxed expression and wide-eyed stare.

Well, well!

CHAPTER 12

Returning home, Jennifer parked a block from her house to free up plenty of closer parking places for shoppers visiting the sale in her driveway.

"Mom, look how many people are there!" Hannah marveled.

"Mornings are usually busiest. Since we're parked on the street, let's lock our own purchases in the car for now," Jennifer suggested.

"Mom, here's Adam's e-mail address." Hannah handed it to her. "Would you mind sending him the photos while I take my turn as cashier?"

Jennifer nodded her agreement.

Walking up the driveway together, Jennifer asked Kaela. "How's the sale going, Honey?"

"Amazingly well, so far, Mom! Haven't added up the other girls' sales yet but I made nearly $200 and it's not even noon! Big crowds of shoppers, and why not: perfect weather, good address, catchy newspaper and Craigs List ads, fifteen signs at nearby intersections, balloons on the mail box and eye-catching furniture near the curb to lure customers." Kaela turned to answer a customer's question and then back to her sister. "Ready to cashier awhile, Hannah?"

"Sure, but remind me again how we're keeping track today. We all wrote our prices on colored sticky labels. Looks like this legend at the top of the page shows blue for Becca, red for you, orange for Bethany, yellow for Mom and the green ones are mine."

Kaela added, "The little kids take their own money at their own tables. When you make a sale put the peeled-off sticker on this page or just write the amount in that person's column. We divvy up at the end. Here's a yard stick for them to measure and that fat orange wire snaking out from under the garage door is an extension cord for testing electrical stuff. Grocery bags and old newspapers to wrap dishes are under the card table. Here's the cashier apron with a calculator, pad and pencils in the left pocket, paper money in the center and change in the right pocket." She removed it from her own waist and tied it around Hannah's.

"I like the apron lots better than worrying about someone lifting a cash box when you're distracted," Hannah said, sitting down at the "check-out" card table near the driveway entrance. The fenced yard with one closed driveway gate created a convenient funnel for customers entering and leaving. Shoppers necessarily moved past scrutiny from the card table before departing, which discouraged "walk-aways."

"Good news for you, Mom," Becca announced. "All your wicker pieces sold: the headboard, lamp, chair, mirror, elephant table, chest, hamper and wastebasket. One person took them all!"

"That'll please Dad since my car will fit in the garage again."

Becca carried a customer's hat tree to the check-out table because his hands were full of other buys. "Mom," she turned to Jennifer, "what do you think about pizza for lunch today? If it's a go, would you mind ordering since we're all so busy? Just in case, we wrote down our choices."

Nodding, Jennifer looked at the neat displays as she meandered up the driveway, through their garage's "people door" and into the house, relieved that the girls remembered to lock that entrance so no buyers could enter the house uninvited.

Once indoors, she spun her Rolodex for the pizza parlor phone number and finished placing the order just as the outside door burst open and Bethany rushed inside!

"Oh, Mom!" she moaned. "You won't believe what just happened!"

Jumping to her feet, Jennifer reached anxiously for Bethany's hand. "Honey, what's wrong?"

"Someone stole Mike's camera! And it's all my fault"

"Your fault?"

"He switched to digital and didn't need his old set-up any more. The camera, the case and all the attachments—he priced it at $300! He wanted to advertise it on Craigs List or E-bay, but I urged him to try our sale first. Now I can't face him! It's gone and I'm responsible! If only I'd watched more closely!" Bethany began to cry.

Jennifer put her arms around her daughter-in-law. "Sometimes shoppers pick up an item and carry it around so nobody else grabs it while they decide whether to buy it. If they don't want it after all, they might put it down anywhere, not necessarily on the table where they found it. Have you checked the other tables?"

"I've looked, the other girls searched, even the children helped. It's just not there! Mike will be so disappointed and so mad at me."

"Another pair of eyes can't hurt. Here, I'll come out to help. And Mike may be more understanding than you think."

They hurried outside, but despite feverish searching, located no camera. None who manned the check-out table recalled seeing anyone carry the camera away.

"I guess a woman with a big purse could smuggle it out," Becca speculated, "or someone pushing a stroller might tuck it under a baby blanket."

"With three hours to go, let's watch everything *very closely* from now on," Hannah said and, grim-faced, they all agreed. But the damage was done.

Besides the many customers drawn by their ads and easy-to-read street signs, the pizza deliveryman browsed their sale, as did the mailman and several construction workers remodeling a house a block away. A van with six women wearing house-cleaning uniforms explained they had a job today in the area, saw the signs and dropped by. All left triumphantly clutching purchases.

When the sale ended at 3 p.m., a few buyers still straggled in but the big crowd peaked about 2:00. At the end, the girls and their children dragged unsold items to their respective cars before gathering in the kitchen to count money and swap "sales tales." All but Bethany felt successful and even she seemed somewhat resigned about the camera theft.

"It's hard to imagine anyone stealing at a garage sale where everything is already so reasonable." Hannah shook her head.

Kaela raised a hand. "Is stealing just about economics? Don't some do it for the thrill?"

"And we thought we were too alert for this to happen to us! Hah!" said Becca.

"It's obvious we're no match for a skilled thief."

"So, we had an actual criminal right in our yard today," Hannah said. "Too bad Adam wasn't here then."

"Who?"

"The policeman, Detective Iverson. He told me to call him Adam." All eyes turned toward Hannah but no one spoke. *"What?"* Hannah blurted defensively, blushing at their combined stares before a self-conscious, almost guilty, smile lighted her face.

Becca changed the subject. "Now that I think about it, we had some odd characters. Remember the foreign women wearing long dresses and head scarves even on this hot day? They insisted on bargaining over *everything* they picked up, big or small. Even those little hotel soaps and shampoos at five cents each. They were adamant, almost belligerent, about buying five for a nickel."

"Bargaining is an accepted way of life in some cultures," Kaela pointed out.

"Don't forget that we sometimes bargain at garage sales, too," Jennifer reminded.

"Yes, but Mom, we back off immediately if our offer isn't accepted. These women persisted and persisted over small stuff until it was downright irritating," said Becca.

"A really scraggly man saw how busy we were and asked to use our bathroom. Knowing Mom's rule, of course I said no," Kaela said.

"One woman asked if her little girl could use our bathroom," Becca admitted. "At first I said no but the kid danced around and whimpered until I felt sorry for her, so I took her inside and stood right by the bathroom door until she reappeared and then escorted her back outside and locked the house door again. Was that okay, Mom, since she was supervised?"

"Supervised is the word."

"By the way, did you notice that strange man, the one who bought Mom's lamp?" asked Becca.

"You mean the big blond muscle man who never smiled?" Kaela volunteered.

"He was weird, Mom," Becca continued. "He also bought your rowing machine and didn't blink at the $75 price, but he wanted the instruction book. When I explained we didn't have it any more, he got mad. While he shopped, he kept looking at me in a way that made me uncomfortable. I mean, not a flirty way but a *scary* way."

"You know how heavy that rowing machine is? Remember how we struggled getting it out to the driveway? He just picked it right up, like a toy, and carried it out to his truck," Bethany said.

" Was… was it a black pickup truck?" Jennifer asked, keeping her voice calm.

"As a matter of fact, it was! He was so strange that I watched him when he left and remember his truck because of the furniture piled up in it. Do you know him, Mom?"

"No," Jennifer said, apprehension mounting at the memory of Wrestler's unflinching determination and unapologetic vice-like grip on her arm when they vied for the painting. Having that frightening man this close to her daughters and grandchildren chilled her, despite the warm afternoon. She shivered.

"Mom, are you okay?" Kaela touched her mother's arm and the others looked over with concern.

"Just lots happening—a busy day!" she covered, not wanting to upset them with her own scare any more than she wished to unsettle Jason with the Wrestler tale the week before. And after all, she did *not* know that awful man and, mercifully, never would!

On the other hand, her daughters *did* listen to her occasional "life-lessons." To imply they shouldn't recognize and avoid threatening people didn't serve her girls well, so instead she said, "Even if your instincts aren't always perfect, listen to them anyway. When something or someone doesn't seem quite right, your mind has made a quick study of the situation and compared it to your other experiences. That very strong uncomfortable feeling is there to protect you!"

Would any of them have occasion to use that advice? She earnestly hoped not.

CHAPTER 13

A thin, young man with curly black hair washed his hands at the bathroom sink. Reaching for a towel, Ralph Forbes thought smugly of the lucrative "business" he masterminded. Heists flowed smoothly, each successful job validating his ingenious formula. His mirrored reflection grinned back at him. A successful entrepreneur: not bad for a 23-year-old high-school dropout.

He hatched his "formula" during the one-year stint at the New Jersey Juvenile Detention Center when he was 17. He hated the boring regimentation of institutional life, being pushed around by fellow juvies and the periodic abuse from the despised staff, those self-styled regal lords reigning over their pathetic inmate inferiors.

Ralph partly escaped the detention center's dreariness through books, eventually reading every volume in their modest library. He treasured the time spent with books, which increased his vocabulary and knowledge. A loner to begin with, he realized the superior attitude the books fostered further distanced him from his fellow inmates and the loathed staff.

Ralph returned again and again to one volume, "Reading and Drawing Blueprints." To kill time, he mapped out all the rooms at the center and kept the growing stack of sketches in a box under his bed. Soon he tried designs on his own. These drawing exercises improved his skill to the point that when Ralph overheard the counselors discussing a new building to house offices and sports equipment, he submitted sketches for the exact structure they eventually built.

He took juvenile detention sullenly in stride until fellow inmate Bill Burdick ransacked his sketches, defacing or destroying them all. Discovering who did this, Ralph punched Burdick, who pulled a spoon handle he'd honed into a shiv. In the ensuing bloody attack, that damned bully nearly killed him. When he finally emerged from the juvie medical wing, his clothing hid healing defensive-wound gashes on his forearms, wrists, hands and across his chest, but the scar on his face advertised a visible reminder of his hatred for that swaggering Burdick. Gazing into the bathroom mirror this morning, he touched the healed slash across his cheek, despising Burdick yet again.

Patiently, Ralph plotted and then executed a wicked revenge that appeared as something quite different. He stifled gloating satisfaction the day a juvie staff member discovered Burdick's body dangling limply below the open beamed ceiling in the eight-bed cottage where he and Ralph lived, an extension cord tightly constricting the bully's bulging neck. Ralph feigned shock like everyone else at this unprecedented *suicide.* An unexpected bonus for Ralph's primary effort came when the ensuing investigation focused blame upon the hated Juvie staff, resulting in the firing of two cottage counselors for negligence.

He could have "gone straight" by capitalizing upon his considerable self-taught blueprint skills, but the astonishing success of his revenge on Burdick infused Ralph with new confidence that he could outsmart most people... and any system.

When he finally tasted freedom, he tried out his heist ideas, at first barely escaping five or six *very* close calls. But he used those mistakes to refine his current winning tactics. While still on probation in New Jersey, he watched with fascination a TV documentary about a master thief named Bernard Welch in a town called Great Falls in Fairfax County, Virginia. The crime-and-punishment show described that place and surrounding neighborhoods as "embarrassingly affluent." Ralph sat forward, watching keenly and mentally pinpointing Welch's old territory as his own target destination. Moreover, he had an angle Welch didn't.

He reached northern Virginia a year later when his probation ended. His primary focus remained his chosen mentor's Great Falls, to which he added select areas of McLean and Vienna. But he and his brother Fred rented in adjacent Arlington County. They selected an inconspicuous house with a large, full basement—close to, but deliberately not within—Fairfax County. Should he ever become a suspect, this foresight might thwart cooperation between adjacent counties' different law enforcement jurisdictions, allowing him to slip through the systems' cracks.

Ralph's plan was simple enough. While ostensibly attending moving sales, he cased the house and afterward drew rough draft indoor/outdoor blueprints of the property, noting security systems and escape routes. Armed with this information, he later burglarized the place. His spineless but doggedly dependable younger brother drove the getaway car and acted as lookout by listening with earphones to the police scanner. During jobs, he communicated with Ralph via a vibrating cell phone should a problem arise when a ring drew unwanted attention. To further minimize identification, they used code names should anyone compromise their cell phones. Ralph wore a ski mask and thin latex gloves during the heist. So far, foolproof!

Thrilled to be part of the action, Fred worshiped his older brother, never challenging Ralph's leadership or their 70-30 split. Fred accepted Ralph's greater role in planning each heist and greater risk as the inside man earning his greater cut. After a job they returned to their house, sorted the loot in the basement and used three South Arlington contacts as fences: one who fielded silver, jewelry, valuable coins, china and figurines; a second who peddled electronics and cameras, and a third for papers like passports, credit cards and checkbooks.

Fred accepted the new situation when Ralph added Celeste as his main squeeze. Far too shy and fearful of rejection to date anyone himself, Fred liked looking at her—the feminine way she moved, the girly way she giggled and the unfamiliar cosmetics and shampoos she left in the bathroom they all shared. Having no sisters, he found living in a house with a woman other than his mother fascinating.

Ralph first spotted Celeste at a garage sale. The way the petite, brown-eyed blond neatly filled her Capri pants and halter top caught his hungry eye. He watched as she lingered over the wares and did a double-take at what he saw her do next. Confidently he followed her down the sidewalk when she left the sale and asked, "Miss, may I speak with you a moment?"

She hesitated and turned toward him. "About what?" she drawled in her heavy West Virginia accent.

They stared at each other for a moment, both aware of an instant physical attraction.

"I saw what you did back there."

A shadow crossed her face as she turned on her heel to walk briskly away from him.

Keeping in stride, he said, "I saw what you did back there and *I liked it.*"

Halting in her tracks, she turned a suspicious eye on him.

"You stole a bracelet and then a hair clip. That was good, but they were small. Slipping the figurine into your purse took more skill. I liked that better."

A half smile played across her mouth, *"You did?"*

"Yeah, I admired how well you did it. So," he paused for emphasis, allowing his eyes to travel over her, "I like what you did and I like how you look." He hoped his Jersey accent sounded foreign to her. "And, I won't tell if you won't tell."

Intrigued now, she asked, "If ah won't tell what?"

"That I want to discuss some business with you over a cup of coffee. What do you say? And I want you to say plenty so I can hear more of that drawl of yours." He felt the chemistry between them heighten another notch right there on the sidewalk.

She hesitated, cautious but also curious. "Well… well ah say, why not?" she decided, waving off the ride that brought her there before climbing into Ralph's car.

That's how it began. In the rush of discovery between the two, the coffee and small-talk became lunch. Ralph spoke little but listened well, deciding just how she might be useful.

Celeste told him her own odyssey began three weeks earlier in a dirt-poor West Virginia "holler." From a broken home like Ralph's, she too quit high school. Bad enough were the pitiful local job prospects, never mind a live-in "step-Daddy" whose advances first disgusted and later frightened her. But the clincher lay when she revealed to her ever-mean mother the "step-Daddy's" attempted rape. The woman slapped her to the ground for daring to speak ill of the man who provided for them both. Celeste realized then that no tolerable future lay ahead for her there.

Gathering her few belongings and her own meager savings, she grabbed every cent from her mother's mayonnaise jar and top bureau drawer, stuffed her "step-Daddy's" prized amber nugget (a plastic imitation, she later learned) into a cloth bag and walked five miles to the bus station in the next town. Nearly penniless after buying a ticket, with Washington, D.C. the coincidental destination of the next bus out, she climbed aboard and didn't look back.

"That's when ah met Amanda," Celeste explained. Amanda Rochester, a gentle-voiced older woman, sat beside her on the bus and coaxed Celeste into conversation. Before long the 16-year-old girl's story spilled out. Amanda clucked over the unfolding tale, muttering frequent "oh dear's" and showing more interest and kindness than the girl could remember. Finally, Amanda suggested Celeste seek her new start in a safer suburb rather than her original big city District of Columbia destination.

"In fact, why don't you just stay at my place for awhile, dear, until you get your feet on the ground?" Amanda patted Celeste's hand. Absent a better plan, the girl nodded.

"Good. Then we'll get off together in Arlington, where I live."

Amanda's small, clean, simply furnished house beat by a mile the weathered, drafty West Virginia shack with an outhouse she'd left that morning. Celeste couldn't fully grasp her extraordinary good fortune in spending her first runaway night in a safe bed instead of drifting along the notoriously dangerous D.C. city streets, where she might not live to see morning. Even so, she vowed to repay this woman's generosity, as was the code of the hills she'd left behind.

Next day, Celeste found a job waitressing and, on a bare-bones budget, began canvassing nearby garage sales, Goodwill and Salvation Army stores to assemble a passable wardrobe, a handful of simple belongings of her own and trinkets for Amanda. She mowed Amanda's lawn, helped her clean house and cooked some meals to earn her keep, but she knew this was only a first step on her path somewhere else. Three weeks later, a restaurant co-worker drove her to the McLean area garage sales where she met Ralph.

"That statue ah took," Celeste explained to Ralph, "it's... it's for Amanda, to thank her. Ah couldn't afford to buy it."

"Don't worry," Ralph soothed, "I understand perfectly."

A week later, over Amanda's warned, "Don't forget, you can come back, dear, if things don't work out," Celeste moved in with Ralph and Fred.

Now she cooked and kept house for the two brothers at their Arlington place. Fred stared at her all the time, which seemed creepy, but Ralph assured her Fred was harmless.

Ralph found her pleasant to have around, liked her efforts to please him and enjoyed the pleasures they shared together. He found Celeste often naïve, given her youth and provincial mountain background, yet conveniently infatuated with him and eager to earn his attention. Watching her carefully, Ralph knew she'd be a natural in his business and an important addition to his team. It was time to begin her training.

CHAPTER 14

With breakfast over on Sunday morning two weeks later, Ralph and Celeste snuggled together on his living room couch, poring over the classified sections of the two major local newspapers.

"Fred's at the grocery buying the stuff on your list." Ralph looked at his watch. "When we finish going over the ads, are you coming with me to sales again today?"

"Oh, Ralphie, of course ah will." She sipped her coffee. "You know, at first ah wondered why you even cared about these silly old sales at houses where people are movin' away, because when they leave, their place is empty, nothin' for you to take! But you taught me that when one rich fella moves out of that big house, another rich one moves right back in an' now we have a little old map of that new fella's house!"

"You've paid attention, Celeste! Anonymity is our goal." Ralph smiled, proud to have added that big word to her vocabulary. "That's the drawback of businesses with easy access into people's houses, like carpet layers, window washers, house cleaners and locksmiths. If you work for them, they have your employee records for a quick trace if a house is heisted after you were there. We want to get our information invisibly, so we do careful homework." He pointed to the stack of floor plans on the coffee table in front of them.

"But Ralphie, how'd you figure all this out? Ah mean, ah used to think all those tag sales were pretty much the same."

"Forget what the sale's called: garage, yard, moving, estate, tag! Only one thing matters to us: getting inside the house. Because that's where we nab any small stuff we see and we memorize the layout for our sketch. *If* we can charm our way inside, we size-up the pay-off for a later heist. If we plan a return, we also pay attention outside: a dog, a fence, an alarm system, convenient windows for the break-in, an escape route and where Fred parks the car. Outdoor information can be just as important as indoor information."

Celeste wiggled with anticipation. "Okay, what about estate sales?"

"They are perfect for us," Ralph said. "You're *supposed* to walk around inside the house since items are sold in place. They expect you to collect purchases as you go and take them to the cashier. But some estate sales are run by amateurs and some by pros, and there's a world of difference."

"Knowin' what we know, you'd think evahbody would hire the pros."

"Yeah, but they don't. People think they're smart to save money by doing themselves what *looks* like an easy job, but two things work against them: they don't have experience and they're vulnerable."

"So not havin' experience means not arrangin' their stuff like a store, not knowin' to price it right and not havin' people to watch out for sticky fingers. Ah think ah got that part figured out, but what's this... 'velderible'?" she asked.

"Vulnerable," Ralph corrected, "you know, distracted and easy to con. Hey, moving is tough! A thousand problems pull at their minds. Their emotions are shot. What's it gonna be like where they're going, are they taking the right stuff, are they selling the right stuff, how can they leave the house empty if everything doesn't sell? Or maybe a parent died and they're dividing up family possessions — what to keep, what to get rid of — yeah, it can be tough for them, but good for us."

"Oh, Ralphie, you're right about when someone in the family dies," Celeste commiserated. "That's just what happened when mah Granny Burkhart died. Mama like to thought she'd die herself, picking through Granny's belongings and fighting her sisters for them. Ah don't like my mama at all, but even ah felt sorry for her that day."

Ralph nodded. "So these sellers are vulnerable and inexperienced, which plays straight into our hands... Yes, sir. And believe it or not, sometimes they just want to talk. They reveal lots about themselves or about the house—like showing you a hidden wall safe or a false-bottom drawer for hiding jewelry in a built-in closet—proud of what their spouse or relative designed. But that information tells us right where to look! One woman told me her house didn't really have an alarm system at all; before her husband died he just put the sign in the front yard to scare away thieves." He laughed, "Imagine telling *me* that!"

Celeste clapped her hands like a five-year-old.

"But there's more. The professionals bring the same staff to every sale they give. They'd recognize us if we're around too often, which we can't risk."

Excited now, Celeste repeated learned lessons. "When an owner gives the estate sale himself, it's a one-time shot. You hit the house a coupla' weeks later when the fella who gave the sale has moved away an' the new owner you just robbed has never seen you before. It's perfect!"

Ralph's eyes narrowed. "But every rule has an exception. In spite of the risk, sometimes it pays to hit the pro's sale anyway." He noted Celeste's puzzled look. "The richer the seller, the likelier he is to hire menial work done for him. He's used to paying others to accomplish things and he doesn't want to be bothered with this trivia. See, the rich guy already took what he values. What's left in his house is a nuisance for him, but a windfall to the estate sale pros. They organize that remaining stuff, price it, sell it and leave the empty mansion 'broom clean.' The rich guy did no work himself, his house is empty and ready to sell and he even gets money back because the pros take only a percentage of what's sold and the owner gets the rest!"

Celeste looked confused. "But with their 'watchers' an' all, what about us?"

"Mapping a rich guy's mansion prepares us for the new owner who rides in on his heels. This area has about ten professional estate sale companies, so we wouldn't necessarily visit the same ones every time, but just in case, we wear disguises."

Celeste brightened. "And that's why you write in your book what we wear each place we go."

"Exactly, to be sure we don't use the same disguise twice for the same company. So," Ralph summarized, "whatever the kind of sale, whoever runs it, we charm our way into the house. And Celeste, you're a natural at that."

"You mean like this?" Celeste jumped to her feet, striking freeze-frame poses as she danced around the room and sang out in a deliberately high falsetto little-girl voice: "May ah please use your bathroom?" she clutched her crotch, pretending extremis.

"Ah'm not feeling at all well, have you a place where I might could lie down for just a minute?" she touched the back of her hand to her forehead as if about to faint.

"Ah used to live in this house long ago an' wonder if ah might just take one last little peek at mah old homestead," her prayerful hands and beseeching expression melting any heart.

"What a *beautiful* garden! Could ah please wander back there to admire your spectacular flowers an' maybe get some landscapin' ideas?" her eyes scanned an imaginary garden.

"Ah see you have several teacups for sale here. Are you a collector, too? Do you have a lot of them? You do? Oh, could ah just look at them? Like, as if ah'm at a museum? As a courtesy, one collector to another?" She raised an imaginary teacup to her lips.

"Oh no, ah just realized my mom said to call her at noon an' she'll be so mad if ah don't. Could ah please, oh pretty-please, use your phone inside for just a quick second?"

Ralph cheered enthusiastically and clapped his hands at her clever, impulsive rendition of their actual tactics. Laughing hard, they both fell back on the couch. This was quite a girl and high time to give deserved praise to his protégé, Ralph decided

"You did great at that place in Woodlea Hills." He put his arm around her. "They were so harassed at that damn sale they didn't realize I was in the house nearly thirty minutes while your fainting act grabbed everyone's attention. And as usual, the cash and jewelry sat right there in the master bedroom closet. I lifted the old lady's jewels clean out of her top drawer and the guy's wallet stuck out on the hat shelf above his clothes hangers. Then I clipped those two little cameras from the den on the way out. Did you see how small these new digitals are now? And then I pocketed those little statues for you from the dining room on the way out."

"Oh, thank you so much, Ralphie! Ah just love them," she squeezed his hand. "Ah know they're called Hummel's because ah saw some over at Tysons Mall and the clerk told me the name."

"You see how I reward you for getting me into a house?"

She hugged him as she thought about another question. "When you took the cash from his wallet, Ralphie, did you get his credit cards, too?"

"Of course, and sold them to our fence so if anybody gets caught, he's the one with trouble! Peddling credit cards backfires if you don't know what you're doing. I know my business and that fence knows his. But $492 in greenbacks from the wallet wasn't bad either."

"Ah guess that was pretty good payback for thirty minutes of work." Celeste agreed.

"True," he said, "but I didn't have much time or hiding space even in my cargo pants that morning. Take that $300 older camera and equipment you hiked from that other sale. My fence said a collector wants that exact model. Your purse works better for those quick grabs. And speaking of grabs... " He pulled her to him and kissed her gently.

Engrossed in each other, they failed to notice Fred's quiet return from the store or that he stood momentsarily transfixed, staring at them through the open kitchen door, his mouth hanging open in surprise and his eyes wide with consternation.

CHAPTER 15

B ack in his office, Adam studied the two snapshots taken at the morning sales. Not bad, working new clues on a stalled case and meeting a cute girl at the same time. He thought about Hannah... beautiful and personable Hannah, good to look at and fun to be around and...

Straightening in his chair, Adam pushed away this intruding distraction, slid the photos aside and ran the five license plates through DMV on his computer. Always uncomfortable about coincidences, he wanted logical explanations. Even if a connection existed between the sales and the burglaries, Mrs. Shannon's "Regulars" might not be involved at all. It was a long-shot, but that was detective work for you: tracking down every possibility to uncover the one that clicked.

He chuckled at the nick-names she'd given her Regulars. She was something else! To his annoyance, he now found himself using them as if they were their real monikers.

Running these vehicle license numbers would net him the vehicle's registration number and whether the car was stolen, as well as the owner's name and address. Using these names, he then looked up their drivers' licenses, learned their date of birth, whether their license was current or suspended and a review of their driving record. He would then run each name through the FBI's National Crime Information Center, which chronicled vast criminal data from stolen cars to missing children, including outstanding arrest warrants.

First he typed Englishman's plate into the Virginia DMV system: Nigel Ridley on Audmar Drive in McLean, vehicle 2009 Ford Taurus, not stolen and a few minor traffic violations.

Next Adam entered Stevedore's tag: Robert Belford on Lost Acre Lane in Great Falls, vehicle a 2010 Dodge Caravan and no significant traffic citations.

The Yugoslavian's info produced his name as Vladimere Karwoski, address on Abbotsford Drive in Vienna, vehicle a 2008 Ford pickup truck with a previous suspended license for DUI, reinstated the previous year.

Duchess came next: Matilda Verling on Arnon Chapel Road in Great Falls, driving a 2010 Lincoln and with no adverse record.

Last was Swordsman: Ralph Forbes on Woodruff in Arlington, driving a 2004 Honda van with another clean driving record.

Printing it all out, Adam paper-clipped the Forbes and Verling information to the photos Mrs. Shannon snapped at the sale. She seemed pretty sharp for an old broad.

Though none of these might be suspects at all, at the sales he took a good look at her Regulars. First impressions were tricky, but experience taught detectives to hone and explore their intuition, while backing it with solid evidence. The knack was pursuing the hunch while remaining open to other facts pointing in new directions. No blinders.

None of the names pulled up rap sheets on the National Crime Information Center, but for some reason, he liked Forbes for these crimes. Mrs. Shannon's uneasiness about the man underscored Adam's own impression since she'd described the others as "colorful," but Forbes as "strange." He'd start with Forbes.

Studying the man's Arlington address, he pulled out a book map and pinpointed the location. Next, he dialed the Arlington County Clerk, explained who he was and inquired about the owner of record of that property: an Orville Thompson with a California address and phone number.

Adam began punching in his number but stopped midway. Some crimes had invisible tentacles involving layers of additional people. What if the landlord were in on the scam? Alerting him to police interest blew any chance of surprise. Adam also knew people tended to trust a female voice on the phone. He strolled down the hall to his favorite secretary, Adrienne, described his dilemma, and asked for her help getting the information.

Adrienne agreed. Smiling broadly at him, she dialed the number he handed her and heard a man's voice say, "Hello."

"Mr. Thompson?" she inquired.

"Yes."

"I'm a secretary here in Virginia updating property ownership information and I just need to verify a few things. Do you still own a house located at 5562 Woodruff in Arlington County? "

"Why, yes I do. Is anything wrong? "

"No, Sir, I'm just collecting information to update our current records. Is that still a rental property?"

"Yes, it is."

"Do you know the name of your current tenant?"

"Actually, a real estate company handles all that since I'm out here on the west coast. My parents lived there for 40 years before they died and I'm hanging onto the property until the housing market improves. Are prices there coming back up?"

"Up then down then up again, always a roller coaster," she said. "Would you mind giving us the rental company's name and phone number?"

"Sure, glad to do it. Wait just a minute while I find it." He did. She thanked Mr. Thompson, hung up the phone and showed Adam the information.

They grinned at their plot's success! "The realty company probably isn't in on this either, but subpoenaing their info would cause suspicion. Would you mind making one more call?"

"Actually, you're in luck," Adrienne volunteered, giving Iverson her most dazzling smile, "because I happen to know someone who works there, so you might not need that subpoena if I get lucky." She dialed the local rent-management company and was put through to her friend, who described Ralph Forbes as a renter at that address for ten months of a one-year lease. A model tenant with no complaints and on-time rent payments.

"Did he fill out any forms for you?"

"Sure did. All our renters do so we can run a credit check to protect our landlords."

"Could you e-mail or FAX me that information?"

After a hesitation, Adrienne's friend said, "No, but I'll read it to you."

Wishing their business relationship could blossom into a personal one, Adrienne basked in Adam's attention as he lavished deserved praise for her nerve, innovation and buddy-in-the-right-place connection. Then he grabbed the information she'd copied and strolled half way down the hall before her expectant smile faded.

Reading as he walked, Adam noticed Forbes listed his occupation as "student," hence no employer. His previous residence was Paramus, New Jersey. Also the location of his bank reference. Person and relationship to notify in case of emergency was "Fred Forbes, brother" at the Woodruff Street address in Arlington. NCIC showed nothing for Forbes, but local police sometimes had another take. Adam dialed the Paramus police department and identified himself.

"I'm looking for information about a 23-year-old Ralph E. Forbes, listing previous address as 2124 Bonfort Street in Paramus. Do you have anything local on this guy?"

"Here's Ralph E. Forbes at that address, but per his birth date, he's 55… maybe the father?"

"Could be. Nothing on the younger one?"

"Ah, this older one has some blips: mostly misdemeanors and a couple of short jail stints for DUI. Oh wait, here comes the one you want, Ralph E. Forbes, Jr., a sealed juvenile file from six years ago. That's about right if he's 23 now, he was 17 then. And here's something: shoplifting arrest in 1999 and burglary in 2000, but charges dropped."

"A criminal family profile?"

"Not a Mafia name but hey, you're raised in it, you step in it. You don't need to be mobbed up for that. You want me to send this to you?"

Adam did, printed out the resulting information and added it to the papers on his desk.

Time for a little off-duty surveillance. Finding Woodruff Street on the map, Adam drove just over the Fairfax County border to one of North Arlington's modest old residential neighborhoods.

Any discovery here counted as research only, because Fairfax County jurisdiction stopped at the Arlington County line. On the other hand, if nothing surfaced here useful to Fairfax County, he could still mention his findings at the multi-jurisdictional monthly meeting where adjacent-county criminal investigators compared notes on crimes, suspects and arrests.

Forbes' Honda van was not visible on the street in front of the house but might be parked in the detached closed garage beside it. Adam pulled to the curb, parked unobtrusively among other cars along the street and pretended to read a newspaper as he watched the house.

He hadn't long to wait. Forbes and the girl walked from the house and entered the closed garage via a people door. Five minutes passed before the motorized garage door lifted and the van backed out. Adam followed them at a safe distance as they drove to an upscale Arlington County neighborhood and stopped at a moving sale.

When the two emerged from their van, Adam did a double take. Forbes now wore a convincing brown wavy wig and compatible moustache. Red hair, cut in a bob style, transformed the girl dramatically. These deliberate disguises raised a red flag for Adam.

The girl went into the sale first while Forbes rummaged for something in the back of their van. A few minutes later, he followed her into the house. Locking his own car as he climbed out, Adam went inside also. Thanks to the Shannon connection, he knew the sale routine now, and he wandered among the rooms, ostensibly shopping while tailing his quarry.

Common at such sales were signs on closets or locked rooms that read "Do Not Enter" or "Nothing in Here for Sale." Most bedroom door locks could be opened effortlessly with a simple tool the size of a toothpick, easily concealed in one's hand. As Adam climbed the stairs to the second floor, he pretended to look the other way as Forbes emerged from one of these closed rooms and sauntered nonchalantly down the hall to shop in the open rooms. The harried couple giving the sale mistakenly posted nobody upstairs to watch buyers.

Adam lingered upstairs long enough after Forbes left to notice the girl ease out of the other closed room. Her bulky purse hung heavily from a shoulder strap. Did it bulge more than when she arrived? Back downstairs, Adam noticed they left the sale separately, pretending not to know each other. Peering out from the corner of a window in the house, he saw them meet down the street at their van.

Returning to his unmarked police car, he recorded the sale address and eyed their car while pretending to study a magazine.

As they drove away, he followed at a distance, back to their house. They parked in the garage and its automatic door closed behind them. When they left the garage for their house, they looked to neighbors exactly as when they originally started out. For Adam, this subterfuge and clandestine behavior at the sale clinched criminal activity.

As he waited to see what they'd do next, Adam turned on his Computer Aided Dispatch and checked the screen. Half an hour later, they came out, got into their van and drove, this time toward McLean. As he followed, something else on the CAD caught his eye. A burglary reported at the very moving sale they'd just left. Wallet missing $1,200 in cash, no doubt profits from the sale which the owners had temporarily stashed for safe-keeping in one of the upstairs "locked" rooms.

Was what he'd seen sufficient probable-cause to toss their house for evidence? If he were an Arlington County cop, he'd try for a search warrant or at least put active surveillance on their activities. If caught red-handed at a house they'd earlier cased, the warrant was a given.

But with this jurisdictional issue, Adam could either alert the local Arlington County police to take over now or he could try to catch Forbes committing another crime in Fairfax County.

He decided to sit tight another half hour to see what they did next.

CHAPTER 16

From Woodruff Avenue, Forbes and the girl drove down Chesterbrook to Kirby Road, a right on Chain Bridge and down to the Dogwoods. Sure enough, another target: an estate sale run by professionals. Even Adam gaped at the mansion's size and grandeur.

Forbes got out first, now clean shaven, wearing a blond wig and different shirt and shoes. He strolled toward the sale. A few minutes later, the girl emerged, now also a blond with short, curly hair and clad in slacks and a jacket. Changing clothes in the van, hidden by the vehicle's deeply tinted windows, resulted in transformations so effective that sellers at the previous sale would describe their burglars *very* differently from those at this house. Clever!

Adam considered the link between garage sales and the subsequent burglaries at the same addresses. While a light-fingered thief might pocket anything handy at a sale, he'd need an accurate sketch for the big heist when he returned. Under the watchful eyes of pros in charge here, this pair who just stole easy pickings at the Arlington sale more likely cased this place for a future burglary. Adam couldn't call for backup *before* they committed a crime and, unlike their activity at the previous sale, this might be a mapping operation only. Though suspicious, *sketching* at an estate sale broke no law!

Before starting into the sale himself, Adam realized his two suspects had seen him numerous times in the past few hours. He might spook them by appearing yet again. Unprepared, he glanced around the car for an impromptu disguise. Borrowing Forbes' strategy, he covered his hair with a baseball cap, slipped on a light windbreaker and donned sun glasses before appraising the results in the rearview mirror. Not a total redo, but not bad!

Inside, the gleaming white marble foyer, gorgeous flower arrangements in stunning vases, expensive Oriental rugs, custom furniture and unique, pricey knick-knacks impressed Adam, as he guessed they would everyone who entered. The house was so very large that Adam moved fast to find either Forbes or the girl, who had deliberately split in different directions. With four rambling stories to cover by himself, he realized he couldn't be everywhere at once. Nor did he choose to alert this pair that he shadowed them. Reluctantly, he resigned himself to wait for them outside in his car.

How long would it take to map a house this size? Unable to do it all from memory, they'd need to draw a layout shortly after their visit when details were fresh. The resulting sketches were likely kept at their house, together with loot from previously burgled houses. If cops could get into Forbes' house, he felt sure they'd find evidence to take these two down.

Cops understood frustration. You invested your time, risked your life and caught your perp, but could you convict him? Sure, law protected the innocent, but the prospect of losing these arrogant young criminals irritated Adam. They would keep scoring, eventually graduating to greater criminal activity, because that's how it worked. The cockier they got and the riskier their heists, the likelier an encounter with a homeowner that could end disastrously for that innocent party. Some called it the "Las Vegas syndrome" because however much you won was never enough once you fancied yourself on an unbeatable roll.

Adam thought of Bernard Welch's legendary case that rocked Fairfax County in 1980. Posing as an antique dealer, Welch bought a house in Great Falls to use as headquarters for burglarizing wealthy homes over a 20-mile radius. Unbelievably successful, he grew increasingly confident and took ever greater risks. Welch's own crime spree would have lasted even longer had a home owner not returned unexpectedly to discover him mid-burglary. Michael Halberstam, a cardiac physician, confronted Welch, who shot him twice at close range and then ran outdoors to escape. Though seriously wounded, Halberstam dragged himself to his car, attempting to drive to a hospital, when he spotted Welch in the road and deliberately ran him over.

Both critically injured men were rushed separately to Sibley Memorial Hospital, their ironic connection unknown. Doctors worked in different operating rooms trying to save each of their lives. They succeeded with Welch but not Halberstam. Welch received sentences totaling 143 years for felony murder, second-degree burglary with a deadly weapon, burglary and grand larceny, while the community lost a celebrated physician and the Halberstams, a beloved family member.

Adam's reflections halted abruptly as he glanced up to see Forbes and then the girl exit the mansion separately and return independently to their van. Follow them again? He looked at his watch. No, time to call it a day. He needed to get ready for his first date with Hannah tonight and he wouldn't miss that! Warm thoughts of her floated into his mind. Not just her great looks, which he'd noted immediately, but her appealing personality. She was smart, funny, clever and desirable... He smiled. She'd needle him when she learned he'd spent his off-duty afternoon still working a case.

His watch showed 5:00 p.m.. Just enough time to go home, shower, shave and pick her up at 7:00. Thinking fast, he called the McLean sub-station and explained the circumstances of this case to Jake Torres, a friend who had duty tonight. " We need to watch out for Forbes' tag number anywhere in Fairfax County. Don't apprehend but follow and observe. Look, I'm off tonight but call my pager if anything breaks on this Forbes case. That's right, day or night."

CHAPTER 17

Cradling luscious Hannah in his arms, Adam covered her with tender kisses as she responded to his every touch. He'd never felt so powerfully drawn to any woman. He pulled her to him and...

His cell phone's insistent chirp jerked him abruptly from deep sleep, melting his consuming dream. Groggy, he blinked awake and sat up. "Iverson here."

"This is the eye on your Forbes guy," said Jake Torres' familiar voice. "He's on the prowl tonight. We're in Vienna. Not much traffic this late, so it's hard to do a close tail without tipping him off. Maybe he's just taking his target's night-time temperature or maybe he's going to hit the place. You want in?"

Already on his feet, Adam held the cell phone with one hand, pulling on his trousers with the other. "I'm on my way. Where in Vienna? Okay, 15 minutes tops. Thanks for the word."

His car sped down Dolly Madison Boulevard and past Tysons Corner's brightly lighted but largely deserted office complexes and shopping malls. A foaming beehive of activity during the day, at this hour even the hotels and restaurants buttoned down. Maple Avenue, Vienna's main street, was nearly abandoned.

Adam spoke into his phone. "Okay, I'm on Maple entering Vienna, just passed Westwood Country Club. Is he still on the move?... where did he stop?... parked there how long?... Okay, I'll park a block away and come in on foot. What are you driving?... no,

I'm plain clothes and packing concealed. Make sure you know who you're shooting at, buddy; I'm the guy wearing dark green." Adam laughed, dropping the phone onto the seat and putting both hands on the wheel as he glided into the wealthy neighborhood of large lots graced with big, pricey houses.

Little transpired in this suburban residential neighborhood's wee hours except for occasional ghostly movements of deer grazing in the lush residential gardens or a dog's distant bark punctuating the monotonous drone of summer insects. Very far away, probably on Route 66, a siren wailed faintly for a moment before the night swallowed the sound.

Grabbing his cell phone, Adam crouched behind bushes in the yard opposite Forbes' van. According to the surveillance team, the van hadn't moved for fifteen minutes. Everyone waited. Due to his hunched position in the shrubbery, Adam felt uncomfortable pressure from the shoulder-holstered gun compressed against his chest.

Slowly, quietly, the passenger door of Forbes' van opened. The inside dome light did *not* illuminate. The figure slipping out the door resembled a shadow more than a person. Clad entirely in black, including shoes, gloves and ski mask, the specter slipped quickly across the road and into the side yard of a large, prestigious house.

Forbes' driver/lookout stayed in his car. He might have a clever way to alert Forbes of trouble, Adam thought. He could follow the thief inside the house, but if the owners were home, apprehending him there could invite risky cross-fire. Adam chose a different tack. He'd wait for Forbes' return to his get-away van with the loot in hand. The on-sight team in the next block provided instant backup if Adam spearheaded an arrest. If the get-away car sped off, they'd call in a Be-On-Look-Out for quick apprehension. Adam recognized Forbes' van from his earlier surveillance in Arlington. What could go wrong? That question always made Adam uneasy!

Long minutes ticked by while the pastoral night-time scene continued unchanged. Adam shifted to a more comfortable position, growing impatient. Waiting was tough!

A large, very old dog plodded along the sidewalk in front of Adam, closely followed by an even older man shuffling behind. At this hour, the master expected no one whose scent the animal might detect. But tonight, the protective old dog stopped to sniff the air. Catching Adam's scent, the graying animal emitted a gravelly bark, persistently repeated despite his old master's efforts to quiet him. Lights snapped on in a neighboring house as this unusual nighttime warning awakened sleeping occupants. If they saw the strange car, they might dial 9-1-1.

Inside the van, Fred froze with fright. He alerted Ralph to trouble by activating the vibrating cell phone and knew his brother would *not* return to the van now. Fred prayed he could remember everything Ralph told him to do. If not, his older brother would be furious later.

They'd rehearsed the contingency plan. Ralph would take off on foot, using his wits and the money in his pocket to eventually find a way home if their subsequent cell phone communication failed. Meanwhile, Fred would drive slowly and inconspicuously out of the residential area until he reached the main road, obeying speed limits. If not followed, he'd circuitously drive home. If followed, he'd head toward the District or Maryland, introducing the jurisdictional complication of *state* lines while leading pursuers away from both the crime scene and from their evidence-filled Arlington house. The brothers would then attempt coded communication on their cell phones every hour on the hour until successful.

Fred hated making decisions on his own because of Ralph's unfailing criticism; therefore he relied totally on his brother's specific instructions for every situation. Turning the key in the ignition, Fred started the engine, shifted into gear and eased down the street. As he crept along the subdivision's residential roads, a car unexpectedly fell in behind him. Fred's eyes widened. He accelerated a little faster. The follower kept pace.

Out of the residential neighborhood at last, Fred ached to head for the safety of their Arlington house but stuck to the memorized drill. As Fred turned onto Vienna's main road, his panic grew as the car behind also turned. Torn between speeding away with at least a chance of escape or continuing at the speed limit and hoping the tail lost interest, Fred struggled to do as he'd been told. His anguish escalated to stark fear when the flashing light of an unmarked police car pulled him over three minutes later on Maple Avenue.

Back on the dark residential street, Adam rushed toward Forbes' target house, hoping to catch the thief in flight. Pausing in the poor light of a moonless night, Adam blindly followed the sounds of movement and pounding feet ahead. He lurched after Forbes as they dashed through yards, over fences and across streets. Several times they both fell quiet, each listening for the other. Then Forbes led the chase again, darting off in yet another direction.

Backup gone but still in hot pursuit, Adam faced a judgment call: to continue solo at increased personal risk or regroup for a safer future try with cover. He forged on. Ahead, he heard metal crashing, more dogs barking. Only a few years older than the perp and in good physical condition, Adam assumed he could keep up, but could he overtake?

The chance light from a porch lamp illuminated the dark ground where Adam spotted and scooped up Forbes' discarded black ski mask. If Forbes shed his other black outer garments, could he emerge normally attired on any residential street and stroll unnoticed to freedom?

Rather than moving toward town, the suspect headed instead for the wooded preserves flanking this suburban area. Possessing only rudimentary Boy Scout survival skills, Adam was no woodsman. But Forbes might be! Out of the residential area now, both men struggled through thick brush and dodged woodland trees. Adam had a cell phone to call for backup, but where the hell was he? He packed a gun, but perhaps Forbes carried, too.

Suddenly, Adam heard crashing in the bushes ahead, followed by a splash and silence. Proceeding cautiously, he peered into darkness under the thick canopy of trees, caught his balance in time to jerk back quickly and avoid sliding down the bank and into a creek.

Adam stood quietly, listening. He couldn't use his flashlight because if Forbes were armed, he'd become an illuminated target. Instead, using his eyes and ears as tools in the darkness, Adam stood absolutely still, straining to hear any sound. He waited, listening.

"Officer, may we be of assistance," said a soft-spoken voice at his elbow. Adam whirled around, gun in hand, to stare at the well-dressed man standing before him. A big dog of unrecognizable breed sat obediently at the man's side.

"Who...?" Adam began.

The man continued in the same quiet voice, "I'm a resident here, Edward Wilford, and also organizer of our neighborhood watch. Here's my ID, though it's hard to read here in the dark. May I see your badge also?" Adam complied and Wilford continued. "This is Jackie," he patted the dog's head. "We spend a lot of time outdoors together and we know this parkland well. We also hunt together and she is well-trained. I see you have a piece of clothing from the man you're chasing. Perhaps Jackie might help you find him."

Processing this improbable development, Adam made a decision. "Thank you for any help you can offer." He handed the ski mask to the man, who waved it near the dog's nose. Ears forward, the dog appeared energized by the scent.

"Find!" Wilford addressed the animal in a normal soft-spoken voice, quite different, Adam thought, from the harsh tone most owners used with their pets. And, for that matter, with their children! The two men waited and watched as the dog raced into the woods.

"And how do *you* happen to be out at this hour?" Adam inquired with caution.

"Back where you parked in my neighborhood, that very old man with the very old dog out at this very late hour was my father with his companion, Maddie. Counting in dog years, they're about the same age. Neither sleeps well so they're often restless at night. I try to keep an eye on Dad but don't always succeed. I'm sorry his arrival interrupted your stake-out."

Three sharp barks drifted through the air. "Ah," said Wilford quietly, "Jackie has your man."

From his own interface with the effective police K-9 unit, Adam respected the uncanny skills of handlers and their well-trained dogs, but he'd never heard of this unprecedented contribution from a volunteering citizen. Still, he and the animal's owner stumbled through the woods until they spotted Jackie looking expectantly up into a large shade tree.

"He'll be up there," Wilford pointed toward the branches.

"Don't go any closer!" Adam warned. "He may be armed. I'll call for backup. Where are we?"

"When you get them on the phone, I'll give you precise directions."

Twenty minutes later, as backup cops pushed a cuffed Ralph Forbes into the back seat of their cruiser, Adam turned to Wilford. "Thank you, Sir, for your invaluable help tonight. Jackie's a remarkable dog, but I don't recognize her breed."

"Perhaps that's because she's a mixture, as most of us are. And we thank *you*, Detective Iverson, and the other police who protect our communities. Here's my contact information if I can be of further service to you." He gave Adam a business card and the two men shook hands before Adam climbed into the waiting police car that would drive him to his own vehicle near the stake-out.

"Can we give you a lift back to your house?" Adam asked.

"No, thanks," Wilford replied in his quiet voice, "Jackie and I will enjoy the walk back."

The next day's newspaper headline read, "Prominent Vienna Attorney Helps Solve Crime," and pictured a pleasantly smiling Edward Wilford standing beside Jackie. The caption below the picture read, "Attorney Says Dog Deserves Credit."

CHAPTER 18

Five months earlier

E xhausted by the long drive from Texas and despite his determination to force this place to fit his plans, Ruger Yates dreaded spending that first night in his mother's old house. Finally, he brought his dog inside and instructed it to lie down on the bedroom floor near him. He willed himself to stretch fully-clothed atop one of the uncomfortable twin beds in the room he'd shared with Mathis when they were young boys. At least the heat and electricity worked and the toilets flushed.

As the nighttime temperature dropped, a bitter February wind howled fiercely across the property, buffeting every cranny of the aged farmhouse and intensifying unfamiliar creaks in the structure's old wood. The wind's shrieks added eeriness to Ruger's anxiety and he tossed fitfully for an hour before finally falling into a deep sleep. Then the awful dreams began...

Aching hunger was Ruger Yates' earliest memory. With no idea of his age, how long he'd been there or anything other than his immediate bleak surroundings, he lay in a cage with bars all around. The boy in the cage with him didn't hurt him. Sometimes the nice girl and the mean man came. Then blackness and fear and thirst and hunger.

His child's remembrance differed only in detail from what actually happened. Ten months younger than the brother sharing his fate, Ruger was four years old when he and Mathis curled on the filthy crib mattress, their emaciated bodies weak from meager food and intermittent beatings. They stared listlessly into black space of the windowless cellar as they lay naked in a feces-strewn enclosure constructed from a baby crib topped with a wooden lid. Wire hinged the lid firmly along one side and a padlock secured the hasp on the other. The acrid stench of human urine filled the immediate area, but the small boys no longer smelled it.

Sometimes the dim overhead light bulbs glowed for days at a time, contrasting with total darkness for other long stretches. The boys had no concept of day or night and thought only of food, despite their knowledge that this yearned-for commodity came with pain, before or after.

When the door opened at the top of the cellar stairs, the crack of light stabbing the darkness should have encouraged hope of rescue from their pitiful plight. Instead, the boys dreaded this moment, for what came next was another installment of the miserable treatment they knew well.

They stared toward the light, unmoving and nearly breathless, as they heard double footfalls on the stairs, one heavy and one very light.

"Are we going to feed them now, Daddy?" asked a little girl's voice.

"We'll see, Miriam. Don't ask so damn many questions," rasped a hoarse, nasty reply.

"Yes, Daddy. I'm sorry."

"Shut up, girl. Damn it, you talk too much."

"Yes, Daddy."

"Look at those disgusting excuses for human beings." The father indicated the crib. "Animals!"

"Animals!" The three-year-old girl mimicked her father's disgusted tone of voice as they reached the bottom of the stairs and approached the boys' cage.

"And why do we keep animals around?"

Miriam recited the memorized litany. "To work for us and do exactly what we teach them."

The father grunted assent. "If they do that, we feed them. What happens if they don't work for us and don't do what we teach them?"

"Then we..." Miriam stared at the cage where her brothers averted their eyes, praying she wouldn't name a punishment he would mete out immediately. Miriam knew the way to avoid being forced into that cage herself meant giving the expected answers, but the boys looked *really* bad today. With a hesitant sideways look up at her father she said, "We feed them anyway?"

An ominous silence charged the still air. The three children knew their father's wrathful temper when displeased with their responses. He grabbed her tightly, clamping his hands so hard on her small arms that she cried out, her head bobbling as he shook her violently. She screamed, "Feed them so they are strong enough to work!"

Hearing this, he dropped her roughly to the concrete floor. Struggling, she got to her feet.

With a mean sneer the father snarled, "Three times those boys had the chance to work with me in the field but they wouldn't keep up. They didn't do what I taught them. They knew they'd get it if they didn't obey and they made their own choice. Tomorrow I'll give them another chance and if they don't make it then, they're not coming out of the cage again except for discipline. I've done my best to train them but they're too lazy and too stupid to learn."

This monologue kindled for the boys vague recall of working in the hot sun to pick vegetables while dragging along impossibly heavy buckets, of pushing hay bales until their bone-tired small arms and legs stopped functioning, of working so many consecutive hours they fell into exhausted sleep in the field. And all for a man they could never please.

The sound of a dog's bark from outside filtered into the cellar. This happened only when strangers visited the farm. All three children focused nervously on their father's reaction.

"Damn, that's the hay customer. Here, you feed them." He handed Miriam the wedge of bread and some bologna slices.

"Daddy," she fingered the food in her hands, food on which the boys' eyes riveted, "don't leave me down here, please."

"Hell, I'll *lock* you down here if you don't do what I say. And don't fill their water pan," he shouted angrily from the top of the stairs before slamming the door.

The boys waved their arms through the cage bars. "Miriam, please... food."

She handed the morsels to Mathis, who deftly tore them apart and handed Ruger half. The food disappeared in a matter of seconds, eaten noisily as fast as they could devour it. Afterward, they licked their fingers for remaining traces of moisture and salt until their tongues were dry.

"Water, please," Ruger begged Miriam. "We thirsty! Pan empty! He not find out."

Glancing furtively toward the stairway, she pushed the watering can spout through the crib bars and poured a stream into the pie pan water dish. They took turns tipping the dish and slurping the welcome liquid. "More water, *please*," Mathis asked and she filled the pan a second time.

"Bring more food when nobody sees," Mathis pleaded.

Miriam shook her head emphatically. "He'd catch me sure and you know what that means for all of us. And Mommy, too. I want to but…" she winced at her brothers' pitiful condition before anguish twisted her little face in fear, "but… I just *can't!*

CHAPTER 19

The February wind rattled with increasing ferocity against the farm house as Ruger Yates sat up abruptly mid-dream. He breathed heavily, the nightmare of the cellar cage profound in his mind. He stared around the farmhouse bedroom and listened to the wind whistling just beyond its walls. Although the dream had ended, a cascade of unwanted memories burst through repression's protective gate and flooded across his mind.

When the man and little girl stopped coming to their basement prison, Ruger remembered the woman descending the basement stairs. She unlocked their cage, dragged the filthy, cringing boys upstairs and rushed them down the hall to a room with tightly drawn window shades. There she prodded them up a ladder into a small, poorly-lit attic space before forcing a flashlight into the frightened older boy's hand and showing him how a button turned it on and off.

"You're out of that cage and you'll have enough food and water up here now but you must be absolutely quiet," she said. "If you make any noise, I'll take it all away and leave you hungry in the dark. Find the food with the flashlight, but then turn the light off or it will stop working. Do you understand?" In response to their terrified silence, she shouted, "Do you understand me?"

Apparently she accepted their muffled grunts as agreement because seconds later their space turned black as she stood on the ladder and pushed the door shut above her. They heard the scratch of a lock and the scrape of the ladder being dragged away.

With no concept of time, the boys awaited the woman bringing food and water often enough to relieve the earlier desperation for nourishment endured in the cage. And when one flashlight died, she gave them another.

After what *seemed* a long time in the attic, one day the trapdoor opened and they were jerked out and dragged down the ladder. Terrified and spooked, like the semi-feral children they'd become, they winced at the dazzling, unfamiliar brightness of daylight in the room. Their mouths gaped open as the woman propelled them through all-but-forgotten parts of the house, its scenes streaking past their disbelieving eyes as she whisked them down the corridor to their next destination.

"After your time out in the sheds and three months in that cellar cage before they took your father away, you were quiet for the month in the attic while the detectives searched," she said. "Now you're going to have another chance."

"Detective" had no meaning for them nor did they understand "months." Their imprisonments spanned their entire conscious memories. They'd heard "another chance" before, but another chance at what? Something worse?

They stared, dumbstruck, as their mother turned a knob to fill the tub and they shrank against the wall at the noisy splash of water against porcelain. They balked at climbing into the bath until she raised threatening fists. As they cowered in the warm water, fearful of new heinous twists at any moment, she roughly demonstrated the use of soap and washcloth, warned them not to splash any water onto the floor and instructed them to clean themselves.

Despite their anxiety at these unknowns, wonder filled the boys with this remarkable unveiling of these parts of the house. Afterward, their mouths hung open in awe when she brought them home-sewn clothes of incorrect but wearable sizes, showed them how to dress themselves and ushered them into a room with twin beds, a shared night table, a lamp and a dresser on which lay a brush and comb. She demonstrated how to use them.

"You'll stay here now. Keep your clothes there." She opened and closed the bureau drawers. "You dress yourselves each day in here and you sleep in these beds at night. You stay in this room except when you do chores, eat or study. In the bathroom, you wash up and use the toilet."

No longer potty trained, the brothers exchanged such puzzled looks that she angrily described to "two very stupid boys" the toilet's exact purpose and threatened punishment for any accidents.

"Now, about the rules…"

"Rules?" Mathis stumbled over the unknown word.

"Yes, rules! You do exactly what I tell you. You get food if you do. You get punished if you don't. Those are the rules. Now, come to the kitchen for lunch."

When she dragged the wary but clean and dressed boys to the kitchen table and slammed half-full plates in front of them, they fell upon the food with both hands.

"Oh, no you don't. You use these or you get nothing to eat." They stared uncomprehendingly at the silverware she pushed toward them. "Watch me," she said, using her fork, then her spoon.

Ravenous from the food aromas, the hungry boys picked up the awkward utensils and tried to imitate what they saw. They spilled at first but started to get the hang of it. Mercifully, she focused on her own meal, ignoring their initial clumsy efforts. They also imitated the way she drank from a glass, but when she turned her back they licked their plates clean.

"We start school tomorrow. I am your teacher. You'll learn your numbers and letters and to read and write."

She might as well speak Chinese. They stared at her, hoping "school" wouldn't hurt.

Within a week, "two very stupid boys" morphed into surprisingly normal-appearing children. Their mother tamed their scruffy, shoulder-length hair using an inverted bowl as a cutting guide. Though still clumsy with silverware, they drank from glasses and ate three regular meals a day. They had no idea how they'd learned to talk.

From household chores indoors, they graduated to simple outdoor tasks such as feeding chickens, gathering eggs and picking vegetables from the garden. Their mother warned, "When you're outdoors you never, ever talk to strangers. Strangers want to *kill* little boys and *eat* them. They're always hunting for a tasty meal. They might *pretend* to be friendly, waiting for their chance to grab you and sink their teeth into you. Always run and hide if you see a stranger." Then she played her trump card. "And if you ever speak to a stranger, I'll know about it…and it's back to the cellar forever."

Any back-to-the-cellar threat resulted in instant obedience.

After awhile, the boys realized their hated father was no longer around, but neither was their small sister who'd often shown them kindness, at her own peril. Despite the risk of consequences, one day Mathis dared to ask his mother, "The man… and the little girl?"

Her composure vanished. An angry voice hissed from her clenched teeth. "Your father's in an insane asylum where that evil fiend always belonged." But then, before their eyes, her face transformed into tragedy. She moaned in a high-pitched wail, "But my little girl… my sweet little Miriam is gone forever. Oh, Miriam, why did he do it?" she sobbed pitifully. "Why did he squeeze you until you couldn't breathe?"

The boys understood tears, for they'd cried together in pain and despair, but didn't know adults could do it, too. Ruger shyly put his hand on her shoulder the way Mathis had comforted him so many times. At his touch she leaped to her feet and shrieked, "Don't you put your hands on me – *ever!*" She shrank back, her hands groping along the wall behind her and her eyes staring wildly at her sons before she rushed from the kitchen, ran down the hall and slammed her bedroom door behind her.

The boys exchanged panicky looks and Ruger clutched his brother's arm. Although she inflicted pain, she also provided food and saved them from the ravenous strangers outdoors. "She'll be all right, won't she?" He searched his older brother's confused face and his voice lifted several octaves as his anxiety increased. He grasped his brother's arm even harder. *"Won't she?"*

"Yes…" Mathis calmed his brother, but he had no idea what to expect next or how much longer they could survive with or without her. "Yes," he repeated until Ruger's fingers, gouging deep into his arm, finally relaxed.

CHAPTER 20

Each day Ruger and Mathis feared their mother's whims, which controlled their lives and their food. Despite her indifference, the little boys craved any scrap of kindness or positive recognition of their efforts to please her. But as weeks passed, her unpredictability escalated. Neurotic and periodically teetering on the edge of sanity, her increasingly irrational tirades found the boys ready targets for her verbal and physical abuse.

Although her schooling wakened the boys' sleeping minds, her harsh punishments for academic mistakes underscored performing well or paying dearly. In their efforts to learn, they made inevitable mistakes. Reprisals hinged on the nearest object transformed into a disciplinary tool: the stinging broom handle, the prodding meat fork or the hot iron skillet.

But the scariest incident happened at the kitchen table when their raving mother shouted to Mathis, "Snake. S-n-a-k-e. I showed it to you, I spelled it for you, I made you repeat it and *still* you wrote it wrong. When you make a mistake you know you must be punished. Why do you make me do this to you?" She cast about for any instrument to drive home the lesson and, grabbing a nearby meat cleaver, she bent back all of the boy's fingers except one which lay flat on the table. Paralyzed with fear, the boys stared at the finger, powerless to defend themselves even if they'd known what came next. "You'll never forget how to spell snake again," she cried and, with a vicious stroke, chopped off Mathis' little finger.

Following the grizzly finger amputation, Mathis disappeared for enough days that Ruger's heart sank, fearing him gone forever. The specter of enduring his mother's madness *alone* frightened Ruger almost as much as losing the brother who was his only companion.

However, no treatment at their mother's hands compared to the bitter nighttime horror two weeks later when a power outage silenced alarms after bed call at the mental institution where Tobias Yates was committed. Taking advantage of this unlikely event for a crazed escape, he hitch-hiked and walked to the farm, where he brutalized his wife and sons for an hour before forcing them outside the house, grabbing a shovel and bludgeoning Mathis to the ground before their eyes.

"Now I'm rid of you at last, you damn parasite," he screamed as the shovel thudded against the boy again and again.

While Ruger and his mother gaped in terror, Tobias forced them both to dig a hole three feet deep, enough for a simple grave. He dumped the child's still body into the yawning trough, where the small inert shape curled piteously at the bottom.

As Tobias flung the first shovelfuls of dirt onto the child's body, the sound of faraway sirens momentarily wrested the madman from his murderous rage. Either they were coming for him or soon would if he didn't return. He stood up, peering through the dark night toward the sound, knowing he had to leave quickly.

He threw down the shovel and turned menacingly toward his two wretched, unwitting accomplices. "Vow to me that you will *never* reveal to *anyone* what happened here tonight or I will return to tear you both into a hundred bloody pieces," the insane man thundered at his terrified wife and son. So acute was their fear that neither Ruger nor his mother ever spoke of this night the rest of their lives.

"You get back into the damn house right now, but tomorrow you come out here and fill in this garbage hole." He gestured toward Mathis' grave.

Scrambling to obey, Ruger and his mother made a desperate dash for the doorway, moving too purposefully to notice their tormentor disappear into the black night.

Tobias Yates reversed the hitch-hike process, returning undetected to his bed at the institution. While aware this confluence of events would never happen again, he took twisted satisfaction in knowing that the two left at the farm would live in perpetual terror of his unexpected return to deliver the promised savage revenge.

***

Now years later, the adult Ruger awoke shaking from this vivid nightmare reliving his childhood memory of Mathis' murder. He stumbled from bed, ran down the hall, out the kitchen door and into the frosty night air. He stared toward the very spot beside the house where the horror unfolded so many years before. Was he losing his mind or did that atrocity really happen?

Stars filled the cold winter night sky and a tree-top high full moon spilled light across the dark gravel driveway. Its pale glow illuminated the small mound near the side of the house, atop which Ruger's mother had plunged a crudely-made cross she crafted the day after the murder. Tonight that cross cast an eerie elongated shadow over the moonlit grave, confirming the reality of Ruger's haunting memory.

Choking and panting for breath, he stood outside in the raw February night while the icy temperature numbed his trembling body.

He'd underestimated the impact of returning to this house. These childhood memories had ignited smoldering embers, fanning a primal urge for the explosive release of *action*, a fiery wave powerful enough to pulse his violent side squarely into the driver's seat.

By the time he reentered the kitchen, the numbness from the outdoor's frosty temperature was replaced by raw rage.

CHAPTER 21

The Present

Jennifer and Jason dozed in bed, half-watching TV, when the bedside telephone's ring jolted them fully awake.

Jason grappled for the handset and mumbled sleepily into the mouthpiece, "Hello."

"This is Denise MacKenzie, Tina's Mom. I'm sorry to bother you this late, Jason, but is... is Tina still over at your house?"

"Hello, Denise. Gee, I don't know. Let me find out. Hang on." He handed the phone to Jennifer, climbed out of bed and padded down the hall toward Becca's room.

Covering the mouthpiece, Jennifer called to her husband, "Ask Becca if she feels any better and she's stopped upchucking." Then into the phone, she said, "Denise? What's doing?"

"Tina isn't home yet and it's late and I'm a little worried."

"Oh?" Jennifer hoped to calm her friend despite vivid memories of her own hand-wringing sessions when a "missing" child of her own was quickly found.

"This isn't like Tina," Denise continued. "Since Scott passed away, we...Tina and I agreed that if we're not home by 10 p.m. weeknights or midnight on weekends we'd phone each other to check in. We've shared a lot of worries lately and that seemed a reasonable way to avoid more. "She's been really good about it, but she is only nineteen. I guess she *could* forget, although she never has. Maybe there has to be a first time?"

"She may still be with Becca, who's got some awful flu bug. Tina kept her company this evening, like the good friend she is. Jason's checking right now." Jennifer studied the bedside clock. "So, it's only 45 minutes since she should have phoned at ten?"

"Yes. That may not seem like much, but Tina's so dependable. This just isn't like her."

Jason shuffled into the bedroom, yawned and took the phone from Jennifer. "She's not here, Denise. Becca says she left around 9:30. That's..." he checked the clock, "...just a bit over an hour ago."

"But it only takes ten minutes to drive here from your house. Even if she stopped for an errand on the way home, what could take so long?"

"She'll probably be home any minute or phone you to say where she is. Call us tonight when she gets back and try not to worry in the meantime." He hung up the phone and climbed wearily back into bed.

"Is Becca feeling any better?" Jennifer asked.

"No," he mumbled, "but maybe a night's sleep will make the difference..." His sentence ended in a shallow snore.

***

They were sleeping soundly when the phone rang next, shattering the bedroom's nighttime quiet. Looking at the clock as he fumbled for the receiver, Jason read midnight. Tina must be home.

"Hello," he said.

"It's Denise," she said, her voice so ragged that even before she spoke, Jason sensed bad news.

"I'm so sorry to bother you again, especially this late, but she isn't back yet and she's never done this before. I'm so worried! I've called her cell phone dozens of times but nobody answers. I've left message after message on voicemail. If Scott were here he'd know what to do next. Should I call hospitals? Should I call the police?"

Jason sat up, wide awake now. "Have you called her other friends?"

"She doesn't have a lot of friends; you know she's kind of shy. But yes, I've called several... without results."

"There's probably a good explanation, Denise, but naturally you're upset until you find it. Look, we know somebody at the police department. I'll run this past him and call you right back. Do you know her car's license plate number?" Denise did.

As Jason hung up the phone, Jennifer mumbled into her pillow, "Tina's not back yet?"

"No, and Denise is a basket case. Do you have Adam's phone number?" She sat up, "Yes, downstairs. Should we ask Becca again what Tina planned when she left?"

"I hate to wake her up a second time this late when she's sick unless it's really necessary, and I asked her that earlier when Denise first called. Becca said Tina headed home at 9:30."

Jennifer climbed out of bed. "Okay, I'll get the Rolodex. Poor Denise!" She hustled toward the stairs.

Phoning Adam at home a few minutes later, Jason apologized for the hour and bothering him off-duty before outlining the situation and giving him Tina's license number.

"I'll find out if she's listed as a traffic accident or if her car's stolen. We need a missing person report to put out a BOLO on her vehicle and we'll want to talk with whoever saw her last."

"Thank you, Adam," Jason said, "Understandably, her mother is *extremely* upset. And as you know, she's Becca's best friend, so we're involved in this by default."

"I understand, Sir. Back to you soon!"

Seven minutes later, Jason snatched up the ringing phone. Adam said, "Sir, our contacts are pretty good so I tapped into recent traffic and emergency medical situations. Tina's name shows on none of them. These situations usually seem worse than they are once we learn what actually happened. She could even be asleep in her car. Believe me, that's not uncommon!"

"So, what's next?"

"Tina's mother can report her daughter missing. If so, we like a recent photo and need to get other facts. That way, besides giving us the information, the mother feels like part of the solution. And we can try to find her daughter's car. What's her name and address?"

Jason read off everything on the Rolodex card Jennifer handed him. "I want to remind you that the mother's already pretty fragile. Her husband died a couple of months ago, and now she's frantic about losing her daughter, too. We're ready to go over there to be with her if necessary."

"There are two ways to do this," Adam explained. "We can send a patrolman to her house to get the information we need or she can go to the Balls Hill Road sub-station to do the same thing. Which is better?"

After conferring with Jennifer, Jason answered, "She should make that choice. We'll find out and call you right back."

He handed the phone to Jennifer, "Your turn," he said. She dialed Denise.

"The good news is that she's not in an accident or a hospital," Jennifer began before explaining the other choices.

Hearing them, Denise said promptly, "I'd rather go there. Our house is a safe harbor now, our comfort zone, our neutral zone. I'll go there."

"Okay then, why don't we come by for you and all go to the station together?"

"Oh, yes, if you don't mind, I'd... I'd really appreciate that. I can be ready in ten minutes."

"Make that twenty because we're still in our pajamas. Can you bring a recent photo of Tina?"

"Yes, but does that mean they think she's in trouble?"

"They just need to see who they're looking for."

"Okay, and Jennifer... thanks," Denise finished.

Next Jason phoned Adam, relaying this latest. "Sorry to call you at home again. Will we see you at the station or are you off duty."

"I'm off, but I'm a phone call away if you need me. I'll let them know you're coming and who you are. You'll have a good reception, even at this hour."

CHAPTER 22

Jason drove while Jennifer sat in the back seat, holding Denise's hand to reassure her. They parked at the police station, went inside and gave their names at the reception window.

"Oh, yes, Detective Gibbs is expecting you. Just a moment," he spoke into his intercom from behind the protective glass.

Almost immediately a beefy detective with graying hair and a business-like smile entered the waiting room. Introducing himself, he invited them into his offce.

Once seated there, Gibbs asked them to repeat what they knew about Tina's disappearance. Besides the when-and-where details, all three emphasized that irresponsible behavior was entirely uncharacteristic of Tina.

"Was she upset, depressed, angry at anyone, afraid of anyone?"

"Not at all," Denise answered. "I've wracked my brain for any kind of explanation."

"Does she have brothers or sisters?" Gibbs asked.

"No, she's an only child so she's always acted more like an adult. Now at 19 she *is* an adult."

"What about school?"

"Good student. Excellent grades. This just makes no sense unless she's in trouble and needs help. We're... both still grieving over my husband's recent death. After Scott got so sick and then died, it's the two of us left, just Tina and me, taking care of each other." At this, Denise gave a convulsive sob and tears rolled down her face.

Gibbs made a mental note. Needy, grieving, possessive mother leaning too heavily on likewise grieving daughter; maybe driving her away? Perhaps, but he needed to know more. "So no other emotional or psychological reason you can think of to explain her failing to phone you tonight? No school problems, no boyfriend problems?" Gibbs probed.

"No," sniffed Denise.

"Excuse me," Gibbs stood, "while I put out a BOLO on her car and then we'll continue. Meantime, please fill out these papers. May I have her Virginia plate number again?"

"BOLO?" Denise asked.

"Be-On-Look-Out," Gibbs explained, handing Denise a pen and taking Tina's license information with him as he left the room.

Denise bent over the papers spread before her on the table and dutifully began writing answers to the many questions, while Jennifer and Jason exchanged tired looks.

Returning, Gibbs began, "Experience suggests we have two possibilities: she hasn't called you because she won't or because she can't."

Denise gave a small gasp and clutched her hands together in her lap.

"We all know that young people can forget tasks like calling home because they're easily distracted, forgetful and not yet very responsible. Sometimes it's on purpose... to get attention, or to punish their parents for a real or imagined slight... or for other personal reasons that make sense only to them. They might magnify small issues. They might run away from home to make a point. From what you tell me, this doesn't sound like Tina, but we can't be sure. In cases like this," Gibbs continued, "time is our friend and time is our enemy."

Gibbs' audience exchanged puzzled looks until Jason asked, "What does that mean, exactly?"

"Time is our friend because a child who forgot to call does *or* he turns up fast with an explanation *or* the one who's punishing his parents relents *or* the one who runs away gets in touch. Many situations like this resolve in a couple of hours and most in a couple of days."

"What about 'time is our enemy'?" Jennifer asked.

"If she's not calling voluntarily, then we consider involuntary possibilities. If she's been abducted, time is our enemy because the trail gets colder every minute. You've heard of the Amber Alert for missing children? That's activated the moment we learn a small child is gone."

Denise jumped to her feet, "But my child is missing and every minute may count right now."

"Ma'am, I understand your concern, but your daughter is nineteen. Amber Alert is only for children below the age of consent."

"Consent! Do you think she consented to being kidnapped? Why can't you use the same tool for a missing nineteen-year-old in the same situation as a young child?" Denise wailed.

Gibbs pressed his temple with the fingers of one hand. "Ma'am, try to calm down. We know you're upset and we're trying to help you as fast as we can and…" he made himself say, "…you asked a good question. Here at the police department, laws govern our procedures and eighteen-year-olds are legal adults, free to come and go as they wish; a totally different category than a minor child without experience, judgment or free will. So let's put Amber Alert completely aside for the moment. We want to help you find your daughter and will use our considerable skills to make that happen. You can help by quickly filling out these forms with important routine information to help focus our search."

"Our daughter, Becca, is best friends with Tina. She's at home now with a bad case of the flu but she's the last person we know was with Tina before she disappeared. They both watched TV at our house until about 9:30 p.m., when Tina said she was heading home," Jason volunteered.

Gibbs made some notes and turned to Denise. "Thank you for bringing her picture; that helps a lot. Does she have a boyfriend or a boyfriend wannabe?"

"No! Well, I mean, not that I know of. She never mentioned one and she didn't bring one home." Denise turned to the Shannons. "Do you know anything about a boyfriend or has Becca mentioned Tina having one? Did they ever double date?"

Jennifer knew too well that parents didn't always know what their "little darlings" were up to but their friends probably would. "Becca might be able to answer that," she told Gibbs.

"Besides a list of all her friends," Gibbs continued, "we'd like to know more about her state of mind that last day. Was she working on any projects that might lead us to others to interview? Someone might know something helpful. We need to know if she had a job so we can talk with her co-workers. You're nodding 'no' about a job. Okay, any hobbies or activities she's involved in, any meetings she attends?"

"She is just a lovely person... a decent, private person," Denise said, tears misting her eyes again.

Gibbs nodded. "And maybe my questions sound like invasion of that privacy, but the more we know about her, the better our chance of finding her. Why don't you take a deep breath and start telling me about her and I'll ask some questions along the way?" To the Shannons he said, "Would you two mind taking a seat outside while Mrs. MacKenzie and I talk together?"

"We don't mind at all," Jennifer said and they closed the door behind them.

Ten minutes later, Gibbs invited them all back to his offce. His phone rang as they sat down and he answered, "Okay, when? Where? Any sign of...," looking at the anxious trio who sat across from his desk, he didn't finish that sentence but listened carefully to the answer. "Any prints? Any leads? Good! Search the immediate area and bring it in for full forensics."

Putting down the phone, Gibbs sighed. "We found her car parked at a McLean fast-food mart, keys in the ignition and driver's side window rolled down. Did anyone use that car other than Tina?"

"No, it's just the two of us at home. We each have our own car," Denise responded, worry lines deepening in her face. "Maybe you'll find her friends' fingerprints, like Becca's for instance, but Tina hadn't too many friends. I rode as a passenger in her car sometimes."

"All right, then I'd like to get your prints tonight for elimination from whatever others we may find. Can you do that right now?"

"Of course, I'll do anything to find Tina faster," Denise said as Gibbs took her to another area to record her prints.

Returning to the Shannons, he said, "If Tina hasn't turned up by morning, send your daughter in ASAP to add her input. We'll also need her fingerprints for elimination."

When Denise rejoined them, Gibbs asked if anyone had questions. "No? Okay, then go home and get some sleep. We may need you alert and on your feet tomorrow. Thanks for giving us this important information. Mrs. MacKenzie, looks like you have some mighty good friends here."

Giving Denise a comforting hug as they wandered out to the car beneath a starry sky, Jennifer wondered how terrible things could unfold on so beautiful a summer night.

Inside the station, Gibbs sighed to himself. No reason to further alarm these already anxious folks but he knew something else, something he deliberately didn't mention. Two women had disappeared without a trace in the last five months in this very part of Fairfax County and Tina might well be the third, perhaps confirming a pattern dreaded by law enforcement personnel. If the girl didn't surface by tomorrow, he'd pass this info directly to the Fairfax County Homicide Division.

As a veteran police detective, he didn't like the way this case felt. He didn't like it at all!

CHAPTER 23

Apall settled over the Shannon house as days passed with Tina still missing. They all ached to *solve* this puzzle, but nothing made sense. What *had* happened to her?

Poor Denise was an understandable wreck trying to cope with her daughter's senseless disappearance and Becca felt devastated with worry over her best friend. Besides sharing their anxiety, Jennifer could think of nothing to do or say to relieve their misery. No progress on the case fueled additional community apprehension about the missing women, producing growing unease and even fear.

Helpless to positively affect the situation, Jennifer sighed. Short of finding Tina herself, she couldn't ease the grieving of those she cared about so much.

Late that Saturday morning this unsolvable dilemma exasperated Jennifer to the point she decided to get out of the house. Driving often cleared her head. Perhaps she'd think of some new angle nobody considered. Problems often cooked to solution in the back of her mind while she was distracted with unrelated tasks.

The kitchen clock read 11 a.m.—later than her usual start to garage sales, but she consulted the newspaper classifieds anyway. At home she felt useless, contrasted with the productive alternative of many upscale addresses. Might she balance the negative with something positive at this morning's sales?

She told those at home her dilemma and, reinforced by their encouragement, started off. Once launched, she skipped lunch to avoid missing the exceptional opportunities advertised on this sunny mid-July day.

She visited sales for nearly five hours, making many stops and several significant purchases. A box of Star Wars figures was a guaranteed thrilling under-the-pillow gift for a grandson, as was the shoulder-high shiny brass spyglass atop an adjustable brass tripod (original tags still attached). Now Jason and the family could get close views of the deer in the wooded parkland behind their house; an amazing value at $45 when she'd priced them in retail stores at $150 and up! At least the telescope might distract them briefly from what was really on all their minds.

Tina's plight assailed her thoughts over and over as she drove, but no light bulb popped on to suggest what might have befallen her.

Finishing McLean, Jennifer went to a few sales in Vienna, then crossed to Route 7 for more in the Springvale area and doubled back through Great Falls for two more at big estates. Under other circumstances, this would have been a rewarding garage sale day! Under these circumstances, it was at least motion.

Losing track of time, she arched her eyebrows in surprise as she checked her watch: after four o'clock. Where had the time gone? Tired and preoccupied with painful thoughts about Tina, she attempted an impromptu shortcut home, in the right general direction but not a route tried before. If she saw just one street sign, she could pull over, consult her book map and pinpoint her location. Dinnertime approached and her family awaited their cook. She must get her bearings soon or retrace her path to familiar roads.

Driving the winding country roads and wooded rolling hills between Great Falls and home in McLean, she knew these back roads could become confusing. Clusters of huge, beautiful homes interspersed with modest houses or even farmland. A couple of landscape nurseries still survived, their owners doggedly resisting developers' staggering sums offered for their land.

Noting this particular winding road was too narrow for a u-turn attempt, she needed a driveway where she could pull in and back out. And soon, because she hated to admit it, but she was pretty much lost. Why had she resisted Jason's offer to install a GPS navigator in her SUV?

Abruptly, the perfect solution came suddenly into focus. "Yes, yes!" she chortled aloud, for rounding a tight curve, she spied an Unadvertised Special. "YARD SALE" read a sign painted on a large piece of plywood. Beneath the words an arrow pointed up the driveway. What extraordinary luck! A last sale for the day, a place to around and to get directions home!

Braking hard, she negotiated a last minute swerve into the graveled driveway. Only in the closing seconds of this maneuver did she notice in her rearview mirror another car materializing directly behind. This little traveled country road had been deserted for miles! She accelerated into the driveway to get out of its way, giving the driver time to brake safely. Instead he over-reacted, forcing his car into a noisy skid. Just shy of plunging into an unforgiving storm water ditch, he careened in a half circle and finally halted his car cross-ways in the road, pointing directly toward the driveway where her car sat.

Years ago, she learned the hard way that law requires following vehicles to be kept under control at all times, thus eliminating excuses for rear- ending a car in front of you. Still, she felt apologetic for braking so suddenly and without a warning turn signal.

She idled her car in the mouth of the driveway to assure herself the other driver was okay. Her rear view mirror showed that his vehicle hadn't moved and the driver seemed to be writing something down. A couple of minutes passed when she reached for the door handle to get out to apologize, but by then the driver had recovered sufficiently to correct direction, pass the driveway entrance where she sat and move slowly up the road. Fortunately, no damage, except perhaps to someone's equilibrium. She sighed, vowing to be more careful and considerate.

She drove ahead up the driveway's long incline. The neglected tangle of overgrown bushes, vines and shrubs along both sides created an abandoned appearance, contrasting sharply with the pristine, cultivated entry ways of most properties nearby. She'd noticed similar neglect at some other sales where owners couldn't maintain their properties as they got sick or old.

At the top of the driveway, gravel covered the expanse between the old house and nearby out-buildings: a large barn and sprinkling of sheds, one looking like a little church or old-fashioned school house. A primitive cross on a small mound beside the house caught her eye; most likely the grave of a cherished pet. If the cross were removed, the mound would blend invisibly with surrounding terrain. Behind the barn, unkempt fields stretched into the distance, though none of this was visible from the road. This small farm, like most of the original land in McLean and Great Falls, doubtless remained from a much larger original tract. After subdividing his acreage, a farmer typically kept the portion with the homestead and surrounding buildings for himself.

Expecting sale items gathered in the driveway or behind the house, she saw none. Maybe the sale was in the barn. The next logical step was getting out of the car to knock on the house door, but she knew canine caution! Farmers usually owned dogs and after her childhood fright, even the he-loves-everybody type scared her. Instead she rolled down the car window.

"Hello," she called. After a moment, she called again louder, "HELLO!"

She knew farm sales and auctions might yield remarkable antiques, quilts, churns, primitive tools, hand-made furniture and vintage household items, so she didn't want to give up too soon. The sign at the driveway entrance hadn't indicated the sale's hours. Perhaps it already ended but they hadn't yet removed the sign. She glanced again at her watch: 4:15 meant she must arrive home soon to start dinner so she wouldn't linger. At least, she hoped for some directions.

If nobody showed soon, she'd turn around and leave. Motor running, window down, Jennifer studied her map. Just as her finger traced the known road she traveled before turning onto this shortcut, a voice at her elbow startled her.

"Here for the sale?" asked the farmer, looking down so his straw hat shielded his face.

"Yes, indeed, but where is it?"

"Inside," he said, walking toward the house. "Come around to the front door."

"Do you have a dog? I'm afraid of dogs," she shouted after him.

"No," he called over his shoulder before turning the corner.

Normally at sales she jumped eagerly from her car, but an unusual hesitation swept over her. She'd come here alone, up a remote driveway to a hidden house for an unadvertised sale. Absolutely no one knew where she was. She picked up her cell phone to call Jason but it wouldn't work. She could press the van's OnStar button to call their operator, but this was no emergency and since she owned a cell phone, she hadn't bought their hands-free phone feature for routine calls.

Still in the car, she vacillated. Pushing the gear shift into "drive," she inched forward to leave, but then pressed the brake hard. This is ridiculous, she admonished herself, on a sunny summer day at a sale in McLean, Virginia. She'd been to hundreds of similar sales, so why would this be any different? *Of course* she would check out this sale! Something wonderful inside might just be calling her name. Shifting into "park," she grabbed her keys, got out of her car and crunched across the gravel parking area to the sidewalk leading toward the front of the house.

The farm house front door stood slightly ajar. She paused, pushed it open and called, "Hello." No answer... "*Hello!*" Silence...

Empowered by the farmer's direction to use this door, she stepped through the foyer and walked ten feet into the living room before a sickening realization gripped her. She froze!

Over the fireplace hung New Husband's painting of the seated nude from the sale a few months ago, and yes, his bachelor furnishings filled this room. She took a step backward, left hand at her throat. That scary man! She *must* get out quickly, dash for the front door, run for her life...

She spun full circle, fingers tightening on her car keys until the metal edges bit into her skin, only to confront a human obstacle, a person who'd waited in the entryway closet until she walked inside before emerging to block her path to the door. She didn't recognize him at all outside, but now she looked up into the unmistakable hard face of *Wrestler*.

Desperately eyeing the door behind him, she gasped, "I must go..."

He didn't speak but his eyes narrowed and a cruel smile crossed his mouth.

"I'm late... my family's waiting," she managed. "You don't understand."

His smile vanished. "No, *you* don't understand!" he growled.

Terror fueled her flight response as she tried rushing past him to the front door, but the tall, stocky man blocked her path. Instinct told her to fight for her life, but he grabbed her wrists and held her at a distance, evading her attempts to kick him in the shins and groin. When she bit his hands holding her wrists, his shrill whistle pierced the air followed by an inhuman scrambling somewhere behind her and the ominous snarl of a large animal as he released her.

She turned her head to see an enormous dog hurtle into the room toward her. Lifting her arms in futile defense against fangs and claws, she felt the heavy animal crash into her, knocking her backward. And then she was falling... falling with no place for her frantically clutching fingers to dig in and hang on!

And then nothing... nothing at all!

CHAPTER 24

How long had Jennifer sprawled unconscious in the blackness before a first pinpoint of awareness pricked her numb mind?

She lay perfectly still, eyes closed, neither asleep nor awake, floating between levels of consciousness. She sensed remote attachment to her body, though no muscle movement verified it.

Was this the passage from life to death, the transition into the spirit world? Was this how that final separation of body and spirit actually felt?

Her mind stirred again, more vigorously this time. Blurred images intruded, too fuzzy to clearly discern. Motionless, Jennifer perceived increasing connection with her fingers, her feet, her eyelids, wondering if her brain could still direct their function from the unworldly dimension she'd already entered. Did a lingering bond remain with the body she left behind, like the amputee detecting sensations in the empty space where his missing limb once grew?

Fear flashed uninvited across her mind as her senses sharpened further, followed by a jolt of alarm... *a house, a man, a dog.* Why couldn't she bring these vital images into focus? Unless...unless remembering would thrust her back to a place so frightening that she must hide inside amnesia's protective cocoon.

Her eyes moved behind their closed lids but registered no hint of light beyond. Taking a shallow breath, she searched the inhaled air for meaningful odor. Nothing! She strained acutely to hear any sound. Silence!

Barely opening her eyes and finding only more darkness, she blinked wide open. Pitch-black! No sound, no smell, no light! Where was she? How did she get here? Was she alone? Was someone nearby who could help, or had someone put her here deliberately because... She extinguished that dangerous unfinished thought!

Moving her fingertips slightly, she felt cloth between her hands and her body. Was she dressed? Barely twitching her toes, she thought she felt shoes upon her feet. She placed her fingertips on the surface where she lay. Wood?

Even these tiny movements revealed a powerful ache toward the back of her head. No light, no sound, no smell. Sensory deprivation and wood beneath her and pain in her skull. What did it mean?

Then a lightning bolt of sheer dread slashed through her confusion. Was she buried alive? That would explain this. Was she inside a coffin?

The murky memory of a news story crossed her mind. A psychotic buried his victims with only a few hours of air to breathe and then left police obscure clues to find his prey before oxygen ran out in their ghastly underground tombs.

She winced at the undeniable facts confronting her; they pointed to her suffering that same grisly death. She stiffened as waves of terror clutched her mind and body. Reacting violently to the doom of suffocating in a coffin beneath six feet of leaden earth, she gasped as a full-blown panic attack overwhelmed her. Her pulse fluctuated wildly, causing her thumping heart to feel enormous inside her chest, its thunderous pounding reverberating in her ears. Sweat coated her skin and she trembled, unable to catch her breath. The headache throbbed violently as nausea twisted her stomach, forcing acidic bile upward to sear her throat and mouth. She swallowed frantically to avoid vomiting and drowning in that awful fluid.

Shaking in the unrelenting grip of acute claustrophobia for long minutes, at last her hysteria lessened. Gradually her ragged breathing evened and she lay in the dark, exhausted and terrified. She fought to wrest control of her emotions so her mind could reason undistracted.

Wherever she was, what could she *do* about it? Had she the courage to explore her surroundings and face whatever fate that knowledge revealed?

She lifted her hands into the inky space above her, fearing what they might feel. Six inches, twelve inches and then even higher into the darkness, fully extending her arms and fingers but touching nothing. Dropping them back to her chest, she struggled to process this information.

A coffin needn't take a funeral casket's conventional shape. One could exhaust the oxygen and perish in any airtight enclosure like a refrigerator or a vault—coffins just the same.

Cautiously, she inched her fingertips down and across the wooden surface on which she lay, exploring away from her body to either side, one hand width, then another and then something unexpected and baffling.

CHAPTER 25

Though in denial, seventy-six-year-old Jeremy Whitehead had become just like the insufferable, tyrannical father he'd despised. Nor did he realize how his father's relentless criticism produced the lifetime inferiority complex which crippled Jeremy emotionally and socially. Like that hated father, Jeremy viewed life through a highly judgmental, ever intolerant, always impatient prism.

Despite Ginger's efforts to share her jollier outlook, whatever leveling balance his wife introduced evaporated with her untimely death five years earlier. Semi-reclusive now with Ginger gone, he thought of himself as a fine-looking, reasonable, intelligent older man who had high expectations and suffered no nonsense. That neighbors viewed him as a beak-nosed, sparse-haired, hunch-shouldered and obnoxious grumpy old man interested him not at all.

"Others" deserved responsibility for whatever diffculties befell him, never Jeremy's own actions. To salve his inferiority complex, he needed to find and criticize someone even more inferior. And he'd created a dandy: *incompetent drivers*! They and the traffic snarls they dependably produced constituted a very *personal* affront to him. Of late, this "calling" bordered on obsession.

Though he excluded himself from this group, in fact his driving skill, reaction time, eyesight and memory were poor and waning.

But to ensure his own virtue, he rationalized that his close calls stemmed from other drivers' obvious inadequacies.

When stickers appeared on trucks and commercial vans inviting "Tell Us How We're Driving" plus a phone number, Jeremy immediately recognized his obligation, if not his mandate! A clipboard with a string-attached pencil lay inches from him on the front seat of his car. He'd reported hundreds of "bad" drivers to their commercial dispatchers and his incessant calls to DMV and Fairfax County police gave him default name recognition.

"Who do you think you're honking at?" Jeremy shouted regularly from his precariously weaving car, for he drove while simultaneously writing down other people's license numbers. "Shaking your fist at me proves you're not only a bad driver, you're a rude driver."

His off-road activity in the few first-floor rooms he still used in his modest two-story house narrowed to sleeping, eating and watching the tube while he snarled disparagingly at TV newscasters, "Aw, you don't know what the hell you're talking about." His on-road excursions consisted mainly of visits to different grocery stores and gas stations to find the cheapest prices; these simple trips lengthened by his increasing inability to find his way straight home.

Lost once more while returning home from an errand, he shouted loudly inside his car to no one. "I pay my taxes, damn it! Can't a citizen expect easy-to-see, easy-to-read signs and the same familiar streets? Criminal how this county allows so damn much new development that a man can't find his way around any more!" Jeremy ranted on, noting at the next *readable* sign that he had turned onto Winding Trail Road. "Worse yet, all this expansion means even *more* traffic. And hell, if there isn't another example just ahead of me."

Even on this narrow back road he wasn't alone. A white Cadillac Crossover sped along the curves just ahead of him until, without warning, the car stopped to turn so abruptly that Jeremy slammed on his brakes and skidded to a ragged sideways halt.

"Damn you," he shouted at the vehicle, grabbing his clipboard to record the offender's license number. "I'll report you before this day ends!" He shook his fist at the driver of the white SUV, which paused where it turned in the gravel driveway. "You'll be sorry!" he yelled, his threat bouncing unheard against his closed car window.

With his usual thoroughness, Jeremy read the street number on the mailbox and wrote on his clipboard "3508 Winding Trail Road, VA tag YRDSALE," oblivious that his own car dangerously straddled the middle of the road near a hazardous blind curve.

At first the license plate made no sense to him until he connected it with the big YARD SALE sign at the driveway entrance of 3508. What a damned fool license plate! What was the world coming to? Yard sale, indeed!

By the time he reached home an hour later via an unsettlingly circuitous route, two other traffic incidents superseded this one on his clipboard. Winding Trail no longer filled his immediate focus, but neither was it forgotten.

CHAPTER 26

In the total blackness where she lay, Jennifer concentrated awareness into her exploring fingers. Still shaken from the panic attack, she calmed enough to reason that she *must* try to understand where she was.

Her right hand traced a vertical wooden wall rising at a 90-degree angle, but her left hand discovered empty space beyond the wooden pallet on which she lay in the dark. Baffling!

Cautiously, she curled her left hand over the edge of that pallet, finding a 90-degree angle going *down*. If only she could see in this cursed blackness!

Lifting onto her elbows, she raised her left arm carefully over her head, her fingers searching for a ceiling. Finding none, she pushed into a sitting position, still touching nothing above her but aware of pulsing pain in her cranium. When she felt the back of her head, her fingers touched a tender baseball-size lump. Pressing it added sharp arrows of pain to the persistent dull ache there. Was the crusty stickiness in her hair blood?

Her head throbbed and her back ached, but why? The dog. Did he knock her down? Did she whack her head? Was she unconscious? If knocked out, she wouldn't remember being brought to wherever this was. From dealing with her children, she knew a head blow could produce a concussion requiring bed rest. But her need to understand her surroundings superseded bed rest and besides, she might not have a concussion at all.

Using both hands, she traced the wall upward as high as she could reach and fanned her hand in circles to determine its contours. The pallet where she lay and the wall behind it were made of the same wooden slats!

Turning on her left side and reaching down as far as she could, she felt the side of a platform that dropped away. Wooden slats again! Sitting up slowly, she dangled a foot downward until it touched something flat. The floor?

Her throbbing head forced her to lie down again but she considered what she'd learned: a platform of wooden slats, with the same slats rising horizontally up the wall in back and down to the floor in front. A wooden bench in a black room?

Piecing together the events before she wakened in this dark place, she knew she was put here deliberately. So the way *in* could be the way *out*. But where was the way in?

Exploring in darkness was risky, but if she was very careful... Sliding to the floor, she felt her way blindly along the base of the bench until it abutted one wall and then back-tracked to where it touched the opposite wall. From garage sales, she knew the distance between her outstretched thumb and little finger measured 7 1/2", so she counted how many times this hand measurement fit the bench from one wall to the other. Six and a half hand lengths times 7 1/2" equaled about 48", so the bench was roughly four feet long and filled one entire end of the enclosure.

Now the dangerous part. Complete blackness hid sharp obstructions, broken glass, creatures, filth or holes, maybe as deep as a well! She winced at these possibilities, but complacency felt the same as cooperating with that deranged man.

Who knew what lay ahead? Maybe no food, no water, no light and no release—ever! At least now she still had energy to think and act, albeit within the limitation of her confined prison. Mercifully, she wasn't tied up, giving her the illusion of at least some control.

Cautiously feeling every inch of the way along each wall, she mapped the perimeter of a roughly 4' x 6' rectangular room, about 5' 2" high, because her head brushed the ceiling when she stood on tiptoes and she knew she was that height.

The wooden bench covered one end and at the other she identified two items by blind feel: a lidded bucket and a roll of toilet paper. The center of the room remained a mystery.

Next, she crawled through the blackness along the now familiar perimeter, brushing her hands in large exploring circles across the floor and up the walls. That's where she felt the outline of a door, locked, of course. On the wall near the door, she felt something sticking out of the wall. Like using Braille in the dark, she felt its shape and guessed at what it might be. But even if it were, did it work? Oh please, she whispered, oh please let it work!

CHAPTER 27

Hoping she'd guessed right, she rotated the little stick on the side of the gadget and held her breath.

At the sudden illumination, her eyes narrowed reflexively while adjusting to this welcome contrast from the ink-black room. She blinked at a small plug-in night light! Tears of gratitude trickled down her cheeks.

Hardly believing such luck, she brushed away her tears to study her surroundings for the first time. Indeed, a small, rectangular room with a door in one wall, no windows, no shelves, and empty except for the bucket toilet at one end and the wide wooden bench at the other. A concrete floor sloped down slightly from the base of the walls toward a 3" wide open drain in the center of the room. She pounded on walls but they were thick enough to be solid. Was this a sauna? If so, could he turn up heat to a stifling, murderous level? What happened when she breathed all the oxygen out of this enclosure's air? And where was this box that explained the total blackness and lack of sound? Underground? Was she buried alive after all?

Her eyes searched across the nearly empty room for a makeshift tool to pry the door open. Nothing! Weary, she sat on the floor to take stock of this crazy situation.

Had she lost consciousness at another stranger's house, they'd call 9-1-1, cover her with blankets and make her comfortable until help arrived. Contrast that with the deliberate dog attack and *imprisonment in a cell.* No mistake, she was in terrible trouble.

Think positively, she counseled herself! Her car cell phone was turned on, though admittedly not working properly. Hadn't police located and rescued a car-jacked child because the mother's cell phone in the seat beside the infant broadcast a beam law enforcement could follow? This madman surely turned off or even destroyed her cell phone, so that wouldn't help. He also had her purse, address and keys. Now her whole family was vulnerable, as well!

With a wrench of longing, she ached for her dear Jason and pictured the sweet faces of her five children, one by one. Would she live to see them again? Even worse, would they fall prey next to this man's insanity?

Stop thinking about *those* things, she counseled herself. Concentrate on positive things! What about her car's OnStar service? Did it include a stolen car tracking feature? If she didn't return home for dinner, wouldn't Jason call the police? Could they track OnStar to her car at that house with the yard sale sign where they'd find Wrestler and make him tell them where he put her?

Unless he disabled it, which he would if he could. Or did OnStar only work with the motor on? She'd never tried it with the ignition off, but how could it work without power? Doubtful.

Her brain-storming continued. This yard sale was not advertised, leaving no newspaper trail to follow. Turning into that driveway was impulsive. The only tangible evidence that the sale ever existed was the hand-painted sign at the road, which was surely removed immediately after her capture. Nobody had any way to know where she was!

So... no cell phone, no OnStar, no trail to follow. No rescue! This left only one alternative: escape! And how in the world could she do that? She knew nothing about this weirdo, his motives, his past or his plan for her. If logic wouldn't help, did survival here depend upon chance? She'd heard that chance favors the prepared person, but how could she prepare for *this?*

Could she distract him? Could she startle or surprise him? Could she talk him out of whatever he planned to do? Could she throw him off guard? Could she learn what makes him tick and somehow use that to...?

Her thoughts shifted to a new worry. Jennifer instantly recognized Wrestler after the graphic impression he made upon her at two garage sales. Did he also remember her since she angered him on both occasions? But wait! She'd worn a scarf on that bad-hair day and used only lipstick due to haste that Saturday morning. Might her natural hair and daytime makeup look different enough that he wouldn't recognize her?

Interrupting her recollections, the throb at the back of her head forced her again toward the wooden bench to lie down. She eased down at one end and surveyed its length, wondering the best way to curl up while protecting the bump on her head and the ache in her back. She thought longingly of her sumptuously comfortable pillow-top mattress at home and wondered if she'd ever delight in its softness again.

By now her eyes adjusted well to the subdued light, allowing her to see more detail than at first. Staring at the bench, she realized all its slats appeared uniform except for the top board of the backrest, where a V-shaped nick had been cut into it. The off-center nick looked deliberately carved. But why? And why had something so irrelevant even caught her attention; because she had time on her hands or because alertness might save her yet?

Something glinted toward the back of the bench. She looked closer. Wedged down between the slats and nearly invisible except for the accidental angle of light falling upon it, lay an object. Using her thumbnail, she tried unsuccessfully to coax it out. Had it fallen there accidentally or was it pushed deliberately? About to give up, she remembered the safety pin used to close her slacks when a button popped off just before she left home this morning. With the pin's sharp point, she dug and dug at the thin metal object, at last prying it out.

Taking it over to the night light, she bent down to examine it. A strangled cry escaped her lips. Her eyes opened wide with shock. Misshapen but clearly recognizable, shimmering in her open palm, lay one of Tina's distinctive earrings.

CHAPTER 28

Ruger's childhood memory of his deranged father's return to their farm house and the ensuing rampage when he watched Mathis beaten to death was real enough, but there was more...

Cowering inside the house with his mother, Ruger heard light rain begin to patter drops on the Yates' farm house roof; drops also fell upon the child's crumpled body outdoors in the open makeshift grave. The warm rain caressed Mathis' still face until his eyelashes fluttered feebly. Eventually, his eyes flickered open. Maimed and dazed, the beaten child struggled to move his limbs, recoiled from the dizzying pain and lay still. But the soft rain woke him again. With slow, deliberate effort he managed to lift onto his elbows. Staring in bewilderment around the bottom of the dark, damp pit in which he found himself, he wondered at the layer of dirt covering him. Pushing very slowly to a sitting position and reeling with pain, he repeatedly tried to drag himself to his knees. Eventually succeeding, he struggled mightily to stand, clinging to the top of the hole for support. After numerous failed attempts to claw his way out of his intended shallow grave, he sprawled at last atop the rim and lay motionless, overcome by fatigue and throbbing aches.

Barely conscious, Mathis had no vision beyond an instinctive urge to distance himself from this place of misery, despite danger from the dreaded strangers. Out of the hole and lying on the ground, he waited for the strength to move again. When it came, at first he crawled and then staggered awkwardly out across the field toward the unknown.

Stopping often and clinging to trees for support, he finally reached and crossed a street before stumbling upon an impromptu roadside dump. After someone unloaded a first derelict appliance, others capitalized upon the convenient opportunity by throwing old washing machines and construction trash down the incline. Discarded wooden kitchen cabinets from a remodeling project comprised the dump's latest clutter. Exhaustion, pain and intensifying rain drove the child to seek shelter. He crawled inside a gutted pantry which lay on its side, wedged securely against a tree, and closed the door as best he could.

Safe inside the dry haven, the exhausted boy instinctively curled his frail, damaged body into a fetal position as the growing storm roared overhead. Oblivious to all but the dreadful hurt everywhere in his body, the child ignored the rain's incessant drumming upon his makeshift shelter and slid mercifully into a deep, anesthetizing sleep. As the storm crisscrossed the countryside, bolts of jagged lightning stabbed the ground nearby, accompanied by explosive thunder booming over the roadside dump, but Mathis slept like death.

Waking the following day and conscious of pain in every part of his body, he opened the pantry's door and squinted against sunlight glinting upon wet woodland leaves and tufts of grass. He didn't know the violent storm had gully-washed enough dirt into the grave where his father threw him to fill it half full of muddy ooze. He didn't know that this morning his mother shoveled the rest of the rim-mounted dirt into the hole and placed a handmade cross on top. He didn't know they all thought he lay forever at the bottom of that grave.

He did know he was hungry and his body hurt everywhere as he crabbed his way with wrenching effort along the unfamiliar terrain. He vividly recalled his mother's warnings that strangers wanted to kill and eat him, but never having left the farm, he had no idea where they lived or how to avoid them. He staggered across another road and stumbled through adjacent woods and farmland, stopping often to muster enough strength to lurch forward another few steps.

During his desperate flight, he traversed an incredible three miles before he saw a farm house from the edge of the woods and smelled tantalizing food aromas wafting toward him on the summer breeze. Underfed even before his newest ordeal began, overwhelmed by exhaustion and grimacing with every painful movement, Mathis could continue no longer. He crumpled to his knees on the forest floor, toppled onto his side and fell into a semi-conscious stupor.

***

Sally rocked on the veranda of her farm house with her dog stretched out languidly at her feet. Two freshly baked pies cooled near the kitchen window and with farm chores to do this afternoon, she reflected that keeping very busy helped some, but not enough. She sighed sadly, hoping the pies, her husband Craig's favorites, might cheer his somber mood a bit at dinner.

Wistful as she was many times each day, she thought of her adored six-year-old boy, Matthew, taken from her only two months earlier by spinal meningitis. Craig grieved at least as hard as she for the son they both loved so much. She felt as if her heart had been ripped open, leaving a raw wound that could never heal. Life, once so full of anticipation when they focused on the boy, consisted now of going through motions because their real purpose existed no more.

A trained nurse before she married, she blamed herself incessantly for failing to identify her son's symptoms sooner. High fever, headache and vomiting were common forerunners of many lesser illnesses. By the time he mentioned a stiff neck, the seizures began. Rushed to the hospital, he rallied briefly, but antibiotics came too late to halt the disease's insidious progress.

He'd have started first grade in a couple of months. She'd already registered him, bought his school clothes and supplies, all of them up in his room, the room with no child.

As a nurse, she'd witnessed grief cripple otherwise strong people, but until losing her own precious child, she hadn't understood how deep anguish could stab. She ached for her missing son all day, and her short nights of troubled sleep continued the hopeless vigil. She cringed, knowing Matthew's diffcult birth left her unable to have another child. Her dream of a family was over.

She wiped away unbidden tears with her sleeve cuff and tried to thread a needle for the mending project in her lap when her dog suddenly jumped to his feet and looked toward the woods.

"What is it, Lucky? What's the matter, boy?"

The dog whimpered, moving restlessly across the porch and staring through its railing at something in the distance. Returning to his mistress, he rested his muzzle in her lap and she patted his head, but this didn't soothe him. He bounded down the porch steps toward the woods, barking an alert. Putting her sewing aside, Sally eased out of the rocker to follow when she noticed Matthew's abandoned baseball bat propped at one end of the porch where he'd left it the day he fell ill. Picking it up, she realized his small hands touched the bat last and caressed the grip with her fingers, feeling an invisible connection with the son she mourned. Sighing again, she picked up the bat and carried it along—just in case!

Following her dog across the yard, she stepped past the outer edge of the mowed lawn and waded into the thick woodland ferns, brushing brambles aside and dodging branches until at last the animal stopped ahead and barked. Catching up, she stared at the ground beneath a bush.

"What's this? Why, it looks like a little tyke and… oh no, he's hurt!" She dropped the bat and eased the unconscious boy onto his back, aghast at his wounds and bruises. "Oh my god, he's hurt *real* bad."

After her nimble fingers ruled out neck or back injuries requiring immobilization, she gently lifted Mathis' limp body into her arms. "Good boy, Lucky," she praised the dog, who followed her, tail wagging, as she carried the boy back to her house.

When Mathis awoke, despite the soft bed and tantalizing smell of food on a tray next to him, he shrank in fear at the sight of a stranger *right beside him.* Although the stranger hadn't yet made a move to grab or bite him, his eyes desperately scanned the room for quick escape.

The stranger smiled and said gently, "Hello there. What happened to you? Why were you out in the woods?"

The boy stared at her, terrified.

"Would you like something to eat?" She handed him a cookie. "Are you hungry?"

The boy eyed the cookie and, although his bruised jaw and split lips ached, he felt drugged by the treat's irresistible smell. He inhaled the aroma deeply and nibbled tentatively at the cookie's edge before wolfing the treat down so fast he choked.

"Here, drink this warm cocoa," the stranger offered and while he gulped the unimaginably delicious drink, she asked in a whisper, "So what happened to you? How did you get all these bruises and cuts?"

Anxious, his eyes followed her finger as she pointed to cuts and black-and-blue marks.

"Who did this to you?" she asked in a soft voice. The boy looked away, but she tried again. "Was it someone you know?"

Maybe if he answered the stranger's questions he wouldn't be eaten. He didn't know what else to do. With effort, his eyes turned to hers and he nodded slightly.

"Was it a grown-up?" she asked softly. He nodded "yes" again.

"Was it your father?" He hesitated and nodded once more.

"Was he the only one who hurt you?" The boy shook his head.

"Your mother hurt you also?" she asked. Tears welled in the boy's eyes and spilled in rivulets down his filthy, gaunt cheeks as he nodded.

"What happened here?" She pointed to the missing finger on his small, dirty hand. The boy gasped back a sob and made a chopping motion with his other hand.

"Someone did that to you? Someone chopped off your finger?" He nodded, and looked hungrily at the cookies. She handed him another, which he devoured greedily. "Did your father cut off your finger?" The boy shook his head. "Did your mother do it?" The boy nodded.

Sally's mind raced. Social Services would put a child like this into their system, where he might bounce from one institution to another or through a string of foster homes. She knew they worked hard at their daunting job, even when underfunded and poorly staffed, but their cases outnumbered them. Once he was removed from his abusive parents, an institution-governed future lay ahead to compound this boy's already tragic start in life. Seeming an unthinkable mistake, a child could even be returned to his abusive parents. The newspaper reported this happening recently, resulting in that child's subsequent death.

After his life-long indoctrination to fear dreaded strangers, Mathis expected blows to begin at any moment and steeled himself for the punch or bite surely coming next. And yet, no one had ever talked so kindly with him or given him such sweet-tasting food or the amazing warm drink. Were strangers different from what he'd been told?

"What's your name?" she asked, wondering if he could speak since so far he communicated with head movements. She held her breath, awaiting his response.

In a weak voice through his cut lips, the child murmured, "Mathis." But what Sally heard was "Matthew."

"Matthew? *Matthew!* Have you come back to us, just as a different little boy?" An expression of radiant happiness lit her face, such as Mathis had never before witnessed on anyone he knew. So contagious was her joy that the child didn't flinch when she touched his cheek with affection.

Beaming gratefully, her heart full of love, Sally whispered, "I'm going to be your new mommy."

CHAPTER 29

Sleeping fitfully on the hard wooden bench inside the small dark room, Jennifer dreamed she ran for her life through dense woods while behind her panted a large black dog, the chain collar and tags around its neck jingling as it pounded after her.

No matter how she swerved, the animal crashed close behind her through the fallen leaves as she dodged tree trunks and fallen branches. She prayed her legs could miraculously keep up with her body as she sped forward headlong. Abruptly, she tripped and smashed down into a leaf-filled crevice, while the chasing animal overshot her. She lay paralyzed with fear and partially covered by dry leaves. Silence! Had she lost him? Then, the jingling tags and heavy breathing returned as the animal doubled back through the leaves, searching for her. As she saw his hairy muzzle appear above the trench and felt his hot, smelly breath on her face, a scream caught in her throat as she stared in helpless horror at the dog's huge spreading jaws and glinting teeth...

Then a sharp click, at which her eyes popped wide open!

Though her dream evaporated at the sudden sound, the panic it created did not. Ripped from her nightmare, she sat upright but disoriented. Was this still the dream or did the room's door move?

As the door opening widened, in the eerie glow of artificial light outside the box, a figure faced her. Wrestler sat on a backward turned chair just outside her room, appraising her coldly.

The grisly nightmare from which she just wakened paled compared to the real one beginning now.

Fear clutched her heart.

This was it, the dreaded moment! She had no knowledge of what he planned next and no tools, real or psychological, to protect herself. Only ominous dread... If she could just think of something startling to do or say, something disarming, something to jolt his predictable pattern—a pattern of which, she knew, Tina was already a casualty. And now... she was next!

Their stares locked because she dared not look away. Perhaps he used no words, just silence and then a quick, chilling lunge toward her.

"The light." In an even voice, he spoke this as a statement, not a question.

She heard herself say, "Yes, I found the light and I'd like to apply for a job." Where did *that* come from?

He leaned forward, watching her face intently. "A *job?*"

Her mind raced! A tumbled recollection of her schooling, training, experience, credentials, jobs and talents cascaded through her mind. What might be useful to him?

"As a servant," at these words she tried not to look as surprised as she felt. What possessed her to mention this hateful task? Would this idiocy seal her fate at the very moment she needed to defend it?

Was it the poor light or wishful thinking or had a nearly imperceptible flicker of interest crossed his face? If so, how could she capitalize quickly on whatever might have triggered this response?

Who was this man? What did he need? Someone weak? Someone strong? Her very survival depended on what she said next.

He shifted confidently in his chair and smirked, keenly aware of her total vulnerability and his complete control. She knew from the garage sale months ago, when they vied for the painting, how single-mindedly he focused and that his muscle could press home any point he chose. The missing McLean women! Tina's earring! Everything pointed to this man! She swallowed hard and held the stare of the specter who sat before her.

"Servant?" he repeated. Was that curiosity or amusement in his eyes?

It was now or never. She felt a sudden burst of energy overtake her. "Look," she found herself saying, "you have many routine chores every day. Because you are very capable, you can do them yourself, but they are dreary, routine, repetitive, time-consuming tasks. Doing them takes time away from... " she groped, uncertain of the pivotal words, "...your important work."

Neither his smirk nor his stare changed appreciably, yet she felt he studied her differently now.

"I have practical skills backed by experience," she went on, "like cleaning, cooking, sewing, ironing and gardening. I work hard and take directions well." She searched his face, hoping for some detectable reaction from him, but he neither moved nor spoke.

Had she already gone too far or was this the moment to lay all her cards on the table? She drew a deep breath and plunged ahead.

"If you have an office, I can use a computer, type, file, pay bills, do payroll and double entry bookkeeping." She waited for any response. His smirk was gone, replaced by that cold-fish expression.

At least this conversation temporarily delayed his attack. "Look, I'm here and my future is whatever it is. You have nothing to lose and everything to gain by using my skills in the interim. For you it's win-win!"

For the first time, he moved, turning his head to look toward the left at something she couldn't see. Was he about to grab a weapon to impale her? Her skin prickled with anxiety.

Looking directly at her again, he wordlessly closed the door and her heart sank as the lock clicked shut.

In a roller coaster of emotions, she breathed deeply to calm herself, grateful to stay alive even minutes longer but fighting despair at her helpless situation. Sitting on the bench, she buried her face in her hands and cried in frustration.

Ten minutes later, another click and the door swung open, revealing Wrestler again astride the chair. He looked at her silently, as if making a decision, before reaching for something outside her field of vision. He pushed an open-topped cardboard box into her enclosure and again shut and secured the door.

Alone in her dim prison, she pushed the container over to the night light and bent forward.

Inside the box lay a rectangular paper sleeve of saltine crackers and a plastic bottle of water.

CHAPTER 30

Jennifer's hand reached gratefully toward the food, but then jerked back. Was it drugged or poisoned; if not the crackers, at least the water? Was this how he incapacitated or dispatched his victims? No, she decided, because his great size and obvious strength could effortlessly overpower a small woman. And didn't killers actually crave their victims' agonized reactions?

With her watch missing, she tried to calculate how long she'd occupied this small room. She drove into his driveway about 4:30 p.m., plus however long she lay unconscious and later slept, plus an hour to map the room and find the light. So maybe this was about 7:00. Dinner time?

Thinking of dinner, she felt visions of her family wash over her, especially mealtimes when they talked together about their days' events. Would she ever share another with them?

She examined the water bottle in the weak glow of the night light. The plastic cap connecters appeared intact, though she remembered a TV show where a narrow hypodermic needle injected chemicals through hard-to-find pinprick holes. What to do? When had she eaten last and how much longer could she hold on? Dashing out mid-morning after gulping coffee and downing a banana for breakfast, she skipped lunch in lieu of attending sales.

Impulsively, she twisted off the water bottle cap, lifted it to her lips and sipped. How wondrously moist and delicious water tasted when you were truly thirsty! Her dry mouth savored the wetness, but she resisted the temptation to down it quickly in case of an adverse reaction. Studying the bottle, she couldn't think how to use it as a weapon. Still, she wished she had something, anything, to defend herself. Could she rip up a bench slat? That attempt failed. Could she punch a hole in the walls of this room or kick the door out? Those didn't work either.

Mentally replaying her conversation with that man, she had no idea where her "servant" idea originated. But with the offer in play, she must make it successful if given any chance. Should he go for it, maybe she'd be out of this prison room to find some way to escape.

When Wrestler opened the room's door earlier, she knew from the light beyond he wasn't sitting outdoors, so where was this room? She'd heard crime rescue stories of captured women held in secret basement dungeons. The thin brightness behind his chair suggested subterranean lighting. If in such a place, might she leave this small room only to find herself in a bigger room with no escape? Yet if he came in and out of this place, potentially so could she.

What if she gained his confidence so he took her to his house to do chores? She'd have a chance there, except for the dog, which would certainly reappear since she'd stupidly revealed to the man in his driveway that she feared them. She cursed her foolishness and trembled at the prospect of facing that animal again.

Her lifelong wariness of dogs stemmed from childhood, when a nasty-tempered Rottweiler chased, cornered and bit her. Since then, she avoided dogs whenever possible but still knew something about them from pet-owning friends. Could she use that knowledge with this animal? Always hungry, dogs loved food, unless this one was trained to accept it from his master only. But would she have access to food? Observing how the man dealt with the dog might offer clues such as its name or the man's commands, which she could later repeat to her advantage.

Absent feeding the dog, might she try petting or kindness? Dream on! This animal viciously knocked her down on one command, yet instantly obeyed other commands not to rip her to pieces or eat her alive! That meant a highly-trained dog responding quickly to complex instructions. Any escape strategy surely hinged on neutralizing the dog's power... unless she could eliminate him entirely. But how?

And what about escape? Even given the opportunity, she had no idea where she was or which way to go. If still at the man's house, should she run into the fields behind the house or back down the driveway to the street, where a car might happen along? Though the road had little traffic earlier, might morning or evening rush hours change that pattern to her advantage? If he caught her running down an empty road, recapture was a given and recapture insured punishment so dire that she'd probably welcome death.

She could run to the nearest neighbor's house, but what if that neighbor was away and his doors locked? The man and the dog would overtake her in no time, away from the street where nobody heard her cries.

If allowed into Wrestler's house, wherever that might be, perhaps she could phone for help. They'd ask for the address. She didn't know the house number or even the street name since she got here taking unfamiliar shortcuts. Did police investigate 9-1-1 hang-ups? Could they trace the call or would they dismiss it as a prank? What if the man had no hard-wired phone but a cell phone with bills sent to a post office box? Hard to trace that!

Even if he tried her "servant plan," that was a short commitment. How long until it no longer amused him, or until her work didn't measure up if he were critical?

This underscored swift action, yet not so fast that she botched her chance to escape. A second chance wouldn't exist! If only she hadn't impulsively gone to his house, if only she could leave this prison, if only she found a way out, if only she could live to see Jason and her children again, if only...

Suffering no ill effects from the water, she took another drink, opened the crackers and inhaled their fragrant, salty aroma. Surprised at the urgency of her hunger and how unexpectedly delicious this food tasted, she munched ravenously, washing the saltines down with swigs of water. Despite her depressing circumstances, the food energized her.

She gave a wry laugh. "Well, at least I'm trying to think outside the box!" she said aloud to her rectangular enclosure, aware of the tragic irony in her words.

CHAPTER 31

D ozing but instantly awake when the lock clicked and the door opened, Jennifer sat up quickly. Wrestler stood in the doorway beside the chair.

"Hello, Sir," she said, hoping this subservience hid the quaver in her voice.

Ignoring her greeting, he dropped a half loaf of bread and something else onto the chair.

"You start the job *now!* Clean up and organize this cellar. Trash in bags over there, cleaning supplies by the sink. And hurry! When you finish, press that buzzer." He pointed at something which lay beside the bread. Her cubicle's door stood open as he disappeared from her view, his retreating footfalls audible on stairs before a distant door slammed and a lock clicked.

Good grief, had the servant idea *worked?* Or was this a trap, masquerading as a short-term edge? Would she emerge from this room only to be bludgeoned just outside? Yet hadn't she heard him, or someone, leaving? Maybe he wasn't the only one...

Cautious, she stepped through the door and *out of the room!* She saw now that her enclosure was a large, heavy wooden box shoved to one side of the cellar.

Six scattered dim bulbs, each suspended from a black cord attached to the bare ceiling rafters, cast poor light in the subterranean room. No clue in this artificially-lighted, windowless room as to the time of day. Unless someone or something lurked unseen, like the dog, she stood alone in a large, clutter-packed cellar.

Was this *a* basement somewhere or *the* basement in his house? If the former, she could be anywhere; if the latter, at least she was still in McLean. She wolfed down several bread slices and finished the water. In the shadowy corners of the basement stood odd-sized cardboard boxes, clusters of dusty cans and jars, old furniture, books, china, kitchen pans, suitcases, decorations, a wardrobe, records, tools, rope, laundry equipment and both full and empty canning jars—a dirty, disorderly scattered accumulation of at *least* thirty years! Heavy dust covered everything, untouched for decades, everything except the door to the box that had been her room and the clear path of activity worn across the dusty floor between it and the basement stairs.

If his house were above this, had he moved here recently? Why else the newly bought garage sale furniture now in his living room? But if so, wouldn't the house sell with an empty basement? Maybe he rented, the landlord's full basement a contingency of their lease agreement? Or maybe he inherited it, a beneficiary who hadn't yet cleaned out this mess in property he now owned? Or maybe this cellar had nothing to do with where he actually lived.

Turning, she considered her task. On the floor by the sink lay broom, mop, bucket, cleansers, rags, trash bags and some empty cardboard boxes. "Clean up and organize," he'd said. She assumed that meant grouping like items together, exactly as one might for a garage sale. She snorted wryly at this sardonic comparison. Hoping she correctly understood what he expected, she plunged ahead to impress him with her work and maybe buy survival a little longer.

The heavy old desk in the corner resisted pushing, so she grouped other furniture around it after first sweeping the floor beneath. Checking the desk drawers one at a time, she found only paper scraps, pencils, rubber bands, paperclips: the usual office debris.

His acceptance of her servant proposal was sheer luck, but now she needed more than luck; she needed a plan. As she swept, four distinct goals crossed her mind.

First, look for clues about this man in items she found here, clues to increase her understanding of him and maybe shape a survival strategy.

Second, look for more evidence of Tina's presence: fresh digging in the floor or recent mortar in a wall where he'd hidden... something? She winced at the chilling portent of such clues.

Third, she must find or create a weapon to defend herself.

Fourth, escape!

Aware her very life might depend upon the outcome of this "job," she bent to the broom with energy. This first job could be her last, irrespective of how well done. Or his satisfaction here *might* lead to cleaning elsewhere, perhaps above ground, with doors and windows offering *escape*. Otherwise, freedom in this enclosed cellar indeed served as a second prison, just one larger than the box. Earning a ticket out of the basement was critical!

The corner sweeping complete, she pushed and carried the other furniture from various spots around the basement to the desk. Her back hurt and her head ached, but concentrating on the work helped her push pain to the back burner. Small end tables and lamps weren't difficult; the ancient overstuffed chairs finally responded to hard shoving, and the rusty old divided laundry tub, complete with ancient wringer, rolled at last on squeaky but functioning wheels.

Beside an aged treadle-style sewing machine sat a big rectangular sewing box. Lifting the lid exposed hundreds of thread spools, needles, pins, thimbles and the myriad accessories of a serious seamstress. "Yard goods" read a big cardboard box on the other side of the sewing machine. Inside, she found stacks of folded fabric and remnant scraps. The owner apparently made her family's clothes and probably the curtains and tablecloths, too.

The scuffed suitcases she gathered together felt empty, but she opened each, finding predictable small trash but no clues like travel stickers or luggage tags showing names and addresses. She also investigated closed tins, old purses and small boxes.

Next, she wiped off the dusty shelves, sliding jars, ceramics and rusted food cans together at one end. From around the basement, she gathered glass, china, household items and rusting tools to line all the remaining shelves but one. There she arranged salvageable books and magazines, previously strewn about helter-skelter. Might the book titles provide insight about their owner, as at some estate sales? No, these seemed random titles without a discernable pattern. Flipping a dozen or so open, she found no owner's name or inscription.

As she lifted a last heavy book, the musty dictionary fell open in her hand. She wondered irrationally if this page, chosen by fate, held an omen. Would it be "E" for Escape or "D" for Death? No, it opened to the "I's". She cringed. "I" as in Imprisoned or Impossible?

But her eye fell upon "Intelligence." She read: "readiness of comprehension; the capacity to meet situations, especially if new and unforeseen, by a rapid and effective adjustment of behavior; also the native ability to grasp the significant factors of a complex problem or situation."

She clung for a moment to the fragment of hope this passage invited, but closing the book and shoving it onto the shelf she wondered how intelligence dealt with an unpredictable maniac. Discouraged, she rubbed her forehead with her hands. Was this madness *really* happening?

Willing herself forward in the gloomy light, she approached piles of cardboard boxes. First she swept. Then she pushed and shoved the largest cardboard containers to an area where she could stack smaller ones on top. Some were so heavy she could hardly inch them across the floor. If only she had time to open and examine every one. "Christmas" on one, "Linens" on another, "Pillows and Cushions," "Clothes" and so on. Should she take time to open them and learn if the contents matched the labels, or were these reused boxes with old labels meaningless to their current contents? She'd investigate them only if she had time at the end.

The few tools she found and arranged didn't translate into lethal weapons, though she needed to defend herself. A garden trowel, a level, bolts, nails, a vice, safety glasses, a set of small graduated wrenches. No hammer, axe, shovel or sharp clippers. A short rusty screwdriver, its rod about 4" long, looked better than nothing; easy to hide, it at least gave her the illusion of some protection. Where to put it? Near the stairs seemed handy. She looked for an inconspicuous but conveniently accessible hiding place. And that's when she saw them.

CHAPTER 32

J ason's first reaction was annoyance. Gone all day and now at six o'clock, no sign of Jennifer and no sign of dinner. Not even the courtesy of a phone call explaining she'd be late. Her obsession with these silly garage sales and the resulting "warehouse" in the garage were generally tolerable, but completely losing track of time... She'd gone too far this time!

He dialed her cell phone, got the recording and at the message prompt said, "Jen, where are you? E.T., phone home!"

His second reaction was concern. At seven o'clock, still no Jennifer, no explanation and no previous behavior like this on her part for comparison. Like anyone, she could focus narrowly on something exciting enough to temporarily block a normal sense of time. He'd done this himself at his computer, swearing he spent only ten minutes while an hour passed. But daydreaming to the exclusion of reality was not like Jennifer, nor was failing to phone to assure him not to worry.

He scrutinized the large scheduling calendar on her desk where she recorded her meetings, appointments, clubs, events, luncheons, family birthdays and anniversaries. Entries filled most of the squares, but this particular Saturday showed a blank.

He tried her cell phone again, first pressing the paging option, then leaving another message. "Jen, where are you? At least phone to let me know you're okay. Do you want me to eat alone or wait for you?"

His third reaction was anxiety. No word by eight o'clock indicated something wrong. His mind wandered over possibilities. Could she be at a meeting she'd forgotten to mention or stopped to visit Denise, or another friend or one of their children? Could she have run out of gas or had an accident with the car? But surely she would call, unless too seriously injured. In that case, was the next step to call the hospitals?

Again, he tried her cell, leaving a curt message this time. "Jen, I'm worried. Please call home ASAP to let me know you're all right."

Should he call the police? He picked up the phone, stared at it a moment, and cradled it. How would it sound? "My wife is two hours late for dinner. Please start a manhunt." Yet how long *should* he wait; wouldn't acting right away make sense if she were in trouble? They involved the police fast when Tina disappeared, but she was *still* missing. He felt the hairs on his neck prickle.

Becca wandered into the kitchen at dinner time. "Where's Mom?"

"Not back yet," Jason said. "Any idea where she might be?"

Hannah joined them at the table. "No, but that's okay, Dad. Don't worry, we'll just snack."

Teenagers. It's all about *them*. Jason watched as they filled plates with leftovers and faded into other rooms, apparently unconcerned. Good old Mom always returned!

He phoned their other children, on the chance she'd stopped by or they'd remember her mentioning plans for tonight. No enlightenment, just polite concern and requests to let them know when she turned up. After all, this was Mom and moms like theirs didn't just *disappear!*

Shortly after 8 p.m. Becca announced, "We're going to a movie, Dad, unless you want us to stay here with you to wait for Mom? There's a good reason she's late. You know Mom!"

He thought he *did* know "Mom." That's precisely why he was so worried. He wondered at his daughters' entirely different take on the same situation, envying their casual lack of worry. They seemed to agree about Jennifer's normal dependability and self-reliance, but did their comfort zone demand such indestructible parents that other possibilities were unthinkable?

"No," he said, not yet wanting to alarm them unnecessarily. "Go on, but take your cell phones."

"Okay, but we can't have them on during the show."

"Good point," he acknowledged. "I forgot about that. Is Adam going along?"

"No, he's on duty tonight."

"Ah," mumbled Jason, as a plan formed. "Well, have fun!"

With effort, he watched the ticking wall clock inch toward nine o'clock. Then he uncoiled like a spring, picked up the phone, dialed the police station and asked for Detective Iverson.

"He's out on a call right now. Would you like his voice mail?"

"I... yes, I guess that's what to do." After the buzzes, Adam's recording and the beep, Jason spoke to the answering machine.

"Hey, Adam, this is Jason Shannon. We seem to have a little problem here and would appreciate your input. Actually, we *need* your input. Please call me, whenever you get this message, no matter how late." He repeated the home phone number.

By ten o'clock, Jason felt fear. He phoned Fairfax police and again asked for Adam, who still wasn't back. "Look," he said to the operator, "this may be... this is an emergency and I must speak with Detective Iverson. Would you contact him to phone me right away, please?" He gave her the call-back information.

Moments later the phone rang and Jason spilled out the story to Adam.

"Sir, I can initiate a few things, checking traffic accident reports just like we did in Tina's case. I can also start some unofficial snooping that might help."

"What if she hit a deer or ran off the road and down an embankment? No collision report would show up for that, but she could still be in trouble."

"True, sir, but we usually hear about those before long. Someone usually sees or hears something. Our patrols also look for unusual roadside situations. Why don't you sit tight for a few minutes while I get some information? I'll call you right back."

"Thanks, Adam. This means a lot!"

"Glad to help, Sir, and try not to worry. There's..."

"...usually a simple explanation." Jason finished the detective's sentence. "Yeah, I know..."

CHAPTER 33

When the phone rang ten minutes later, Jason grabbed the receiver and gripped it hard against his ear. Could it be Jennifer?

"Hello," he said expectantly.

"Sir, it's Adam. We have no recent reports of serious traffic accidents involving your wife or of injuries to anyone unidentified. No reports of off-road one-car incidents, although that remains a possibility. Why don't you come down to the police station? I'll meet you there and we'll talk about what to do next. And Sir, could you bring a recent photo of your wife?"

"All right, I'll be there as fast as I can. And Adam, thank you again. Thank you!"

"See you shortly, Sir."

Jason's mind raced. Where could he quickly find a picture of Jennifer? Boxes of photographs sat in a closet upstairs, but shuffling through them would take too long. A wonderful picture of Jennifer sat on his desk at work, inaccessible at the moment.

He hurried to his desk in the study and searched the passport file. Finding hers, he opened it and studied the picture. Though several years old, the flattering color photo captured her smiling face, alert blue eyes and shoulder length honey-blond hair. His breath caught as he thought of her perfume and that this woman he loved might be in terrible trouble somewhere this very moment.

Pocketing the passport, he scribbled a hasty note for the girls and started out the door, only to halt abruptly at the garage. What if Jennifer returned after he left? He dashed off a second note to her, taping both to a dining room chair where anyone entering the house couldn't miss them.

Ten minutes later he arrived at the police station.

Adam met him in the lobby and they shook hands. "Hello, Sir, still no word from her? Okay, have you her vehicle license plate number handy so we can post an alert? Good," he handed the information to the reception desk with some instructions. "Let's go back to my office."

Minutes after they sat down, another policeman joined them, introducing himself as he shook Jason's hand. "I'm Detective Bardonner. Glad to meet you, Sir. I'd like to sit in on this."

"Fine," said Jason. They pulled chairs up to the desk. " What do we do now?"

Bardonner spoke first, "We don't want to alarm you with what we're about to say, but may we speak frankly?"

"Of course," Jason agreed, stiffening.

"Absent probable explanations for your wife's disappearance, a traffic accident, for instance, we must consider other possibilities," Bardonner explained.

Jason looked expectantly from one detective to the other, overtaken by uncomfortable déjà vu. His last visit to this police station with Denise involved filing Tina's missing person report, her disappearance still a frightening unsolved enigma.

Adam cleared his throat, "As you know, Sir, from the MacKenzie situation, we've had three women mysteriously go missing from this area in the last five months."

Jason's polite smile faded instantly, alarm registering upon his weary face.

Bardonner shifted in his seat, leaning closer to Jason. "In situations like this, we look for patterns, but we've had trouble profiling this since their ages, appearances and circumstances of disappearance differ. Also, none of them have turned up, alive or dead, so we have no matches there. The common denominator we do know is they're all females and all from this part of Fairfax County. This could be coincidental to your wife's absence or..." Bardonner wondered whether to describe their serial-killer theory, "...or it could be related," he finished.

Jason lurched forward in his chair. "You think someone kidnapped her?"

Seeing the worry on Jason's face, Adam said, "Sir, technically anything is possible until we learn what actually happened, but what this means for you and for us is rather than treating your wife's case as a routine missing person, we can throw more ammunition at this."

"Did any of the other women's families get ransom notes?" Jason asked.

The detectives exchanged patient looks. "No ransom notes so far, Sir," Adam said.

"Where does that leave us? If not kidnapped for ransom, then..." Jason's voice trailed away.

"We can only guess at that answer," said Bardonner, quickly changing the subject. "What we want now is your wife's description, when you saw her last and when you realized she hadn't returned home... that sort of stuff. Plus we'll post her picture, if you brought one for us."

Jason handed him the passport.

Bardonner stood. "Adam, will you help him complete these forms while I get her picture copied and distributed?" Turning to Jason, he added. "Then we'll have a few more questions. Okay?"

"Okay."

Bardonner left, closing the office door on his way out. Each case took its own direction, but he didn't like where this one pointed.

CHAPTER 34

Adam indicated the papers on the desk. "These questions are pretty straightforward, Sir. Her name, birth date, weight, height, hair and eye color." He slid the forms toward Jason, who bent over them in concentration, his pen moving carefully across each page.

Bardonner returned about the time Jason finished. "Would you like coffee or something to eat?" Jason declined. "Okay, then, let's get started. When did you see her last?" Bardonner asked, taking notes.

"At breakfast. Then she headed out to garage sales about 11:00," Jason recalled. "The newspapers should list many of those addresses, telling us some of the places she went, though we wouldn't know in what order or whether she found others not advertised."

"Do you remember what she was wearing?" Bardonner asked.

He wracked his brain. "Black slacks and a black T-shirt with white dots."

"What time did you expect her home?"

"Well, it varies. Sometimes she returns for lunch, sometimes she doesn't. "Since she left at 11:00 today, I didn't expect her home for lunch. Typically, she's home no later than mid-afternoon. Occasionally 4 p.m. Rarely 5 p.m. But if that late, she would call from her cell phone with a game plan. At 6:00, I began to feel uncomfortable, more so at 7 and 8 p.m. I left a message for Adam at nine and then asked the dispatcher to contact him immediately at 10:00, when I knew something was very wrong."

"Has she seemed moody or depressed lately?" Bardonner asked.

Jason didn't hesitate. "Hardly! She's always high-energy and upbeat, but she's especially happy right now because Hannah has come back to life."

Adam tried hiding his immediate interest at hearing Hannah's name and listened intently as Bardonner said, "Oh?"

"Our daughter, Hannah, had a romantic disappointment about five months ago and took a nosedive. She temporarily lost faith in people and shut down to a low burner to heal her wounds. Jennifer worried some about her, but then just recently, our bright, fun-loving Hannah is back," Jason explained, before returning to the real reason he was here. "So I guess that was a long-winded 'no' to your question. Jennifer definitely is *not* moody or depressed."

Bardonner leaned forward. "Did she have any enemies?"

Jason looked pensive before shaking his head.

Bardonner studied the forms Jason completed. "Maybe a neighborhood dispute or a problem where she works?"

"Hers is a temp job, filling in for someone on medical leave. But no, she loves her work and the people there. And ours is just a quiet residential neighborhood. No problem there."

She hadn't told Jason of any difficulties at school where she mentored once a week. He considered her bridge group and tennis friends. "She volunteers with Childhelp, the organization that rehabilitates victims of child abuse. She belongs to an auxiliary that supports the organization in various ways. She's told me some awful stories about unbelievable things some parents do to their kids, but she wouldn't be exposed to any danger there."

Bardonner tapped his pencil against his chin. "Sir, from a police standpoint, citizens can be exposed to danger any time, anywhere. A false sense of security is your enemy because you are always your own first line of defense wherever you are."

Jason stared uncomfortably as he absorbed this information.

"Okay, has she any friction with relatives? Any situation at all that might cause her to leave voluntarily?" Bardonner asked.

"Nothing I know of. I'm certain. No."

"Forgive my asking this but I have to," Bardonner said. "Are you having any marital problems?"

Jason chuckled, "Every marriage has little glitches, but something big? Definitely not."

"Is there any possibility that she has an admirer or a boyfriend?"

Jason's startled expression answered that question for Bardonner. If she did, this husband knew nothing about it.

"You need to rule out the family, don't you?" Jason asked. "At least, that's how it works on the police shows. They always suspect the family first," Jason said.

Bardonner sighed. "We're trained to look at every possibility. Over 80 percent of victims are harmed by people they know, relatives or acquaintances, so you see the reason..."

Jason leaned forward, locking eyes with first Adam and then Bardonner. "Please do whatever you need to in order to find her. I promise my family will do *everything* in our power to cooperate and to help you." He brought a clenched fist to his lips and tears glistened in his eyes as he added in a faltering voice, "We are desperate to find her."

Adam said nothing as this man, old enough to be his own father, fought for composure. Bardonner also waited.

"Should I gather the family so you can talk to them?" Jason finally managed.

"That's not necessary at the moment," Bardonner said. "Just let us know how to reach them and we'll follow up if we need to. I can see how worried you are, but if there isn't a reasonable explanation for her apparent disappearance, we're pretty good at what we do. We'll try to have some news for you soon. Go on home and we'll get to work. Do you need help getting back?"

"No, thanks." The smile of gratitude Jason intended for the detectives twisted into a grimace as he fought to control his emotions. Bardonner shook his hand, said good-bye and left the room.

Rising to his feet with unusual effort, Jason thanked Adam again for his help. On his way out the door, he turned back to ask, "Who was that Detective Bardonner?"

Adam cleared his throat, unable to think how to soften the truth. "Sir, he's from Homicide."

Open-mouthed, Jason stumbled from the police station into the parking lot and leaned against his car, groping for his keys and the strength to use them.

CHAPTER 35

Jeremy Whitehead wakened late and headed for the bathroom when the first strange feeling hit him. He brushed this indigestion away as a morning hunger pang until a wave of dizziness forced him to lie down.

When he arose, he still didn't feel right but ate a small breakfast while watching TV. He flipped channels between programs to find the news, having cancelled his newspaper subscription a few years ago. Reading blurred news type made his head spin, likely because he needed new glasses. But he no longer trusted the medical profession, particularly after their proven incompetence in letting Ginger die.

Despite decades of sleeping eight-hour nights, Jeremy couldn't remember ever sleeping twelve straight hours until last night. So what? Things changed when you were seventy-six!

He opened all the first-floor windows and turned on the kitchen fan. Without air conditioning, he knew ventilation on these hot July days was mandatory. He turned up the TV volume partly because the commentators just whispered and partly because the background sound gave the illusion of human company without its annoyances. Real people were an intolerable nuisance.

Therefore, he did not welcome an insistent knock on his front door. A pause and even louder knocking the second time. He opened the door slightly and growled through the crack, "What do you want?"

"Hello there, Mr. Whitehead. I'm Bob Wolf, your neighbor from next door," said a pleasant voice from a friendly face.

"Well?"

"Any chance I might come inside for a minute, Sir?"

"No!"

"Oh, ah, okay. Well, we just wanted to see how you are getting along."

"I'm perfectly fine."

"My wife's baking today. She asked me to bring these cookies over to you. They're on a paper plate so no dish to return."

Silence from inside the house.

"And," Wolf continued, "what with it being summertime, of course it's natural to open windows to let in the breeze, but we wonder if you realize your TV might be tuned up a bit loud. The sound carries all up and down the block every day. You know, this is a pretty quiet neighborhood and we just thought maybe you wouldn't mind turning it down a little so that..."

"You young whippersnapper!" Jeremy pulled the door wide, his frail body framed in the opening. "You mind your own damn business!" he snarled. "My TV is not too loud, because my hearing is perfectly good. But even if I wanted it loud, this is America and in my own house I'll do whatever I want. You stuff your cookies you-know-where and leave me alone! You hear?"

Jeremy glared at him as Wolf groped for some way to break through this cantankerous old goat's wall of anger. As neighborhood spokesman, he hoped yet again to befriend the old man and perhaps also solve the community nuisance of Whitehead's blaring TV.

"You hear?" Jeremy shouted and slammed the door with a crash so mighty, the sash of the adjacent open window thudded shut.

Having rudely slammed the door right in Bob Wolf's face, Jeremy didn't see his neighbor stare at the plate of cookies in his hand, sigh deeply and reluctantly turn toward his home next door.

Inside his own house, Jeremy dialed the TV volume even higher. "I'll show them," he muttered to no one. "Now look what they've done; I'm all riled up. Why can't they just leave me alone? Is that asking too much, damn it all?"

The odd feeling swept over him again and he leaned against the table, trying to clear his head. The fingers on his left hand tingled and his vision blurred until out of the fuzziness materialized an absolutely clear thought: call in yesterday's bad driver reports.

Jeremy stepped out the side door of his house to the carport and paused for breath. What was this tightness in his chest? Had he eaten breakfast too fast? No, it was that insufferable neighbor, trying to upset him. Well, they wouldn't get the best of Jeremy Whitehead, no sir.

He opened his car door, pulled out the clipboard and stumbled back into the house. From his chair facing the TV, he heard the newscaster announce, "And here is a local news flash. Another woman is reported missing in the McLean area. In the past five months three other Fairfax County women have disappeared. Police suspect these cases may be related."

Jeremy closed his eyes. His legs felt heavy, his left arm numb, and he had trouble catching his breath. The newscaster continued, "The latest missing woman is Jennifer Shannon, last seen on Saturday in McLean, Virginia, driving a white Cadillac SRX Crossover SUV with Virginia license plate YRDSALE. If you have any information about her whereabouts or the circumstances of her disappearance, call Fairfax County Police Crime Stoppers at the phone number on your screen."

His eyes snapped open wide. Printed on the screen were a woman's name, a license plate number and the Fairfax County Police phone number. Why did that license number look so familiar? Fumbling to pick up the pencil, he hadn't time to copy the Crime Stoppers number before it faded from the screen, but he knew the Fairfax County Police number by heart.

Jeremy felt a surge of energy born of vindication. When he reported his information, the media would interview him and tell the world of his tireless efforts to rid roads of incompetent drivers. Showcasing his cause, this public platform would *finally* bring the recognition he richly deserved.

He sat still and tried to breathe deeply but a sharp pain stabbed his chest each time he inhaled. The phone... in the kitchen. More dizziness doubled him over as he rose from the chair, one hand clutching its armrest. He staggered into the kitchen, fell heavily into a chair and reached across the table for the phone.

With the clipboard in one hand and phone receiver in the other, he grunted with discomfort and focused on his task. There was the tag number he needed to report the white SUV. His hand trembled as he slowly punched buttons on the phone.

"Fairfax County Police," said the voice.

"This is Jeremy Whitehead."

"Ah, yes, Mr. Whitehead. What can we do for you today?"

"I want to report... " He was breathing rapidly now with the increasing effort for his leaden body to draw and expel breath.

"Another bad driver, Mr. Whitehead? Okay! Where did the violation occur?"

His large script blurred on his clipboard. He shook his head to clear his vision and amazingly, the page came into focus.

"3508 Winding Trail Road," he read hoarsely.

"Okay, Mr. Whitehead. I've copied that. And what was the violation?"

His mind reeled back to the serpentine road and the white van, its sudden stop demanding his brilliant, skillful maneuvering. "Jammed on the brakes right in front of me, forced me to swerve nearly off the road or crash into that damn car. Nearly killed me," he managed. Sweat broke out on his face and he felt clammy, even though the kitchen fan blew directly toward him.

"Sounds like a scary experience for you, Mr. Whitehead."

"Yes, it was."

"Can you describe the car for me?"

"It was a... a white Cadillac SUV."

"Okay, now can you give me the license plate number?"

His left arm was useless now, his body so heavy and every breath a gasping effort.

"It's... " he wheezed audibly and stared at the writing on his clipboard, "Virginia tag YR...," another gasp and a long silence.

"Mr. Whitehead, we need that license number to finish your complaint."

"I can't breathe!" The pressure in his chest intensified.

"Mr. Whitehead, are you all right? Do you need help?"

"I...I can't breathe! My heart feels like it's on fire! Yes...help me! *Please!*"

Clutching his chest, Jeremy Whitehead toppled to the floor; arms flung outward, eyes glazed.

CHAPTER 36

As she looked for a place to hide the screwdriver, three distinctive black-and-white striped boxes tucked under the basement stairs caught Jennifer's eye in the artificial light. Identically sized and entirely different from the brown cardboard packing cartons stacked elsewhere, these old-fashioned round hatboxes were labeled: "Papa," "Junior" and "The Boys." Clearly these boxes hadn't been opened for a long time. Were vintage hats inside?

Considering how much work this basement cleanup required, she'd moved surprisingly fast. Her garage sale experience in organizing disorderly items helped enormously. This unexpected "extra" time, coupled with her curiosity, allowed a hasty peek into these three boxes.

Blowing dust from the top, she slid the cover off the box marked "Papa" and stared inside. A scarf-size flag with a swastika, medals and battle ribbons and the photo of a middle-aged man standing in front of a foreign-looking bombed out building. The soldier wore a WW II uniform, much like the one belonging to her own father. Another photo, but this one of a letter. She vaguely remembered mail like this received long ago from her dad when he fought in Europe. V-mail, was it called? Examining the photo-letter in the thin light beneath a hanging light bulb, she squinted at the small photographed print and read:

"Martha — You know I can't describe my whereabouts. Loose lips sink ships. I am still okay and eager for this damn war to end. The problems we faced there on the farm were a picnic compared to this god-awful mess. Sorry the boy is such a problem. I know you're strict with him but you need to break his spirit, like you saw me do with the horse. When I get home, I'll whip him into shape all right. The army has taught me a lot more about discipline, which you know better than anybody I could already dish out pretty well. I will straighten everything and everyone out when I get back. Junior will obey us, I promise you that. Your husband, Charles"

This letter slid from Jennifer's fingers back into the hatbox. She tried to absorb its content before carefully unfolding the yellowed paper of a second letter. Under an official seal at the top was typed, "June 9, 1944. From Department of the Army of the United States of America to Mrs. Charles Yates: We regret to inform you that your husband, Charles Mathis Yates, was killed on June 6th during the Normandy invasion in the European theater of action. Please accept my sincere condolences and know that our entire nation is grateful to you and your family for his and your sacrifice."

She refolded and returned the second letter before replacing the box's cover. Had she heard a sound from up above? What if the man dashed down the stairs to find her snooping instead of working? Motionless, she listened. Convinced at last that no one was coming, she hastily opened the next box labeled "Junior."

Inside lay a wedding ring, a small bouquet of dried, faded flowers, a crumpled paper and a stack of photos. The first pictured a young man beside a beautiful young woman who wore a modest tiara with a short veil. They held hands, looking at the camera — she smiling, he stern. A wedding picture? The second photo showed the same two standing in front of a store, neither smiling. A third photo captured the two of them again, she very pregnant and clearly unhappy, he with a menacing grimace. Fourth photo caught her holding a young baby, a haunted expression on her face. The next picture showed the same woman standing before a barn. She held the hand of a sad little girl while at her side sat two unhappy boys atop a hay bale. All their expressions seemed like deer in the headlights. The final photo showed two little boys, perhaps three and two, with gaunt, serious expressions. Did one sport a black eye and the other a large bruise on his left arm, or were those oddly placed shadows of years-old amateur photography?

Carefully replacing these photos, Jennifer gently spread open the tightly wadded paper:

"Wendey, you bitch. You are an abomination and a scourge on my name. When you dared to question my authority and you refused to obey me, I gave you the discipline you deserved. I couldn't beat the poison out of you or starve it out of you in the confinement box but even though I won't be there to continue your lessons, I promise you will suffer even after they take me away to that place. I will destroy everything you care about. You doted on the little girl and I got rid of her, didn't I? Never doubt my power! You cannot escape my wrath because each time you look at your sons, my scalding hate will stare back at you from their eyes and in their faces you will see my face. You might think I am not there, but through my boys I will torment you every minute of every day for the rest of your life, exactly as you deserve. – Tobias"

Jennifer's hands trembled. The cruel face of the man in the photo and now this! Did the basement's damp chill trigger her shiver or what she'd just read? She hesitated; dare she even look inside the final box? Despite a morbid fascination to do so, she shrank at what she might find. Yet she *had* to know. What if information inside helped her gain freedom?

Slowly she lifted the lid from the last hat box labeled "The Boys." On top lay a photo of two little boys, maybe four and five, dressed in tattered clothes. Both looked wretched, though the older had his arm protectively around the younger. The younger one's face favored the cruel man, even more noticeable since he shared his father's identical sour expression. But did either of the boys in this grainy photograph resemble the man upstairs or was this someone else's tragic story?

Two more photos: in the first, one of the boys stood at attention in front of a military school, looking so young, maybe five or six, in a uniform too large. Other cadets hovered in front of an institutional building in the background, but she couldn't make out the school's name above the door. Was this the younger or older boy of the previous pictures?

The second photo pictured a little old-fashioned schoolhouse the size of a playhouse. In this black and white photo she saw painted-on windows and a bell tower on the cupola at one end of the roof.

She remembered a weathered version of this shed, odd looking enough for a second glance when her car rumbled to the top of the farm's gravel driveway. What else was different about that shed? A heavy board nailed across the door had looked new compared to the gray, sun-bleached lumber beneath. Was that a place for these boys to play? If so, why would it be boarded now?

In the bottom of the hatbox, beneath the photos, something clinked. A number of large and small keys. Next to the keys lay an old rag rolled tight and secured with a rubber band, its rotted strands still loosely circling the wad of cloth. As she started to unwrap it, she heard footsteps somewhere above. Quickly closing the box, she tucked it under the stairs with the other two, hid the screwdriver beside them and hurriedly picked up the broom.

Were these items relevant to the man upstairs or to some unrelated owner of this cellar?

Tired from strenuous work, she'd nevertheless transformed the basement. Similar items were neatly grouped, the floor swept, the sink cleaned and the trash bagged. Certain now of footsteps overhead, she pressed the buzzer he'd given her.

Seconds later, a beam of light widened overhead as the door opened, followed by the man's heavy tread descending the aging stairs. At the bottom, he circled the basement and, she hoped, observed her dramatic changes. She watched his face for any reaction to the difference she'd made but saw none. Then without looking at her, he returned wordlessly to the stairs, walked up and closed the door.

Her heart sank! Had this diligent labor accomplished nothing? How could she actually have thought this plan could work? Instead, she'd exhausted herself, making subduing her even easier for him when the time came, and surely it would come. Probably *soon!*

Without doubt, Jason had called the police by now. Why, since logic told her otherwise, did she cling to the irrational notion they might somehow find her if only given enough time?

Frantically, she tried to conjure a new strategy, but no idea came. What would the man do next? Lock her again in that stifling box? Or worse? She struggled to keep her head clear, but despair welled inside her as tears of helpless frustration pooled in her eyes.

Startling her back to reality, a noise near the top of the stairs again interrupted the stillness as the door above banged open. He started down the stairs, carrying something in one hand. A weapon? Fear clutched her heart. Were these the last seconds of her life?

He tossed a bundle down the steps. "Press the buzzer in five minutes." He ordered before closing the door at the top. The turning key rasped metallically before his footsteps faded above.

Jennifer crept to the stairs, almost afraid to see what the man had left. Maybe the severed hand or foot of a previous victim as a deadly warning? Wary, she picked up the bundle to find it was a rubber-banded sack. Removing the elastic and spreading open the brown paper bag to look inside, she gave a sharp intake of breath at what she saw.

At the bottom of the sack lay a crudely made sandwich atop a bag of potato chips and beside them a bottle of water. He wanted her alive a little longer!

CHAPTER 37

The alert Fairfax County Police Department operator rattled off Jeremy Whitehead's name and address to the 9-1-1 fast response team. She realized that besides his actual request for help, Whitehead's usually loud and angry voice sounded uncharacteristically weak and pathetic. She felt she almost knew the old curmudgeon, having fielded his incessant phone calls more times than she could remember.

Whitehead's partial report would remain a matter of record, but there was no point forwarding his incomplete information for further action.

While she ruminated about the old man, an ambulance rescue team sped toward Jeremy Whitehead's house. When their knock remained unanswered, they easily broke open the ill-fitting door to find him sprawled on the kitchen floor, barely breathing. They administered emergency care, loaded him into the ambulance and tore off toward Fairfax County Hospital. Though not dead, he'd suffered a massive heart attack. Before leaving Whitehead's house, the paramedics turned off his television set, tuned to such deafening loudness that it vibrated.

Shortly afterward, two Fairfax County policemen entered Jeremy's house to secure the broken door against opportunistic vandalism and to rule out foul play. After checking the house and chatting with neighbors, the cops reviewed their assembled facts.

"So," said the first uniform, "a 76-year-old male has a severe heart attack while on the phone with headquarters, reporting a bad driver. He's known at the district station as a semi-kook. He's known in the neighborhood as an ill-tempered recluse. No apparent friends or contacts since the wife died. So what are we looking for here? Smash and grab? Homicide? I don't *think* so!"

The other cop pointed. "Hey, check the last entry on this clipboard! Is that what he called in?"

"Probably! So what!"

"What's this? An address and a VA license number: YRDSALE? Weird! But makes no sense! Should we take it in as evidence?

"Evidence of what? Hey, we came, we looked, we checked. The old guy's ticker acted up. Does this look like a crime scene to you?"

"No, well… I just thought… "

"Nah! Look, so some jerk who drives like a maniac gets lucky and isn't reported today. How bad can it be?"

"Yeah, I guess you're right. Let's secure the front door and go."

On impulse, just before they left, the second uniform copied the clipboard's last entry on a scrap of paper found in the wastebasket and stuffed the note into his pocket.

At that same moment miles away, temporarily revived at the hospital ER, Jeremy struggled hard to tell the doctors his crucial information. Focused upon the nearly impossible challenge of keeping him alive, the medical staff initially overlooked his feeble efforts to get their attention, instead urging him to quiet down.

He finally grabbed a nurse's arm with surprising force, pulling her close to his mouth. "Important!" he whispered hoarsely. "Very important!"

"What is it, Sir? What's important?" she asked.

"Yard Sale," he whispered.

"Yard Sale?" she repeated doubtfully.

"The tag said Yard Sale. Tell the…the poleeeesss." He hissed the word "police," in a final exhalation as his attached monitors changed from a heartbeat's audible beeps to the monotone buzz of a flat-liner.

"Code Blue," shouted the nurse as additional medical personnel rushed into the room to assist with CPR. They worked feverishly for ten minutes, but to no avail.

"He's gone," the doctor announced. "Note the time for the record."

The nurse shook her head sadly and turned to the doctor. "Poor old man! I'd like to think someone understood my last words on earth, but could you make out what he said?"

"The words, yes, but the meaning, no: 'tell the police the tag said yard sale'? Makes no sense!"

The nurse agreed. "Not to me either, but isn't it too bad since he seemed to think it was mighty important?"

The doctor took a last look at Jeremy's still body, alive only minutes ago.

"Not any more," he said and turned away.

CHAPTER 38

Her exertion cleaning the basement and relief at still being alive honed Jennifer's appetite. With no idea when or if she might eat again, she wolfed down the food and refilled the plastic bottle at the basement sink, praying the water was potable. She drank in great gulps.

Newly fortified, though still anxious, she stood at the bottom of the stairs and pressed the buzzer.

The door at the top of the stairs opened almost immediately.

"Come," he ordered, as one might command a dog.

She crept up the stairs. His bulk no longer filled the doorway and, reaching the top, she tried to quell an irrational surge of hope. Emerging alive from that dreaded dungeon, even if only temporarily, was an unimaginable victory.

Head submissively lowered to avoid eye contact, she stood at the top of the stairs, determined to play out the role of cowed servant. This ruse parlayed into a ticket out of the basement and with a world of luck, maybe, *somehow*, a ticket to freedom.

"The kitchen," he barked. "Clean it. Over there," he pointed to an adjacent anti-room. "Do the laundry. The dog guards you every minute. Don't leave these two rooms. Finish and buzz." He stepped through the door, back into the hall, and locked the kitchen door behind him.

She blinked into sunshine spilling through the window above the sink. What an appealing contrast to the bleak artificial light in the cellar below! But the window meant more than welcome sunlight. It framed a view of the outdoors she'd doubted ever seeing again, and somewhere beyond lay those she loved… and *home*.

She leaned forward over the sink to increase her field of vision and memorize what she saw outside. This was the same house, all right: the yard, the barn, the sheds scattered outside beneath several large shade trees. This was still McLean! A long field stretched far behind the house, bordered in the far distance by another stand of trees, but no sign of her car or the black pickup truck. How she wished she'd paid closer attention to details when she originally drove in here, never dreaming such information might affect her departure.

The clock above the sink read noon. Looking through cupboards, she found a box of tea bags and longed for a cup of that hot, soothing beverage to calm her nerves. What could it hurt? She extracted a bag, filled the teakettle with enough water for a single cup and turned on the burner.

Behind a modern table and four chairs at one end of the eat-in kitchen were three tall side-by-side windows with the center window unscreened. Outside, the glass panes spread a wide angle of the same back yard barn-and-shed view. Were these big windows painted shut? If not, were they on a security system like those at her house? No visible wires or plastic pads! If caught, could she excuse lifting a sash as part of cleaning if an alarm sounded?

With a cloth and some glass cleaner in hand to camouflage her true intent, she carefully opened the lock atop the center window's lower sash and lifted slightly. When no alarm sounded, she edged it up another few inches. Suddenly a heart-stopping, high-pitched shriek pierced the air!

Oh god, a bugged window! Prickles of adrenalin moved over her skin as her ears followed the sound… not from a window alarm but from the *teakettle*. Jamming the window down but with no time to relock it, she rushed toward the stove as two frightening events unfolded.

The dog's toenails clicked a staccato trill across the vinyl floor as he careened snarling from the laundry room into the kitchen, his fangs glinting and his metal tags jingling that sound she hated. Simultaneously, the door crashed open and the man loomed, glaring furiously at her quaking finger pointed toward the whistling teakettle.

"No!" he shouted, whether to her or the dog, she couldn't know. "Water at the sink only!" He glared, his jaw and neck veins working. She cowered, praying he wouldn't notice the unlocked window as his glance swept the room for irregularities. She tensed for the ensuing pain. Staring dumbly at the floor, she felt his electric energy as he shaped his next move. Would he strike her? Throw her down the basement stairs? Cut her? Blind her? Rape her?

She hunched vulnerably before him, trembling with fear. Seconds passed as she steeled herself for violent retaliation, the wait for that terrible pain creating its own grisly torture.

But minutes passed and nothing happened. Did he prefer storing this situation's rage to extend her agony later? Did he think once his hands touched her, he couldn't stop himself until he beat her to death? Did he not want that satisfying termination just yet?

"Door," he screamed to the dog as it spun around and scrambled to that post. When she looked up, the man was gone and the kitchen door once more shut and locked.

Cursing her idiocy with the teakettle, her heart pounded from that horrific close call even though this perilous experience bought a vital piece of information. The doors might be bugged, but that window was not! No alarm and no screen. A possible way *out!*

To avoid angering him further, the teakettle incident warned her to be more cautious than ever. On the other hand, she must escape, which wasn't cautious at all! How could she do both?

Vigorously polishing the table, she surreptitiously re-locked the opened window fastener. At that moment she realized that having no person in the room didn't mean she wasn't observed. Stores sold plenty of hidden camera technology, so anyone with money, determination and skill could install them, or pay professionals to do so. Maybe he even was such a professional. Who knew what his background included? Trying not to be obvious, she moved around the kitchen toward the sink, searching for a camera lens, but finding none.

Back at the sink, she washed the dishes and opened drawers to find a weapon. No sharp kitchen knives and even the silverware knives were gone. He was a step ahead of her.

She looked out the smaller window over the sink, at the barn and sheds, wondering about outdoor lighting at night. Her own driveway had motion-activated floodlights over the garage. Was the worn light fixture on the barn operated by a switch, photocell or motion-sensor? It didn't look new or like hers at home, but maybe a different model. If motion floods existed outside above the back door, they'd affect a night getaway—the likeliest time, while he slept—by triggering a back yard brilliant with light when cover of darkness was crucial.

Finished at the sink, she entered the laundry room. A pull shade covered most of the window in the door's upper half. If she could press her face against the glass and look up she'd learn if floodlights existed in the eaves above. But as she approached the door, the dog leaped to his feet and growled a warning, his alert eyes focused single-mindedly upon her.

She stopped in her tracks, looked away and moved the laundry around atop the machine. But when she edged a tiny step in the outside door's direction, the dog growled a decibel higher and drew back his lips in a low snarl revealing his teeth.

No way!

CHAPTER 39

Jennifer stepped back from the dog, turned to the washing machine and added detergent and the laundry: the usual men's socks, shirts, T-shirts, pajamas, underwear, handkerchiefs, and trousers, plus sheets and towels. This volume of dirty laundry required two loads. Unexpected in an old house, the washer and dryer looked *new*. Multiple hangers crowded the adjacent wall-mounted rack; beside it sat an iron and folded ironing board. In the right situation, several of these might become weapons.

From the corner of her eye, she confirmed that the dog watched her every move. What had he been trained to do? Bark if he saw a weapon in her hand? Bite if she reached for the door knob? Knock her to the floor and rip out her throat? The teakettle whistle certainly sent him into orbit!

The dog barricaded any escape attempt through the back door. What could she do to neutralize him? Stab him, poison him, trap him? Befriend him? She flinched at the last idea… because of her dog phobia in general and this menacing brute in particular.

Returning to the kitchen, Jennifer peered into the oven: a real mess! Steeling herself for the filthy task, she put the racks in the sink, sprayed oven cleaner inside the oven and closed its door. Studying the can, she knew this would be an excellent weapon if sprayed into face and eyes. But could she get away while it disabled her captor? No, because of the dog! Could she spray the dog, too? The dog was the key! Even if she miraculously eluded the man, the dog would find her and finish her. Still, she left the oven cleaning canister on the counter... just in case!

The surprisingly well-stocked refrigerator needed cleaning also. Maybe some food here for the dog? She saw several pounds of raw ground beef stuffed into a plastic bag, the original packaging gone. She gouged out a bite-size chunk of the hamburger meat and squeezed the remainder in the bag smooth again. Sticking the small ball of meat on the end of a fork, she crept back to the laundry room. Again, the low growl as she entered.

She loathed nearing the animal, but she *had* to try. If the dog barked, signaling the man to rush in to find her with the meat in her hand, she'd be done for. Back to the basement or far worse! Was it worth the try, and if she *did* try, what was the best way to go about it? Perhaps a variation of Pavlov's famous experiment? The dog would need to connect her with a sound she made and the food she offered. But what sound? She clicked her tongue and very slowly placed the meat fork on the floor between the dryer and the dog so he couldn't reach it without getting up.

At first he ignored it, but then his nostrils twitched as he caught the scent. The animal stared directly at the meat and sniffed the air again. No question, he recognized food! She'd read that guard dogs could be specifically trained to *attack* a stranger offering food or to bark this alert to their master.

Was food rationing a cruel part of the dog's training? If so, could that work in her favor? The animal's ribs showed through his scarred hide. Not emaciated, like many Fairfax County Animal Shelter foundlings that friends volunteering there described to her, but neither was he well-fed.

Clicking her tongue, she bent down slowly, picked up the meat fork and removed it... to build his anticipation. The animal watched, sensing danger. After a moment, she replaced the fork on the floor. The dog licked his lips, stared at the meat and changed position but didn't get up. The third time the dog leaned toward the meat but pulled back. Who says the third time is the charm?

A fourth time she pushed the fork closer to him, clicking her sound. He did not leave his post but stared at the meat, shifted his position slightly closer and extended his head toward the meat. Edging nearer, she lifted the hamburger until it was directly between them, reinforcing the animal's connection with her, the sound she made and the anticipated food. Nudging it to within inches of his mouth, she held her breath as the dog pushed his muzzle forward, moistened his lips and jerked the meat from the fork. "Good dog," she crooned.

Whew! She leaned against the washer for support. This could so easily have gone the other way. Had the dog barked, sealing her fate, at this very moment the man would be standing over her to kill her. She sighed in relief. So far so good!

Not knowledgeable about dog training, she *did* know something about children, having raised five of her own. Some parenting hinged upon encouragement and positive reinforcement. Other methods stressed strictness and punishment. If animal training were similar, she could guess which this scarred dog had experienced.

Facing her task once more, she realized wryly that cleaning a kitchen is second nature to one who's tackled that task thousands of times. In between the scouring, wiping, drying, scrubbing, polishing, sweeping and laundry, she managed to feed the dog, using her same technique, *four* more times. The smaller mound of ground beef in the refrigerator presented another risk, but with luck he wouldn't notice.

Putting the first laundry load into the dryer, she added the remaining clothes to a second washer load. After tackling the onerous oven cleaning job, she folded the dry garments atop the laundry machines.

Jennifer saw no telephone in the kitchen. Did this mean he had no phones or few phones or cell phones? A hard wired phone for her 9-1-1 call was too much to ask! The kitchen clock read 2:30 p.m. If accurate, and if her calculations were correct, she'd been captive about twenty-two hours.

Glancing around the kitchen one last time, she pressed the buzzer. The door opened quickly and the man whisked past her to inspect the kitchen. Then he collected the hangers with his clean shirts and trousers from the laundry room.

"Bring that," he indicated the stack of folded laundry, "and follow me."

Obediently, she did; toward what, she knew not...

CHAPTER 40

They moved quickly down a hallway, along which she counted five closed doors. He opened all three doors on the left side of the hall and said, "The vacuum cleaner is here," he pointed to the linen closet behind the first door. "Put the laundry in there," he indicated the bedroom through the third door. "And then clean the bedroom after you finish the bathroom," he gestured toward the middle open door.

The man's sharp whistle startled her, foretelling the immediate appearance of the dog, who watched her intently. She fought the urge to recoil as the large animal moved nearer. "Guard," he commanded the animal. To Jennifer, *"Don't* close the doors while you're working. The dog will keep you in sight at all times. Press the buzzer when you're through."

"I am also an experienced cook," she volunteered, eyes submissively downcast.

Staring at the floor, she couldn't read his expression but thought he hesitated a moment before walking to the end of the hall, entering a room on the hallway's right side and closing its door after him.

A dead-end at one end of the hall prevented escape and the animal, only a few feet away, blocked the other. The old fear gripped her at close proximity to any unpredictable dog, never mind one with specific instructions to guard — or maybe — *kill* her. The dog returned her stare, as if daring her to try a wrong move. She must face it; she hadn't won him over at all!

Struggling for positive focus, she turned to her work. Maybe she'd find clues about the man in the bathroom medicine cabinet like a prescription revealing his name. But first she closed the door enough to elicit a warning growl from the dog. Gratefully she used the toilet. So much better than the bucket in the basement.

Besides the toilet, the bathroom had a claw-foot tub next to a large sink set into a dresser-size cabinet with storage drawers and doors. At the end of the room, a fixed window with a high-transom above it framed two rectangles of daylight. The small, high opening wasn't a way out, but the pole that operated the transom looked like a potential weapon.

Brown towels hung neatly on the racks, a brown shower mat draped over the side of the tub and several matching brown rugs lay across the floor. Brown, she thought, was about as understated as you can get. A brush and a comb lay atop the toilet tank.

Reaching toward the medicine cabinet, she gasped suddenly, confronted by the shock in the mirror above the sink! A woman's haggard face—ringed by a tangle of disheveled, dirty hair—stared back at her. She nodded to be certain the awful mirrored face moved when hers did. Could this be her actual reflection? Far worse than any early-morning, no make-up visage she'd faced at home. The purplish circles under her eyes, their haunted look, the drawn mouth, cheeks smudged with dirt and that mop of dull, clumped hair surrounding her face…she looked like a war refugee.

Hypnotized, she gazed in disbelief at this pathetic stranger. Her hand grabbed the comb atop the toilet tank and she watched in the mirror as the comb rose in her fingers and attempted to work through a few strands of her matted hair. Rinsing her cleaning rag, she dabbed at the sticky bump on the back of her head. The cloth's resulting rust-colored smear confirmed dried blood. She stared dumbly at her reflected apparition as both her hands lifted to force the comb through the snarls.

Her eyes wandered from the mirror down to her clothes, the same ones she'd worn two days, slept in last night and cleaned house in today. What could she expect but the dirty, rumpled slacks and stained shirt that encased her body? Leaning forward over the sink, she finished combing her hair and splashed cold water on her face to jar her back to reality. Rinsing the rag, she washed her face with warm water and soap. Never had this simple act felt so redeeming, as if she were cleaning away a foreign mask to uncover the real Jennifer hidden beneath.

But now the "real Jennifer" must move forward. Hurrying, she cleaned the bathroom, removed strands of her hair from his comb, washed it and placed it back beside the brush.

With a last brave look in the mirror, she opened the medicine cabinet to reveal an electric razor and small hotel-size shampoo bottles. In the under-sink cabinet were more towels, toilet paper and bar soap. Had he sanitized this room on purpose or did he live like a monk? Except for her own frightening reflection in the mirror, she'd learned nothing new.

Returning to the hall, where the dog jumped to attention, she grabbed the vacuum cleaner and pushed it ahead of her into the bedroom. The animal moved quickly into the room's open doorway while she glanced around for a phone or hidden camera. If this were his bedroom, perhaps she'd discover something about her captor here.

Immediately recognizing her lamp on the bedside table, she felt surprise. Her daughters said he bought it at their garage sale but seeing it here, something of hers in his house, struck her as incongruous and disheartening.

Making up the queen-size bed with the sheets she'd laundered, she covered them with the rumpled comforter lying on the floor. Moving to the two windows, she lifted each shade and peered out. Like the kitchen, one faced the back of the house, but from here she could see the other side of the barn, where pieces of long-abandoned farm equipment rusted in the sunshine. She also had a better view of the long field with a wood of tall trees at the opposite end, the field itself overgrown with saplings and bushes. The second window looked out on the yard at the end of the house, where a sprawling thicket blanketed the area from the house to a dense stand of trees thirty feet away. In which direction should she head if ever she could get away?

Moving around the Spartan room, she quietly slid open every drawer and examined the contents as she dusted and vacuumed. She'd use the putting-away-your-laundry excuse if he caught her doing so. She felt around the neatly stacked but sparse clothing, socks, handkerchiefs, belts, pajamas and underwear in the dresser drawers, finding no new clues. On top of the dresser sat a magnifying glass and an electric clock-radio, the alarm hand set for 6:00, presumably his morning wake-up call. Good for her to know.

In the closet hung a dress shirt, casual shirts, trousers, work clothes and one suit. She checked all pockets, discovering only a wadded Kleenex, a pocket comb and some coins. The room had no wall decorations, framed photos, books, magazines or jewelry. Not even a jar of pennies or something under the bed, where one could usually count on a stray sock.

Looking around to see if she'd missed anything, she realized she'd forgotten the second night stand. While dusting the lamp and shade, she inched the drawer open. Inside lay a framed photograph of two little boys, a different background and grainier, but unquestionably the same serious-faced boys pictured in the hatbox downstairs. He must be one of the two, but which? She recalled before-and-after photos of missing children on milk cartons where artists projected their appearance today. Would adding years to one of these little faces equal the man across the hall?

Her time was running out! She scrutinized the faded photograph again, grabbed the magnifying glass from the dresser, turned on the night table lamp and studied the picture under the light.

The photo captured two unhappy boys sitting on a high-backed wooden bench, their hands in their laps except for the older boy's left arm placed protectively around the younger one's shoulder. Unhappy or frightened, stunned or resigned, strain showed in their eyes. Jennifer searched for any obvious identifier — a birth mark, a scar, a deformity — to compare against her captor. And do it fast, for if he appeared at the door and found her like this, she was toast!

Her eyes moved to their hands. Closing in with the magnifying glass brought two surprising discoveries. The fingers hung loose on the bigger boy's left hand draped over the smaller boy's shoulder, but she saw only three fingers and a thumb. Was his little finger folded up behind his hand? She tried folding her own little finger back, but her adjacent finger curled also. Unlike her simulation, the boy's fingers lay relaxed. He had no little finger! Next, she looked at the smaller boy's hands, spread open on his knees. On his left hand she saw a dark line several inches long. A scar, the scab of a burn from a metal rod or a birth mark? Each boy's left hand! So if she glimpsed her captor's left hand, she'd know!

Something else about the photo stirred in the back of her mind. Pushing the magnifying glass closer, she searched for background details, seeking something familiar. But what? Then she saw it and focused the magnifying glass. Behind the boys was a v-shaped nick in the bench's top board. These boys huddled on the bench in the confinement box, the very same box where the boys' mother had been imprisoned, according to the hatbox letter! And Tina. And Jennifer herself.

And who knew how many others?

No sooner did she stuff the photo back into the drawer and turn off the lamp than the man abruptly appeared at the door. Holding her breath, she covered the magnifying glass with her cleaning rag and continued laboriously dusting the lamp and table top. Turning, she appeared to dust the dresser, slipping the magnifying glass subtly from the cloth back onto the dresser as she moved past.

"Finished, Sir!" she said, looking not at his face but carefully at his hands, both thrust deep into his trouser pockets.

Her mind reeled. What if this ended her tasks? Should she stall for time? Had she idiotically misread the situation by thinking swift efficiency would earn more work when cleaning fast actually lessened the time he'd need a servant? Moreover, given the remote chance he allowed her to clean the whole house, if not already dispensable, she would be then!

He glanced around the room then jerked his head, "Follow me!" The man snapped his fingers, causing the dog to follow them so closely that she felt its hot animal breath against the back of her slacks as they moved along the hallway.

Jennifer tried to prepare herself for any eventuality: to clean another room, to desperately run for her life, to grab any object and aggressively defend herself? She simply had no idea what to expect next...

CHAPTER 41

He led the way to the living room, which she remembered uneasily from her arrival the day before. Here she'd recognized the painting above the fireplace, realized the farmer was the dreaded Wrestler, grasped her peril when he blocked her escape and crashed to the floor when the dog attacked her.

Had she ever really been that *other* Jennifer Shannon, living a happy life with her family, innocently attending weekend sales, harming no one, oblivious to the remotest possibility of abduction by a madman? One minute the clear identity of her full, rich, trouble-free life, and the next at the mercy of a tormentor intending to kill her. She swallowed hard.

Now more than ever, she needed her wits about her! These large windows faced the front yard and, beyond that, the road. However fleeting the chance, she needed to focus on this scene, because this could be where she'd run headlong if...

His expressionless voice interrupted her train of thought. "Clean this room. The dog guards you constantly. When you finish, press the buzzer." He placed the familiar electronic pad on the coffee table and, turning on his heel, disappeared down the hall.

Plugging in the vacuum cleaner, she shoved and yanked it while studying the view out the window. A long, rectangular yard between the house and the road looked football-field size and overgrown with waist-high brush. Kudzu vines draped many trees. She wondered if the grass were tall enough to hide in, but what was she thinking? She couldn't crouch there undetected with the dog in pursuit.

This outdoor view reminded her of the *long* driveway down the side of the rectangle from the house to the road. If only she'd jogged daily! Now, even if she reached the outside, how fast could she move and for how long? Had she enough stamina to run down that driveway and then along the road to find help? Even so, she could *never* outrun the dog.

Parking the sweeper in front of the window, she went to the entryway alcove to look for a front door alarm system. No keypad, but one might be inside the front hall closet. Her approach elicited a warning growl from the dog standing in the foyer, head alert and eyeing her closely.

From a pocket she retrieved the last piece of plastic-wrapped meat for the dog and, making the clicking sound, fed him the bite. "Good dog," she praised, pretending to dust the foyer. The dog watched her closely but didn't move as she satisfied herself no alarm system existed inside the closet. "Such a good dog," she encouraged the animal, who licked his lips anticipating another treat.

Would the living room tell anything personal about her captor? She knew the furniture's origin. Maybe the man didn't live here, but only "camped" here. Did he lead a double life? What best fit the few facts she understood?

Under the lamp on a corner end table sat a small travel clock, the kind that folded up flat into a case the size of a cracker. Its second hand moved rhythmically and the time shown mirrored a wall clock. Without a clock or window to gauge outside light, in the cellar time stopped.

Ostensibly dusting the little clock, she folded it shut and slipped it into her pocket, but in doing so felt a small lump already there. Investigating this brought a smile: Tina's tiny frog. These must be the same slacks she wore on her birthday when she tucked away the special gift. Wishing the Chinese good-luck legend to apply now, when only magic could help her through this insane situation, she slipped the clock into her other pants' pocket.

She was running out of options. She'd already cleaned much of the house while discovering few clues except in the nightstand drawer and the basement's three hat boxes, clues which might be important or not. Outside of escape or rescue — and she had ruled out rescue in her untraceable location—if Wrestler locked her back in the basement, she probably wouldn't emerge alive.

She finished the living room but did *not* press the buzzer. Buying time made sense now. She fluttered the dust cloth, creating make-work. "Good dog," she said several times and each time the animal let her move quite close to him before his warning growl. Was she becoming less fearful of dogs? After enduring a fifty-five year phobia, this subtle change amazed her.

What would unfold next? She'd earlier planted the seed about cooking. Buying this much time seemed incredible, but once she finished cleaning the house and, if allowed, cooked a meal, her usefulness ended. Tonight was the night! One way or another! If her attempt failed, she was out of options.

She pressed the buzzer.

CHAPTER 42

When he strode into the living room to survey her work, she willed him not to notice the missing clock. His eyes scanned the room and lingered near the table where it belonged, but after a few agonizing seconds, passed by.

"Follow me," he ordered again.

Awash with relief, she trailed him back down the hallway, where he opened a door across the hall from the bedroom she earlier cleaned. "Clean this room," he said, again directing the dog to guard the open doorway before he returned to the same room as before and closed the door.

Jennifer gaped in surprise at a home work-out room! But of course! This tracked with his body-builder physique, earning him the name "Wrestler." No gym-enthusiast herself, she still recognized most machines: treadmill, stationary bike, rowing machine, stair-stepper and weight bench. These machines cramming the room insured variety for a serious cross-trainer.

Putting down the cleaning equipment, Jennifer wandered to the window, lifted the shade and studied the overgrown front yard. Somewhere beyond lay the county road and freedom. Was this her last glimpse of this tantalizing view? She sighed wistfully before turning to her job.

She vacuumed the wood floor, mopped, then wiped down the machines. Her daughters said Wrestler bought her rowing machine at their sale, a machine she herself bought used two years earlier to start a fledgling exercise program. Such machines looked alike but she could identify hers by a white paint spatter unintentionally flicked across a corner of the machine during a decorating project at home. Crouching down, she spotted the familiar mark. To think one of her own belongings improved the daily health and strength of a man scheming to kill her felt eerily unjust. This bitter irony nauseated her. She swallowed hard until the urge to vomit passed.

When steady again, she resumed cleaning the remaining machines. Only one closed door remained in the hallway: his office, she guessed, because he spent most of his time there and because she'd found almost nothing personal or revealing anywhere else upstairs. There he must do his "important work," as she'd improvised in the basement, whatever that might be. Harking back to their first encounter at the garage sale, he did buy that collection of Playboy magazines. Were they stacked in his office for regular attention or the unwanted part of a package deal which he later tossed?

If his office held sensitive secrets, work or play, he still might instruct her to clean there. At last she'd satisfy her curiosity by learning what he did, even if she could never use the information because he'd kill her first. She gulped at this incongruity.

If Wrestler were one of the boys in the hatbox photos, how did the facts connect? The letters suggested first their cruel father abused the boys and then their broken mother, who saw her despised, insane husband in his sons. Jennifer couldn't imagine hurting a helpless child, but from Childhelp volunteering she recalled the sobering statistic that five youngsters *die* every day in America from abuse or neglect.

She thought of the school house outside. What if it weren't a playhouse at all, but a dementedly different kind of "learning" house? If so, what had the boys endured there? And that pet grave under the cross. Was an animal buried there… or something else?

Tina?

Even if the savage cruelty of Wrestler's mother triggered his hatred of women, despising that horrible woman was one thing but randomly murdering innocent women to defy her, quite another. How differently it might have turned out if he'd broken that chain of violence, by himself or with outside help. She knew the statistics: without intervention, one-third of abused waifs would then abuse their own kids and on and on... What a sickening spiral of vicious human behavior.

Jennifer's earlier idea to gain an edge by psyching out her captor had faded. Unable to defend herself physically, she'd hoped at least to defend herself verbally, perhaps with a tirade of discovered truths he thought no one else knew. Or would that further enrage him, intensifying his resolve to extinguish her knowledge in ways too terrible to imagine? Or maybe she could calmly talk him out of his plan for her, proposing treatment alternatives instead of further brutality. Sure! Who was she kidding?

Opening the closet to clean inside, she found a zippered plastic suit bag pushed to one end. Glancing anxiously toward the open door, she slid the zipper down and spread the bag open. A military uniform hung inside with two shirts on adjacent hangers and two sets of fatigues behind those. On the hat shelf above the suit bag gleamed a pair of highly polished black dress shoes and a second pair of worn high-top combat boots. Looking furtively again toward the door, she unzipped the bag far enough to see the name stitched above the fatigue uniform shirt pocket. "Yates," she read before zipping the bag closed, a hasty glance toward the open door confirming that only the dog observed her stealth.

Only one machine left to clean. Two books lay on the treadmill's stand, one closed and atop it a smaller open book, apparently material he studied when working out the last time.

Sliding the top book aside, she read the title beneath: "The Militia Handbook." Covering it again with the small opened book, she saw the picture of a small frog with reddish orange upper body above blue legs and hind quarters, almost as if the tiny creature wore blue trousers.

She read:

"Red and Blue Poison Dart Frog (dendrobates pumilio) and its 'cousins'; small, 2-3 cm brightly colored frogs found in Costa Rica, Panama and Ecuador, eat small insects and beetles. Their toxin, batrachotoxin, more potent than curare and ten times more potent than tetrodotoxin from the puffer fish, affects the nervous system. Currently no effective antidote exists for the treatment of batrachotoxin poisoning. Each frog contains enough poison to kill 20,000 mice. Humans can get sick just by touching the frog's skin. Central and South American natives use the frog's poison on their

hunting darts. The frog's consumption of certain beetles, which either make the toxin or get it from their own food chain, appears strategic to the manufacture of the frog's toxin because captured frogs fed a different diet lose their poison."

Impossible! Frogs, snails, turtles and butterflies were the "safe" wild creatures she'd *encouraged* her growing children to catch and play with. She didn't dream frogs anywhere were dangerous. She riffled curiously through succeeding pages, which pictured more brightly colored frogs with similarly descriptive text. Flipping back to the cover, she read the title, "Poison Frogs and Toads of Central and South America." Was this her intended fate? Would a poisoned nervous system cause her excruciating end?

No, she guessed, he'd do that job with his own two hands. And thinking of those hands, she realized with resignation that looking at the man's left hand might serve her curiosity, but not her escape.

She patted her pants' pockets, feeling the small clock in one and Tina's frog in the other. She rubbed the little frog. This one containing no poison. But perhaps, a miracle? If ever she needed good luck, now was the time.

The cleaning finished, her finger hovered over the buzzer. If she pressed it, would her life end in the next few minutes? She'd wait, buying time, until he appeared next. But at that very moment, he materialized, nearly filling the doorway with his stocky frame.

"Well?"

"Finished," Jennifer said, hoping to god it wasn't the literal truth.

CHAPTER 43

Approaching Hannah's house to spend some brief time with her before he went to work, Adam fought the triple frustration of getting nowhere fast on an important case, of his personal stake in its outcome and of witnessing Hannah's anxiety.

He liked Jennifer Shannon from the moment she marched into his office with her logical theories about the moving-sale burglaries. Since then, his tender feelings for Hannah had grown until he felt personally entwined in everything surrounding this case. Now that he and Hannah dated regularly, he enjoyed not only the companionship of this lovely, bright girl, but also the dynamics of her big, affectionate family. He'd missed out on this as an only child.

Working on a case involving people he knew and liked, he vowed early not to let his subjectivity compromise the objectivity the case demanded. In fact, he felt his focus and dedication *increased* because of his personal involvement, providing heightened motivation that could make a positive difference. For Adam, this wasn't "just another case."

Adam hated seeing Hannah so forlorn, his attempt at calming platitudes ringing hollow even to his own ears. What you most want to do is comfort someone you care about who suffers distress. Yet, short of finding her missing mother, he knew his well-meant words sounded ineffective. And despite his best efforts, never mind those of the entire police force, would Mrs. Shannon ever be found—alive or dead? His heart twisted when Hannah looked up at him and said, "You're a detective. Can't you do *something?*"

"If only I could! The department just has no leads, Hannah. We've shown your mom's photo to all the people who listed sales in the paper that day. Some remember her, some don't, but nobody noticed when she left, what direction she went or recalls her mentioning where she'd go next. You know what a zoo those sales can be. We've shown her picture, description and license number on the media. We're doing everything we can."

"Adam, I'm so scared. I can't stand thinking something terrible happened to her." Hannah whispered.

"The radio and TV broadcasts have netted lots of tips. Nothing productive yet, which is typical, but we check out each one and that's our best hope at the moment. Someone somewhere surely saw something!"

"Oh, Adam," Hannah threw her arms around him. "Please find her. I miss her so much!"

To her surprise, Adam revealed, "I do, too. It's as if I've been waiting most of my life for your big family... and most especially for you. The minute I met you I wanted you in my life."

Hannah let him fold her into his strong arms and looked up. They shared a light kiss, this stolen moment of pleasure a sharp contrast to their shared worry over her vanished mother.

But unbidden thoughts of Kevin crept again into Hannah's mind. She'd promised herself to avoid vulnerability. True, she liked Adam, his good looks, his appealing sense of humor, his intelligence, kindness and dedication to work. But Kevin had many of those qualities also, which he used to earn her trust, loyalty and love... only to betray her. No one wanted that kind of hurt again. How different could Adam be? After all, he was a man.

Shouldn't she protect herself from heartache by using the valuable lesson she'd learned the hard way? Or might she someday trust and love again, as her dad predicted?

"Oh, Adam," she pulled away, not wanting to share her perplexing thoughts with him. "I... I do care for you, but..."

"But...?"

"But so much is happening now. I'm sorry to be upset all the time because my mom's in trouble. I understand how hard you're trying to find her. Since you've been with the police, this is the only case you haven't been able to solve, much as you want to." She started to cry softly.

"That I haven't solved *yet!*" He hugged her close and then held her at arm's length. "Hannah, if ever I've seen a survivor, it's your mom. She's a land-on-her-feet person. I can just feel it." He stroked her hair. "Look, at the department we're trained to deal with facts. But intuition can take you places facts don't. I might not be this optimistic in other situations, but my gut feeling is this will work out okay. I don't know how, I don't know why, but I believe it will." He hugged her close again, wrapping her in his protective arms.

"Just hearing you say that helps. Thank you, dear Adam." They shared a real kiss.

Reluctantly he broke from their embrace. "Look, I'm going back to the station to stay on this. I may be up all night, but if anything breaks, you know I'll call immediately. Keep your cell phone on. Try to calm your family and I'll see you tomorrow, no matter what happens tonight."

"Thank you for trying so hard, Adam." She squeezed his arm affectionately as he walked toward his car and sped away.

Brushing away tears of confusion, Hannah blew a heartfelt kiss toward his departing vehicle. She smiled at the silhouette of his continuing farewell wave through the vehicle's rear window and watched his car grow ever smaller as it receded down the street, turned the corner and was gone.

CHAPTER 44

The phone on Adam's office desk rang. "Detective Iverson," he said into the mouthpiece.

"Hello, Adam. It's Jason Shannon. I don't want to be a nuisance, but any news yet about Jennifer?"

"No, Sir, nothing yet, but we're working hard on it."

"Well, this morning I remembered something that might help. Her car has something called OnStar. I think they offer a service for finding your car if you forget where you parked."

Adam sat up in his chair. Even if Mrs. Shannon weren't still in her van, forensics might comb out helpful evidence. The location itself might even be significant, if abandoned at or near the crime scene. With zero clues at the moment, Adam salivated for any new lead.

"I pulled the OnStar file from her desk drawer." Jason studied the papers as he spoke. "This contract shows her account number, her password and OnStar's contact number."

"Right, Sir. I'd appreciate all three." Adam's pen flew across the paper as he copied the information in bold handwriting.

"Thank you very much, Mr. Shannon, for calling about this. I'll get right on it."

Adam cradled the receiver against his ear, jabbed the phone's disconnect button and punched in OnStar's number. At their menu's prompt, he pressed the button for "Urgent Situations."

"Hello, this is Detective Adam Iverson of Fairfax County Police in McLean, Virginia. We're trying to locate the driver and vehicle of your member, Jennifer Shannon." He read them her member number and password.

"Sir, I've copied that. Let me transfer you to a special operator who can help you."

Adam tapped his fingers impatiently.

"Hello, Detective," the voice answered. "I'm Brad Billings. How can I help you?"

Adam identified himself again. "We have a missing adult female, last seen driving her vehicle yesterday. Her husband just advised us she subscribes to OnStar. Locating her vehicle could mean locating her. Can you help us?"

"Has a missing person report already been filed?"

"Yes, yesterday."

"Good. Okay, we cooperate with law enforcement, but at the same time are legally bound to protect our members' privacy. To do both, we have procedures for police requests like yours, Detective. Basically, we need to verify key pieces of information: that you're who you say you are, that a missing person report exists, and so on. Then if we find something, we have more procedures for giving you that info. But if we don't find anything, we may not get to that."

Adam stiffened, "How long will this run-around take?" he asked impatiently. "We may have an abduction here, we may have a serial... "

"Detective, we understand your urgency and will process this quickly. Give me your full name, badge number, precinct, city and state so we can verify. Your headquarters will put us through to you when we call back. You should hear from me in ten minutes or less and we'll get to work. Meantime, FAX me your missing person report. Here's the number...."

Sighing, Adam provided the information they requested, hung up and strolled down the hall to send the required report to OnStar.

Unbidden, the vision of Hannah's face floated into his mind. In four years on the force, he'd seen his grim share of frightened family members struggling to absorb terrible news about their loved ones. All policemen dreaded that messenger role. He imagined Hannah's winning smile crumbling in despair at receiving news of her mother's death. Rising frustration at his inability to unravel this mystery again swept over him. Hell, solving crimes was his job! Of all he'd encountered, why was this one the toughest?

Back in his office, the sharp ring of his phone jarred him back to the present. Impatiently, he snapped the receiver off the cradle.

"Iverson here."

"This is Brad Billings of OnStar again, Detective. I have Jennifer Shannon's screen on my computer. Let's see, do you know how our system works?"

"Why don't you tell me?"

"OnStar offers services through two different links that reach a member's vehicle; one is a cell phone feature and the other a global positioning satellite locator or GPS."

"Same way Lo-Jack tracks stolen vehicles?"

"The location technology is similar, although they use a different radio frequency, but unlike OnStar, that's all they do. Both technologies bounce a signal up to a satellite, telling it to locate the receiver they've installed in a particular vehicle. Now, let's see if I can locate our member's van."

Computer keyboard clicks sounded in Adam's ear, as the pen in his hand hovered restlessly over his notebook. This could be the breakthrough he needed... this could be it!

Listening with anticipation as Brad's voice returned to the line, Adam registered a look of disbelief before shouting into the phone, " What? Are you sure?"

Brad repeated, "That's right, Detective. Our system is excellent, but not foolproof. We can't locate this car right now. Conditions on the ground can influence the GPS's ability to tell us a location, because the satellite can only communicate with what the satellite can reach. Usually we're successful, but sometimes not. A little like that well-known cell phone phrase, 'can you hear me now?' For example, the GPS signal may not respond if the vehicle is shielded."

"Shielded?"

"....in a covered situation, like a concrete parking garage, or sometimes certain carports or even a very thickly wooded area. The satellite beams down well enough through the atmosphere, but if the car's receiver is shielded, not even GPS can perform magic."

"Damn," Adam muttered, blanching at the disheartening realization that her car could be in any one of hundreds of parking garages around the shopping malls, office complexes, apartment buildings, restaurants and hotels comprising the adjacent city of Tysons Corner.

Equally discouraging were the thousands upon thousands of single family homes with potentially "shielding" garages, never mind the naturally wooded character of this part of Fairfax County.

"Now there could be another explanation," Brad resumed. "It's like this: the car's battery energizes the GPS response to the satellite, so when the battery's dead, the GPS is, too. And," more clicking of computer keys before he spoke again, "her car automatically shuts down the electrical system 48 hours after the vehicle is parked and turned off. The auto manufacturer designs it that way to preserve the battery. When the electrical shuts down, the OnStar GPS shuts down. When the ignition turns on again, OnStar GPS wakes up when the car wakes up."

Adam slumped dejectedly in his chair. "She's been missing less than that 48 hour cut-off, so GPS should still work and it's a fairly new car so a dead battery isn't likely. Did she use any other services very recently?"

"Well, there's vehicle diagnostic advice if a member has car trouble, remote door unlock... "

"Remote door unlock?" Adam recalled the irritating number of police calls from citizens who'd locked keys in their cars, usually with the motor running, asking for police help. Police cruisers used to routinely carry slim-jims, but no longer because of potentially unintended damage to the newer electronic door locks. Adam knew their current procedure involved calling a locksmith or AAA for stranded motorists. Compared to that, this OnStar service seemed sci-fi.

"That's right," Brad said, "The locked-out member calls our toll-free number with his name and password. OnStar beams up to the GPS satellite, which locates his car so we can electronically unlock the door via our cell network. Slick, isn't it? The members really like that one."

"So did she use the car advice or door unlock recently?"

"No, but this still might tell you something."

"For instance?" Adam asked.

"No air bag deployment, as is typical in a high speed crash, which automatically calls OnStar. No voluntary request for help, directions, proximity of a gas station, or medical or roadside assistance. Hmmmm... she could have contacted Triple-A or a local gas station directly on a cell phone. You've probably already checked that out."

"Yeah, we have." Adam's fatigue showed in his voice.

"Tough case?"

Adam sighed, "Yeah, but thanks for the earful. This info might help with a future case."

Brad Billings stared at his desk photo of his little daughter's grinning face. He'd had a panic of his own when she wandered away and disappeared for five awful minutes at Home Depot. He remembered how store clerks pitched in to help him search and one of them found her in a nearby aisle, playing hide-and-seek behind a display. How gratefully he valued their instant "good Samaritan" help. Maybe he could pass that good deed along.

"How long has your person been missing?" Brad asked.

Adam calculated rapidly. "About 24 hours."

"Look, I have an idea. Since her car shuts down after 48 hours, you have 24 hours to go. I could do a periodic GPS check on it during that time in case it's relocated from wherever it is now. After that, GPS can't help unless the ignition is turned on again."

"Great idea, Brad! That would really help. Thanks for going the extra mile to help us out."

"If my GPS check is successful, you'll hear from me. Since a missing person report is filed, we won't have to take more time with a subpoena."

"Thanks, again, Brad. I appreciate your doing this."

Hanging up, Adam pushed back his chair, locked his hands behind his head, and stared at the ceiling. After any crime, the longer elapsed time, the colder the trail. Every single lead invited thorough investigation. Would this be just another time-consuming futile exercise, or might OnStar actually locate the missing car in the next 24 hours?

Geez, he hoped so!

CHAPTER 45

"You cook." Wrestler spoke this as a statement, not a question.

"I am an experienced cook."

"Take this cleaning stuff to the kitchen."

Her mind raced. When her useful activity ended, so did her future. Cooking a meal, if allowed, might well be her farewell chore. What then? Uneasy and exhausted, she trudged ahead of him down the hall, pulling the vacuum cleaner behind her.

"Fix dinner," he ordered when she reached the kitchen. He snapped his fingers twice. The dog rushed forward, looking up at him expectantly.

"Door," he said to the animal. It hurried to guard duty by the laundry room door. "When the food's ready, hit the buzzer." He left so quickly, locking the kitchen door behind him, that she still stood with one hand on the sweeper and a pail of rags and supplies in the other.

Grateful for the mercy of another assignment, she clung to the hope that wowing him with this meal might mean he'd want her to cook again. Another meal equaled another day alive!

Though she'd cooked thousands of meals for her big family in her forty-one years of marriage, she'd truthfully described herself as an *experienced* cook, not Julia Child. Nor had her very *life* ever hinged upon the success of a single meal, as this one might.

Unlike dinner parties she hosted at home, with carefully planned menus and ingredients bought specifically for them, today's situation was a different challenge. Ingredients already in this kitchen determined the dinner's possibilities and *her* outcome depended upon *that* outcome. Complicating this further, meal preparation excluded using sharp knives, which he'd removed.

Stowing the cleaning items in the laundry room, she examined the contents of the refrigerator, freezer and pantry shelves. Should she use the hamburger, or save it for the dog? If only she could lace the dog's snack with sleeping pills... or put them into the man's dinner, for that matter.

With that thought, she rummaged again under the sink for rat poison or other toxic ingredient. Oven cleaner, cleanser, 409, Windex—enough of it could make them sick but the awful taste nixed that idea. She stopped short. What if he forced her to taste the food first to ensure its safety? She'd be in the same traumatized state they were. Not a good plan.

In a novel she once read, a prisoner escaped by starting a fire and this kitchen was the ideal place. No matches, but paper towels could ignite on a stove burner to torch window shades. Fires create confusion. This old house would burn fast. Smoke and flames could attract outsiders to rescue her. Maybe the man and dog would be trapped in the flames. She could escape.

This proactive idea appealed to Jennifer. Any size fire guaranteed distraction, but how would the man react? Would he chase her while his house burned to the ground or ignore her while he put out the fire. She frowned. What if he ordered the dog to guard her while he extinguished the flames? Then he'd save the house and, afterward, punish her.

What if the man imprisoned others somewhere in this house? They'd be burned to death as well. The earring proved Tina's presence here once. Perhaps she was still here! What if Jennifer were trapped in the flames herself? A horrible way to die! No, she'd try to think of something else...

A mountain of a man, Wrestler's size suggested a huge appetite, with quantity more important than quality. She considered her narrowed meal options even with a well-stocked larder. Unable to picture him enjoying restaurant dining, she guessed he ate all meals here.

While mulling a menu, she slipped the dog another small piece of hamburger, hoping to repeat this during meal preparation. No longer growling, the animal now responded to her approach with guarded anticipation. He acted the way he looked: half-starved! Lacking a way to subdue or eliminate him, she needed the dog's acceptance, even his cooperation, to get away.

She decided on meatloaf for four reasons. Cooked meat would still entice the dog, using all the hamburger prevented discovery of its reduced amount, the dish was tasty yet easy to prepare and plentiful in amount if her captor's appetite matched his size.

Gathering the hamburger, two eggs and numerous seasonings, she mixed the ingredients, shaped two loaves in a baking pan and spread each with catsup before sliding them into a hot oven.

Unable to peel potatoes without a knife, she knew they'd mash with a fork if boiled until soft. She selected frozen green beans, adding bottled bacon bits and a can of diced tomatoes. For dessert, she poured canned peaches into another baking dish, sprinkled a mixture of brown sugar, flour and cinnamon over them and fitted this into the oven beside the meatloaf.

Setting the table with a paper towel placemat and napkin, she poured him a glass of water and added a bowl of apples as centerpiece. Would he care about the convenience of prepared food enough to want her to cook again? Probably not, but she had to try!

An hour after starting, she pressed the buzzer, indicating dinner was ready. He stalked into the kitchen, walked directly to the table and sat down. "Prepare two plates. Put mine on the table. Take yours downstairs," he ordered gruffly.

"Do you want me to clean up afterward?" she looked at the counter as she spoke.

"No!" She must have hesitated a moment too long, the hot pad in her hand, because he shouted impatiently, "*Now!*" and rose to his feet as the dog rushed into the room at the sound of his raised voice.

Nerves frayed and hands shaking, she filled the man's dinner and dessert plates quickly and put them on the table. Returning to the stove, she served herself, grabbed a fork and moved toward the basement door. Following right behind her, he opened the door so forcefully that for a moment she feared he would fling her down the stairs.

Balancing her plate in one hand, she grabbed the hand rail for support. As she started down the basement stairs, her downcast eyes fell upon the pencil-shaped scar on his left hand just as he closed and locked the door behind her. She stopped still on the third step down, clinging to the banister with one hand and frantically trying to quiet the plate trembling in her other hand.

Ten fingers and the angry scar. The younger brother!

CHAPTER 46

Locked in the basement, she sat on the bottom stair step to eat her dinner. Putting aside several pieces of her meatloaf for the dog, she realized that despite her efforts to please the man with her good performance, he seemed angrier as the day wore on. Did anger make him even more unpredictable? He was a killer and something would trigger his inevitable attack on her. Would it be frustration about something else that he took out on her?

She needed to get out very soon!

Escape tomorrow in daylight made little sense since she'd be easily visible. If she even saw tomorrow! No, tonight while he slept. She needed the cover of darkness.

She tried to shrug off the triple whammy of physical labor, minimal sleep and emotional stress. The overpowering urge to lie down, shut her eyes and drift into healing sleep made waking up doubtful once her eyes closed. Even with an alarm. She couldn't escape tonight if she fell asleep! No, she *must* stay awake, whatever it took.

Patting her slacks, she rubbed the lucky frog in one pocket and removed the small clock from the other. She tested its alarm, which worked, but could she stake her life upon its dependability? Setting the alarm for midnight as "insurance" even though she intended staying awake, she hid the small timepiece on a shelf where she could see it but he wouldn't.

Though captive in the cellar, at least she wasn't locked in the awful confinement box. She peered inside that prison, unwilling to climb in for a better look. At its door, she noticed an unpleasant smell emanating from inside, probably from the toilet bucket. If her escape tonight were successful, she'd leave that for *him* to empty.

The night light inside the confinement box still glowed so she needn't get inside to verify the V-shaped nick in the top board of the bench. Definitely where the boys sat in the night stand's photo. Poor, frightened little guys. Thirty-five years ago, "disciplining" children was considered the prerogative of parents who were barely accountable to society. Even schools meted out corporal punishment then. Kids like these boys hadn't much chance of rescue, isolated as they were. Had they run away, foster homes and orphanages during that era offered their own documented insensitivities and occasional atrocities. Brutality to children was an issue mostly swept under the rug.

As her fatigue grew, even the basement floor looked inviting. She thought of stretching out, just to relax her aching body for a few minutes, but she knew she'd fall sound asleep. She slapped her cheeks. She pinched her arms. She did some stretches. She stamped her feet.

Then she remembered the three boxes under the stairs. Pulling out the one marked "The Boys," she opened it and spread the photos side by side. She returned the "schoolhouse" and studied the remaining two.

The young boys together, with the older one's arm around the younger one's shoulder, looked much like the night-stand picture upstairs, except they were younger here, maybe three or four. She wished for the magnifying glass or at least better light. Holding the pictures directly under one of the six naked bulbs hanging from the ceiling, she counted five fingers on the older boy's hand and no scar on the younger one's. Assuming these were the same children, whatever caused those injuries happened after this photo.

Next, she studied the boy pictured in the too-large military school uniform. Based on her children's sizes, he looked about six or seven. At first she thought he stood at attention, but then his hands would be pressed flat against the sides of his trousers. He stood stiffly with his feet together, but his arms hung loosely in front of him, the hands showing enough below the jacket sleeves to reveal a pencil-shaped scar on his left hand. Again, the younger brother! Was this dress-up or a Halloween costume? She didn't think kids could attend military school at so young an age.

Placing the photos beside the hatbox, she again lifted out the old, rolled rag. The puckered rubber band fell away as she unrolled the small bundle. So many folds, but when at last the ancient cloth fell open, inside lay a thin, brown shriveled stick about two inches long. But was it a stick? On closer examination, one end had a flat side that looked a little like...

She shrank back, covering her mouth to stifle the scream filling her throat. "Oh," she cried out to the empty room, *"Oh, no...."*

She stared dumbly at the still visibly intact nail and slightly bent knuckle. Atop the rag lay a child's mummified finger.

CHAPTER 47

Jennifer gazed in shock at the wizened finger. What *had* these little boys endured at the hands of their parents? You could never excuse Wrestler's murderous retaliation, but you could certainly grasp the grisly chain of events pointing him there.

Hastily re-wrapping the finger in the rag, she put the ghastly bundle on the floor beside the photos and fumbled through the rest of the box's contents. She remembered keys of various sizes lay at the bottom. No clue what the small ones fit, but what about the three large old ones? She remembered keys like these from childhood visits to her grandparents' house. Maybe they opened the barn or the "schoolhouse" or the front entry or... maybe the basement door?

Taking the three big keys, she crept up the stairs and gently rotated the doorknob. While the knob turned easily, the door held. She pushed gently, then firmly. Locked tight!

She pulled out the three big keys and knelt down to peer out the 3/4 inch crack under the door. Light shone on the other side, but she saw and heard no sign of the dog or the man. The left half of the under-door view faced the opposite wall, about four feet away. The right half view stretched down the dark hallway. Other than the possibly irrelevant 6:00 alarm setting on his bedroom clock and with no other clue to the man's sleeping habits, she crossed her fingers that he was in bed.

Closing one eye, she peered again into the keyhole. Some light there, but the hole wasn't empty. After locking the door on the other side, he had no reason to pocket the key with only himself and the dog upstairs, so he'd left it in the lock. She remembered from her grandparents' house that you couldn't fully insert a key into one side of such locks with another key engaged on the other side. She needed to bump his key out of the hole to use hers.

Jiggling her key against his would make noise which could attract the man or the dog. Even if the man weren't near, the dog's keen hearing would surely prompt investigation, if not a barked alert. If the man jerked the door open to find her at the top of the stairs with keys, she was through! Also the successfully nudged-out key would fall and clatter onto the bare floor. Once it fell, how could she retrieve it if none of the keys in her hand opened the basement door?

She eased her way quietly back down the stairs and looked around. A carton marked "Linens" caught her eye. Opening it, she pawed through sheets and table cloths to find what she needed, pulling out a terrycloth bath towel.

While cleaning the basement earlier, she threw several rusty coat hangers into the trash by the sink. Retrieving one, she tried to unbend it with stiff old pliers found among the tools. Gritting her teeth and using all her strength, she untwisted the hanger's neck and bent the sprung wire fairly straight, leaving the top in the same shepherd's hook that hangs over a closet pole.

She pulled her stolen clock forward on its shelf to check the time: almost midnight! She turned off the alarm. Was he asleep?

Collecting the meatloaf saved from dinner, she wrapped the pieces in paper from the corner trash pile, slid the hidden screwdriver into her belt and picked up the towel and hanger. Creeping back up the stairs, she paused at the top to listen. No sound! She poked one end of the towel through the crack under the door. Then she used the coat hanger to push the towel through and straightened it with the hanger until it lay spread out on the other side of the door beneath the key hole.

Retrieving the coat hanger without disturbing the flattened towel, she pushed one end of it into the key hole and wiggled it, flinching at the scratching noise this created. She paused, listening for any reaction on the other side, and hearing none, cautiously jiggled the key again. Squinting into the lock, she saw the hole filled with light! Crouching back down, she peeked out the crack under the door. An irrepressible smile crossed her lips at the sight of the metal key lying on the towel after its silent fall.

Quickly getting to her feet again, she tried the first key from the hatbox, then the second, finally the third. None worked! She needed next to retrieve the fallen key from the other side.

Crouching down with the extended coat hanger, she used it to gently pull the towel, inching it back toward her through the crack under the door.

Her movements froze at the sound of nails clicking on the floor. *The dog!*

With shaking hands, she fumbled the paper open, clicked her tongue and pushed a piece of meatloaf under the door. Wet smacking sounds came from the other side as the dog gobbled the piece of food. Slowly, carefully she pulled on the towel again. Looking through the crack, she saw the key coming closer... closer. It was almost under the door, almost within her grasp.

And then, the unimaginable happened. The dog grabbed the towel, as she'd seen dogs at the park grab and shake a toy or a stick, tumbling the key across the floor. Oh my god, she thought, he thinks this is a game!

The dog gave a playful snort, but at least didn't growl or bark. Could she reach the key with the coat hanger while the towel still distracted the dog? Crouching to peer through the crack, she spotted the key and inched the coat hanger toward it. Miraculously, the hanger's length reached just far enough so that after several efforts she managed to hook the shepherd's crook through the key's loop and draw it slowly toward her.

Just as the key was almost to the door, the dog put his paw heavily upon it, giving a satisfied grunt. With one hand she kept the wire hooked in the key's loop and with the other hand she put a second piece of meatloaf at the edge of the crack and shot it into the room as one might flick a marble. As the dog dashed after the meat, she quickly pulled in the key.

Before unlocking the door, she had to be sure the dog's activity hadn't drawn the man's attention. She crouched, watching down the hall through the crack beneath the door. She waited. Nothing. Standing up, she put the key into the lock, turned it *very* slowly, pushed gently on the door and felt tears of relief prick her eyes as it slowly swung open.

The dog frisked near her, eager to continue the game. With no idea what signals he was trained to recognize, she put her finger to her lips and whispered, "Shhh." This seemed to sober him as he followed her across the kitchen. She lifted the window and held her next-to-the-last-piece of meatloaf in his direction.

If she got outside without the dog and shut the window in his face, he'd surely bark wildly. Crazy as it was, with no other choice she could think of, the dog would have to come with her!

She let him smell the meat but didn't give it to him. "Good dog," she whispered, climbing out through the window. "Come on. Good dog."

The animal hesitated, a warning rumble sounding in his throat, but when she held out the meat for him, he bounded through the window to get it. Closing the window, she gave him the snack, patted his head, said "come" and started running across the gravel toward the driveway.

She hadn't taken ten steps when the parking area abruptly flooded with light.

CHAPTER 48

Arriving at headquarters, Adam called his police dispatcher contact, Akeesha Williams. Upbeat and alert, she was an excellent choice for her particular job. Nothing flapped her and she was rumored to own a photographic memory, because her recall amazed everyone.

On her shift, she typed many CAD bulletins and messages that appeared on each cruiser's computer screen. The soft cadence of her distinctive voice gave clear information to patrolling police cruisers when a situation called for voice communication.

"Hello, Akeesha," Adam said into his cell phone. "Got anything new on the Shannon case?"

"We have one unit following up on a woman in a white Cadillac SUV seen buying gas in Woodbridge. Tipster said she matched the description and looked just like the picture on TV, but they didn't catch her tag number. They said there was a man in the passenger seat, too. We ought to hear back from them any minute. That's it for now."

"Thanks. I'll be in my office."

He just sat down at his desk when his phone rang. "Iverson."

"Detective Iverson," Akeesha spoke, "We just got another traffic report. Woman in a white Cadillac SUV hit a tree down on Georgetown Pike."

"Any identification?"

"Not yet, but there's just one thing…."

"What?"

"She's dead."

Adam's heart sank. This terrible development meant crushing news for some family, hopefully, not the Shannons. If it were Jennifer, he should be the one to tell them, however much he dreaded the task. "Can you put me through to them?"

"Sure."

He imagined the despair such news would wring from Hannah. Wanting to protect her, he yearned instead to bring her news that her mother was safe. Was that even probable as the trail grew colder with every passing minute and Jennifer's disappearance — he consulted his watch and did the math — thirty-one hours ago?

A voice crackled into the phone at his ear, "Unit 21."

"Iverson, here," he identified himself. "Got an ID on the passenger in the white van?"

"Yeah, it's," more static, "Matilda Wong and this scene is a mess. Need anything else?"

"No, that's it. Thanks."

He hung up the phone and eased back into his desk chair. He heard coughing echo down the hall even before Jake Torres reached Adam's door.

"Geez, I just can't shake this cold," Jake spoke in a nasal voice as he ambled up to Adam's desk. "No, I won't infect you, but let me stay long enough to find my last cough drops. I know I have a couple left here somewhere." He patted and then emptied several of his pockets onto the corner of Adam's desk. Out came a handful of change, a comb, some paper clips, three wadded up cough drop wrappers, a bolt with a washer and nut attached, a pocket pack of Kleenex tissues, a crumpled piece of paper and a box of breath freshener mints. Jake patted more pockets, stifled another cough, and at last triumphantly produced the two elusive cough drops.

Adam splayed his hands open and drummed his fingertips impatiently on his desk top.

"Hey, buddy," Jake looked at Adam's hands. "I never did ask you what happened to your hand."

Adam glanced down. "It's a birth defect. I never notice it since it's been like this since the day I was born."

"Didn't affect your getting into the police academy?"

"No. See, my writing hand is my shooting hand. The left hand just goes underneath to steady the gun hand." He demonstrated this familiar position, simulating the pistol barrel with his right index finger.

Adam started to reach into his desk drawer for something when the phone rang and instead, he answered. "Iverson here!"

Akeesha's voice came over the line, "The Woodbridge tip didn't check out for your case," she said. "Some husband and wife in a *tan* Cadillac van, not a white one. Sorry."

"Thanks for the input, Akeesha." Adam hung up and leaned forward. "Quite a cache of stuff you carry around with you, Jake-Boy. What's the bolt for?"

Jake talked around the cough drop in his mouth, "Oh, it's for a drawer at home. Got to match the size and threads next trip to the hardware store."

"Is this a silver dollar?" Adam examined one of Jake's coins with interest.

"Yeah, it was my grandfather's. Check the date: 1928! I carry it for luck."

"And what's this, a love note?" Adam smoothed the wrinkled paper out flat and looked at the writing. Suddenly he jumped to his feet.

"Where'd you get this?" he shouted.

Jake held out his hand for the paper, examined it and tossed it back down on the desk. "It's nothing. That old guy, Whitehead, the one who pesters us with those driver reports, he started to call that in this morning and had a heart attack instead. The big one! It's just another of his bad driver reports, you know, the address, the tag number."

Electrified, Adam moved around the desk. "Not just any tag number. This is Jennifer Shannon's tag number. You got this information this *morning?*"

"Well, yeah," more coughing from Jake until the lozenge took effect. "The medics took him away and we went over to check the house as a possible crime scene and then secure the place because EMS broke the door open to get to him. It was kind of weird, actually. I mean, he basically died calling in this report and I saw it there on his clipboard and I don't know why, I just copied it down on impulse and then forgot about it."

Adam snatched up the phone and dialed, "Akeesha?"

"One and the same," she purred.

"That guy, Whitehead, who calls us a lot."

"Called us a lot," she corrected.

"Ah... right. Can you remember a pattern? Did he call in those violations the day they happened or a week later or what?"

Pause. "Very timely, usually right after his encounter but always within a few hours, as I recall."

Adam brightened. "Okay, were you on when he made that last call?"

"I was and I sent him the rescue bus."

Adam knew a record was made of any type incoming call and asked, "Would you look up what time that call came in?" He heard her clicking computer keys.

"This morning at 10:45."

"And did he give the tag number or say when and where the incident happened?"

"That's a 'yes' and a 'no'? He gave only the first two digits of the license plate before he needed emergency assistance, but he said it happened yesterday around 4:00 and the address was 3508 Winding Trail Road." She studied her computer screen, "And that partial plate number he gave...actually they weren't numbers, they were letters: YR."

As he listened to Akeesha, Adam's eyes followed the identical address information in Jake's handwriting on the note before him, except Jake had copied down the *entire* tag number.

"Thanks, Akeesha. You're the greatest."

"That's true," she allowed with a mischievous chuckle.

In one fluid movement, Adam hung up the phone, snatched something from his open desk drawer and threw it to Jake, who grabbed it in a one-handed catch before identifying it as an unopened bag of cough drops.

Accepting Adam's gift, a grateful Jake said, "Geez, just what I need! Thanks, good buddy!"

"You're welcome!" Except for the note, Adam pushed Jake's pocket contents back across the desk to him. "Now gather up your stuff. We're going for a ride!"

CHAPTER 49

Illuminating the stretch between the farm house and out-
buildings, the motion-activated flood lights blinded Jennifer
as she ran across the parking area toward the driveway. She
hated the loud gravel crunch beneath her every footfall which
broadcast her location to anyone listening, but the unforgiving
tangle of prickly bushes on both sides of the driveway prevented
any quieter choice.

Instead of barking or pinning her down, the dog surprised
Jennifer by bounding along beside her, perhaps thinking this more
of the game. Distancing themselves from the harsh, bright backyard
light, they raced into the driveway's shadows and toward the dark
street at the end.

This part of Fairfax County actually prided itself on few, if
any, street lights; a misguided attempt at preserving the one-time
"country" atmosphere. If she reached the street on this moonless
night, she might hide in the underbrush. Unused to sprinting, she
felt a pain in her side grow with every pounding step. How long
was this damnable driveway? Huffing vigorously now, at last she
felt the gravel give way to firm asphalt underfoot.

She'd reached the road, but which way to turn? Uphill would
double her physical exertion. She turned downhill and ran full out
when she heard the man's pickup truck roar to life back by the
house, tires skidding in the gravel as he barreled the vehicle toward
the driveway.

Why couldn't she run faster? The pain in her side sharpened! Was she slowing down? Where was that legendary secondwind? Rushing onward as best she could on the dark, deserted road, she realized the dog kept pace beside her. Was this a desperate freedom run for them *both?*

Reaching the street, the truck's headlights pierced the night at the foot of the driveway and hesitated. Jennifer flung herself deep into the thick bushes along the side of the road and burrowed in just before the vehicle also turned downhill. *"Come!"* she'd commanded the dog, her earlier gentle approach replaced with the raw urgency of a sharp order. If the dog failed to follow and instead stayed visible beside the road, he'd instantly compromise her location. To come this far only to be recaptured tore at her heart. So did her terror of the man's unthinkable retaliation *after!*

She felt amazement and relief as the dog eagerly followed her deep into the wild bushes, hunkering down, out of sight, right beside her. More game for him? Was his eagerness to play a welcome contrast from cruel treatment at the hands of his sadistic master, treatment reflected in the animal's scars and hunger?

Panting, she held onto the dog—stunned that he allowed it and just as stunned she could do it—partly to quiet him and partly to share this hysterical experience with any companion, however unlikely. Lying against her, he seemed impervious to the brambles that scratched mercilessly at her exposed arms and face.

"Shhh! she whispered to him, as they pressed deeper into the underbrush-covered ditch alongside the road. Realizing that without this animal's unexpected cooperation she could never have made it this far, Jennifer whispered "Good, good dog." Putting her cheek against his fur, she meant every word.

The truck crept around the curve of the empty road. They watched transfixed as the pickup's headlights rolled an illuminating arc across the trees. The vehicle moved toward them slowly and paused for a terrifying moment right in front of them. She held her breath. At last it passed by, moved down the road and around another curve.

Just before the truck disappeared at the bend, its headlights high-lighted an opening in the bushes that looked like a driveway about 40 feet further downhill and on the other side of the road. A place to get help? Would the owners even answer the door to a stranger after midnight? Did they have their own patrolling dogs to rip her and this animal to shreds?

The driveway appeared to angle up into the woods, but no house lights shone through the trees; maybe not a house there at all, but the road into an unimproved wooded lot. In those split seconds of truck-light illumination, had she seen a black mailbox or imagined one?

Headlights flickered again far down the road. A vehicle coming. Were these the man's headlights or those of someone to help her? Nighttime headlights looked alike, bright and blinding. Unable to distinguish his beams from a rescuer's, she couldn't risk a mistake. The engine sounded like a truck, but she wasn't sure.

Desperate for help from any stranger happening along this road, should she jump out to flag down this driver before her only chance disappeared? She hesitated, her heart pounding. Sensing her agitation, the dog shifted position. She held on to him, agonizing about what to do.

A pair of headlights rounded the turn as the vehicle slowed and shined a spotlight slowly along each side of the road. It was his truck! Thank god she stayed put.

"Shhhh," she whispered again to the dog, her fingers pressing a warning against his side as they lay motionless deep in the bushes. The spotlight moved first along the other side of the road, then moved to their side of the road, inching along the edge of the bushes. Suddenly the light stopped. Moving only her eyes, she saw the glint of a metal soda can in the brambles only about ten feet away from where they huddled. The truck door opened as the man focused the spotlight there and stepped around the front of the truck for a closer look. The dog trembled but held.

Scanning the bushes left and right of the soda can, the man's eyes seemed to linger directly on them but *finally* moved on. Shuffling back to the truck, he turned the spotlight ahead, shifted into drive and worked his spotlight search of the roadside on up the hill to the curve, then slowly around it and out of sight.

As the sound of the truck's motor receded, she jerked herself out of the thorns, leaped from the ditch and raced downhill toward the new driveway. The dog followed, matching her stride.

Reaching the entrance illuminated minutes earlier by the truck's lights, she realized she *had* seen a mailbox by the opening. She and the dog hurtled past it and up this new driveway in the dark.

Unable to see more than a few feet in front of her and running fast, she barely avoided tripping over a large branch fallen across the asphalt. To her surprise, the dog took the lead up the long, winding stretch. She followed the sound of his jingling tags more than his scarcely visible shape.

The curling driveway ended in a clearing atop a hill, where a huge house rose majestically against the stars in the dark night sky. A light burned above the center of four garage doors, but no lights at all showed in the windows of the house. At midnight they'd be asleep!

Moving quickly from the driveway to the sidewalk, she struggled up the tiers of terraced stone steps to the front door, the dog bounding along beside her. She found the doorbell, rang it twice and pounded on the door. No response. Stepping back, she looked for lights to appear in the windows. None. More ringing, more pounding. The doorbell's musical notes sounding in the foyer were audible outside, so she knew it worked. Oh please! She rang the bell again.

And then she heard something ominous.

CHAPTER 50

From the distance came the now unmistakable rasp of the truck grinding back along the road. Unable to rouse anyone inside, Jennifer stood anxiously on the mansion's front porch before reaching down to reassure the dog and herself as she struggled to think what to do next. Suddenly, the animal froze and stared fixedly toward the road, body alert, eyes focused. For the first time since their sojourn began, he whined. He took a step forward but stopped, turned and looked back at her. "Would you like to be my dog?" she asked softly. At her touch, his ears momentarily relaxed, he lifted his face and nuzzled her hand. But rather than pliant as he'd been earlier, the dog again acted edgy and distracted. "Good dog," she soothed, crouching to give him a confidence-restoring hug.

He pressed against her in response but then, for no apparent reason, reverted again, standing stiffly, staring rigidly down the hill before whimpering in obvious distress. "Good dog," she repeated, petting the top of his head to soothe his plaintive sounds. His ears pointed tensely forward, his muscles tight, his focus on the road as he emitted a low growl.

The man must be calling the dog, probably with a high-pitched whistle, because she heard nothing. How cruelly had he trained this animal for it to react this fearfully to that sound?

The dog looked up at her, then jumped off the porch, moved toward the driveway, ears forward, and whined again. It turned toward her one last time, as if apologizing for a decision made, and then rocketed away down the driveway toward the road.

Frantically, she rang the door bell again and again. No response. When the dog emerged from this driveway, the man would know her whereabouts. Maybe he knew this house was unoccupied. With the dog back under his spell, the man would command it to find her.

Fumbling in the dark, Jennifer picked up a small concrete flower pot from the front porch and pounded it against the etched oval of glass on the front door. The sound of shattering glass rent the still night, but after the tinkling shards cascaded onto the floor, an encompassing silence returned. Bashing out the remaining jagged shards for a safer entry, she jumped through the resulting hole in the door and ran inside the dark house, desperate to find a phone. Afraid to turn on lights to show the man coming up the driveway exactly where to find her, she stumbled into the kitchen where a tiny night light provided weak illumination.

Seeing a wall-mounted phone, she picked it up and with shaking hands dialed 9-1-1, lifted the receiver to her ear and waited impatiently. No sound! Clicking the hang-up bar, she listened again. No dial tone. Disconnected!

The wealthy owners must be on a long vacation.

The man and dog would reach the house any minute, where they'd barrel non-stop through the hole she bashed in the front door. She dropped the receiver, wondering where to hide. Desperate, she opened the kitchen door, hoping for some solution in the back yard, but the impenetrable darkness revealed no quick safe place and no lights visible through the trees from other houses where she might run to safety.

Where to hide? Under no circumstances the basement. She'd had enough underground horror for a lifetime.

Running back toward the entry, she tore up the wide, graceful staircase to the second floor, ran down the hall, jerked open a door at random, dashed inside and locked the door behind her. Only her jerky breathing sounded in the dark room. She looked around. Curtains drawn, the room very dark. In the gloom, she barely made out a bed and dresser.

Looking for a weapon, almost anything, she grabbed a lamp, jerked the cord out from the wall, ripped off the shade and held it upside down like a club. She flattened herself against the wall so he wouldn't see her until the door swung wide and when he entered the room she would smash the lamp against his head again and again.

Listening for sound in the hall, she waited as endless, silent minutes passed. Her shoulders ached, her head throbbed, her back hurt, her energy drained. She couldn't take much more. When would it end?

Worse, *how* would it end?

Then a sound: the whine of a dog. He'd led the man straight to her door! When that door opened, she'd have not only the man to fear but the dog, which appeared to relapse to its original training. Silence. The dog whined again. She watched the doorknob turn slowly, stopping when the man discovered it was locked. With trembling hands she lifted the lamp above her head. Dreading what she knew came next, her heart pounded so loudly she feared he could hear it.

With a deafening smash, the door crashed open, slamming against the wall where she would have been crushed if standing directly behind it. As he burst into the room, she realized to her horror that she'd dangerously miscalculated. He was so tall and she so short that the lamp only smashed ineffectively against his broad shoulder. Halted more by surprise than injury, he turned in a menacing rage to grab her.

Still holding the lamp in her right hand, she pulled the screwdriver out of her belt with her left hand and stabbed all four inches to the hilt into his lower torso. She twisted it left and right before letting go of the imbedded handle and ducked aside as his earlier momentum lurched him against the wall where she'd just stood. Startled, he staggered, clutching his stomach, and bent over, grunting. With a moan he stumbled to the floor.

The dog rushed into the room, sniffing at the slumped, moaning man before looking squarely at her. With the man no longer a threat to the dog, would its loyalty to him also end? In that poignant moment, the animal's allegiance could shift either way—the man's cruel beatings and starvation or her food and kindness?

She stared pleadingly into the animal's eyes, fixed upon her. "You don't have to be his dog. Be *my* dog! Please, *please* be my dog!" she begged.

As if reading her mind, the animal made its answering decision. Snarling ferociously, he leaped toward her, fangs bared.

The screwdriver gone, she lifted the broken lamp, forcing the twisted harp and bulb deep into the animal's open jaws. The dog fell back in surprise, shaking out the obstruction jammed in his throat, while she dashed from the room. She saw the man rise onto one knee as she slammed the door behind her and ran for her life.

The dog couldn't open the door, but the man could. If only he were too injured to do so!

Rushing headlong down the staircase toward the front door, she leaped across the shattered glass slivers strewn across the entryway floor, through the door's yawning oval hole and into the dark night.

CHAPTER 51

L egs pumping, Jennifer reeled off the porch, down the tiers of stone steps to the sidewalk, and rushed across the top of the driveway toward the man's parked truck. She prayed his keys were inside as she jerked the door open and blinked at the pickup's automatic ceiling light that illuminated her in the otherwise black night. Her fingers brushed an empty ignition.

Leaving the door ajar, she hopped into the driver's seat. No keys on the seat, under the floor mats or behind the visors. If she stayed here, locked the doors and leaned on the horn, would someone nearby hear the noise and call police or investigate themselves? Not likely, with houses spread sparsely across these multi-acre lots. And honking the horn would tell him exactly where she was, to open the truck door with his own keys, grab her and...

If only she could disable the truck, but with no handy tool and none visible in the car she couldn't slash his tires. Nor dared she take precious time to unscrew their valves to let out air. Sliding out, she closed the pickup's door, spun away from the truck and ran as fast as she could into the darkness down the long, twisting driveway toward the street.

She couldn't see well and hoped to avoid the fallen log she knew lay somewhere ahead. Nor dared she slow down to choose her way more carefully. Had her screwdriver jab crippled the man or only further enraged him? His size and strength boded granite resilience, making her too-short screwdriver wound likely superficial. If he could drag himself far enough to open the bedroom door, he'd release the dog. She knew she couldn't risk pausing to grab a stick or find a rock, and with no weapon to fight off the dog, running became her only option.

***

"Aw, geez," Jake growled, hearing the computer aided dispatch report "a residential silent burglar alarm at 3509 Winding Trail Drive."

Adam grumbled his own annoyance. Focused exclusively on the 3508 address identified by Jeremy Whitehead and verified by the dispatcher, Adam hated getting this close to the possible rescue of his quarry and instead being diverted to cover this alarm. The new address might halt a crime in progress, but at the other address he might save someone he knew. Grudgingly, he admitted the residential alarm identified a known incident while the other was still only a hunch. And the call's address was very close. They had no choice.

"Just tell me where to turn," Adam said with resignation to Jake, who searched for house numbers on mail boxes and brick columns along the dark street.

"3503, 3505 we're getting close," Jake chronicled the advancing street numbers. "Here's 3507, must be the next left."

***

Dashing down the driveway, Jennifer heard the dog's faint bark back near the mansion. Then his tags jingling metallically, that sound growing closer. Simultaneously, Wrestler's pick-up truck engine roared to life and its headlights flashed on. Swiftly circling the area in front of the garage to angle downhill, its lights would spotlight her in seconds.

Her lungs ready to explode, she glimpsed the main road another fifty feet ahead, though reaching it hardly meant safety. Directly behind her, she heard the dog's heavy panting, his tags jingling loudly now. The animal was closing in, her gruesome nightmare hideously *real* this time! She couldn't go on, couldn't breathe or make her exhausted legs speed forward any longer. Suddenly she felt sharp pain as the dog's teeth grabbed her arm. At the same moment, her foot caught on something in the darkness. The downed branch. She tripped and as the fall pitched her forward, it jerked her arm from the dog's jaws. She plunged headlong and skidded forward, scraping her hands, arms and face on the driveway's unforgiving asphalt surface and twisting her ankle. Triumphantly, the dog leaped for the kill.

In a sudden surrounding bath of ultra-bright illumination, she shuddered at the vivid view of the dog's huge jaws, red mouth and gleaming teeth opening directly over her face, the last horrible sight she would ever see.

And then a firecracker! She lay on her back in the driveway, elbows and knees flailing in futile life-and-death desperation to fend away the mauling dog. But after fevered jerking without the searing pain of his fangs sinking into her flesh, she realized the dog was no longer there. Still terrified, she struggled to sit up, blinking into powerful lights blinding her from two directions: the man's truck at the top of the driveway and more lights at the mouth of the driveway.

Immobile, open mouthed and uncomprehending, she saw two forms emerge from the lower set of lights. Her captor's cronies? Would three men subdue and torture her now instead of one? She cringed, unable to see them until they were only a few feet from her. She tried desperately to scramble away from this new danger, but her spent body wouldn't respond. A uniformed policeman and another man, both with guns drawn, hurried up the driveway in her direction. As comprehension took hold at the sight of police, so did mingled waves of relief and exhaustion. Before they spoke she cried out, "Help me, please! He's trying to kill me! That man in the truck up there, he... " Surprised at how loud her voice had sounded despite how weak she felt, she cradled her head in her hands and began to sob.

The man not in uniform pounded on up the driveway toward the man's pickup truck while the uniformed cop called for backup.

Aware that a dark shape lay on the ground beside her in a widening pool of blood, she jerked back from the dog's motionless body. The sound hadn't been a firecracker at all, but a gunshot.

"Did you...? Is he...?"

"Dead, yeah," Jake confirmed. The first man out of the police car, he witnessed the dog's attack and fired immediately. "Hated to do it but he was going in for the kill, Ma'am. You or him; couldn't be both. Even if you are a suspect, we need you in one piece," he added, referring to the silent residential alarm and identifying this scruffy female derelict as the probable person-of-interest.

"A suspect, but...?"

As he checked out the pickup, Adam shouted from too far up the driveway for her to recognize his voice. "Nobody here... but blood on the seat. I'm turning off the truck's headlights to cut the glare," he added, using a Kleenex to preserve existing fingerprints.

"I called for backup," Jake shouted back. Turning his full attention to Jennifer, he said, "Now tell me... who are you and what's going on here?" Confused and dismayed to be labeled a suspect after what she'd been through, she tried quieting her sobs to answer the uniform's questions when Adam's face appeared inches from hers.

"Oh, my god, it's Mrs. Shannon. Quick, get her into the cruiser. Here, Ma'am, let me help you. Are you okay?" he asked in an anxious voice.

"Yes. Except for this ankle... but mostly just... just tired and scared." Supported by his arm, she limped on her tender ankle to the police vehicle and crawled gratefully into the protective walls of the cruiser's back seat. The policemen got into the front seat, locked the car's doors for protection and both turned to Jennifer.

"Can you tell us what happened?" Adam asked.

Calmed by the secure surroundings, she did. When she finished, a side of Adam she barely recognized transformed him from the pleasantly charming young man who dated Hannah into a trained police professional. All business, he spoke into his cell phone, "Located missing female, Jennifer Shannon, while responding to residential silent alarm at 3509 Winding Trail Road. She is alive with apparent minor injuries. Besides backup already requested, we need Rescue to stabilize her. We need K-9 assist ASAP for suspected abductor still in vicinity. We need a cruiser to secure the broken front door at this location. Copy?" He waited for the acknowledgement before continuing.

"Suspected abductor's domicile is across the street at 3508 Winding Trail Road. That is a crime scene. We need cruisers to apprehend the suspect if there. No sight or sound. If not there, he can't be far, so let's flush this guy out tonight. We also need an Animal Warden to remove a dog we shot and a rabies screening, since he bit the victim." He then described the essence of the crime information Jennifer gave him.

While he finished his transmission, Jennifer dried her tears on a tissue the uniformed cop handed her. "Thank you a billion times for finding me. But... but how did you know where to look?"

Jake explained the silent residential burglar alarm. "Broken windows and opened doors set off the signal. We always investigate, especially in these neighborhoods with the big houses. Turned out, we were almost on top of this driveway when the call came in. When we saw the dog mid-attack, we had to cap him. As I said up there, burglar or not, we wanted you alive. We've had several recent incidents of dogs running loose in this area. I covered an attack on a young girl two days ago, less than a mile down the road. She was hurt pretty bad. Some of these mutts are worth a bundle and their owners scream if we harm them, although they admit their animals sometimes get loose and roam out of control. For us, protecting human life always comes first."

She nodded numbly. "What does that mean, 'no sight or sound'?"

"No blinking cruiser lights or sirens," Adam explained.

Safe at last and unaware how mentally overwhelmed and physically taxed her ordeal had left her, she relaxed into a fear-free stupor for the first time in nearly two days. Leaning her head back, she closed her eyes.

CHAPTER 52

Adam backed out of the driveway and repositioned the cruiser by the unoccupied mansion's mailbox in a cleared area intended for the postman's access. As they waited for the summoned assistance, Adam asked his partner, "Do you think we ought to call for a chopper?"

"I like the idea. Fairfax One's million candle-power searchlight and heat-seeking infrared would cover a lot of ground fast, especially in woods like these."

"True, but it's a judgment call," Adam said. "If we nab him right across the street, we don't need to waste that manpower and fuel. Still, this is a high-profile case. There'll be hell to pay if we lose him. Let's do it. We don't want any mistakes so let's also get a quick search warrant. We want a good look around once we're in the guy's house. Who knows what the hell we might find there. Get on the phone fast and order 'em both!"

As Jake did, a rumble of traffic swelled along this little-traveled road as a string of police vehicles moved up Winding Trail Drive. When numerous cruisers pulled to the top of the farm house driveway at 3508, their headlights blended with the farm's automatic motion lights to illuminate the graveled back yard, making the weathered barn and old sheds appear gray and ghost-like in the background shadows. This glow, though faint at a distance, shone through the woods from the mailbox area across the road at 3509, where Adam's cruiser waited.

Rescue and K-9 pulled into the 3509 driveway, followed by uniforms assigned to secure the mansion. The medical techs took Jennifer in hand while Adam and Jake gave K-9 an overview, beginning with the suspect's truck where the handler's dog got a good whiff of the suspect's scent. Jennifer watched from the ambulance while the Animal Warden placed the remains of her captor's dog in a canine body bag and removed it from the scene.

"You treat your charges kindly." Jennifer managed a smile for the medical techs.

"Ma'am, we know that besides physical injuries, crime victims are usually pretty upset about what's happened to them. So we take that emotional stress into account and just treat you the way we'd want someone to help us if we were in your spot."

"So, what's the verdict?" Jennifer asked the head tech when they finished their examination.

"Luckily, the dog bite is superficial, but teeth pierced your skin in several places so we cleaned it out and bandaged it, the same as your deeper scratches. You twisted, maybe sprained, your ankle. It doesn't look broken, but better see your doctor tomorrow for X-rays. We've taped it to keep swelling down and make walking easier. We also cleaned up the bump on the back of your head and again, your doctor may want a head X-ray. Those bruises on your back just take time to heal. We disinfected the scrapes you got in your tumble on the asphalt. All in all, you're looking pretty good and in a couple of weeks you ought to be perfect again!"

The other tech added, "Sometimes folks who go through situations like this benefit from post-trauma counseling. Your doctor may have some ideas about that and we also have information at the station if you decide to look into it. Take care and we hope you're 100% again very soon."

Jennifer thanked both techs for their gentle care, and they returned to their parked vehicle.

Adam spoke with Rescue briefly before returning to the cruiser where Jennifer waited. "How are you doing?"

"Surprisingly well, considering..."

"Now that the techs are finished, we can take you right home. The worst of your ordeal is over!"

Blinking to clear her eyes and her mind, she stared out the cruiser window. He didn't understand. Her ordeal wouldn't end while that man who possessed all her identification remained at large.

She and her family were at terrible risk. This dangerous maniac must be captured. He could be getting away this very minute. Fear lined her scratched, weary face, followed shortly by resolve.

"No," she said firmly. "We need to find him now, before he disappears completely. I can save you time by substantiating everything I've told you and showing you what is where. I described the screwdriver and you said you found blood in his truck. Maybe he returned to his house for first aid. And what about Tina's earring?"

"Tina? Who's Tina?" Jake looked confused, although Adam understood immediately.

"Tina MacKenzie, my daughter's friend," Jennifer told Jake. "She went missing nearly a week ago. I found her earring in that man's basement. It proves she's been there. And even if she isn't now, we might find other clues. I can take you right to the place where I found it. Look, I *am* okay, Adam, and I can't go home yet. This isn't over for me until he's caught. Please take me across to the farm house so we can finish this. *Please…*" Adam and Jake conferred quietly in the front seat while Jennifer leaned back against the rear seat, closing her eyes.

"She has important first-hand information and this is a *very* high profile case," Jake pointed out.

Adam nodded. "I get your point, but if the suspect's at the house, she could be at risk. And look at her, what she's been through. She's just barely hanging on!"

"She hasn't had time to tell us everything she knows, and she may have information critical to the crime. The BOLO says she's sixty years old. She'll never remember the details better than she does tonight," Jake countered.

Adam glanced back at her, knowing she'd bristle at Jake's memory comment and glad she hadn't heard it. "Look," he said quietly to Jake, "she's convinced protecting her family hinges on catching this guy, and she could be right. I won't jeopardize her safety but if other units go in first to secure the place, I agree. Let's see what we can find out."

Adam contacted the cars across the street, where police had emerged from their vehicles, pistols drawn. "Found anything so far?" he asked. "No? The victim says she stuck a four-inch screwdriver into his gut so the suspect has an abdominal wound… We don't know how serious. If he returned to his house from across the street here, he could be anywhere in any condition. K-9 is trying to sniff him out on this side as we speak. Shall I hold Rescue here in case you find him? ...All right. Did you get an okay on that search warrant request? Great! So once you have the situation under control they'll start taking pictures? Good!"

"Ah, listen," Adam continued into the phone, "we're suggesting something a little unusual we think will help. The victim has important information to show us and since we're pushing the clock, once it's safe over there I'd like to bring her in for an eye-witness take on what she knows. Yeah, I know we usually take her statement and verify what she says on our own, but I think her participation may speed up our case and she really wants this guy caught. Okay? So let me know when you're ready for us to bring her over... okay."

Twenty minutes later, Adam got the call and Jennifer's eyes widened as they drove up the farmhouse driveway, the very one down which her frantic escape took place only an hour and a half earlier. At the top, Adam parked near the waiting Rescue ambulance.

Adam turned to Jennifer, "You stay here for now. I'm going in first to check the situation. Be back in a few minutes. Meantime, Jake can keep you company." Jake looked disappointed, preferring instead to be part of the action inside. They watched Adam pull out his pistol and take a quick overview of the outdoor layout before crossing the driveway and entering the house.

Back in the locked cruiser, the phone beeped. Jake punched the button and a concerned voice crackled into the car. "This is the Supervisor. How is Mrs. Shannon?"

Tailoring his response for Jennifer's ears as well as his superior's, Jake said, "Sir, she has minor injuries which Rescue has stabilized. Scared and worn out, Sir, but alive and alert."

"Good, I'll advise PSCC and her family. And what else?" Jake described the crime scene so far.

When they finished talking, she asked wearily, "What's PSCC, Jake?"

"Public Safety Communication Center," he explained. "Their Special Command department contacts families in situations like this." Then Jake sighed, "You know, Ma'am, you are one *extremely* lucky lady. Looks like you lead a *charmed life.*"

At these words, Jennifer's eyes opened wide as she did a double take!

"Did you just say a charmed life?"

"Yes, Ma'am, I sure did."

She'd last heard that phrase from an old man presumably now in a house in a California vineyard. To her surprise, an exceptionally clear image of him popped into her mind. She saw him, smiling at her from his rocker on the veranda of a quaint cottage. Behind it, rows of grape vines climbed a hill. Before it, his grandchildren played on the porch steps. Was this some crazy ESP? Was this even what Gilbert Snowden meant? Was she at last losing her mind?

On impulse, she asked, "Jake, what day is this?"

"July 15th."

One month *exactly* since she and the Professor agreed to remember each other in thirty days! Weird, *spooky!* She remembered his last words to her, "Be careful, *very careful.*"

Somehow he *knew?* No, impossible! Yet, against *all* odds, here she was. Still!

CHAPTER 53

Adam reappeared, unlocked the cruiser door and got in. "Jake, they need you inside."

Glad to enter the fray, Jake trotted over to join the others inside the house. Adam holstered his own pistol before re-locking the vehicle's doors.

Turning to look at Jennifer, he said, "You can't even *imagine* how glad I am that you're okay!"

Leaning forward from the back seat she hugged his shoulder and cried, "Does my family know?"

"Yes, Jake says the Supervisor just called them and PSCC is in contact. I've been to your house half-a-dozen times since you disappeared. Your family *really* misses you!"

"Thanks, Adam. I guess they've... they've been confused and worried."

"You don't know the half of it," Adam chuckled so contagiously that for the first time in thirty-six terrifying hours, she laughed too, wondering if she sounded as deranged as she felt.

"I guess I'll be seeing them soon, Adam. How do I look?" she asked. "Tell me the truth."

Adam studied her. Rescue's medical team bandaged the puncture marks on her arm, treated the zipper-shaped bramble scratches across her face and hands, the asphalt scrapes on her arms, nose and cheek and cleaned up the smudges on her haggard face. But antiseptic and bandages did not change her dirty clothes, leaf-matted hair, dirt-caked fingernails or her tear-streaked cheeks. "You look mighty good to me." He smiled. He meant every word.

A scurry of feverish activity erupted outside their cruiser, as a policeman loped toward them from the sheds, knocking hard on the Rescue ambulance window and shouting at the medics to open their door. The techs immediately jumped from their vehicle carrying medical bags and ran after the cop toward one of the sheds.

Thank god, Jennifer thought with relief. They caught him; they caught that awful man. At last I can stop worrying.

The cruiser door opened as Jake said, "We're ready for you now, Mrs. Shannon, if you're up to it." Looking toward the shed, she steeled herself for a last glimpse of her captor but saw only a cluster of police and medics.

Limping slightly, she held onto Adam's arm for moral support as much as physical. They went in the back door, moved through the sickeningly familiar laundry room, where she half-expected to see the dog guarding the door, through the kitchen and to the basement entrance.

"Can you make it down the stairs with that sore ankle?"

She nodded and winced, not at the pain but the irony. She'd vowed if she ever escaped this sinister house, *nothing* could bring her back. Instead she *insisted* on returning, forced to relive her nightmare after barely wakening from it. Was it a mistake to revisit this place she ached to forget?

Jake trotted down the steps first. Leaning heavily on the rail, she took a deep breath and descended slowly, Adam following behind. At the bottom, several cops awaited them.

"Would you tell us what happened here?" one of them began, and noticing her tense expression, added quickly, "take your time... anything you think will help us."

She pointed a trembling finger and said very quietly, "That's the room. 'The confinement box', they call it, where the man locked me up the first day." She described the dog's attack, being moved while unconscious and waking up in the box fearing she'd been buried alive. The uniforms each looked inside, making faces at the covered bucket's distinct odor. Jennifer stayed near the stairs, avoiding closeness to her former prison as she told of finding the night light and then Tina's earring. She pulled the bent metal object from her blouse pocket and a police woman bagged it as evidence. Adam reminded the group of Tina's missing person status.

"To know what it's like with the door closed and the light off, maybe one of you would like to go inside?" she said.

"Not until the forensic team works on it so we don't disturb fingerprints or other evidence," Adam explained, "but I can imagine it's unpleasant."

Unpleasant, Jennifer thought, hardly covered it!

Pointing out the three hat boxes under the stairs, she described their contents, including the severed finger. "Letters, pictures and other things in there tell about the man and his brother being brutalized as children and, before that, a whole family history of abuse."

"I don't know what's in these other cardboard boxes because I didn't have time to look inside them all...." Her voice drifted away as the police stared at her.

Moving back up the stairs, some cops went ahead, others behind, keeping her protectively in the center. Once upstairs, they guided her down the hall to the first bedroom.

"From cleaning the house, I know my way around some rooms." She showed them the military uniform in the gym closet and the name on the pocket. She showed them the two books he read while exercising. "And I wondered about that place in the closet ceiling—maybe access to attic storage? I have some of those in my own house, but see the hook-and-eye lock on the panel? Strange, as if they thought someone might break in from the attic."

A cop dispatched to bring a step ladder arrived and, activating his flashlight, Jake climbed up to take a look. "Whew! What an odor: smells like a latrine up here," he reported, aiming his flashlight beam around. "It's a small room about 5' x 7', wallboard sides and ceiling, and there's been activity here," he called down to the others. "Dirt, food wrappers, a dish, a cup, a lot of something dried up... looks like vomit or excrement. Wait, something written on the wall in... in something that dripped. It's kind of scrawled but I think I can make it out. Looks like it says," he twisted awkwardly, his ample waist nearly filling the ceiling opening, and focused his flashlight against the far wallboard. "Looks like it spells: 'H-E-L-P'." Jake cleared his throat, "And there's... " his voice faltered, "... and there's a child's hand print with..." Jake's eyes glistened as he climbed heavily back down the ladder and faced the other policemen, "...with only four fingers."

The other cops averted their eyes and one blew his nose loudly.

As Jake descended the ladder, a photographer climbed up to film what he'd described.

As they filed out of the bedroom, Jake said, "You know, I have an attic space like that and my wife makes me go up too often for something stored there. It's insufferable in the hot summer and freezing in the winter. How could *anyone...?*" His voice trailed away.

Back in the hallway, Jennifer entered another room. "I think this is his bedroom. It's where he told me to put the clean laundry and a man's clothes are in the dresser and closet, but everything's very basic. No personal touches here or in the bathroom... with one exception." She showed them the framed photo in the nightstand and explained about the distinguishing hands and the bench nick that pinpointed the picture's location.

Once again in the hallway, Jennifer said, "I don't know what's in that last room because I didn't clean it, but I'm mighty curious to find out. With the rest of the house so sparse, that *must* be where he keeps anything personal and does his work." Her hand reached for the doorknob before Jake gently steered her back.

"Sorry, Mrs. Shannon, but that room is sealed off, waiting for forensics and computer guys, so we can't go in right now. But we thank you for all your valuable information. Now, wouldn't you like to go home to your waiting family?"

"Oh, yes... yes, I really would," she answered with a widening smile.

As they walked back down the hall, through the kitchen and out the laundry room door, she shuddered. She wanted to erase all memory of this house. But she knew its haunting grip would never entirely free her.

As harrowing experiences brand a soldier during battle, so too would she be forever marked by this grisly war zone in which she could have been tortured to death.

They stepped outside, where Rescue personnel huddled over their gurney, administering medical care while police and EMS radio speakers blared loud messages into the summer night.

"Where did you find the man?" Jennifer asked Jake. " Was he in the barn? Will he recover from my screwdriver wound or is he..."

"Not exactly, Ma'am."

Jennifer focused on the stretcher, "Then...?"

"A female was locked in that schoolhouse shed. Alive but barely. They're working on her now."

Jennifer limped toward the ambulance. "Sorry, Ma'am, we need to move out now to get this patient to the hospital."

She stared at the unmoving blanket-swathed figure on the stretcher, IV tubes running from a plastic bag on a pole to an arm tucked under the covers. Jolted by an idea, Jennifer cried urgently, *"Wait!* I... I might know her. Wouldn't it help you if I did?"

"Make it fast, Ma'am." The medic stepped aside impatiently to allow Jennifer a quick look.

The outdoor floodlights in the middle of the night cast an ashen glow over the scene as she neared the gurney. She flinched at the patient's grotesquely swollen face, cut lips and disheveled hair. This wasn't anyone she recognized!

A bandage covered the left half of the face. Leaning closer, Jennifer pushed aside the matted hair to reveal the right side of the victim's face showing deep cheek scratches under a puffy black eye. Ripped nearly in half and caked with dried blood she saw the remnant of an earlobe and clinging precariously to the torn skin... a familiar earring!

CHAPTER 54

"Tina!" Jennifer cried out before consciously changing her tone from the anguish she felt to the healing voice Tina needed to hear. "Tina, its Mrs. Shannon. The man who hurt you is gone. Police are here to keep you safe and doctors will help you get well. Caring people are all around you. You're going to the hospital, where your mom is waiting for you and where Becca and all the rest of us will see you very soon." She touched her shoulder. "You're going to be fine. Hang on! You can do it! We all love you, Tina."

Useless as her words might seem, Jennifer had read that some anesthetized surgery patients later described entire conversations heard during their procedures. Encouragement didn't hurt and the words gave Jennifer the illusion of offering Tina *something* positive in this gruesome situation.

When no flicker of response showed from the corpse-like form lying on the stretcher, Jennifer's heart sank.

Gently pushing Jennifer aside, a medic said, "We're shoving the gurney in and closing the doors now, ma'am. Out of the way, please." The EMT collapsed the cart's shiny aluminum legs and slid his deathly-still patient into the vehicle.

"Should I come along? We're like her second family; she practically lives at our house. She's my daughter's closest friend. Could I comfort her if she wakes up in the ambulance?"

"We're the ones who can help her best right now, Ma'am. But if she gets through this day, she'll need a *lot* of help from all her family and friends."

Jennifer shouted after him, "At least you should know... her name is Tina MacKenzie."

Climbing into the ambulance cab, the medic shouted back, "Tell these cops to call that in. We're taking her to Fairfax ER. Her parents can meet us there."

The tech slammed his passenger door as the vehicle, already underway, rolled down the driveway. Reaching the road, the ambulance's tires screeched, peeling onto the asphalt, its ear-splitting siren shrieking into the night. As it hurtled away, the siren's haunting whine faded and finally disappeared completely, as if it had never existed at all. Jennifer stared after it, agonizing for Tina... and for Becca. Tina's ordeal would dramatically affect her best friend, whatever the outcome.

Feeling a tug at her sleeve, Jennifer turned toward Jake. "Should we send that information to the hospital and call her parents now?"

Jennifer told him what she knew about Tina and her mother, and as Jake relayed it onto the CAD, her mind filled with a stark vision of the cruel maniac who tortured Tina.

Suddenly her hand flew to her throat. If her captor wasn't the injured person in the ambulance, then where *was* he?

***

When unexpected headlights appeared earlier at the foot of his neighbor's driveway, Ruger Yates immediately abandoned his pursuit of Jennifer Shannon. He jumped from his truck at the top of the deserted mansion's driveway, rushed into the dark woods and plummeted down the sloping, forested hill. Dodging trees, fallen trunks and underbrush as he ran, he used the receding glow filtering from the headlight-illuminated driveway at the empty mansion to thinly light his way in the blackness.

He and his dog damn near caught that woman. They were inches away from disposing of her once and for all. Who intruded to botch her final punishment? The mansion's owner? Curious neighbors? Cops?

Whoever they were, their intervention created a *major* problem for Ruger. The Shannon woman would spill what little she knew, but it was enough. And when they discovered the other girl's dead body in the shed, he couldn't defend against such evidence.

Relieved to feel surprisingly little pain from his newly inflicted wound, Ruger cursed the bitch who'd stabbed him. She would pay for this... dearly!

Hearing a gunshot echo through the woods as he ran, he zig-zagged to foil their aim if they'd spotted him. Likely they took out his dog, though he hoped the animal had ripped the woman apart before being wasted or, better still, that they'd accidentally plugged the woman instead.

After all the hours Ruger invested in training—the rigorous discipline, the punishment and the strict food control—that damn dog turned out a total loser. While on guard, he failed to attack or bark a warning when the woman escaped; in fact, he *went with her!* If the dog weren't already dead, he'd kill it himself. But only after teaching painful lessons!

He willfully compartmentalized his fury at the dog in order to focus on flight. No room now for mistakes. Woods like these didn't provide the dense jungle cover he used to advantage in Central America, making this dash in the dark through towering trees and scattered underbrush easier and faster but far less concealing. Yet Ruger knew a deer could vanish seconds after being sighted in woods like these. So could the trained human.

He traversed his neighbor's property swiftly, the glaring headlights, police conversation and vehicle radio static fading with each distancing step. By the time cruiser searchlights raked the forested hill, Ruger had crossed the road and sprinted up his own long driveway to the place he'd concealed Jennifer's van.

Swinging open the barn's aging doors, he grabbed an emergency knapsack hidden inside and flung it into Jennifer's vehicle. Hastily donning plastic gloves lying on the driver's seat, he grabbed her keys from the floor mat, started the car and backed out of the ancient building, stopping only long enough to close the barn so they wouldn't know to look there first.

Besides Ruger, probably no one alive remembered a narrow, overgrown dirt road crossing the field behind the barn. Once active, where plowing and harvesting equipment moved daily to the fields of the working farm, the path had languished under years of overgrowth.

Nevertheless, Ruger's trained eye spotted the obscure pattern of parallel tracks while walking the property with his dog. Trained to prepare for all possibilities, he carefully removed obstructions such as fallen branches, protruding rocks, scrub trees and pieces of abandoned machinery in anticipation of a situation like tonight's. He also learned exactly where this path ended: at a paved county road two miles in the *opposite* direction from the current activity on Winding Trail.

Consistent with military tactics requiring contingency alternatives, he'd rehearsed an escape plan. The duct-taped light-switch inside Jennifer's car door frame would *not* turn on when he climbed into the vehicle. Headlights off, he drove slowly but confidently, bumping lightly along the abandoned, overgrown secret dirt road. Given the dark night, they wouldn't discover his route until morning light revealed foliage crushed by his vehicle's tires. If it rained in the interim, coaxing the weeds to rebound and stand tall again, they'd detect almost nothing.

Bouncing at last to the far end of the lane, the SUV's ride smoothed immediately when its tires touched the asphalt county road. He turned on the headlights and with a self-congratulatory grin at his success, proceeded at normal speed along the deserted secondary roads toward crowded Tysons Corner.

Ten minutes later, as the Fairfax County helicopter's blades throbbed deafeningly overhead and its brilliant searchlight raked the countryside below, Ruger was long gone.

CHAPTER 55

Even inside the cruiser, Jennifer had to shout over the hovering helicopter's whomping thunder above them. "Adam," she cried, "if the man isn't here at the farm, could he have gone back to his truck across the street? What if he's getting away in it right now?"

Adam rolled the window down. "Jake," he shouted, "have you heard from backup about the guy's truck in the driveway across the street?"

"No, we've been too busy here," came the barely audible answer.

Adam put the window up and grabbed his phone. "What's with the pickup truck at 3509 Winding Trail Road, the house that had the B&E residential alarm?"

The phone crackled, "Two units here now and forensics on the way."

"Any sign of the suspect?"

"No, K-9 didn't score yet but still trying. He's not in this house and we're securing the front door.

"Got it! Thanks!"

Overhearing that conversation and clearly upset, Jennifer said in a wavering voice, "Adam, as long as he's out there, my family's in danger. Where could he be?"

"Ma'am, he could hide in the fields or the woods; he could be alive or dead; remember, you wounded him! We're bringing in more dogs for the ground search. The helicopter doesn't miss much upstairs. Chances are we'll find him yet tonight. If not, tomorrow's search has the added advantage of daylight.

"I... I'm very tired," she said softly, her fatigue multiplied by this added worry. "Adam, could I just get my car and drive home now?"

"Your car?"

"Remember, I told you I drove here to what looked like a garage sale. Isn't my car still here?"

"We haven't found it yet, but we've just begun to look. Maybe he ditched it somewhere else. If so, it should turn up fast because we've had a BOLO on it since you disappeared."

"I'm ready to go home."

"Okay. I'll take you there right now."

"Oh, that noise is awful." She covered her ears.

"Be glad you're in the car and not outside. The president's plane is called 'Airforce One,' so we named our chopper 'Fairfax One'."

"How did it get here so fast?" Jennifer asked.

"It's hangared next to the landfill on West Ox Road, only a short distance in flying time."

"Do you think it will find him?"

"If anything can, it can," Adam replied with conviction. "Its spotlight is as bright as daylight and from the air it has machinery to detect and follow anything moving on the ground."

Adam turned the patrol car around, reached the road and headed for McLean. The chopper's throbbing drone gradually diminished as they distanced themselves from the crime scene. "I can hardly wait to see... " his mind focused specifically on Hannah, but instead he said, "...all your family's glad faces when you arrive home."

"Me, too!"

She looked down at Adam's holstered gun, visible in the dashboard light. Could armed police protect her loved ones from a predator like Wrestler or should her family buy guns for the house? She hated the thought of transforming their home into a fortress, where defending themselves might accidentally risk her own loved ones. The faces of her trusting little Grands flitted across her mind. That was no way to live.

Sitting stiffly in the patrol car's seat, Jennifer shouldered the burden that her family would never be safe while that terrible man remained free. What if he headed toward her house this very second? Besides her own abduction, her rescue also exposed his torment of Tina. From the contents of Jennifer's purse, the man knew her address. She had to acknowledge responsibility that her own actions in choosing to attend that "sale" resulted in her family's current danger. But Wrestler's convoluted mind might also hold her responsible for *his* crumbling world.

She sat up straight, grasping the dash with both hands.

Looking at her in surprise, Adam asked, "Is... is something wrong?"

"Adam, aren't there two possibilities? Either this guy is *not* a danger, because he's caught or dead, or he *is* a danger because he's alive and loose. Don't we need to prepare for the worst until we know for certain it's safe?"

Silent as he processed her logic, Adam wordlessly pressed a dashboard control. Instantly, flashing blue lights speckled the dark night as he accelerated the cruiser, racing unimpeded along McLean's empty nighttime streets and intersections in a rush toward the Shannons' home.

CHAPTER 56

Reaching residential Lewinsville Road, empty of traffic at this early morning hour, Adam dispensed with the cruiser's lights. Responsive to Jennifer's concerns, he slowed as they approached her house, alert for anything unusual. No suspicious cars along the street approaching her cul-de-sac, but he remembered that the Shannons' wooded back yard bordered parkland, offering additional access for a determined criminal.

When Adam pulled up at the front gate, most windows in Jennifer's house blazed with light, even though Adam's watch read 4:30 a.m.

"Why not stay here in the cruiser while I ring the doorbell?" he suggested. Wearily, she nodded.

Moments later, her family streamed out of the house, down the sidewalk, through the front gate and surrounded the police car. Their unrestrained squeals of delight at seeing Jennifer caused lights to turn on in several curious neighbors' houses. Adam stood back, scanning the surrounding area for any potential trouble, as Jason opened the cruiser door, and Jennifer staggered out into his arms.

Her husband and children swept her into the house. She was home. She was safe.

The family was exuberant!

After describing Adam as her rescuing White Knight, Jen hugged all of her family members one by one, with a few special words for each. To Becca she whispered, "Adam has something to tell you about later." Hannah could only stare at her.

By then, overwhelmed with physical and mental exhaustion, she asked, "Do you mind if I curl up on the den couch while Adam tells you what happened?" She smiled and waved as Jason gently guided her to the next room.

He returned minutes later. "She's out like a light!"

Hannah moved closer to Adam, grinned and twined her arm in his. "You *did* it! You *found* her. We'd nearly given up. You're our hero and my hero especially. Thank you, thank you!"

More grateful than Hannah could ever know at this wished-for development in his most difficult case, Adam hugged her close and lightly kissed the top of her head.

Every face turned toward the detective, who gave them a broad brush description of Jennifer's imprisonment, escape and rescue.

"We have an unusual situation here," Adam continued. "Mrs. Shannon's had a frightening experience. In the process she discovered compromising information about her captor. He is," Adam tactfully did not say "a probable killer," but instead, "… an extremely dangerous person who, I'm sorry to say, is still at large at this moment."

Hearing this, murmurs of nervous conjecture rippled through the assembled group.

Adam continued. "She stabbed him in the belly with a screwdriver. We don't know how seriously he's injured. So this dangerous guy is doubly mad at her. He has her purse with her address and keys. If payback is on his mind, he knows where to find her. The police have a BOLO out for her car, in case he's driving it. If he has revenge in mind, he'll find police protection around this house. That is, until he's apprehended, which should be soon.

"Rallying around Mrs. Shannon is good. But until he's caught, if you don't live here at the house, the best way to help is to return to your homes. Take everyone who lives here along with you. We may capture the man later tonight, or tomorrow, but pack to stay away for several days. Meantime, the police will give him a reception here if he comes looking for trouble. If that happens, the fewer of you here, the better."

Jason stepped forward. "Words can't describe our worry when Jennifer was missing and now we have you to thank that she's safely back with us. Let's hear it for Detective Adam Iverson!"

A wildly enthusiastic response of cheers, clapping and whistles erupted from the family, their faces beaming with gratitude.

"Adam's plan makes good sense," Jason said. "Let's decide right now who goes where, pack overnight bags quickly and turn this situation over to the police."

Becca approached Adam, "Mom said you have news for me?"

"Let's sit down somewhere quiet." Adam suggested.

"May I come, too?" Hannah asked.

"Of course," Adam agreed. They sat at the wicker table in the sunroom.

Searching for the right words, Adam wanted to recount the facts yet soften the shock, an unfortunate art forced by circumstance upon detectives early in their careers. "The good news is that at the man's farm, we found your friend Tina and she's alive."

After a week of anguish and dread when Tina vanished, followed by their mother's disappearance, the sisters couldn't hide their unabashed delight that *both* at last were found!

"The bad news," Adam continued, "is that the man hurt Tina and when the medics arrived, she was in shock."

Jumping to her feet, a hand at her mouth and tears in her eyes, Becca cried out, "Where is she?"

Adam told her, explaining they'd already alerted Tina's mother.

"She'll need me. I'm going there *now!*"

Hannah grabbed her arm. "I'll come with you, but first let's throw our stuff into a suitcase so we can go from the hospital directly over to Bethany and Mike's house." The sisters rushed upstairs.

After the girls hurried to the second floor, Jason strolled into the sunroom and Adam repeated his information about Tina. "And, Sir," he added, "it's a good idea to change your house locks before our police surveillance here ends."

"Thanks for your outstanding work, Adam! I'm also going upstairs to pack for my wife and me, but after the terrible news about Tina, I need to ask you about Jennifer... man to man." He looked directly into the detective's eyes. "Is she *really* all right? Was she... did he...?"

"Sir, my understanding is that she survived a harrowing time. Physically, a dog bite, some scrapes, scratches and a twisted ankle. Emotionally, a terrifying and exhausting episode. Certainly, a doctor should look her over tomorrow. She was incredibly lucky,

Sir. What happened to Tina was in store for her next. Hers could easily have been a very different story."

Jason exhaled with relief. "Thank god we have her back! And thanks to you and your fine police work," he added.

"Unlike a lot of victims with almost nobody to fall back on, your wife has this amazing family support system. And, Sir, she's... she's *resilient.*"

To Adam's surprise, Jason began chuckling and then laughed out loud as he felt the tension of the last nerve-wracking thirty-seven hours melting away. To the detective, he finally managed to say, "After forty years with her, Adam, I assure you 'resilient' is an *understatement!*"

CHAPTER 57

Certain of BOLO and NCIC lookouts broadcast for Jennifer's van, Ruger knew to ditch it quickly despite having earlier altered her license plates. Her vanity tag's white background with blue border and blue letters simplified that task. Using office white-out correction fluid, he obliterated the letter "Y," the curved part of the "D" and the lower bars of the "L" and "E."

"YRDSALE" now read "RISAIF." Ruger knew this forgery would fail close inspection, but it should escape the casual scrutiny of passing vehicles, such as a rolling police cruiser. He also knew this subterfuge bought him critical time because white vans similar to this turned up everywhere. Until they located this particular one, they had no idea where to look for him.

Even when the cops found it, his inside/outside wipe-down and protective gloves afterward guaranteed no fingerprints. Still, he'd envisioned this scene unfolding years hence, when this missing woman was old news. Then he could easily drop her van in another city or even another state: Maryland, the District of Columbia, Pennsylvania and West Virginia were all within about an hour's drive. They'd find the vehicle but not Jennifer Shannon, who would occupy a grave on his farm. Given that future "clean" car and no corpse, anybody could be responsible for her disappearance, which by then would be a dusty cold case.

Her escape destroyed that perfect strategy. He gritted his teeth and slammed a tightly clenched fist hard against the steering wheel. That woman! She ruined everything!

When she spilled her story, cops would swarm over his house. They'd investigate his computer, which his hasty midnight departure left no time to booby-trap. They'd discover his clandestine consulting for Special Forces and side-line activities with militia, both groups operating at the edge of the law. Besides losing the painstakingly compiled files he'd never see again, their discovery would turn the very friends who could help him create a new identity into enemies. Enemies determined to find and kill him for failing to secure their super-sensitive information entrusted to him. Now he had to dodge everybody — cops *and* clients.

Driving toward Tysons Corner, his life in a shambles, he took stock of his situation. He'd survived a bitter childhood, succeeded in a tough Army career, made a new start at the inherited house and worked with organizations where his unique military experience contributed importantly. He didn't expect the unstoppable need to punish those women. But when the rage overpowered him with the uncontrollable need to punish as he was punished, he acted. Then the unimaginable physical and emotional satisfaction that followed, a catharsis experienced only by *humiliating* and *controlling* and *eliminating* them, justified all the risks.

Even so, except for the first woman in the bar, he'd planned carefully, proceeded efficiently, used them savagely and buried the evidence. That is, until this last one escaped. The decision for her to clean and cook allowed him critical hours to concentrate on his time-sensitive computer work and, when she reorganized the basement, to neutralize his mother's power over the cellar. He'd captured Jennifer Shannon for his own whims. Why not use her that way, he'd decided, before he used her the other ways?

Everything went well until she caused the crescendo of events turning his life upside down. Now, as with perilous Army missions, new situations required new strategies. He needed a plan.

Pulling into a Tysons Corner hotel parking lot, he parked his car among the dozens belonging to guests asleep in their rooms. Leaning back in the seat, he closed his eyes to concentrate and fought a powerful urge to sleep, an unthinkable luxury at the moment! "On duty" now, as surely as with any Army assignment, he must fall back on his survival instincts, a natural acuity reinforced by rigorous military training.

Eyes closed, he focused his mind on the problem at hand. To accomplish his dual missions, avoiding capture and punishing Jennifer Shannon, he could flee or hide in plain sight, each with risks and rewards. If he left tonight, returning months later to teach that woman her painful lesson, she'd live in constant fear in the interim. The subtle cruelty of this psychological torture excited him. Police protection and interest eventually waned in such cases as new crises overshadowed old ones. In time, he'd get to her unimpeded.

He couldn't use her stolen van to escape because that vehicle might be stopped at any time. Police would have a lock on all commercial transportation now, so scratch planes, buses and trains. Even driving to a truck stop to hitch a ride with a driver he encountered in the diner would be safer months from now. With the Shannon case currently top priority on every cruiser's BOLO list, the sooner he fled, the likelier his apprehension.

As for hiding in plain sight, he again considered nearby big cities where he'd eventually planned to lose Jennifer's van but could lose himself as well. For that matter, northern Virginia housed a dense population. A fact he collected for the militia listed Fairfax County with 1.4 million people. Add to that adjacent Arlington County and the city of Alexandria, never mind Washington, DC across the Potomac River. Hell, he could disappear right here!

A twinge of discomfort distracted his focus to the wound in his abdomen. He pulled a clean wash cloth from his knapsack, opened his trouser belt and studied the small hole on the lower left side of his belly for the first time. It hurt like hell when he prodded the spot with a finger, but absent that, he felt surprisingly little pain. Maybe this indicated a superficial wound that could heal on its own. The small quantity of external bloody ooze wouldn't explain his weariness, but internal bleeding might. He could consult a doctor, passing off the injury as a workbench accident, but only as a last resort. Rubbing the area with antiseptic wipes from his knapsack and using the washcloth as a makeshift bandage, he anchored it top and bottom under the elastic of his briefs and refastened his trousers.

Leaning back again, Ruger felt a second wave of fatigue affect his concentration. His mind quieted as he lay back against the headrest. He wouldn't fall asleep, but only rest a moment.

CHAPTER 58

Despite Ruger's resolve to stay awake at all costs, moments after his eyelids drooped his breathing slowed to long, deep inhalations, his lips parted and his jaw relaxed. Soon his eyes began moving beneath their closed lids as he passed into deep REM sleep. His mouth hung open and he snored slightly as his mind shifted into the imaginary world of dreams.

The unwanted, nearly forgotten memory of a woman's face floated into his dream. From afar, the face seemed placid, even beautiful. But as it came closer, the features morphed into a leer and from its twisted mouth shrilled his mother's unmistakable derisive voice.

"Failed again, did you? You dim-witted piece of garbage, I knew you would! You never could get anything right! Ever since you returned to my house, I watched from the basement as you threw away my furniture and defiled my bedroom. Just look at you now. You didn't protect your computer and didn't control the woman who escaped to tell the world what a loser you are. You couldn't even train your dog right. Well, I'll show you, you Cretan!"

Gripped by the teeth of his nightmare, Ruger contorted in the seat, arms protectively over his head to ward off the biting blows raining down from his past. The woman's voice in his head shrieked on. "Why must you do everything wrong? Why do you make me do this to you? When you make mistakes you know you *must be punished.* Here it comes."

"No," Ruger half-screamed, cringing and squirming. *"No, please..."*

Ruger twisted and writhed in the van's front seat, reliving futile childhood efforts to tear himself away from the cruel face and unwanted pain. Yet the dream roiled on, and the punishment. How could she *know* about his recent failures, to ridicule and taunt and humiliate him with them? His eyes rolled back, his hands stiffened into claws and his body trembled. Minutes ticked past.

He lay spent, his powerful body curled into a fetal position and his eyes staring trance-like, as a rivulet of saliva trickled from the corner of his mouth. For several semi-conscious minutes, he remained inert until awareness crept back through vaguely overheard sounds: the grinding of a garbage truck emptying dumpsters, the rumble of a passing car and far away, a fading fire truck siren: waaaah, wah-wah-wah-wah...

The noises drew him back to reality. He sat up, blinked his eyes several times and shook his head to clear the dream's fear and confusion. Finding his chin wet, he dragged a wrist across his mouth to remove the drool. The screwdriver wound throbbed on the lower left side of his gut, aggravated by his recent convolutions. Reaching into his knapsack, he took a long swig from a water bottle.

As Ruger's waking mind processed this terrifying episode, he drew the protective, self-serving conclusion that he'd done nothing wrong, but Jennifer Shannon had. He had total control before she came. The others were easy; they obeyed. She could have too; he thought she had, but instead she did everything wrong.

The dreaded childhood commandment preceding each discipline flooded his mind: " When you do something wrong, you *must* be punished." Jennifer Shannon must be punished! His hate escalated into rage, pulsing adrenalin into his body and feeding an insatiable desire for vicious, satisfying revenge. As passion further displaced logic, a new mandate filled his mind. Forget postponing her discipline until it was safer for him. Do it *now!*

Face red, neck veins bulging, jaw clenched and muscles tensed for action, he narrowed his plan to four simple steps: ditch this car, steal another, find the woman, punish her!

Still wearing rubber gloves, he took her purse from his knapsack, extracted her wallet and again read her driver's license address. From her box of garage sale paraphernalia conveniently next to him on the passenger seat of her van, he removed and opened her northern Virginia book map.

A feral grin creased Ruger's face, as he translated her address into exact map coordinates. Now, where to get rid of this car and steal another? He drove slowly through the hotel parking lot, searching for an older model car without an electronic alarm system to hoot relentlessly if violated. Damn! He saw only newer models not worth the risk. Reluctantly, he moved on.

Driving down Route 123 toward McLean, he sought a strip mall with an all-night grocery or drugstore, where parked cars and traffic around open stores drew no special attention even in these early morning hours. Improved security lighting and people locking their vehicles heightened the challenge as he looked for an inconspicuous dark-colored, older model car, preferably unlocked. Cruising slowly, he entered the Chain Bridge Corner shopping center, glided by the Giant Supermarket, CVS drugstore and Kazan Restaurant.

He surveyed several nearby lots, tentatively identifying two cars. Parking away from them on a dark nearby street behind the old McLean Fire Station, he stuffed Jennifer's purse and keys into his knapsack. Then he slung it onto his shoulder, locked the van and slipped into the shadows.

If lucky, he'd select a car belonging to a night-shift employee, which bought him several hours before the owner would discover its theft. Such employees usually parked a distance from the store to free closer spaces for paying customers. He walked toward the larger lot, aware the success of his remaining plan hinged on this step. Otherwise, he might have to retrieve Jennifer's van and scout another area. The longer he drove her car, the likelier that police would spot him.

Walking up to the older model black sedan he noticed earlier, he couldn't believe his luck: a locked passenger-side door but its window wide-open! In a hurry to get to work, the driver apparently pressed the four-door lock button without first ensuring all windows were closed.

Ruger got in. He could hot-wire the ignition but knew a faster way. Using a screwdriver from his bag, he pushed the sharp end into the key slot and rotated it to the right. The vehicle purred to life and the gas gauge revealed a nearly full tank. No failure here, he congratulated himself!

Picking up the piece of paper on which he'd written directions, he turned his new ride toward her McLean neighborhood to deliver Jennifer Shannon's date with destiny.

CHAPTER 59

Becca and Hannah hurried down the stairs, clutching their purses and overnight bags. As they dashed out the door, Hannah asked Adam, "Shall I call you on my cell from the hospital or later when we get to my brother's house?"

"From the hospital. You can tell me how Tina's doing. Here, I'll walk you to your car," Adam volunteered to be sure they were safe until their last minute here. "Do you know how to get there?"

"Actually we do. We've visited sick friends there before… and Tina's dad." The girls climbed into their small car and rolled down the windows, still conversing with Adam.

"Both of you keep your cell phones turned on. I want to be able to reach you with any new developments."

The girls checked their phones. "Okay, they're on."

"You shouldn't run into much traffic this early. I know you're impatient to see her, but…" Adam looked directly into Hannah's eyes, "be careful," he said, touching her arm resting on the car's window ledge. His hand lingered, reluctant to let her go. "Cops see some terrible accidents. We never want to find somebody we know in one."

She put her free hand over his and gave it a warm squeeze. "We'll be fine. *You* watch out, Adam." Genuine concern clouded her pretty face. "You're the one in danger here, guarding the house from that maniac. Adam, *please* be very careful." She held his gaze.

"Enough, you two! Let's get going," Becca prompted.

He waved as their Volkswagen beetle circled out of the cul-de-sac, raced down the road and swerved around the corner.

As he turned toward the house, thoughts of Hannah filled his mind. He realized his rescue of her mother and Tina accomplished more than saving their lives or doing his job competently. The "ripple effect" also saved the Shannon and MacKenzie families from the shattering experience of losing a loved one in the grotesque manner Yates, if that was his name, intended.

A vision of Hannah's sunny smile floated before his eyes. Something about her really got to him. Her quick mind, graceful body, clever humor and the way she looked *into* him with her bright, intelligent eyes stirred a new and compelling need for her. He stared down the quiet street, her absence creating emptiness. How could he miss her already when she'd been beside him only moments ago?

Then, he realized he didn't want to miss her any more. He wanted to be near her all the time, to devote his life to enjoying her, protecting her and sharing happiness with her.

"I'm going to marry this girl!" he said aloud to the dark, empty street, startled to hear his own words clarify the confused personal thoughts nudging him the past few weeks. He grinned as this decision opened a purposeful path, but then frowned. Leery of serious commitment after her broken relationship with Kevin, how would *she* react to this?

Pushing his personal thoughts aside with effort, he knew he needed to assure the Shannon family's safety by positioning his people in and around their property. He turned to his task.

***

Ruger parked the black sedan far enough down Jennifer's street to watch her house without being conspicuous. Taking a swig from his water bottle, he thought about how much he'd learned from the contents of her purse.

The day he discovered and opened his mother's purse held vivid memory for Ruger. Odd, he thought now, that she even owned a purse since she never left the farm. Perhaps old habits died hard. He thought of her purse as her secret hiding place. Since the purse rarely left her bedroom, where the boys were forbidden to go, finding it unattended one day in the kitchen transfixed him. Though dreading consequences if caught, he discovered his powerful curiosity coupled with extraordinary opportunity overcame fear. Although he was never allowed to touch or hug his mother, opening her forbidden handbag and touching its contents thrilled Ruger with the illusion of closeness to her. This sensation of intimacy translated to future purses he'd investigate with similar results. After that, women's pocketbooks held irresistible fascination for him.

This first connection between the excitement of risk and the palpable satisfaction in overcoming it would surface repeatedly in Ruger's life, drawing him toward the elite covert branch of the military where nearly every assignment exposed him to deadly danger.

Handling the array of items inside a woman's purse intrigued him. It was more than learning confidential information about the person who assembled them. Touching these personal items felt like caressing a secret part of the owner.

When a woman at a bar near his military base joked that if he kept kissing her he'd "have to be punished," Ruger froze. Outside that bar, he punched and kicked her until she stopped moving, then threw her body into his car and buried her in a trench at an abandoned training field on base. He kept her purse, a lingering memento of his satisfaction and triumph, stashed in a wooden box in the woods. He visited it frequently. Now, Jennifer Shannon cost him his entire coveted collection of purses, sequestered at the farmhouse he could never enter again. She would pay for that sin!

He reached for her purse on the seat beside him. The mother of a big family, Jennifer needed a lot of items at her fingertips. What he found were the usual comb, mirror, nail file and cosmetics plus emergency items like Bandaids, wet wipes and hand sanitizer; child amusers like crayons, notepad and miniature flashlight; practical items like a tape measure, postage stamps and eyeglass repair kit; and health items like cough drops, Kleenex, allergy tablets and aspirin. Besides $62 in cash, her wallet held numerous credit, ID and membership cards. Add sunglasses, earrings, shopping lists and key ring. The amount and variety in her purse surpassed anything in Ruger's experience.

But her two most-valued purse items were a small photo album containing family pictures and a thin calendar book. It not only detailed her scheduled activities, but on its back pages listed names, birthdays, clothing and shoe sizes, phone numbers and *addresses* of her children. Her driver's license simplified finding her house, and entering it later with her own keys would become almost too easy.

He fondled each item before returning it to her handbag.

Then he waited…

***

Absorbed in conversation as Hannah's VW bug sped around the corner, the sisters failed to notice an older black sedan parked farther down their street ease away from the curb and into the road behind them.

Following at a distance, Ruger Yates used his free hand to press another clean cloth from his knapsack against the gouge in his abdomen. That done, he lay that same hand confidently atop several items assembled on the seat beside him: his unique Special Forces ceramic pistol and a case containing a hypodermic set, together with a cardigan sweater to cover blood on his shirt and upper trousers. Useful items for whatever unfolded next.

Surely they didn't think he'd continue driving that woman's easily identified SUV. Like his parents, like all of his foes and like the women he destroyed, the cops too had underestimated him.

As he drove, he couldn't repress a smug smile; for he possessed sole knowledge of a tightly held secret which had served him well and would again. Deployed in a remote Central American mountain village, he was worshiped by those natives as a bona fide god for his obvious magic with fire (matches), talking box (cell phone), food in hard bark (rations in tin cans), traveling-river-face (mirror) and stick-that-throws-fire-and-kills (pistol). To earn favor with this "god," the ancient medicine man one night confided his own unique knowledge, passed to him alone from generations of revered predecessors: the cryptic method for *preserving* the poisonous extracted frog toxin indefinitely. Knowledge is power and power is control, Ruger reminded himself.

After jerking out the screwdriver that *idiot woman* had rammed into his belly, he felt little pain until now. The gentle pressure he applied nearly stanched the slight bleeding, but he needn't re-examine his wound to know that if this new pain increased, he'd need a doctor.

How he hated that woman! Why hadn't he dealt with her as he had the others? The police cars at her house thwarted putting his hands on her tonight, but there were other ways to even the score, after which he'd ultimately deal with her.

Revenge could take various forms. For now, he'd follow and eliminate the two girls. Harming her daughters would tear at the heart of this woman who, unlike his own mother, apparently cherished her children.

Her purse revealed a roadmap of her life. Hating her superficially was easy enough, but through the purse, he *knew* her. Such knowledge gave him so much more to despise. He grinned menacingly, savoring *very special* plans for her and her family once inside her house. Drawing upon his considerable practice during interrogations, where he instigated human suffering while carefully sustaining life, he would save the *worst* torments he could inflict for Jennifer Shannon.

He gloated, anticipating her suffering and screams.

CHAPTER 60

As Jennifer's two daughters drove toward Fairfax Hospital, they paused at the Dulles access tollbooth, threw three quarters into the coin basket, waited for the bar to lift, and sped through.

Following at a discreet distance, Ruger hadn't anticipated this. Did he have quarters? Damn! He did not. He didn't want the attendant in the manned booth to get a look at him, and tearing off the crossbar barrier by driving through without paying triggered the automatic camera to photograph his license plate. What to do? He spotted numerous coins on the ground under the basket, where drivers missing a toss lobbed in additional quarters rather than retrieving the fallen ones. Opening the car door quickly, he leaned out, scooped up several, popped them into the basket and sped through when the crossbar lifted.

Even this brief delay cost time, and he barely glimpsed the VW ahead taking the I-495 South turnoff. He accelerated onto the beltway behind them, determined to keep them in sight and concentrating even harder on staving off a fleeting light-headedness.

Major road arteries around America's largest cities experienced traffic 24/7. Washington, DC and the surrounding Maryland and Virginia suburbs were no exception. Nothing like the paralyzing grind of morning and evening rush hours, yet even in these wee hours, a steady flow of vehicles persisted.

Moving aggressively, the VW bug wove in and out of traffic, obviously hurrying. Cursing each time the bug switched lanes, Ruger managed to maintain sight of the small vehicle. What are they up to? he wondered, when they finally nosed onto the Gallows Road ramp and a moment later swerved into the hospital's parking lot.

While crammed with cars in the daytime, the lot was only partially full at this hour, and he found a spot not far from the bug. Taking a look at himself in the rear view mirror, he poured a trickle from the water bottle onto the corner of the wash cloth and hastily cleaned up his face and the hand he scraped during his earlier dash through the woods. Getting out of his car, he refolded and stuffed the cloth between his wound and his trouser belt, before slipping on the cardigan sweater to cover the washcloth's bulge and dried blood on his lower shirt. Gathering the pistol and hypodermic case, he slipped them into a sweater pocket.

Following the two girls as they hurried up the hill to the hospital's main entrance, he knew he could get near them undetected because he knew them but they had no knowledge of him. He smirked at this advantage because he needed to get *very* close to use the hypodermic. Maybe he could even take care of them outside? But a look around at bystanders squelched that option. As the girls passed through the automatic doors into the hospital's lobby, Ruger trailed behind but paused within earshot as Hannah stopped at the information desk.

Listening over her shoulder, Ruger couldn't believe his ears when she asked for Tina MacKenzie. He knew that name from the driver's license in the girl's purse. She was the one he took before the Shannon woman. Tina, the girl who gave up too easily, who didn't fight back and whose small purse contained so few uninteresting items: a comb, a lipstick, her license, one credit card and a little cash.

But he left Tina in the cramped schoolhouse, too close to death to survive. Tomorrow he planned to extricate any last bit of life still in her and bury her in the field with the others, thus emptying the schoolhouse for his next victim, Jennifer Shannon. He grimaced. Now that plan and all his plans were in chaos because of that *woman*. With disciplined will, he suppressed his rising anger in order to focus clearly and listen carefully.

The receptionist studied her computer and smiled at the girls. "I'm sorry, but we show no one here by that name."

"But she arrived by ambulance only a couple of hours ago. The police told us she's here and... "

"Oh, well that could be a different situation. If it's a police matter her name might very well not appear on our list. She might be under protection. If that's the case, you'll need that information directly from the police."

"Thanks" said Becca, while Hannah whipped out her cell phone and punched in Adam's number.

When he answered, she briefly described the situation and said to Becca, "He's finding out. Would you write this down?"

As Becca fumbled in her purse for pencil and paper and Hannah waited for Adam to come back on the line, both girls eased into waiting room chairs. Ruger picked up a discarded newspaper, slipped into a nearby chair and pretended to read.

Hannah motioned her sister to write and spoke into her cell phone again. "Okay, she's in Tower 10 West, Room 1074 and if we're asked for a password code it's..." Hannah looked puzzled, "Are you sure? Okay... would you spell that? E-u-p-h-r-a-t-e-s? Euphrates—like the river? Weird. We're on our way up. Oh, by the way, the signs in the lobby say to turn off cell phones in the hospital." Pause. "Well, if you're sure. So we just tell them we have police permission?" Hannah giggled, "Okay, but remember, if we're caught, we know where to find you!" Snapping off the phone, she was all business again. Motioning Becca to follow, she returned to the information desk.

"Visiting hours ended at 8:00 p.m.," said the receptionist. "If you're going to try anyway, ask for directions on the 10th floor. Elevators are that way," she pointed the direction.

The girls passed through the nighttime security detection point and followed the receptionist's directions. Ruger waited until they disappeared down the hall and deftly transferred the ceramic pistol from his sweater to his trouser pocket. He knew its unique materials would escape metal detection and that only a very few Special Forces personnel, like him, were issued these state-of-the-art weapons. He approached security himself, where the guard eyed him cautiously.

"Put your sweater on the belt, please," and seeing blood the sweater had covered when Ruger complied, the guard added, "You okay, Mister?" he asked.

"Yeah," Ruger joked, "just tired and a little roughed up. You should see the other guy."

The guard smiled in commiseration. "What's this?" he pointed to a hypodermic in the sweater's pocket now pictured on the monitor screen? Prepared for the question, Ruger said without hesitation, "I'm diabetic and carry my insulin with me." The guard passed him through and he slipped into his sweater again.

Now in the hospital proper, Ruger scanned the lobby signs to locate a restroom. Following appropriate arrows, he soon stared at himself in the large mirror over a sink in the public men's room. Pulling a fistful of paper towels from the holder, he dampened them, added liquid soap and cleaned his face and hands. A man at the next sink eyed him curiously as the water in the sink ran red. Hell, this was a hospital. A little blood shouldn't attract undue attention.

Whatever the other man thought, he said nothing and averted his eyes when Ruger looked his way. Wetting his comb, Ruger smoothed down his hair. Not bad, if it weren't for the beard stubble. The other man left and he was alone in the public bathroom.

Taking advantage of this unobserved moment, he removed, folded and pocketed the Out-of-Order sign from one of the stall doors, being careful to include the tape affixing it. The sign might come in handy or could be easily jettisoned if not. Now for the next step of his plan. Ruger grinned with anticipation: he who looks, finds.

CHAPTER 61

"This is 10 *East,*" the night nurse at the 10th floor desk explained when Hannah and Becca emerged from the elevator. "10 *West* is at the other end of this floor. Take either the even or odd numbered corridor and when the woodwork color changes from cream to light blue, you're in 10 West. Be sure to check in at the West desk."

The girls hurried down the tweed carpet to the 10 West nurses' station and gave Tina's name plus the special password. They waited as the nurse confirmed that it was correct. "You know this is way past regular visiting hours." The nurse frowned.

"But this situation is special. Tina's mother was recently widowed so this is the second terrible blow for her in two months. We'd like to comfort her. Couldn't you make an exception, *please?*" she asked.

The nurse smiled, "Well, this patient is unusual but you know the password so perhaps we can be a bit flexible. Her mother's alone with her now and I think could use some moral support." Pointing toward a hallway, she added, "Room 1074 is that way. Our rooms on this floor are all two-bed, but we've blocked the other bed in 1074, so your friend is the only patient and you'll have privacy."

Thanking her, the girls hustled down the corridor and eased open the door. Waving silently to Mrs. MacKenzie, they tiptoed in and each gave her a reassuring hug before walking to Tina's bedside.

Shocked at the sight of their friend's ravaged condition, they choked back their reactions to avoid further upsetting her mother.

On the far side of the bed, Becca pulled a chair close to Tina's mother and held her hand, while Hannah stayed on the side nearer the door and peered anxiously at the blotched, swollen face of their sleeping friend. An oxygen canula clung to Tina's nostrils and an IV cord snaked from the plastic bag hanging above her to the needle taped near her wrist. A blood pressure cuff encircled one arm, while a telemetry machine monitoring heart activity beeped rhythmically in the otherwise quiet room.

"They brought her here from the Intensive Care Unit about an hour ago," whispered Denise. "They say her vital signs are stable now. I think that means her organs no longer show signs of shutting down. Something in the IV helps her sleep, but the bag is nearly empty so she should wake up soon."

The girls nodded and Hannah asked, "And what about *you?* Are you all right?"

Denise sighed, staring at her hands. "Tina is all..." she fought tears, "...all I have left now that Scott's gone. When I thought I might lose her too, I... " Her shoulders shook with silent sobs.

Becca hugged her again and said with greater conviction than she felt, "At least the worst is over." Seeing Denise's concerned face, she added quickly, "She'll get wonderful care here. We know *lots* of people who rave about this place. They say that the care is very personal yet very professional at the same time."

"...and that the food is good," Hannah added.

When Denise's troubled expression didn't change, Hannah continued, "You know, being out of the ICU is a *really* positive sign! And Adam, a policeman I know, says the only trauma center in northern Virginia is right here. So this was the ideal place for the ambulance to bring her."

After a long silence, Becca tried even lighter conversation to distract Tina's mother, who remained on the verge of tears.

"How did you ever pick that unusual password?" she asked.

It worked! The woman brightened slightly. "As you know, Tina owns two cats."

"That's right, Tiger and Fraidy," Hannah said.

"Ah, but those are only their nicknames. Their real names are Tigris and Euphrates. I tried to select a password nobody could guess."

"Well, you sure succeeded." Becca nodded and after a pause asked, "When did you get here?"

"The police called me as the ambulance brought her in and I guess I arrived about 30 minutes after that. She was still in the FACT room when I got here."

"Excuse me, the 'what' room?" asked Hannah.

"That acronym stands for—let me think if I can remember—Forensic Assessment and Consultation Team. I think that's it." She spelled it out, "F-A-C-T."

Responding to both girls' puzzled expressions, she said, "In the emergency room when a crime is involved like... like sexual assaults, they take the person to a special room where the medical care is the same as a regular emergency room; but the FACT people add other procedures."

"Like...?" Palms up, Becca gestured her confusion.

"They try to learn more about the crime... to answer who-where-what-when-and-how questions is the way they explained it to me. If the patient can talk, I guess they *ask* for those answers and if the patient can't, I guess they *look* for those answers. Besides the rape kit, they do other tests like checking under fingernails for evidence, that sort of thing. I... I didn't actually see them working because they wouldn't let me in until they finished and then they rushed her away on a stretcher to ICU. I finally got to see her there."

The nurse bustled into the room to check Tina's vital signs. "Looking good," she said. "I'll be back in about 30 minutes, but call me if she wakes up sooner. Here's her call button." She indicated a button on the bedrail. "Okay?"

They all nodded.

Tina's mother turned to the Shannon girls. "Thank you for coming. It's good to have someone help shoulder the... " her eyes misted again and she fell silent.

"You know you can count on us and our whole family. We'll help get Tina through this..." Becca searched for the right words, and at last said, "...through this rough patch."

CHAPTER 62

Ruger knew what he needed next, but where to find it without drawing attention?

He wandered from the public restroom along the main floor corridors. Besides his reason for following the two daughters here, discovering Tina *alive* posed new risks for him. Externally and internally, her body bore indisputable evidence of his physical brutality. But her ruinous *verbal* testimony threatened only if she were alive!

Of course, he must first kill Tina, then the daughters, and then he'd punish the Shannon woman. Pounding his right fist into his open left hand, he again cursed his stupidity in letting her escape.

Hearing the sound of the slamming fist, a doctor who strolled down the corridor ahead of Ruger looked back. Thinking fast, Ruger said, "Smacked a fly. Got him, too!" The doctor nodded, continued down the hall toward the administrative offices, opened a door and went inside. Reaching that door himself, Ruger read "Men's Restroom, Staff Only." Well now, how convenient! Ruger listened outside a moment, then entered and closed the door behind him.

Inside, Ruger saw two cubicles, two urinals and a clipboard lying on the sink. While the doctor occupied one cubicle, Ruger crafted a quick plan.

When the doctor emerged and saw Ruger, he said, "The public restroom is down the hall." He headed to the sink, looked in the mirror, stuck out his chin and rubbed it with one hand. From the pocket of his white lab coat he removed a disposable razor, set it on the sink and washed his hands. "I said the public restroom is down the hall," he repeated to Ruger's mirrored reflection.

Advancing swiftly to the sink, Ruger stepped directly behind the doctor and instantly grabbed him in a vice-like chokehold. Ruger had used this basic, effective close-quarters combat technique many times. The beauty of it was that you could either temporarily control or disable or kill with this method, depending upon the amount of pressure and length of its application.

The startled doctor's eyes bulged in his reddening face as he gurgled incoherently. His hands clawed frantically, ineffectively, toward his neck, where Ruger's sinewy forearm pressed relentlessly against his trachea. Increasing the pressure, Ruger gave a sudden snap to the right, instantly breaking his victim's neck. Neat, quick and no blood, exactly as the Army taught him, Ruger thought as he removed the lab coat from the man's warm but lifeless body.

He would also need the doctor's badge, hanging on a colored string around his neck and, of course, his wallet. Flipping the billfold open, Ruger smiled in appreciation at the ID credentials and cash to grease his escape once his task at the hospital ended.

Slipping into the lab coat, Ruger dragged the man into the first cubicle, propped him into a sitting position on the commode and eased his lolling head against the wall. He bent the dead man's limp, compliant legs, forcing them into a secure cross-legged position so someone outside the cubicle couldn't see them. He exited the cubicle and closed the door. But how to lock it from the inside?

Standing on the edge of the toilet in the adjacent cubicle, Ruger leaned over the top of that stall's divider wall and reached his long arms down to lock the doctor's cubicle door from the inside. Removing the Out-of-Order sign from his sweater pocket, he taped it firmly outside the closed stall's door and stepped back to survey the result. Perfect!

Returning to the sink, he picked up the doctor's razor, soaped his chin from the dispenser and eliminated his own whisker stubble. Substituting clean paper towels for the blood-stained cloth stuffed into his trousers, he examined the badge hanging around his neck.

"Morton Prescott, MD," Ruger read aloud. Although he bore little resemblance to Prescott's photo, who would question him in a hospital where doctors ruled? Into the roomy right lab coat pocket, he transferred the gun and hypodermic case from his cardigan and hid the sweater under papers in the trash. From his left lab coat pocket, Ruger withdrew the stethoscope he found there, draped it around his neck, picked up the clipboard and grinned at his commanding reflection in the mirror. Seconds later, the new Dr. Prescott stepped from the restroom and strode with purpose down the hall toward the elevators to Tower 10 West.

As the elevator doors opened on the tenth floor, Ruger studied the sign directing him to the even-numbered hallway and walked briskly to Room 1074. The door stood slightly ajar. Pressing it open, he surveyed the room. Good, no medical personnel inside. He entered the room with confidence, closing the door behind him.

Tina lay motionless on the closer of two patient beds, the light blue blankets drawn up to her chin. On the far side of the bed sat a woman with one of the Shannon daughters and on the near side of the bed stood the other girl.

"Ladies," he addressed them, "I am... Dr. Prescott," and nodded as the women introduced themselves. Good, this *confirmed* who they were!

Studying his clipboard, Ruger said, "I have Tina's chart here," and pretended to read it while remembering what he'd heard during their earlier lobby conversation. Looking at the chart, he announced in a low voice, "What this patient needs now is rest and quiet." He needed to curtail their communication options. "We rely on these machines to monitor her progress. Do any of you have cell phones?"

Each of them raised a hand.

"As on an airplane, their frequencies might interfere with our specialized electronic equipment, so please turn those phones off now."

He watched sternly while all three complied. Hannah opened her mouth to mention their "police permission," but remembering the lobby signs, she certainly didn't want responsibility for a medical machine malfunction compromising her friend's survival.

Walking to Tina's bedside, Ruger touched her forehead above the raw, red scrapes, the bluish swollen cheeks and the puffy black eyes, the irregular splits across her lips and the gash on her chin. But this was only her face. They'd *really* blanch if he pulled back the blankets to show them the rest of her traumatized body, hidden beneath the covers.

He thought he remembered the very blows creating these bruises, or did he? Sometimes after the discipline began he became so agitated that he simultaneously lost control and memory. In those instances, he could only recreate what must have taken place by later witnessing the indisputable evidence of his actions.

Pretending to take Tina's pulse, Ruger looked importantly at the IV bag and fingered its tube, as if assessing proper function. Then he turned to the three women. "Good. Now, have you any questions?" This would distract them while he implemented his next step.

"What can you tell us about her condition?" Denise MacKenzie whispered tensely, clasping her hands so tightly the knuckles whitened.

Who knew better than he what Tina had endured? This would be easy and he rather liked the powerful role of respected, god-like physician, the sort of attention and esteem he'd come closest to in covert forces, though such acknowledgment necessarily remained largely secret outside his unit and even then, nothing like this.

"Well, she had no food or water for many days..." and now he drew upon his covert forces medical training lingo, "...leaving her dehydrated and malnourished." He was beginning to enjoy this. "And," his voice became husky, "she was raped... repeatedly." He looked at his listeners' faces, gratified that his words triggered the desired demoralizing effect.

"And she was..." he wanted to say *punished*, but substituted, "... beaten... beaten numerous times." Inadvertently, his hand grasped at a sharp pain in his lower left side. He glanced down quickly, relieved to see no blood leaching onto his white lab coat.

Hannah and Becca exchanged significant looks, appalled at this physician's distinctly odd bedside manner, but Tina's mother stared at him, transfixed.

"Due to her confinement in an unventilated shed where she spent those hot summer days, she also suffered severe," he fished his medic's memory for the right word, "hyperthermia. And then she went into shock, which involves dangerously low blood pressure and," he glanced at the beeping machine above the bed before further inventing, "erratic heartbeat. This machine," he gestured toward the telemetry unit, "tells us her heart is beating normally now. Thanks to modern medicine, we have her stabilized. Basically, she'll pull through this physically."

"Physically, yes. But...what about emotionally?" Tina's mother whispered.

"That will be tougher," Ruger spoke quietly, inadvertently clenching his teeth at the uninvited recall of his own grotesque childhood, one he'd scarcely survived physically, never mind mentally. "*Much* tougher," he added thickly, and noted with satisfaction that all three women paled at this pronouncement.

"Any other questions?" Ruger reached into the right pocket of his white coat, his fingers curling around the hypodermic case. With a full syringe and only one drop of poison needed to kill, why not inject a small amount into Tina's IV tube and save the remainder to inoculate the other three women? How stupid were they? Could he explain this as an antibiotic to prevent their further endangering his fragile patient with accidental infections she couldn't tolerate? In their eagerness to help Tina, they just might fall for it.

He pulled the case from his pocket and extracted the hypodermic syringe. Removing the plunger shield, he snapped off the needle protector and reached for Tina's IV tube.

CHAPTER 63

Twenty minutes after the girls rushed toward the hospital, Adam sat quietly in the Shannons' darkened living room and stared at his cell phone. Something tickled the back of his mind, something unspecific yet nagging.

Had he overlooked an important detail? Again, he reviewed the circumstances, focusing his detective's experience on what he knew about this case. Still at large, if this "Yates" were in this area he couldn't return to his house, now a guarded crime scene. He apparently escaped the farm either in Mrs. Shannon's missing van or another car stashed there. Assuming he had wheels, if unable to exact revenge on her due to police presence at her house, what would he do next?

As a *wanted* man, Yates could flee the area, perhaps returning to seek vengeance in the future, or remain inconspicuous to risk revenge now, the latter justifying Adam's protection of the Shannon family. As a *wounded* man, he might seek medical attention. Adam already started that search through police channels to hospitals and physicians.

Was Ruger on the run or did he lurk nearby? Adam drew upon all his training, experience and intuition, to get inside the perp's head and psych out his next move. He'd dispatched Shannon family members to various locations, knew where to reach them. This protected them against the worst eventuality, but his nagging concern persisted. What had he overlooked?

He'd stationed other cops outside the house, while he covered the inside. The existing security alarm and new locks tomorrow would offer some protection, although who knew better than a cop that determined perps could always gain entry if sufficiently clever and fearless? Would Hannah and the others eventually be safe here from that vengeful maniac?

Lost in thought, Adam startled at the ring of his cell phone. Had the girls reached the hospital? Had Tina taken a turn for the worst? Bracing for bad news, he flipped the phone on and identified himself.

"This is the McLean District Station calling. Two things: forensics made a fingerprint ID on the abductor in the Shannon case. His name is Ruger Yates."

"Okay, got it. And the second thing?"

"You just received an urgent call. It's about the Shannon case. He won't talk with anyone but you. Can you copy the number?"

Fumbling for pen and paper, Adam wrote rapidly as he listened.

"Thanks."

Dialing the unfamiliar number and extension, Adam identified himself and heard, "Brad Billings from OnStar, Detective. Remember me?"

"Of course!"

"I offered to do a periodic GPS check on Mrs. Shannon's van for another twenty-four hours. Well, I'm on night duty and followed through on that."

"Yes," Adam's voice reflected immediate interest.

"The van's been moved, all right, and we've pinpointed the new location. The vehicle was no longer in transit when I found it on the screen, so we don't know where it was before, but we know the location now and it appears to be parked."

"Where?" Adam hoped he hadn't shouted his excitement into the phone.

"In downtown McLean, on a street near the intersection of Center Road and Redmond Road."

Adam scribbled the information quickly. "I know right where that is, by Chain Bridge Corner shopping center. Brad, thanks, man! This information is *really* important right now."

"Is the woman still missing?"

Antsy to get on this new lead, Adam owed an explanation to someone volunteering so vital a clue. "We found her alive just a few hours ago. Now we're after her abductor, who we think has her car. Got to go! Again, thanks Brad, for sticking with this."

"Glad to learn she's safe. Good-bye."

Adam hurried to phone this new information to the dispatcher. "Get Crime Scene on it as fast as you can for forensics. Check stolen car reports in that general area in case he traded wheels. Let me know right away what you find. Thanks."

His thoughts turned again to Hannah. The girls should be at the hospital by now. Certainly, they'd be safe en route, driving in their locked car. And at the hospital, with lots of people around, how could the girls be vulnerable there?

Now, how to fit this new OnStar puzzle piece into the picture? The man could have changed cars in a dozen crowded places safer than McLean, suggesting his presence here was deliberate. But where was he this very minute? Absent the perp's focus on Jennifer Shannon, who else posed a threat to him besides the police?

It came to him in a flash: Tina MacKenzie! After the man's merciless treatment of her, if she survived she'd describe first-hand her captivity and abuse. Would he silence her first before Mrs. Shannon? Had he called local hospitals, asking about her? No, that wouldn't work because of her admission alias, the "Jane Doe" name known only to certain high level hospital staff and to police, neither of whom acknowledge these victims were in the facility in order to protect them. No, the man couldn't know Tina's whereabouts, unless...

Grabbing his cell phone, Adam dialed Hannah. "Your call has been forwarded to an automatic voice answering machine," the recorded voice droned. But Hannah's cell phone was supposed to be turned on! He dialed Becca's number. Same message!

Quickly he phoned headquarters. "Iverson here. Reason to believe suspected killer in two abduction cases may be at Fairfax County Hospital, possibly targeting Tina MacKenzie, a former victim currently a patient there. Send nearest available unit to secure. That's Room 1074 in Tower 10 West. Do you copy?"

"Affirmative!"

"And hurry," Adam shouted into the phone. Rushing to the back door of the Shannon house, he called outside, "Miguel, I need to get to the hospital *now*. Tell the others to cover for you on the outside perimeter and take over for me inside."

"You got it," Miguel called back.

Adam rushed out the front door, threw himself into his cruiser and tore away from the house. At 80-90 miles an hour, with little traffic and his siren whooping, he might get there in 10 minutes or less. He roared out of the development, past the elementary school and careened left onto Spring Hill Road. His police speed-pass automatically opened the tollbooth barrier as he sped through and turned south onto the beltway, his speedometer nudging 100 mph.

Reaching Gallows Road, he rocketed onto the exit ramp and two minutes later turned into the hospital complex. Driving straight up under the hospital's porte-cochere entrance, he braked to a skidding halt on the far side of the horseshoe driveway. Hoping for the first time ever that his hunch was wrong, he jumped out of the cruiser, his hand on his holster.

CHAPTER 64

While Tina breathed evenly in her drug-induced slumber, the three women focused in unison on Dr. Prescott. He held Tina's IV tube in his left hand as his right hand raised the hypodermic. A cruel smile crossed his lips as he calculated which would kill her first, the air bubble which doctors meticulously avoid injecting or the toxic serum he was about to administer.

But aware the women's eyes followed his every gesture and reveling in his doctor role, he couldn't resist posturing one more time for this riveted audience. Lifting the hypodermic up toward the light and gently inserting the plunger until a tiny drop of liquid glistened on the needle's point, he eliminated the possibility of any air in the syringe. Relishing his on-lookers' reverent gazes, he felt almost disappointed that this part of his plan must end so soon.

A nurse bustled into the room and closed the door, stepping back quickly when she saw the man in the white coat. Her surprise entrance and her anxious expression shifted everyone's attention and put Ruger on guard.

"Oh, Doctor, I... I didn't realize you were here. Have you a moment to... to step outside and go over the patient's chart?" Her voice rose, "It's an *urgent* question about the patient's meds!"

Just then the door flew open, bashing against the adjacent wall. Everyone in the room—including Ruger—recoiled at the sharp noise as all eyes turned to the armed policeman crouching in the doorway, his pistol trained directly on Ruger.

The three women gasped in confusion and shock. Sneering, Ruger dropped the IV tube in his left hand and grabbed Hannah, who stood right next to him. In one swift movement, his beefy left arm encircled her small waist and he jerked her so tight against him that she choked for air. Holding the needle menacingly near her throat, he edged the two of them toward the door.

"It's an easy decision for you, copper," Ruger hissed. "I escape with my hostage or she gets a shot of poison in her carotid artery. One drop and she's dead in seconds. Your call, Mister. Now throw down your gun and kick it over here."

Still crouching, the policeman thought fast. Give up the pistol and you give up the advantage, his police academy training drilled. He stared uncomfortably at the terrified girl with instant death centimeters from her neck. What if his own teenage daughter was this hostage and a different policeman stood in his place? Would he want that cop to risk a shot, perhaps sacrificing his daughter's life?

"Don't move," he shouted to Ruger, recognizing this as a hostage situation requiring the experienced crisis team. Still pointing his weapon at Ruger with one hand, he lifted out his cell phone with the other to call them when Tina moaned loudly, stirred on the bed, and for the first time since her rescue, opened her eyes.

Her first glance fell upon her mother and she managed a frail smile, then toward Becca and the smile increased as much as cut lips and swollen face allowed. Encouraged by these loving faces, her eyes moved cautiously across the unfamiliar hospital room, first passing by and then snapping back in revulsion to where Ruger stood, clutching Hannah.

Tina's eyes widened in horror at the nightmarish sight of the very tormenter who'd captured, tortured and tried to kill her. *HERE!* Right next to her! A ragged cry formed in her damaged throat, then escaped her lips in a hideous half-animal scream of anguish.

While the others cringed at Tina's wrenching cries, Ruger reveled in them, having deliberately elicited such screams from victims. But even before Tina recognized him, Ruger knew he had the upper hand the moment the policeman decided not to risk the hostage by shooting him. This knowledge gave a new twist to his earlier plan and Tina's hysteria provided the perfect distraction for his next move.

With the same brash confidence displayed in daring escapes during jungle warfare, he gripped Hannah so tightly that she gasped again while he side-stepped them both right up to the door, inches from the policeman's pointed pistol. With a sinister smile, Ruger looked directly into the policeman's eyes as he edged himself and the girl past the pistol's muzzle and out the door. As the cop's gun trained impotently toward him, Ruger backed down the hallway, the girl shielding him.

Moments later they entered the elevator and as its mechanical door slid shut, Ruger purred into Hannah's ear, "Now you listen to me very carefully, sweetheart. Besides this syringe, I have a gun in my pocket. Both are deadly. If you don't do exactly as I say, you're a goner. Do you understand?" He jerked Hannah's stomach so sharply that she cried out in pain and coughed to regain her breath. Struggling to inhale, she nodded.

"You walk right in front of me through the lobby as if everything's okay, and once outside we're going to take a little ride. If you're good, I'll drop you unharmed at the nearest corner." In truth, once at his car, he would inject her and kick her body under the next parked car, guaranteeing a grisly find for some unwitting motorist. "So do exactly as I say and I won't hurt you," he lied.

Ruger's knees trembled as a film of sweat formed on his forehead. With one arm clutching Hannah and the syringe in his other hand, he leaned on the elevator wall for support. Even without sleep on lengthy missions, his stamina was legendary, so it must be this damned hole in his gut. Looking down at his white coat, he cursed the pinkish ooze staining the cloth.

Before the elevator door opened on the main floor, Ruger released his grip on Hannah just long enough to snap the plastic guard back on the hypodermic needle and place it into his trouser pocket, exchanging it for his pistol. Nearly asphyxiated by the pressure of Ruger's powerful arm squeezing her ribcage, Hannah gulped air in a frantic attempt to fill her starving lungs.

Ruger waved his gun before her eyes. "You see this? You'll feel it in your back the whole way." In fact, he dropped the weapon out of sight into his pocket, instead prodding her back hard with his forefinger as she faltered, too frightened to walk.

"Move," he growled in her ear and prodded again until, eyes wide with fright, she struggled forward. They crossed the lobby, nearly deserted at this hour except for the information receptionist absorbed at her computer and the security guard, distracted by someone asking a question.

Ruger pushed Hannah across the waiting room to the entrance, where the automatic doors flared open for their exit. He again withdrew his pistol, using its barrel to shove her roughly through the hospital door ahead of him.

Stumbling along in front of Ruger, her brain fogged with terror, Hannah thought she envisioned a policeman on the sidewalk, his weapon pointed at them. And not just any policeman, but Adam! She shook her head to clear this mirage, but the policeman remained in place. Deciphering this apparent hallucination as reality propelled her into action.

"Run, Hannah!" Adam shouted, and she did.

Ruger Yates swung his weapon toward the fleeing Hannah and prepared to fire as a wave of dizziness clouded his aim. He rocked in place, his left hand clutching his throbbing belly.

Desperate to distract the gunman's attention from Hannah, Adam taunted, "So, you like bullying girls but piss your pants when you face a man? Give it up, Yates. We know what you've done."

Ruger turned his menacing attention to Adam, lifting his weapon and aiming it at Adam's heart.

"Then one more won't matter," Ruger roared and, fixing his sharpshooter accuracy on Adam's chest, he squeezed the trigger.

Seconds before Ruger's shot, the policeman earlier dispatched to guard Tina upstairs had dashed down ten flights of stairs and across the lobby. Weapon in hand, he aimed toward and blasted Ruger's gun hand, deflecting the bullet intended for Adam. Grimacing, Ruger dropped his pistol and clutched his temporarily paralyzed fingers. As the other cop rushed to subdue and cuff him, Adam trained his weapon on Ruger.

Despite his numbed hand and the oozing hole in his side, Ruger fought too wildly for the other cop to get the upper hand. Holding the pistol in his right hand, Adam closed in to assist the take-down with his left hand, when Ruger abruptly kicked the weapon from his fingers.

Adam joined in the melee. He had never seen anyone with such devastating close-quarters fighting skill. Ruger roared savagely, landing blow after blow. Adam doubted now that even the two of them could overpower him.

As if sensing Adam's thought, the second cop grunted as they struggled, "Backup's rolling... here... any minute. And... hospital security."

Skilled by years of hand-to-hand combat, even in his weakened condition Ruger landed enough crushing blows, chops and kicks on both cops to break free. As Adam vainly sought his gun, he realized the other cop lay on the pavement, unconscious from Ruger's barrage of punches to his head and chest. The sight of his comrade down galvanized Adam with new energy. He lunged after Ruger and with a flying tackle, grabbed him hard enough around the hips to send them both sprawling on the ground.

As Adam raised his fist for a smashing blow to his opponent's upturned face, he hesitated. Something was wrong. Ruger lay limp and unresisting on the pavement, his arms askew, eyes staring and a stain spreading across his trousers at the loss of control over his body functions.

"What the hell... a heart attack?" Panting from exertion, Adam lurched to his feet, spied and grabbed his weapon. Confused at his seemingly lifeless quarry, he still pointed his loaded pistol into Ruger's face to foil any trick.

Moaning, the second cop sat up, rubbed the bruise on his forehead, and wheezed through bleeding lips, "Upstairs he waved a hypodermic, said it contained poison. Maybe..."

"Cover me," Adam said as he kneeled to check Ruger's carotid pulse, then shook his head. "This guy's gone. Let's take a look."

"Careful, *careful!* He said even one drop could kill!"

Together they eased open Ruger's lab coat. Beneath it, jutting from a torn trouser pocket, they saw the top of a syringe. Cutting the pocket open revealed an intact hypodermic, its needle jammed through the cloth of the man's trousers and imbedded to the hilt into his flesh, the plunger pushed home.

Police sirens wailed, growing louder every second as cruisers closed in from several directions and hospital security personnel rushed out to assist them.

Just before the cruisers screeched onto the scene, the second policeman spoke through his broken teeth, "Geez, it must have stabbed into him when you brought him down."

Wiping the sweat from his forehead, Adam holstered his weapon. "Damn," he breathed heavily, "if that needle pointed in a different direction, I'd be lying there dead instead of him!"

CHAPTER 65

A day later, Adam investigated the case's newest clue: utility company payment history for 3508 Winding Trail Road. A prominent McLean attorney had signed those monthly checks for at least twenty-five years.

Curious about the direction this might take, Adam anticipated brief, guarded answers, since lawyers tended to give law enforcement the minimum information legally required. Attorney-client privilege justified this, plus the strategy that fewer facts given meant fewer to bite back in the courtroom. Adam expected little from the interview.

"Come in, Detective Iverson. I'm Greg Bromley." The attorney welcomed Adam into his office. "Coffee, soda, homemade cookies?" Bromley asked, indicating two comfortably facing chairs with a low table between.

"Thank you, Sir, and okay to the cookies. They smell good." Shaking his hand, Adam did a double-take of this man, momentarily feeling the familiar "haven't-we-met-before" connection, yet knowing they had not.

"I'm absolutely shocked at what I read in this morning's newspaper," Bromley began as a secretary brought in the cookies. "It's unbelievable. Multiple murders at a place I often visited... by a boy I tried to help. I had no idea... no idea at all." His voice trailed away as he shook his head in disbelief and stared vacantly out the window for a long moment.

Finally, Adam cleared his throat, the sound drawing Bromley back to the present. In a stronger voice, the attorney said, "Actually, I intended contacting you today, but you beat me to it! Good detective work," the older man congratulated him. "My finding you as the detective working this case would have been easy, but how did you find me?"

Cautious with this likeable individual who played an as yet undetermined role in an important case, Adam answered, "I followed the money, Sir."

"Of course! I not only was Mrs. Yates's attorney but also paid her bills, which would be a matter of record. Now I'll bet you're wondering what light I can shed on this bizarre situation?"

"Exactly," the detective agreed. Despite Bromley's well-respected reputation and pleasant demeanor, Adam would evaluate this man as they talked, because everyone connected with a case was a person of interest until otherwise categorized.

"All right, how can I help you?"

"Why not just tell me everything about your experience with the Yates family."

Bromley leaned back in his chair to collect his thoughts. "This case really troubles me, Detective." He sighed. "With all the principals dead I think attorney-client privilege is flexible. Besides, I want to understand it just as you do, so I'll tell you the whole story."

Adam tried to hide his surprise. Reaching for a cookie, he maintained eye contact with Bromley.

"You want to 'know everything,'" the attorney repeated. "I'm nearly sixty now, so this starts *way* back! Long before she married Yates, Ruger's mother Wendey and I were high school sweethearts and again in college. She was a vision: lovely, cheerful, intelligent. A beautiful person in every sense." He smiled at his memory of her. "We graduated in the same Virginia Tech class. Then she taught school in McLean and I was a summer intern here for an attorney before entering law school. We were inseparable! We were in love! We wanted to spend our lives together. The truth is, even after what happened, I never married… because I didn't stop loving her."

"After what happened?" Adam repeated.

"We were the perfect couple until that day when we met for lunch. We each had something important to tell the other, but she insisted I tell my news first. We were both laughing and I was so excited I could hardly talk. I told her I'd been accepted at law school that very morning. This news clinched our future together because we always planned to wait until I earned my law degree before we married. We discussed it often and agreed it made sense since we were both young, had little money and I needed loans to pay for law school. I wanted to be able to support a wife and the children we hoped for, which meant graduating first. She heard me talk about it often enough since I'd dreamed of becoming a lawyer ever since I could remember."

Bromley shifted in his chair as if the memory still made him uncomfortable.

"Naturally, I thought she'd be thrilled with my news, but instead she clasped her hands across her stomach and I can still see her stricken expression when I spoke about waiting. Instead of welcoming my news, she changed in an instant from the glowing person who walked into that restaurant into someone with a broken heart. She said she loved me too much to destroy my dreams and ran from the restaurant. I was flabbergasted! I ran after her but she disappeared. I phoned her dozens of times, but she wouldn't answer. I pounded on her front door, begging her to talk to me, but she wouldn't. I was half crazy because she was the love of my life. And..."

After an awkward silence, Adam prompted, "And...?"

"And two weeks later she eloped with Tobias Yates, an awful man. She'd joked about rebuffing his coarse advances for months. When I learned they'd eloped, I was stunned, hurt, angry and jealous, but at the same time I felt guilty. Whatever I said at lunch that day changed our relationship. What seemed so logical to me seemed to devastate her. I didn't understand it then and I don't understand it now."

"What happened next?" Adam asked.

"When I learned about her sudden marriage and their move to his farm, I went there to ask for an explanation, but Tobias found us talking in the farm driveway and went ballistic. He beat me up, physically threw me off his property and said he'd kill me if I came near her again. I believed him! So I tried adjusting to the reality that she married someone else, that I couldn't undo it and that I must accept it. But I couldn't stop loving her. I'd drive by their house, hoping for just the sight of her, but to no avail."

"Did you see her again?"

"Yes, about seven years later but under terrible circumstances. Are you familiar with the Miriam Yates murder case?

"Why don't you refresh my memory?"

"Wendey's mean, crazy husband suffocated their three-year-old daughter, Miriam. He said he couldn't revive the child after she fell down the cellar steps, but the police found signs of physical and sexual abuse that didn't track with his explanation. Remember, this was over thirty-five years ago, before anyone knew about DNA, so we couldn't pinpoint guilt as we can now."

"How did you get involved?" Adam reached for another cookie.

"Wendey sent me a letter, begging me to defend her husband. I don't know if it was her idea or his, but she was a gentle person who I knew didn't believe in capital punishment. Frankly, I took the case in order to be near her again. But when I saw her, she'd changed almost unrecognizably in those seven years... from the neat, happy, capable person I'd known and loved into the disheveled, depressed neurotic she'd become."

Bromley stared into space as if seeing her ghost in the room with them.

"I pled insanity for Tobias and it wasn't hard to convince the jury since he looked and acted like a madman every day in court. By the time he was sent to a nearby mental institution, Wendey's deterioration had progressed too far beyond normal to restart our romance. Still, I loved her 'in sickness and in health.' She was my lady!"

"With Yates gone, did she improve?" Adam asked.

"No, I think she had a nervous breakdown — not surprising with her daughter's terrible death, her husband a murderer in an insane asylum and a farm to run. Turns out she also had two little boys to raise. I begged her to get psychiatric help, but she flatly refused. She also wouldn't accept my offer to find a person to help with housework and farm chores. The more I pressed, the more upset she became, so I decided to care for her the best I could."

"How did she manage there alone?"

"She convinced me she'd mastered a simple, mostly self-sufficient life on the farm and *refused* to leave her home voluntarily. I hated the idea of removing her forcibly, a change which might even destroy her remaining sanity. Also, I hoped in time I could persuade her to get the psychiatric help she needed. I agonized after every visit about how best to help her and finally concluded not to interfere...unless necessary for her safety. Neurotic and eccentric yes, but at the farm she lived free as opposed to a drugged, dehumanizing existence in a mental institution. I'd seen a few such facilities and balked at the thought of committing her to one."

"Did she have any other contacts outside the farm besides you?"

"I was the only person she trusted, so I began visiting her; every week at first, then every two weeks, then at least once a month. She made short lists of things she needed, so I brought flour, sugar, coffee and so on, to supplement food from the farm."

"And how does Ruger fit in to this?" Adam asked.

"Ah, here the plot thickens. First, her three children were born at home and I found no birth certificates recorded for any of them. I suspect that creepy Tobias masterminded that. Eventually, I legally prepared one for Ruger, to enter him into society. Second, when the home and farm buildings were searched during the little girl's murder investigation, they found no other children and both parents denied having any. Wendey apparently hid her two boys and all evidence that they existed. I didn't know about them myself until several months afterward. In most homes, children and their toys are easily visible inside or outdoors. But there? No trace."

"Then how did you learn about the boys?"

"Of necessity my visits were unannounced because Wendey had no phone and wouldn't let me install one. When I finally saw the boys at a distance and asked about them, she told me their names but when I went outside to say hello, they disappeared. The next time I came they were in the house, but when they saw me they ran like scared rabbits. That happened to be one of Wendey's better days and she revealed they were indeed her sons but very shy and afraid of strangers. When I asked to talk to them, she said they weren't 'social' and besides they had chores."

Adam wrote some notes on his pad. "So you were curious about them."

"You're right. When I asked their ages and where they went to school, she said they were five and six and she home-schooled them, which tracked with her teaching background. After that, I always looked for them, brought them school supplies, candy bars and little gifts for her to give them at Christmas. I rarely saw them, even then always at a distance, and so never spoke to them. Of course, I asked myself if she was in any condition to raise kids, but the house looked tidy, she showed me the boys' bedroom, the refrigerator had enough food and from a distance I personally had seen nothing to suggest mistreatment or neglect."

Bromley walked to his office wet-bar and filled a glass with water."Would you like something to drink?"

"Oh, no thanks. So how did you discover there was a problem?"

"On one visit when I asked after the boys, she told me Mathis was 'gone,' but where would a child his age go? She'd mentioned earlier having no living relatives, so who would he visit? I pressed her about Mathis, but she clammed up tight. I chalked it up to temporary confusion. She gave the same explanation about him on my future visits. Then, as I left the farm one day, I found the younger boy examining my car in the driveway. Before he could bolt, I grabbed his arm and took a really close look at him for the first time, sickened at what I saw."

"What *did* you see?"

"Bruises, scars… It was obvious he'd been abused. I knew then I had to get both boys, or at least Ruger, out of that environment. But I wanted to do it in a way that avoided the authorities taking Wendey also. My problem was how to make that happen."

CHAPTER 66

A mazed at Bromley's unexpected "need to talk" and the resulting cathartic stream-of-consciousness, Adam paid close attention. "So did you make that happen?"

"I had the younger boy by the arm and knew he'd vanish again if I didn't hold on. He was really terrified. He fought me like a wild animal, almost as if he thought I was going to take a bite out of him. I finally maneuvered him back into the house where he calmed down a little when Wendey told him I was not a stranger but a friend. Funny, he looked at us as if he didn't know what 'friend' meant. But now that I had him, I wracked my brain for some solution."

"What did you come up with?"

"When I was young, my parents sent me to board for a semester at a prep school to bring up my grades and," he chuckled, "to improve my behavior. Back then, I hated trading my comfortable life at home for a 24/7 academic environment, but I looked back on it later as a positive experience. Still, I expected Wendey to veto such a plan for her son, given her mental state and fear of 'outsiders.' "

"How *did* she react?"

"Imagine my surprise when she offered no resistance to my boarding school suggestion! She said she didn't want Ruger in the first place and hoped he never came back. She said it right in front of him! This had to be her illness talking. Now, I was always gentle with her before, but this time I needed her attention so I shouted that I wanted to take the bigger boy as well. This seemed to terrify her *and* the younger boy, as if they knew something but dared not tell. They both stared at me wild-eyed as she screamed again and again that Mathis was *gone* and would never come back."

"What did you do?"

"I took Ruger away that day, spruced him up presentably, fed him well and drove him to a military school in southern Virginia. I'd known the commandant there from earlier days when we served together in Vietnam. I convinced my friend the boy's miserable home life meant he'd be safer and better prepared for life at the academy."

"And he agreed?"

"In an odd twist of fate, my proposal played right into the commandant's own need at that time. He was trying to keep his academy afloat financially and the long-term enrollment of every student counted toward his school's solvency. So he and I struck a special bargain. Ruger's mother would pay extra for him to stay for summer school and holidays, besides his regular tuition. Like the military service itself, these academies are well-versed in 'straightening out' troubled boys, so Ruger fit right in. He enrolled at age six and didn't return home during his twelve years at the academy. This arrangement sounds extraordinary now but was uniquely possible back then."

"How did that work out?"

"The commandant knew the real story, but the boy understood himself to be an orphan with a guardian who paid his bills. He seemed to accept this and adjust quickly to his new environment. He made above-average grades with high scores in military aptitude and marksmanship. Remember, in contrast to his chaotic home life, the order, predictability, nutritious food, regular meals, reasonable discipline and health care at the school were immediate pluses for the boy. They sent me regular reports about his progress and, although I gave the originals to Ruger about five months ago, I made copies you're welcome to look at here in the office."

"How did he spend summers?" Adam asked.

"He went to the academy's summer school and then the commandant paid members of his academic staff to care for Ruger in their homes the remaining month. The staff liked earning extra money and Ruger seemed a quiet child, offering little trouble except for suspicion that he mistreated their pets.

Some animals disappeared during Ruger's visits, which might have been coincidental except for what we now know about him."

"What about holidays during the school year?"

"The academy pretty much closed down during Easter, Christmas and Thanksgiving, leaving only a few cadets on campus. With the mess hall dark, the school ordered special meals for this handful of students and a skeleton staff stayed to supervise them. Occasionally, a compassionate teacher at the school invited Ruger to spend a holiday at his home, or he was invited to the home of another classmate, but those visits must not have worked out well because they were infrequent and not repeated at the same places. The school sent me this information in their regular reports."

"Did you make contact with Ruger during that time?"

"I wish now I had, but wrestling with the decision then, I thought it would complicate more than improve his life. He'd want to know who I was and about his mother, with whom no productive connection existed. I thought of entertaining him for holidays or cheering at his graduation but drew back each time. Hell, I even thought once about adopting the little tyke, but with no wife, I hadn't a traditional home life to offer him. While I loved his mother, I detested his father, and he was that man's spitting image. Somehow, I just couldn't warm up to the kid for the kind of commitment which, once started, should continue." Bromley grew pensive again.

Adam broke another long silence, "And when he graduated...?"

Bromley nodded, "With no welcoming home and life-skills learned at academy, joining a uniformed service was logical and he did. Afterward, I lost track of him, but at least knew where to start looking when his mother died."

"Can you think of anything else?"

"No, except I'll tell you, Detective, I'm really broken up about this whole thing. I never imagined the situation could turn out this way. If I hadn't brought Ruger back to McLean, two local women would be alive today and that poor girl he tortured would be whole again. If I'd thought back then that I might have made a positive difference in Ruger's life, perhaps I'd have acted differently, but now that's in the past."

Adam's silence encouraged Bromley to fill the conversation's void again. "Strange, but I'm haunted as well by that other boy, Mathis. I have an awful feeling that your digging at the farm might uncover his body, which would be a grisly explanation for his being 'gone.' If so, I also failed to rescue *him* in time. This twenty-twenty hindsight is cruel stuff."

Looking haggard, Bromley changed the subject, "Now will you tell me something? What about Wendey? Have you found the explanation for her transformation once she married that man?"

"We have evidence that Tobias Yates savagely abused his three children and their mother. It must have been a nightmarish environment for them all."

Ashen, Bromley held his head in his hands, "My beloved Wendey… put through that horror, not in some medieval dungeon centuries ago but right here, today, in McLean, Virginia. It just doesn't seem possible!"

"Sir, you'd be shocked at what police see every day in Fairfax County. In fact, it's…" Adam's voice wavered, thinking of gory situations detectives confronted, "…unbelievable."

"If only she hadn't married that man, so many lives would be different!" Bromley produced a handkerchief and blew his nose several times.

Standing, Adam laid his business card on the table. "If you think of anything else, please contact me, Sir. I'll let myself out."

"Why did she do it?" Bromley muttered as Adam stepped into the hall, closing the door quietly behind him.

A few minutes later in Bromley's conference room, Adam sat alone, contemplating the unopened file of Ruger's school reports the secretary had placed on the table in front of him.

He thought about Bromley's tale, marveling that this otherwise intelligent, capable lawyer remained so blind to the obvious. *Bromley* was the one who'd pushed this iceberg into the water, creating the ripples that ultimately washed against so many other lives.

Why did Wendey do it? Adam had a hunch: She was pregnant thirty-five years ago when abortion was illegal and out-of-wedlock babies brought scandal and ridicule. She loved Bromley too much to trap him into an inconvenient marriage. So to avoid ruining his life-plan and presumed brilliant future career, her solution was wedding Tobias Yates! Bad enough to willingly resign herself to a loveless marriage, but catastrophic to discover too late that instead of a man, she'd married a monster!

Though circumstantial, the evidence fit perfectly.

Mathis was Bromley's son!

CHAPTER 67

Following his morning meeting with Greg Bromley, Adam drove across the gently rolling green hills of pastoral Virginia countryside to his impromptu appointment with the commandant of the military school which Ruger once attended. After a productive forty-five minute interview there, he returned to Fairfax County by 3:30 p.m. to meet with the Medical Examiner. His watch showed 4:00 as he drove toward the police station to prepare his case report.

When his phone rang, dispatcher Akeesha's melodic voice sounded in his ear. "If this is hero-of-the-moment, Detective Iverson, McManus wants to see you in his office when you finish with the M. E. Oh, and you have two messages from a pretty little voice named Hannah."

Adam brightened. "Thanks, Akeesha."

Twenty minutes later, he pulled into the police station parking lot and in another five he knocked on Number One's door.

"Come on in, Adam," Jim McManus welcomed him enthusiastically.

A big, broad, animated, fiftyish man of Irish descent, McManus had a thick head of wavy gray-streaked black hair and bushy brows above expressive hazel eyes that brimmed with life — twinkling when he joked, which was often, and piercingly inquisitive when all-business. Above his disarming smile were the keen mind and sharp eyes of the detective he was for twenty-three years.

Demanding as it was, straight police work comprised only part of McManus' challenge in privileged Vienna, McLean and Great Falls; inevitable exposure to politics, the rest. Congressmen, senators, lobbyists and all the wealthy in Fairfax County expected — sometimes demanded — preferential treatment. Moreover, the proximity of this upscale suburb to the nation's capital lured embassy personnel, adding confusion where cultural distinctions, language differences and diplomatic immunity complicated police issues. All things considered, McManus handled his nearly impossible task with remarkable skill.

Sure, he was the boss, but Adam liked him anyway.

"Good to see you, lad. You're here straight from the M.E.? Good! So, what did we learn from Mr. Ruger Yates?"

"Remember telling me to pay attention and I'd learn something new every day on the job?" Adam began as his boss nodded and leaned back in his chair. "I thought the plastic safety cap that snaps over a hypodermic needle gave foolproof accident protection. But the M.E. reminded me those needle caps snap right off when ready for use. In Yates's case, the needle cap worked free and unsnapped so that when he fought with us, the unprotected part of the needle broke off. The larger piece of the broken needle stayed in the detached cap, but enough needle stub remained on the syringe to jab through his clothes and into his skin. The plunger must have pushed home when I tackled him at the end of our scuffle."

"Scuffle, was it? I hear that hardly describes it," McManus chuckled. "So what was in the syringe?"

"The toxicology report says it's a deadly poison taken from certain dart frogs in Central and South America. Sounded sci-fi to me since frogs here are harmless, but Yates had access to bizarre stuff through his Special Forces connections."

"Frog poison? Hah, I thought I'd heard everything but that is a new one. And just how do they get the frog to cooperate?" McManus flashed his famous smile, eyebrows raised.

"Toxicology says they 'agitate' the frog so he excretes this poison out of pores in his back."

McManus chuckled. "Now, how the hell do you *agitate* a frog?"

"The natives poke a stick down its throat and if that doesn't do it, they use the stick as a handle to hold the frog over fire. Stuff like that."

"So poison he intended for others got him instead! Some poetic justice there, don't you think?"

"Yes, but he was also stabbed in the abdomen with a four-inch screwdriver. The M.E. says," Adam read from his notes, "'a two centimeter laceration punctured the subject's descending sigmoid colon on the lower left side. Besides causing pain and some bleeding, that wound would have needed suturing and a drain within another few hours for him to survive.' Obviously, the fist fight with us messed it up even more."

"So he was going out one way or the other, eh? Well, he *did* save the taxpayers the bundle for his prosecution, jailing and execution. And who knows better than we do that sometimes the guilty get off during trial after all, despite our efforts." McManus sat up. "What else?"

Adam told him about the Bromley interview. "The man honestly thought he rescued the boy and put him in a safe place. But knowing now about the nine murders, he's carrying a load of guilt for not intervening differently." Adam then described his visit with the military school's commandant that corroborated Bromley's earlier information. "Bromley located her surviving son and heir in the US Army after Mrs. Yates died. That soldier was Ruger Yates."

"Anything revealing in his service report?"

"Actually, yes. You know how secretive those covert guys are, so most of his file is censored. But I phoned a friend of mine in Special Forces. He didn't know Yates but knew of him. He told me Yates was under suspicion for the disappearances of three women near different bases where he was stationed. Their bodies were never found but he was the last known person seen with them. With only circumstantial evidence against him, they took no official action. Instead, they got rid of their problem each time by transferring him to a new assignment."

"So a pattern fits?"

"Yes, Sir," Adam agreed. "According to my friend, Yates had impressive sharpshooter rifle skills. Even so, with those unresolved cases, the Army wasn't entirely disappointed when he resigned to go home to take over the property he inherited."

"And we inherited something too, didn't we..." McManus said, "...a serial killer!"

CHAPTER 68

cManus answered the phone, made the call short, and returned to Adam's briefing. "So it turns out the perp had a wee fetish, did he?" McManus queried.

"He sure did! Until we found his victims' purses hidden under his office floorboards, those Army cases remained unsolved. What a break that the handbags contained their original contents, expecially the women's ID's."

"He liked trophies, eh?" McManus said. "So we solved nine crimes with one: the two lucky women you rescued here in the nick of time, the three he did in the service, another from Maryland plus one from Pennsylvania and the two who were our own unfortunate McLean casualties. What about the digging at the Yates property?"

"It's a fifteen-acre farm. Graves could be anywhere. We're using cadaver dogs to locate bodies. The remains of the two local adult females you just mentioned were found five feet deep and not near each other. We assume who they are from the degree of corpse decomposition and the purse information under the floorboards, but not which one is which. Their dental and DNA should be in tomorrow. We're still looking for more bodies. But here's an odd twist. The graves with the women's bodies were unmarked, but the mound near the house with a cross on top that looks like a grave was empty.

"Figure that one!" McManus gave a mirthless chuckle.

"Here's another hard one: why did the mother continue the abuse the father started once he was sent away to that institution? She had to be half nuts herself by then to keep assaulting her children. We've pieced together things done to these little boys that were..." he groped for words, "...worse than POW interrogations, and these were just kids! Whatever child protection programs they had back then must have been underfunded and overworked."

McManus gave another wry laugh, "...just as they are now. It's mighty tough work they do."

"Sir, I happen to know firsthand that our county's Child Protective Service is an effective operation. I investigated one report myself and saw how they rescued the kid, arranged his rehabilitation treatment and provided information for us to arrest and prosecute the abuser."

A frown darkened McManus' expression as he shook his head in disgust. "After all these years on the force, I still can't stomach this damn brutality to the little ones. We think we've seen everything, don't we, lad? Then this comes along." McManus changed the subject. "Mrs. Shannon stumbled into Yates via that garage sale ruse, right? The other dead women can't tell us how he lured them, but has the young girl revealed how he got her?"

"Yes and, Sir, you may want to advise the media about this for public awareness. He took Tina MacKenzie at a fast-mart store around 10:00 p.m. She says the area was nearly deserted except for a black pickup truck that pulled up next to her. She made a purchase, returned to her vehicle and locked its door. She was about to start her car when he tapped on her window. She was wary but the man was neatly-dressed, gave her a friendly smile and didn't try to jerk her car door open. This was a public place, so she felt safe. Then he held up a five dollar bill and told her through the closed window that she'd dropped it when she left the store. She thought he was nice to return the money instead of pocketing it. So she rolled down the window to take the cash and thank him for his honesty. Adam paused, picturing the scene.

"And..." McManus pressed.

"And when the window was open he pressed a smelly, damp cloth hard against her face. Probably chloroform or an equivalent. It happened so fast, she couldn't scream or defend herself. Nobody witnessed the incident to help her. The store clerk saw and heard nothing, or so he said. He didn't even recognize her picture...

and no surveillance tapes because their cameras were broken. Possibly Yates disabled them earlier. The girl woke up gagged and restrained in the front seat of Yates's pickup truck. Back at his house, he locked her in that cellar 'confinement box,' the same one where he put Mrs. Shannon. So that probably was part of his regular routine with captives."

"What a shame law-abiding citizens must be suspicious to be safe. But we can't be everywhere." McManus sat forward, elbows on his desk. "Anything else I should know up front before I get your final report?"

"Actually, Sir, one more thing. I guess you'd call it a jurisdictional issue."

"What?" McManus looked up in surprise.

"Before I talked with the friend I mentioned earlier, I first called Army Special Forces about Yates's military history. They said they'd send someone right over to help us with the case. Turns out their rep just wanted to get his hands on Yates's office computer, which he *impounded*. We raised hell, but he had an order signed by the Secretary of the Army. Legal says they supersede our authority. Now they're not telling a single thing to help our case."

"Give me their contact's name and I'll look into it. Detective work would be a snap around here if it wasn't for the damned politics, the spooks and the military. But here in Fairfax County, I'm lucky enough to have 'em all!" McManus smiled at Adam. "Thanks, lad."

As Adam stood and moved toward the door, McManus added, "By the way, Detective, you did a hell of a fine job all around. Good police work! Thanks." He stuck out his hand.

Adam turned and grabbed his captain's hand. "Thank you, Sir."

Adam left, knowing he needed to get ready for dinner tonight at the Shannons' house. Hannah revealed their ulterior motive was learning the latest about this case that had so dramatically affected their lives. Then he frowned, thinking of another piece of unexpected information he had to deliver that could upset them even more.

CHAPTER 69

"How many are coming tonight to hear Adam's update?" Jason asked Jennifer as she bustled around the kitchen. "The whole family. I set places for twenty-one, including us. Would you mind opening the wines?" She checked the clock. "They shouldn't arrive for another hour so let's eat about 7:00."

Jason uncorked several bottles, poured a glass for each of them and sat thoughtfully at the kitchen table, sipping his drink. "You know, Jen, in a strange way maybe Adam and Ruger have some things in common."

"*What?*" Jennifer halted mid-stir, her eyebrows raised in shock. "*How* can you compare that do-good policeman with a murdering psychopath?"

"Well now, hear me out. Both were rejected by their mothers for reasons they didn't understand. Both grew up in adoptive homes, if you consider military school an adoptive home. Both ended up in uniformed services, if you include the police in that group. And both excelled in their chosen careers."

"But, Jay," she interrupted, "what about their differences? Ruger was negative and Adam is positive. Ruger suffered horrible abuse when he was very young and Adam didn't!"

"Oh?"

"Hannah says when they talked about childhood Adam said he couldn't ask for better parents than the Iversons, who adopted him. That's worlds different from Ruger's parents, who *tortured* him."

"They were both about six when they went to other homes," Jason continued, "if you think of the academy as a home. We know the misery of Ruger's early years. Adam never speaks about his."

"Hannah says he was too little to remember. And what if Adam had double luck... loving people around when he was a baby and then a wonderful adoptive family? If that's true, they had *opposite* experiences because Ruger went from a cruel home to a military school, which you'd hardly call loving."

"Didn't you learn from those letters you found in the cellar that several generations of the Yates family were dysfunctional? Is that just a coincidence?"

"Ah, the old nature-nurture question: are we the way we are because of heredity or environment? I think the old college-knowledge said it's the interaction of both!"

"But Jen, that's from forty years ago. Maybe this kind of behavior is better understood now."

Mincing garlic for mashed potatoes, she said. "Actually, Jay, there might be another explanation for Ruger's behavior."

Jason looked up. "Oh?"

"The doctor who x-rayed my ankle asked how I twisted it and my answer included describing Ruger. He reminded me that doctors are legally responsible for reporting signs of physical abuse, which aren't always obvious like bruises and scars and broken bones. They can be invisible."

Jason frowned, "Invisible?"

"Like brain damage from too little oxygen if a child is choked or smothered or if his head is held under water. Or if a child is shaken so hard his brain moves inside his skull. Or if a child's head is banged or slammed hard during a beating to cause brain injury. Or if he's forced to take pills or drink chemicals like cleaning products that harm his brain or nervous system. Or even starvation, if a child hasn't nutrition to grow a normal brain, especially infants and toddlers."

"Geez, I never thought about that."

"And Jay, there's more." She slid sliced onions into the green beans. "After what happened to me, the doctor asked if I wanted counseling. I said no because while my experience was awful at the time, Ruger was the threat and the danger ended when he died. Not so for poor Tina, of course, but her terrible treatment was different from mine. Anyway, the doctor explained that besides invisible physical damage, emotional damage is also invisible. He talked about Post Traumatic Stress Disorder, which we know is that thing soldiers with battle fatigue or shell-shock have. But it can happen to anybody exposed to a terrifying experience; whether a group trauma like a plane crash or a tornado or a house fire, or an individual one such as a car crash or mugging or abuse like Ruger's."

"So how do you know if you have this PTSD or not?" Jason asked.

"That's the puzzle. Some heal and recover, some don't."

"Well then," he said, "let's pick Hannah as an example. An event left her heart-broken and disillusioned. After a five-month funk, she managed to heal and is functioning normally again."

"Oh, Jay, I wish you'd picked a different example. Hannah is functioning, but we won't know how normally until she tries to love someone again. And even if she does, can she make a go of it or will the old trauma return to cripple her new relationship? She's made good progress and I want her happiness more than anybody, but Jay, I don't know if she's out of the woods yet."

"Gee, I guess you're right. I wanted so much to see her okay again, I looked only at the surface."

"My doctor said it can take months or years of *safe* living for someone with PTSD to balance that terror, if ever. We know Ruger had too many strikes against him to recover, but I'd like to think, given a normal home life, he might have been a very different person."

Jason countered, "I'd like to think so, too, Jen, but even if that explains what happened to him, it doesn't excuse what he became. Society can't allow killers on the loose."

"Right. The trick is to find and rescue kids like Ruger and help them recover."

Jason tapped the newspaper, "Believe it or not, here's an article about a study that says gene changes might explain why two people exposed to the same experience can have such different reactions. It says..." he read from the page, "'...the common denominator among those with serious stress reactions to a current trauma appears to be a previous trauma at a young age.'"

"Like my dog bite? Hey, I learned a good lesson: it's sensible to be cautious around strange dogs. But if I had PTSD, wouldn't I be afraid to leave the house for fear a dog would get me?"

Jason chuckled, "Well, you *certainly* aren't afraid to leave the house." He put the newspaper down. "It's only one study, Jen, but unlike your dog situation, I think it means people with serious PTSD *did* have early trauma and just when they thought they were safe at last as adults, terror found them once more and now they'll never feel safe again."

"But I thought genes took generations to make even tiny changes. How can a gene change in just one lifetime? Instead of gene changes, didn't they just learn fear from a couple of unfortunate experiences?"

They both fell silent, wondering at these complex questions.

Jennifer thought of Ruger's scarred, half-starved dog and its positive response to her food and kind voice. For a time, she thought they became bizarre fox-hole buddies of a sort. Had the dog made a different choice in the deserted mansion's bedroom, rejecting the cruel man and joining her instead of attacking, she'd have brought the animal home and tried to rehabilitate him, despite her phobia.

Would she have been successful or could animals—and people—become broken beyond repair?

CHAPTER 70

The doorbell rang thirty minutes later and Jennifer greeted the detective at the front door. "Hello, Adam, come on in. Glad you're early. Hannah's still in the shower so would you like to visit with me in the kitchen until she comes downstairs? Do you mind slicing tomatoes while I finish getting dinner ready?"

He agreed enthusiastically and they chatted as they worked. "Hannah tells me that you and your mother live in downtown McLean now?" Jennifer began.

"Yes. My dad died four years ago. Mom felt isolated in the country. I lived there too and helped out when I could. But you know police work… odd hours. She got lonely out there. Besides, builders bugged her daily to sell her property. Finally she agreed. She's glad she did."

"Where was the other house?"

"Out Old Dominion Drive, near Great Falls. That northern Virginia book map, the one you use for garage sales. If it's handy, I could show you."

"Great idea. Mine is still in my van, but I think you'll find another one on the desk in the study."

Putting the tomatoes he'd prepared aside, Adam wiped his hands on a dish towel, retrieved the map book and riffled the pages. "Here, this is where our four acres were and where the builder's two new mega-mansions stand now," he pointed and she put the salad aside to take a look.

"I see it. And you say she's happier in town now?"

"Oh, yes. She found a beautiful house. It has what they call a mother-in-law suite added on. Now it's my bachelor apartment. Got my own entrance and kitchen. Mom likes to cook breakfast for me. So I eat there to keep her company most mornings. Unless my work schedule interferes. And I do handyman jobs around the house, mow the lawn and such. She loves the house and the neighborhood is friendly. Her life's a lot quieter now that Dad's gone."

"She's lucky to have you so near and involved."

"I'm happy to do whatever I can for her." Glancing at his watch, Adam fished through his pockets but came up empty-handed. "Hannah should be down in a minute. By any chance, do you have a comb I could borrow?"

"Why, yes. You should find five or six in the laundry room on top of the washing machine. I cleaned them just today."

Alone in the kitchen, Jennifer's mind wandered back to her earlier conversation that evening with Jason. Something bothered her... something just beyond her ability to draw it in.

Ten minutes later, when Jennifer used the bathroom herself, she noticed a comb on the edge of the sink. She stared at it a moment before tidying that area for company.

***

After dinner, the smaller Grands left the table to play elsewhere while the adults nibbled at dessert and sipped coffee.

"Well, Adam," Jason began as those around the dining tables leaned closer, "You know we're all curious about this case that put our family through such a scare. Anything more to tell us?"

All eyes focused on Adam, who sat beside Hannah. He put down his coffee cup and stood. "I know you want closure, but anything I say here tonight is off the record, not to be discussed elsewhere. Okay?" He looked around expectantly and all nodded agreement.

Adam recounted the general information he'd given his boss earlier that afternoon. Then he described the attorney who visited Wendey, sent Ruger to the military academy and sold the mother's land to pay her bills. "Over time, this reduced the original 260-acre farm to the current 15."

"And golden acres they are!" Mike said. "Given the chance, hungry developers will carve that prime property into big lots topped with McMansions." Agreement rippled through the group.

"So this lawyer filled in a lot of gaps? What did you say his name is?" Becca asked.

"Greg Bromley. He's a respected McLean attorney and heck of a nice guy. He's very upset about the whole situation. We talked at length and he showed me his files on the Yates family. Then I visited Ruger's military school. Fortunately, it's still in business today. The earlier personnel were gone but the school kept good records. Their rules have changed a *lot* in the meantime. They wouldn't admit a cadet now on the terms Ruger needed.

"So how did this guy become a serial killer?" Bethany wanted to know.

"I guess the bottom line is that cruelty has consequences," Adam said. "The father terrorized his wife and children. When he was institutionalized, the mother was too damaged mentally to break the chain of abuse. Ruger was just the next link. Did you know three *million* cases of abuse or neglect are reported in America every year? Right here in Fairfax County last year we received 5,400 calls reporting child abuse. Of those, 2,700 were documentable cases. And we're not talking low-income areas. Some happened right here in McLean. Yet for all that *are* reported, many are not. Like the nightmare at the Yate's house. Those are the children we can't protect."

Murmurs of disbelief traveled around the table. No one realized the problem existed in McLean.

Hannah said, "Adam, you must be a very good detective to discover all this."

Embarrassed, he nodded to her. "Part effort and part luck, like all cases. One person says a name or a place that leads to the next. And so on. Considering how many years back the clues led, the story came together pretty fast. One interesting fact is that detectives are often the first to pull a *whole* puzzle together. That's because they try to interview *everyone* involved in a case. Others just know isolated pieces of the total picture. Say, for instance, the academy commandant or the medical examiner or the toxicologist or the neighbors or the Army."

"So after Ruger left home for the military school, did the mother change?" Bethany asked.

"Not for the better. Our investigation includes talking with neighbors. They said local kids occasionally sneaked onto her property. They called her 'The Witch' and described her with wild hair, a shrill voice and weird behavior. If she caught sight of them, she screamed at them to leave her property. In fairness, signs were posted along the outside of her property, so the kids *were* trespassing."

Jennifer shook her head sadly. "Except for the dreadful way she treated her little boys, I feel sorry for her. I mean you told me she started out a normal, bright, healthy person; yet look at the miserable direction her life took. Makes us count our own blessings."

The group chatted amiably a few minutes before Kaela interrupted. "Didn't you say Ruger had a brother? What happened to him?"

"Good question, but we don't know." Adam kept to himself that the grave search at the farm included the tragic expectation of finding the boy's remains.

CHAPTER 71

Adam leaned down for a sip of his coffee, grateful for Hannah's encouraging smile shining up at him. "How am I doing?" he asked her quietly.

"Magnificently!" she answered back.

He stood again and asked the family, "Any other questions?"

"Given his awful childhood, how did Ruger adjust to school?" Kaela asked. "Hey, I'm a first grade teacher. I need to know these things."

"No public school record exists for either brother, but they also had no birth certificates! The mother was a teacher and presumably home-schooled her sons. Academy files show Ruger could read and write when he arrived. He made good marks and excelled in military skills. Compared to his dysfunctional home life, the orderly academy routine had to be an improvement."

Jennifer said, "Hard for you all to believe now, but thirty years ago obedient kids were the popular objective, and the majority thought tough discipline and physical punishment were the ways to make that happen. So even if those boys had attended public school in those days and someone noticed their abuse, there might not have been intervention. Public and parochial schools doled out physical punishment, with or without parents' consent. So did some fundamentalist churches. And a child's parents might punish him again when he got home for causing trouble at school. Spare-the-rod-and-spoil-the-child actually passed for wisdom then."

"Mom's right," Hannah added. "I saw a TV documentary last week that said only in the last fifty years did mistreatment of children create enough public outcry for the federal government to pass protective laws. And guess how it originally began?"

"How?" Mike asked.

"Laws existed to protect animals way before they did children. So a family in New York City called their local Society for the Prevention of Cruelty to Animals and asked them to investigate a neighbor who treated his daughter worse than any dog. The SPCA did, and from that incident gradually grew the child protection laws we have now in every state."

Adam added, "And those laws now include missing and exploited kids, not just abused or neglected ones. No question, current law offers the best child protection ever. Still, staffing, funding and enforcing are always challenges. In Ruger's case, their deliberately isolated family discouraged outsiders. Only Bromley was in a position to read the situation at the farm and help the boy. Law enforcement today holds as suspicious this same kind of isolation and secrecy that cults practice and often tries to investigate their treatment of children."

Mumbles about cults animated the listeners.

"Anything else?" Adam asked.

Mike said, "My own six-year-old's behavior still seems to be growing and forming, not set in stone. If Ruger left that environment at age six, couldn't he still recover? What tipped him from abused kid over to psychopathic killer?"

Jennifer and Jason exchanged looks, listening for Adam's answer. Perhaps he'd add information to their conversation earlier that evening.

"It's easy enough to hate someone who tortures you. Our psychologist thinks Ruger subconsciously wanted his mother's love but consciously hated her for withholding that love... and hurting him besides. Reaching puberty and adulthood complicated this situation. As a result, he didn't trust women, although he wanted and needed the normal relationships any adult male would. When rejected, that latent anger against his mother spilled out on the nearest handy female victim. The hate-the-thing-you-love syndrome is explosive stuff. To compensate for his helplessness as a child, he reinvented himself with power and control."

Thinking back to her curiosity about the remaining mysterious room at Ruger's house, Jennifer asked, "So what was the 'important work' he did in his office?"

"The short answer is that we don't know. The long answer is the Army confiscated Ruger's computer. They promised to tell us facts found there relating to our case. So far, they've volunteered nothing, saying it's classified. But we can make some guesses. His office had lots of books about the militia movement and covert operations. He owned an attention-getting arsenal of guns. And stacked in one corner were hundreds of copies of Playboy Magazines."

Jennifer's hand went up. "I know where he got those," and she told her story.

"Any other questions?" Adam asked the group.

Jennifer raised her hand again, "Two quick ones: when do I get my stolen van back and are the things I bought at garage sales that day still inside?"

Above the chorus of patronizing groans from the other family members, Becca said, "Only our mom would think about that at a time like this!"

Smiling with amusement, Adam responded, "The police inventoried everything in the van and your vehicle comes back tomorrow. Let's presume everything's still inside."

"If not," Hannah joked, "she knows where to find you, Adam!" This gave everyone a very good laugh and seemed to end the evening on a high note.

Jason stood, clinked his fork against a glass for attention and when the room quieted said, "Adam, we *all* thank you again for your crucial role in solving this crime, for rescuing Jennifer and Tina from the farm and Hannah at the hospital. We are each and every one in your debt for your priceless gifts to our family." Enthusiastic applause echoed through the dining room, together with "here-here" and "hurray, Adam!" Hannah snuggled her shoulder against him.

This was Adam's cue to sit down, but he did not.

CHAPTER 72

A s the tumult of appreciation died down, Adam still stood before the group. "Just one more thing," he began, "I know you've already absorbed many shocks the past few weeks, but I'm afraid there's one more." He paused, readying himself to lob another.

Jennifer reached nervously for her husband's hand, murmuring her apprehension into his ear, "Jason, can our family handle more bad news right now?"

Adam looked at the group nervously. "A couple of things I say next may surprise you, but please listen anyway." Looking uncomfortable, he drew a deep breath. Then, turning to the girl seated beside him, he said, "Hannah, I love you and I think we can share a wonderful life together. Please, will you marry me?"

Shocked silence filled the room as Hannah stared up at him in stunned surprise. Absorbing the impact of his words, her serious expression furrowed more as she rose to her feet beside Adam and looked at him as if for the first time.

Everyone at the table knew about the disastrous end of Hannah's long relationship with Kevin. They remembered her months of gloom, distrusting both men and her own judgment. Jennifer's fingers tightened anxiously on her husband's hand.

The electrified silence hung in the hushed room and Hannah searched Adam's eyes as if her answer lay somewhere within them. At last she spoke. "Detective Iverson," she looked up at his hopeful face, *"Yes!"* she cried, beaming her dazzling smile up at him and then to the room full of family faces. "Yes, Adam, I *will* marry you!"

Immediate wild applause, whooping, foot stomping and whistles filled the room as the handsome young couple shared a kiss, their happiness radiating out to those gathered around them.

Slipping a ring onto Hannah's finger, Adam kissed her to seal their bargain. Then, flushed with relief and success, he shifted his gaze from his new fiancé and turned to the others. His eyes moist and the corners of his mouth tight with emotion, he forced himself to continue.

"In my line of work, I see a lot of sad and scary family situations. Being adopted, I'm always amazed at my luck that such wonderful parents chose me. But growing up as an only child was a very different experience from yours. I missed the fun of a big family. So besides asking Hannah to accept me in her life, I guess I'm hoping the rest of you will let me be part of yours also."

The room erupted into lively cheers. Everyone hugged the engaged couple. The men shook Adam's hand, clapped him on the back and welcomed him into the family. Even the small children converged from their scattered play areas to get in on the loud, contagious excitement.

Standing by Jason, Jennifer clutched his hand, tears in her own eyes. "You're taking this news too calmly. You rascal, did you know about this beforehand?" she asked suspiciously.

"Adam asked me for her hand yesterday. He said it was old-fashioned, but he wanted to show his respect for her and us that way. And he wanted to surprise everyone else, even you and Hannah. I didn't know he'd ask the family to accept him also, but wasn't that touching?"

"My eyes aren't dry yet." Jennifer sighed, "But Jay, what about their age difference? He's *sixteen years* older than our Hannah!"

"If they don't think that's a problem, then I guess it isn't."

"And what about his dangerous job? Will she worry every time he goes to work?"

"It's certainly riskier than a desk job, but other police families deal with it, much the way we did when I went to war in the Army, and somehow they will, too."

"And, Jay, do you think she's ready? I mean... remember what we talked about earlier?"

"I guess we're going to find out."

Looking over at her daughter, Jennifer said, "She… she just seems so young. Only twenty."

"And how old were you?'

"Nineteen! And somehow we made it, didn't we?"

"Well, some days the jury's out…"

She slapped playfully at his arm.

"Adam told me he wants her to finish college as he did, so she'll probably transfer to a local school now that they're engaged," Jason explained.

"That's great news!"

Jason put an arm around his wife and she snuggled against him as he said, "I must say, I have to admire Adam. And now, it seems, he's going to be our son-in-law."

Jennifer again fought a strange uncertainty. The idea eluding her earlier this evening troubled her again, this time taking clearer shape and inviting further exploration. Where would it lead? She shivered.

"Hon, are you cold? Shall I get a sweater?" Jason asked with concern.

"No thanks, Jay. Just a bunch on my mind and with the proposal tonight… it's a lot to process!"

She hugged him and they looked together out into the room, filled with their lively, beloved family. "What a fine man," she said.

Jason's eyes rested on Adam. "Yes, I believe he is."

"No," she whispered, "I meant you."

CHAPTER 73

B rimming with purposeful resolve the next morning, Jennifer propelled her finally-returned van into the parking lot at the Tysons Corner office of her temporary job. Today was the day! Her hunch probably would lead nowhere, but she wanted to follow through, whatever the direction.

Hurrying inside, she shuffled through papers on her desk to see if anything required immediate attention. Finding only routine tasks for the day ahead, she removed an envelope from her purse, eased it into her pocket and asked the receptionist, "Have you seen Ronnie this morning?"

"I think he's in the kitchen getting coffee," she said.

Finding him there alone, Jennifer began, "Hi, Ron. Are you in a good mood today?"

"Office managers are always in a good mood. You know that. But you seem like a lady with something on her mind. I hope it's me!"

Jennifer brushed aside his usual harmless flirting. "Of course you are, Ronnie, but today so is something else."

"Go on…"

"In all the years we've worked together I've never before asked for a favor, but I wonder if you might do a special one for me now."

Attracted to Jennifer since the first day they'd met at the office and ever hopeful of escalating their relationship past business to personal, Ronnie saw this as a possible way to earn payback. "What do you have in mind?" He grinned, wiggling his eyebrows suggestively.

"Now Ron, be serious! I need a DNA sample tested against any match in the system. Of course, I'll pay for it but I want the results to come straight to me rather than going through the usual office channels. Do you think that's possible?"

"As they say in New 'Joysey,'" he adopted his best Mafia persona, "we wouldn't do dis fuh nobody else in da whole world, but fuh you, sweetie!'" He chucked her under the chin.

She laughed at his outrageous performance. How could you not find Ronnie amusing? She handed him an envelope. "Thanks, Ron. *You're* the sweetie to do this for me! Will it take long?"

He continued his nasal Jersey accent, "Da DNA test or your seduction?"

She nudged his arm, "Ron!"

"Normally, two days is the fastest, but we recently bought a new technique which processes the information in a matter of hours. It's just as accurate and will eventually eclipse the previous methods. Right now, we're one of very few companies using it. Let me see how busy we are. I put your desires ahead of all others. Will you do the same for me?" He did the eyebrows again. She had to smile at his parting comment as he whisked the envelope out the door. "Just remembuh, Doll, yuh *owe* me now!"

"Oh, Ron, and there's something else. If… if there is a match, this needs to be confidential. I'm smart enough to know you'll have a look, but promise me this will stay between us?"

"I like the thought of having something between us." Again, the eyebrows.

"I'm serious about this. Will you promise? Please, Ronnie."

"Okay, I promise."

Anticipating the test results made her jumpy all day. The probability of no match outweighed any alternative, but she wouldn't feel calm until she knew. She looked at her watch: almost the end of the day. She'd already cleaned off her desk and gathered her belongings to leave when Ronnie popped into her office. "I did your test and surprise, surprise!"

She held her breath!

"We got an exact match."

Jennifer jumped from her chair. He returned her envelope plus the paperwork with lab results. She read it slowly, gasped and then read it again to be sure. "Oh!" she cried, still clutching the paper as she fell back into her chair.

All seriousness now, Ronnie said, "Would you like to tell me what this is all about, Jen? You can guess that I'm pretty curious."

"Ron, I... I will, I promise, but not yet, because I need to find out two more things to understand this myself."

"And when might that be?"

"If I had the day off tomorrow, I think I'd have the answer."

"I see. Well, that would be a second favor!" More eyebrows. "And now that I look closely, you do, ah, look rather pale and we don't want you to infect the rest of the staff with your, ah, contagious germs. Yep, you better take a sick day tomorrow."

"Oh, Ronnie," she kissed his cheek. "You're the very best!"

As she left the office and hurried down the hall toward her car, he called after her good-naturedly, "You're right, I am."

Driving home, she tried to fit this DNA information into place by recalling details overheard during past conversations. She longed to discuss this with Jason, but he'd doubtless regard this as just another one of her "far-out ideas." No, she would unravel this herself and present it to him as a done deal!

Finding no one at home when she arrived, she searched through the phone book and, putting her finger on a particular number, called for an appointment in McLean the next morning at 9:00 a.m.

CHAPTER 74

"Mrs. Shannon? Please come in," Greg Bromley held the door and motioned toward his comfortable office. She thought he might recognize her name from newspaper reports about the case, but apparently not. When they both were seated comfortably and exchanged superficial small talk, he asked, "What can I do for you today?"

"Mr. Bromley, I am the woman who recently escaped from Ruger Yates."

Bromley did a double-take, blanching at her significant role in this case that plagued him with such remorse. He apologized for failing to identify her name immediately.

"I... I wonder if you could help me with a legal problem."

"I'll certainly try. Why don't you tell me about it?"

"Imagine you discovered conclusive DNA information showing that two people with no idea they are related are actually father and son. Imagine how this information would shock each of them. Imagine how this knowledge would change their lives. Legally, what would be your responsibility?"

"This sounds more like an ethical question than a legal one. You have no legal responsibility to share what you know. Objectively, whatever furthers the truth is generally considered positive. Subjectively, not everyone is brave enough to reveal such a truth or to accept it if on the receiving end. So, it's a judgment call. You might ask yourself if the good accomplished by the news outweighs or balances the bad. But that's another subjective judgment call."

"Is DNA in national data banks considered public knowledge, like fingerprints?"

"Mmmm… for the most part, yes."

"For example, is your DNA in the national data bank?"

Bromley's eyes narrowed. You heard just about everything in a law office, but where was this going? This woman seemed rational enough but who knew better than lawyers that what you *thought* you saw wasn't always what you got? He studied her a moment, admitting she'd piqued his curiosity. What did he have to lose? Why not humor her along?

"Yes. I belonged to the National Guard for many years. At one time they sent me abroad as legal advisor with a task force on a *very* sensitive issue which I can't discuss. They took our DNA to identify our remains if… if things didn't go well."

"I see. Thank you for explaining that." She changed the subject. "I think you've already met Detective Adam Iverson, the policeman who solved the Yates case."

"Yes. Pleasant, bright young man."

"He is engaged to my daughter Hannah and so is already considered part of our family. As her fiancé, he visits our house often. When I first noticed his missing little finger, I thought of the mummified child's finger I found while captured in the cellar at the Yates house. I knew it must be coincidence, but that fact nagged at me. Adam was adopted at age six. My daughter told me Adam had no memories of his first six years but happy memories after his adoption. He and his adoptive mother live in downtown McLean now, but when I learned their original family home was only a few miles from the Yates property, my hunch grew. I happen to work part-time at a forensic lab where DNA samples are tested. One day when Adam borrowed a comb at my house, I collected the hairs he left in it and had them analyzed at the lab. Adam is the son in the situation I asked you earlier to imagine."

Bromley sat forward in his chair. "Six or seven is just about the right age when Ruger's older brother disappeared. So you think that brother and Adam may be the same person? But you said you had DNA matches for a son *and* his father. Wouldn't that prove conclusively it's Adam?"

She had his riveted attention. "You're right, DNA doesn't lie. Hold onto your hat. Adam's DNA exactly matches *yours.*"

Bromley stared dumfounded, trying to process this staggering implication. Absolute silence filled the room as he struggled to absorb her information and she to shape her next question. She knew what she needed to learn but not how to approach a stranger for such personal information.

"Can... can you think how that DNA match could be possible? For you to be his father?"

Looking stunned, Bromley finally cleared his throat and stammered, "I...I guess it *might* be possible, though... just too incredible to believe. Are you certain about the results?"

Jennifer pulled the report from her purse and pushed it across the desk to him. He read it and then re-read it as cautious acceptance supplanted his initial doubt at this extraordinary piece of information.

Taking a deep breath, he began, "Wendey and I were together for six years and engaged for four of them. We were very much in love. Yes, we were intimate. But this," he closed his eyes and shook his head as if to clear it, "...this information puts a whole new, wrenching twist on what happened... why she ran off with Yates. Oh god, my poor Wendey! I can scarcely believe this is true, and yet it explains the greatest unsolved mystery of my life. All these years I couldn't imagine why she rejected me for that awful man. Now, thanks to you, I... I begin to understand."

"Mr. Bromley, there's more. Adam's parents told him they adopted him from an agency when he was six years old. If that's true and she has records to prove it, then we need to figure how that meshes with what we know. I think we need to visit Adam's adoptive mother to learn more about his adoption."

"You're right!" He reached for his phone. "My secretary can call her here to the office and..."

"Is that really the best way?" Jennifer asked quickly. "Our questions are bound to upset her, maybe make her angry or defensive. Won't we need her cooperation to get at the truth?"

"We could subpoena the adoption records if necessary..."

"If necessary, yes, but think long term. I don't know how you feel, but if you want to become part of Adam's life, being on good terms with his adoptive mother might be more important than forcing the truth out of her with legal muscle."

"Obviously, you've given this some thought. What do you suggest?"

Jennifer explained her plan.

CHAPTER 75

Mrs. Iverson felt uneasy. Why would her son's prospective mother-in-law call this morning, asking to drop by the house to meet her today? And why would she bring a friend instead of her husband?

True, Adam had brought Hannah to the house to meet her after the two began dating, and only yesterday he excitedly told her about his accepted marriage proposal of the previous night. Yes, he mentioned wanting the parents to meet soon, which his mother agreed was a good idea; but wouldn't the five of them going out to lunch or dinner be a likelier venue for getting acquainted?

This didn't make sense, especially since Mrs. Shannon said the friend was an *attorney*. She reflected again, as she had so many times during the four years since her husband died, that if only he were here, he'd know what to do. She missed him. She missed his experience and support in challenging situations like this. In fact, she missed the companionship of a man in her life. But that situation wasn't likely to change.

Startled when the doorbell chimed, she curbed her apprehension to greet them at the door with what she hoped passed for a confident smile. After introductions and offered refreshments, they sat in the living room, where the opening chatter flowed more easily than Mrs. Iverson expected. Despite her anxiety at this improbable meeting, she relaxed enough to warm a little toward this pleasant woman and the charming attorney accompanying her.

As for Bromley, an attraction toward Mrs. Iverson bloomed the moment he recognized her disarming resemblance to his Wendey... Wendey as she would look now had she led a normal life and aged gently instead of as the broken pariah she became.

Oblivious to their rapport, Jennifer concentrated on how best to uncover the needed information. As the conversation grew ever friendlier, Jennifer gently guided the talk toward the clues that prompted her hunch and the subsequent actions leading her to the DNA discovery and Bromley.

Picking up the story's thread, Bromley described his youthful romance with Wendey and subsequent involvement with the Yates family, which included Wendey's insistence that her older son "disappeared." Jennifer noticed he slipped into that conversation the fact that he'd never married.

Together, they showed her on the northern Virginia map the close proximity of the Yates farm to the original Iverson home and that the final step in finding the truth hinged on Adam's adoption.

"For instance," Jennifer began, "he told Hannah his missing finger was a birth defect. So was it gone when you adopted him?"

"Yes. We called it a birth defect because we couldn't know what really happened and we thought he would accept it more easily if he thought it a natural condition."

"And how did you decide to adopt him?"

" We... we lost a child to illness and because of a hysterectomy I couldn't have more. So we contacted an agency and they found Adam for us."

Bromley pressed, "And the name of that agency that has his adoption records?"

"Tri-State Adoption Company," Mrs. Iverson replied.

"I recognize that name," Bromley acknowledged. "They're defunct now, but they operated in Fairfax County at that time. A well-run organization. I did legal work for them a few times."

"Would you mind too much showing us Adam's adoption papers?" Jennifer asked.

"I... I lost them three years ago during the move to this house."

Brushing away that excuse, Bromley said, "No problem. I may be able to get them from the agency's stored files. If not," he threw this idea on the table, unsure whether he could actually follow through, "the information can be retrieved from court records which my office should be able to access easily."

His ploy worked. Mrs. Iverson paled and brought a trembling hand to her lips. She'd feared this day for three decades, knowing she'd randomly picked the agency's name from the phone book yellow pages the day Adam entered their lives. She realized her ruse could buy only a few days' time before Bromley's search unearthed no recorded facts to support her invented story. She always hoped if it came to this, spontaneously volunteering a legitimate agency's name would satisfy curiosity enough to discourage further checking. She searched her mind for *any* plausible explanation short of the truth, but nothing believable emerged. Cornered at last, she realized the deception guarded for nearly thirty years was finally over.

But when she told that truth, what devastating reprisals awaited?

She sighed in resignation as her face clouded with anguish. Worse than the revelation that she'd broken laws, she feared her son's outrage when he learned the parents he trusted had lied to him all his life. If she lost Adam, what little was left of her world would disintegrate. Tears welled in her eyes and rolled down her cheeks.

Just then, the front door opened and in walked Adam.

CHAPTER 76

"Hi, Mom! I'm home," Adam began. But his smile melted, replaced by confusion at the unlikely group before him. "Mrs. Shannon? Mr. Bromley? What...?" his incomplete question faded as a sob caught his attention. Following the sound, he did a double take. "Mom! You're *crying*." Striding quickly to the couch where his mother slumped, he put his hands protectively on her shoulders and turned sternly toward the others. "What's going on here?" he asked, piercing first Jennifer, then Bromley with steely eyes.

Sally Iverson pulled a tissue from her pocket and dabbed at her streaming tears. "Adam, I... guess it's time to tell you something... something your father and I hoped never to reveal." Her hands twisted the tissue as she gathered resolve to continue. "You see, we had a little boy before you came to live with us... our son, Matthew. He died of spinal meningitis when he was only six years old. Losing him broke our hearts and your dad and I thought we couldn't go on living without him." She blew her nose. "Then two months later, when we were just about at the end of our rope, we found you curled up in the woods by our house. You'd been beaten and starved. You were covered with bruises and cuts and your little ribs showed through the skin on your chest... "

She stifled more sobs at the memory of his emaciated condition. "Clearly, you'd been neglected... and even worse, abused, but we were afraid if we called the police, you'd be returned to those same cruel parents or put in a system with foster families. We feared you'd be scarred by more bad experiences until *maybe* someone like us eventually adopted you. We needed you so much, and you needed us, so that *finding* each other seemed like a miracle. We instantly took you into our hearts and into our lives and no parents could love you more than we have."

Mouth agape, a startled Adam finally managed, "You *found* me in the woods? This is a joke, right?" He laughed nervously, but their sober expressions told him it was not. "But... you told me you adopted me from an agency."

"We said that because we loved you too much to lose you. We thought if all our family told the same story, everyone would believe it. If the world knew the truth, you would have been taken away from us and, worse, maybe even returned to the people who hurt you. We read several terrible newspaper stories about that happening."

Adam took a step back, trying to absorb these lightning bolts. Finally he managed, "Mom, I... I couldn't ask for better parents than you and Dad and I knew from the start that I wasn't your own child, but *found in the woods?*"

Sally stumbled on. "Son, there's more! We used our dead son Matthew's birth certificate for you. You became Matthew Adam Iverson. We held our breath when you started kindergarten, but nobody questioned your birth certificate then or in college or on your job applications. Nobody ever has... until now. Yes, we told you we'd adopted you in case you remembered your awful early years. If you did, we wanted you to know that other life was separate from the safe one you shared with us."

"So, if that's not my birth certificate, who the hell *am* I?"

"We didn't know," Sally admitted, "but legally adopted children often don't know that either. Adam, we *did* adopt you in every sense except for the legal papers. You looked about six when we found you and that age fit perfectly with our little Matthew's certificate."

"So if you used Matthew's information, I also don't know how old I really am."

"But that can happen with legal adoptions, too." Sally wiped her eyes with the tissue. "Children abandoned by their parents on the street or left on church doorsteps don't come with statistics."

Jennifer asked, "Adam, do you recall anything at all about your early years?"

He reached back in memory as best he could. "No, it was always too scary to think about. I... I just completely blocked it out." He turned toward his mother. "And actually, because of that black hole, I was all the more grateful to you and Dad for your care and love." He shrugged, trying now to think about this from a detective's standpoint. "So, where did I spend my first six years and how *did* I end up beside your house?"

"That's what we're all trying to figure out," Jennifer explained.

"Did my other parents file a missing person report?"

"No, they did not," Bromley explained. "I checked."

"Did the newspapers or media report the disappearance of a little boy?" Adam asked.

"No," Sally said with certainty. " We checked every single day for months after you came to us."

"Then was I kidnapped somewhere else, abused and eventually dumped in the Virginia woods?"

"Or did you escape from a very cruel home, wander a few miles through the woods and collapse near the Iverson house?" Bromley suggested.

Thinking like a policeman, Adam asked suspiciously, "And of the many possible scenarios that could fit this situation, why do you pick that particular one?"

"Good question, Adam! We couldn't figure any of this out except for an amazing piece of information Jennifer uncovered. Why don't you sit down. Good! When we tell you this, you'll understand how the rest might fit together. Now get ready for a... a big surprise!" Bromley drew a breath. "It turns out your DNA and mine are an exact match!"

"*What?*" Adam jumped to his feet. "But how... how could that be?"

Then his mind reeled back to his interview with Bromley and his own conclusion then that Mathis, the boy who disappeared from the Yates's home, the boy with the missing finger, was actually Bromley's son.

Adam's voice rose an octave as he cried out, "You mean you are my *biological father?*"

Bromley nodded.

Gasping, Adam looked at the four fingers on his left hand. Then his eyes opened very wide. *Was he Mathis?*

CHAPTER 77

Dazed with this mind-numbing revelation, Adam recalled the night of Jennifer's rescue when they returned to the Yates house and she showed police what she'd learned while captive. As they moved through the rooms and dim cellar, he didn't *dream* that dreadful house and its terrible secrets related to him personally. Yet he surely endured years of horror in that very place. How could anyone suppress ghastly memories that tightly? Yet the undeniable facts proved he and Mathis Yates *must* be the same person! And detectives understood facts, convenient or not.

Adam groaned, shaking his head in disbelief. "Oh my god," he cried out, slumping down heavily onto an empty chair. "Does this mean that awful Ruger is my *brother?*"

"Half-brother,"Jennifer corrected. "Remember, you had different fathers."

"Does this mean I accidentally *killed* my brother outside the hospital?"

"'*Accidentally*' is the key word here," Bromley added quickly. "You meant to subdue and arrest him. You couldn't have known about the syringe in his pocket."

"Good lord, this is just... just too *much!* In a matter of minutes I've learned I'm not who I thought I was, that I don't know how old I am, that I suffered a dreadful childhood, that a crazy woman—who is also my *mother*—chopped off my finger, that I have a new father I knew nothing about, that my brother is a serial murderer and that I *killed* him!" Adam hunched forward in the chair, holding his head in his hands and moaning softly. "Will Hannah even want me when she learns my missing finger is the least of my scars?" His voice cracked in misery.

For the first time in his life, he felt as if he were outside himself, looking down from above upon a stranger while simultaneously being the very stranger he gazed upon.

A heavy silence hung in the room as each of the others realized how their parts in this drama paled compared to Adam's life-wrenching revelations. Their instinct to comfort him warred against the guilt that they brought him the very information causing this suffering.

Minutes passed as he struggled to assimilate the magnitude of these disclosures!

Groping for *anything* that might help, Jennifer ventured carefully, "Adam, believe it or not, there may be plus-sides to all this."

He choked and managed sarcastically, "My entire life has changed in a matter of minutes and you say there are *plus sides?*"

"Well… for example," she continued with great caution, "you escaped from an impossible childhood and overcame that awful start without permanent scars like Ruger's. You ended up with loving parents, which he never had. You made a successful, well-adjusted life, which he couldn't. You found a wonderful girl who loves you so much she wants to marry you, and he didn't. And while the dad you loved died four years ago, now you have a second chance to get acquainted with another father, one who's eager to know you."

Adam listened. A long moment passed before he straightened ever so slightly as Jennifer's spin on this new situation penetrated his troubled thinking. But anguish still shrouded his mind and face.

"And that's not all," Bromley added. "You're now the rightful living heir to the Yates's farm property. That extremely valuable location potentially makes you a millionaire. Wearing my 'attorney hat,' I think I can help straighten out the legal details very quietly so only a handful of people close to you need to know."

Imagining the impact of this information at the police station where he worked or the media circus inevitable with a story like this, Adam asked doubtfully, "You could hush it up?"

"I think so." Bromley confirmed. "And wearing my 'father hat,' I could introduce you to another branch of law enforcement:

the legal profession. Every law firm needs a good private investigator, and you're already an experienced detective. Once you have a family, you might find such investigating safer and better paid than your current job. And if law school interests you, I'll be looking for an eventual successor to take over my practice."

Adam straightened a bit more, lifted his head and looked at others in the room. Sally touched his hand and eyed him anxiously. "Son, can you ever forgive me for not telling you the whole truth about your adoption?"

Adam sighed and stared at his hands. Finally, he put his arm around her in a tight hug. "Mom..., dear Mom. You just tried to protect me. Can I forgive you for wanting me and loving me? That's what every child hopes for! You're my mom and I've loved you ever since I can remember. That hasn't changed... although lord knows everything else has."

Sally beamed through tears of relief at her son's unexpected forgiveness. Jennifer hugged her. "I'm glad to know someone like you, someone brave enough to risk everything to get to the truth. Thank you and welcome to the Shannon family. We'll plan a get-together very soon to introduce everyone to you."

Sally dried her last tears. Her son still loved her and after four years of widowhood, she was about to be swept into the Shannon clan, a family Adam liked and respected.

"And to think," Adam marveled, "this morning when I woke up I was just a poor, simple, everyday Fairfax County police detective."

Bromley chuckled. "Now wait! You're not the only detective here! We'd know none of this without Jennifer's hunch and follow through."

"Her hunch?" Adam asked.

Jennifer explained the clues sparking her curiosity and the sequence of events bringing them to his mother's house today.

Adam looked at Jennifer with new respect. "So when I marry Hannah, we'll have two detectives in the Shannon family?"

"And if you're getting married soon," Bromley interrupted hopefully, "does this mean I may have grandchildren one of these days?"

"Well, yes. I suppose it could... someday, Sir."

"You don't need to call me Dad yet, unless you want to, but I hope one day you will."

"Well, I... well, thanks... ah, Dad."

As Jennifer and Bromley prepared to leave, Greg turned to Sally. "How would you and Adam like to have dinner with me tonight?"

Adam shrugged. "Sorry, Sir...er, Dad, but I'm on duty tonight."

"Well then, perhaps you'll join us next time. Sally, why don't we go anyway to talk about suddenly finding ourselves the mother and father of the same son?"

"Why, thank you, Greg. That's a wonderful idea," she agreed with a smile.

Jennifer chuckled to herself as she stepped out the door. Well, well!

***

Back in her car, she reached quickly for her cell phone and speed-dialed her husband. Her excitement was electric as she waited for him to answer.

"Hello."

"Jason, any chance you can get away from work early? I have something *really big* to tell you!"

"Jen, what is it? Are you all right? Are the kids okay?"

"Yes, yes, but this news is *colossal!* Please come home as soon as you can. And Jason..."

"Yes?"

"....*hold on to your hat!!!*"

ACKNOWLEDGMENTS

Though my story is fiction, I researched for factual accuracy. Thanks to all who shared their time, knowledge and insights. If errors exist, they are my mistakes alone.

At **OnStar (by GM)**, **Michael McNamee** helped me understand their system and how it operates in police situations.

At the well-respected **INOVA Fairfax Hospital, Maria T. Huber** answered my questions and toured me through the areas relevant to my story.

In Virginia, the public sector group called **Fairfax County Child Protective Services (FCCPS)** partners with a private sector group called **Childhelp,** a national organization devoted to meeting the physical, educational, emotional and spiritual needs of traumatized children. Several individuals at FCCPS gave me valuable information, including **Jim Gogan**, Hotline Supervisor and retired police officer. Many at **Childhelp** (http://www.childhelp.org; phone: 480-922-8212) provided important facts.

The **Fairfax County Police Citizens Academy Class #15,** under **Police Chief David M. Rohrer,** offered ten weeks of in-depth, on-site exposure to their objectives and procedures, besides a 12- hour citizen "ride-along" when I was able to observe first-hand all patrol responses and activities during that period.

Guy Morgan, Professional Standards Fairfax County Fire and Rescue Department (retired Fairfax County Police Officer with 22 years of service, 17 of them in Major Crime Investigation) read and reread my manuscript, offering dozens of relevant ideas and corrections.

Two physicians advising me on medical accuracy were **Martin G . Prosky, M.D.** of Washington, D. C., and **Tony Fiore, M.D**. of Fredericksburg, VA. A third doctor, **Daniel B. Kaplan, D.O**. of Naples, FL (a fellow writer) offered not only medical knowledge but his valuable time, encouragement and many excellent suggestions for improving my story.

Carole J. Greene entered my world when I was about to give up on my novel. Capable literary agent and editor extraordinaire, she made *invaluable* contributions by stimulating, instructing, inspiring and prodding my original rough draft into this book. She's not only my mentor but has become a dear friend.

Beth Iddings used her valuable time to provide me with important information.

Fred Getty, Attorney at Law in Locust Grove, VA, graciously provided legal insights.

Others who read and offered ideas to better my story are **Bill Wilson** (a fellow author), **Hugh Gibbs, Ruth Geils, Sally Eatmon** and **Kathy Weinert.** Special thanks to my sister, **Margo Gibbs,** for her constructive coaching and enthusiastic cheerleading.

READING GROUP DISCUSSION QUESTIONS

1. How would you describe Jennifer Shannon and her relationship with her husband?

2. Explain her interest and insights into garage sales. What tactics did you learn about giving or attending these sales?

3. Jennifer Shannon discovers human interest stories at garage sales from people she doesn't know. Have you ever learned an interesting story from a complete stranger?

4. How was Jennifer Shannon able to escape from her captor? What might you do in such a desperate situation?

5. How would you describe the lasting effects of Ruger Yates' childhood? Do you consider him a victim or a villain? Do you think his Special Forces training played a role in who he became?

6. Compare the lives of Ruger and Mathis Yates. Discuss the likelihood of siblings from the same home environment turning out very differently.

7. How did Greg Bromley try to protect Wendy and Ruger? Discuss how the best of intentions can have tragic results.

8. Since the police can't protect citizens at all times, discuss the contradictory roles of trust and suspicion in shaping one's own self-defense.

9. What chance events affected Jennifer Shannon's fate? Has your life been similarly impacted by random occurences?

10. Given their painful past experiences, what do you think the future holds for Hannah or Adam?

11. If Ruger's dog had made a different decision about who to side with in the bedroom of the uninhabited mansion, do you think an alternate outcome with Jennifer might have unfolded successfully?

CPSIA information can be obtained
at www.ICGtesting.com
Printed in the USA
FFHW02n2008151018
48814623-52987FF